# MURDER IN HIGHBURY

## VANESSA KELLY

KENSINGTON
PUBLISHING CORP.

www.kensingtonbooks.com

KENSINGTON BOOKS are published by

Kensington Publishing Corp.
900 Third Avenue
New York, NY 10022

Copyright © 2024 by Vanessa Kelly

All Kensington titles, imprints, and distributed lines are available at special quantity discounts for bulk purchases for sales promotion, premiums, fund-raising, educational, or institutional use.

Special book excerpts or customized printings can also be created to fit specific needs. For details, write or phone the office of the Kensington Special Sales Manager: Attn. Special Sales Department, Kensington Publishing Corp., 900 Third Avenue, New York, NY 10022. Phone: 1-800-221-2647.

The K with book logo Reg. US Pat. & TM Off.

Library of Congress Card Catalogue Number: 2024939439

ISBN: 978-1-4967-4597-2
First Kensington Hardcover Edition: November 2024

ISBN: 978-1-4967-4599-6 (ebook)

10 9 8 7 6 5 4 3 2 1

Printed in the United States of America

This one is for Laurie and Anne, who have been with me
every step of the way. No one could ask for better
(or funnier) friends. Love you—and don't forget the snacks!

# ACKNOWLEDGMENTS

When my editor asked if I would be interested in writing a mystery series based on the character of Emma Woodhouse, I might have literally shrieked for joy. *Emma* is not only my favorite Austen novel but is probably THE book I would choose in the event that I was marooned on a deserted island. So, it is with deep gratitude that I thank my editor, John Scognamiglio, for supporting me throughout my career and giving me this opportunity. To say that I enjoyed writing this book is a massive understatement.

Evan Marshall, my agent, also played a huge role in bringing this book to fruition, and I am deeply grateful for his advice and support. I doubt I could have survived this business without him.

I am also grateful to Larissa Ackerman, Alex Nicolajsen, Vida Engstrand, Lauren Jernigan, and the marketing and social media teams at Kensington. Thank you so much for your support for *Murder in Highbury,* and for your kindness over the years. Many thanks are also proffered to the Kensington art department (the best in the business, IMHO), to Rosemary Silva for her eagle eye, and to the Kensington production department.

As a bit of hermit, I have a tendency to live too much in my head (an occupational hazard), so I'm grateful to the family who keep me grounded in the real world, especially my sister Trish, my stepmother Anne, my brother Brian, along with Liz Sykes and Wendy Durante. I'm also fortunate to have wonderful friends who encouraged me at various stages in the writing process, including Debbie Mason, Minerva Spencer, Terri Brisbin, Digby Ricci, Teresa Wilde, Sharon Page, and Moze Mossanen. As Ted Lasso would say . . . I appreciate you!

And a special shout-out goes to Nick Rudman, my ubertalented nephew, who created the awesome book trailer for *Murder in Highbury.*

I would also like to thank Louisa Cornell, whose knowledge of all things criminal in the Regency period is truly gobsmacking. Louisa, you saved me from more than one spectacular bungle, and any mistakes in the book are certainly mine! I'm also grateful to the Regency Fiction Writers group, whose collective wisdom has been so helpful.

It's no exaggeration to say that I would have given up writing years ago without the steadfast love and encouragement of my husband. He not only cheers me on, he reads every word I write, plugging up plot holes and rescuing me from any number of grammatical and lexical mishaps. He not only does the laundry, he remains calm whenever I have a computer/technology/writing-related breakdown. And then usually fixes the problem. Randy, you are the best thing that ever happened to me, and I love you more than mere words can express.

Finally (and rightfully), my deepest thanks go to Jane Austen for creating such an iconic character. It has been a privilege to spend time in Highbury with Emma, and I add my voice to the legions of readers who rightly adore Austen for the novels she gifted to the world.

# CHAPTER 1

*Highbury, England*
*Summer 1815*

Emma Knightley fancied herself quite adept at managing awkward social situations. Murder, however, was not one of them, especially murder in their village church. Those circumstances struck her as *particularly* awkward.

"Is she dead?" Harriet Martin asked in a horrified whisper.

Emma took a hesitant step toward the crumpled heap lying on the shallow steps that led up to the chancel. Steeling herself, she leaned down to press two fingers to the woman's exposed wrist and felt for a pulse.

Hastily straightening up, she had to swallow twice before she could answer. "I'm afraid she is dead, Harriet. I cannot feel a pulse, and you can see there is quite a lot of blood."

Mrs. Elton's blond ringlets were dark with the sticky substance. A fair amount of blood was congealed beneath her head, and there was also something odd about the angle of her neck. As for her bonnet, the over-trimmed hat was decidedly askew.

Harriet dropped her wicker basket, spilling an assortment of roses and larkspur onto the gray stone floor of the nave. "Mrs. Knightley, how can this be? Poor Mrs. Elton!"

"Indeed," Emma replied, staring at the corpse of the vicar's wife. "Poor Mrs. Elton."

Never could she have imagined herself referring to her social nemesis as *poor* anything. Such, however, was the awful magnitude of the scene before them.

Harriet, wide-eyed and pale, pressed a trembling hand to her bodice. "How . . . how can you be so calm, Mrs. Knightley? I feel terribly sick and lightheaded."

Emma didn't feel the slightest bit calm. In fact, she wanted either to shriek so loud it would shake the old bell tower to its foundations or to cast up her crumpets. But since neither reaction would be helpful, she ordered her stomach back in place and tried to collect her scattered wits.

"No fainting, Harriet. I cannot manage two bodies at once."

When her friend let out a curdled moan, Emma took her by the elbow and steered her to a pew. "Put your head down and breathe slowly, dear. You'll feel better in a moment."

Biddable girl that she was, Harriet sank into the pew and rested her bonneted head on her knees. Emma was very fond of her young friend, but Harriet often displayed an unfortunate excess of emotion when distressed as well as a tendency to faint. Neither characteristic was welcome under the circumstances.

With Harriet sorted for the moment, Emma could gather her thoughts and determine what must be done next. As mistress of Hartfield, her father's manor house, and of Donwell Abbey since her marriage to George, she was used to making decisions. Still, while Emma generally trusted her judgment and intellect, a dead Mrs. Elton was a challenge that taxed even her ability to think clearly.

She glanced around the church—a cool, silent refuge on a

bright summer's day. Or, at least, it would have been a refuge without a corpse lying in the middle of it.

Yet she saw no other signs of disturbance. All was as it should be on a quiet Saturday, the day she and Harriet always brought flowers from Hartfield's gardens to refresh the floral arrangements for Sunday services. As usual, the caretaker had left the main door in the south porch unlocked for them. Emma doubted anyone else was expected in the church, and certainly not Mrs. Elton. The vicar's wife set foot in the place only for the Sunday service or the rare meeting of the altar guild, where decisions were made about the state of the linens and vestments. Even then, she usually left the details to others, deeming such tasks beneath a woman of her dignity. It had been so since her arrival in Highbury as Philip Elton's bride early last year. Mrs. Elton had possessed a highly elevated sense of superiority and so had believed that parish business was merely an irritation best ignored.

So why was she here on a Saturday afternoon, and who could have possibly . . . ?

*Murdered her.*

Emma finally allowed that horrible thought to fully sink in. She dearly hoped she was wrong, but only a fool wouldn't consider the possibility of foul play, given the odd disposition of the body and the distressing amount of blood. Perhaps she was overly imaginative, though. George had accused her of that particular flaw more than once in the past, and with some degree of merit, she was sorry to say.

She pressed a hand to her forehead, trying to think. Should she send for Mr. Elton? While this was his church, seeing his wife in so dreadful a state would be too great a shock. He might even descend into hysterics, and Emma was quite certain she couldn't manage Mr. Elton in a state of hysteria. Managing Harriet was challenge enough.

*You need George.*

Emma's still-racing heart started to settle. Her husband was the most intelligent and levelheaded person she'd ever met, and he always knew exactly how to proceed. As the local magistrate, George would be responsible for managing this horrid situation, including breaking the news to Mr. Elton.

With that decision made, her mind turned in a more orderly direction. Death had come to their quiet corner of Surrey, and in a most unexpected fashion. It would be up to Mr. and Mrs. Knightley, as the first family of the parish, to see that all legal and social matters were conducted with as much care and delicacy as possible. The residents of Highbury would depend upon them for guidance and support, and Emma was determined not to fail them.

Looking away from the body because, really, it was easier to think without Mrs. Elton's hideously blank gaze staring up at her, Emma turned to her friend.

"Harriet, are you feeling better? Do you think you might be able to exert yourself?"

With a shuddering breath, the girl pulled herself upright, her normally placid features taut with distress. Even though Mrs. Elton had always been rather cruel to her, Harriet possessed a sensitive nature easily overpowered by such a scene.

Mrs. Elton's unkind behavior had stemmed from the fact that Harriet had been in love with the vicar while he was still a bachelor. Once apprised of that fact by her new husband—a most uncharitable deed, as far as Emma was concerned—Mrs. Elton had never passed up an opportunity to snub the poor girl. But kindhearted Harriet had rarely held it against her tormenter, which was a tribute to her sweet temperament.

Emma was forced to admit that she was neither as sweet nor as sensitive as Harriet, since she was already getting used to the fact that they'd stumbled upon a bloody corpse.

"But, Miss Woodhouse . . . , I mean, Mrs. Knightley," Harriet said, her voice breathy with distress. "What is to be done?"

"First, we must fetch Mr. Knightley. He will take charge of this unfortunate scene."

"Of course," Harriet replied with immediate relief. "Mr. Knightley always knows what to do."

Emma gave her an encouraging smile. "He is the magistrate, after all."

"Should we fetch Robert, too? He would be happy to help."

"We should leave that decision up to Mr. Knightley, dear."

Harriet looked disappointed. No doubt she was longing for her husband's support. And while Robert Martin was a very sensible young man and Donwell Abbey's best tenant farmer, Emma was reluctant to involve others without her husband's knowledge—especially if foul play had been involved.

"But we should fetch Dr. Hughes, as well," Emma added.

Harriet blinked. "But you said Mrs. Elton was . . ." She swallowed. "Dead. How can Dr. Hughes be of any help?"

Emma repressed an impulse to sigh and reminded herself that Harriet was still very rattled. "Dr. Hughes will know what to do with the . . . er, Mrs. Elton, since he is also our local coroner."

She didn't know Dr. Hughes very well, because her family had always relied on Mr. Perry, the village apothecary, for their doctoring. But George had consulted with Highbury's physician on a few legal matters over the years, when a coroner's opinion was needed.

"Would it not be better to fetch Mr. Perry?" Harriet asked. "That's who Mr. Elton always relied on for health matters, I think."

"The coroner will need to determine the cause of death."

Harriet frowned, obviously confused. "Surely she must have slipped on the steps and hit her head."

Emma turned again to peruse the body, ignoring the squeamish sensation in the pit of her stomach. "If Mrs. Elton simply slipped, she might certainly have received a nasty knock to the head. But a fatal injury? I think not."

The fact that Mrs. Elton's neck was at such an angle seemed too odd for a simple slip and fall on the chancel steps. She also looked quite disheveled, and for all her bad sartorial taste, she would never dream of stepping out her door without every frivolous bow and too-large button firmly in place.

Emma frowned and took a step forward to get a closer look. Mrs. Elton was garbed in a bright blue gown and matching spencer, the top button undone so her neck was partially exposed. Normally, the woman wore a necklace or some sort of choker, but today her throat was bare.

She crouched down a bit. "Are those marks on her neck?" she asked, more to herself than to Harriet.

Her friend crept up beside her. "What did you say, Mrs. Knightley?"

Emma pointed. "Look at her throat, Harriet." She hadn't initially noticed any bruises there, but now the marks were quite evident on a closer inspection.

Harriet clutched Emma's arm. "Why would she have bruises on her throat?"

"Mrs. Elton usually wore a necklace. Perhaps someone took it and injured her in the process."

"Mrs. Knightley, I do think I'm about to be sick!"

"You most certainly will not," Emma said in a firm voice. "We have too much to do."

She took Harriet by the arm and steered her back down the nave.

"Harriet, you need to find Dr. Hughes and tell him to come to the church. Then go to the Crown Inn and ask one of the stable boys to run for Mr. Knightley. Simply say that I need to see my husband as soon as possible on a matter of urgent church business."

"But what do I tell Dr. Hughes?"

"Simply say there's been an accident, and that he's needed at the church immediately."

"So you do think it's an accident?" Harriet asked in a hopeful voice.

*Unlikely.*

Emma hesitated. "I don't know, Harriet."

In the past, she'd too often let her imagination run away with her. It had resulted in a number of unhappy misunderstandings, including the belief that Mr. Elton returned Harriet's affections. But in this fraught situation, she was determined to rely on reason over imagination. After all, what did she know about murder? There might be a perfectly rational explanation for Mrs. Elton's unfortunate demise.

Firmly ignoring her mind's efforts to conjure up lurid scenarios, she escorted Harriet to the vestibule. The door was still open, and sunlight streamed into the old stone porch that sheltered the entrance. Birds flitted between the majestic oaks that stood guard over the tombstones in the graveyard, and a marbled white butterfly danced past, then landed on a lavender bush. Outside, all appeared ordinary and peaceful in Highbury.

For a moment, she was tempted to march out of the church and into the sunlight. Inside lurked a nightmare and a hideous intrusion into the tranquility of daily life. If she tried very hard, perhaps she could pretend it hadn't happened at all. Pretend that Mrs. Elton was alive and well, her usual supercilious self, snubbing Emma the first chance she got.

"Mrs. Knightley? Are you unwell?" Harriet asked.

Emma had never thought of herself as a coward or someone unequal to dealing with even the most vexing of challenges, including a possible murder. She would indulge in a bout of nerves later, alone in the privacy of her bedroom.

"I'm well, Harriet. Now, you'd best be off. First to Dr. Hughes and then to the Crown."

Harriet nodded and started down the path toward the street. Then she stopped and spun around.

"But, Mrs. Knightley, what are you going to do while I'm gone?" Her eyes had grown as round as tea saucers. "Surely you cannot stay here by yourself, with the . . . with Mrs. Elton."

"I cannot leave her alone, Harriet."

Harriet rushed back and grabbed Emma's hands. "But you cannot! It would be simply too dreadful."

While Emma did not relish the notion of sitting alone with a corpse—possibly a murdered one at that—she knew George would wish her to keep people out of the church until he arrived. Besides, if Mr. Elton were to come, she must try to prevent him from entering. He must not be allowed to see his wife without adequate preparation.

"Harriet, you must calm yourself. I'll be perfectly fine."

Of course, her robust imagination chose that exact moment to cast up images of desperate villains lurking in the vestry or the bell tower, waiting to pounce on the next unsuspecting victim.

"But surely Mr. Knightley would be shocked if I left you alone," Harriet exclaimed.

"He would be even more shocked if we left poor Mrs. Elton alone. Truly, Harriet, there is no need to worry about me."

Her friend adopted an uncharacteristically stubborn attitude. "No, I cannot leave you, Mrs. Knightley. If you can be brave, then I will be brave, too."

Emma repressed a flare of impatience. "That's very kind, but one of us must go and fetch help. And I must remain here, just in case Mr. Elton comes by."

"I forgot about Mr. Elton." Harriet fell to wringing her hands. "Poor Mr. Elton. Whatever will he do when he finds out?"

"You're not to think of that now. I am relying on you, Harriet, as no doubt will Mr. Elton. We must do everything in our power to help him in this dreadful situation."

Harriet gave her a tremulous smile. "You're right, Mrs. Knightley. You are always right. I will run to the Crown—"

"No, go to Dr. Hughes first, and no running. You must be calm. We do not wish to raise the alarm, at least not just yet."

Harriet turned to go but then spun around again. "But what if something dreadful and evil did happen to Mrs. Elton? And what if a dreadful person is still lurking about?"

"Really, Harriet, your imagination is even worse than mine. If there was foul play, I'm sure the perpetrator is long gone by now."

"But—"

"I promise to stand just at the door, right here. If I see or hear anything to alarm me, I will rush off immediately." She turned Harriet around and gave her a gentle shove. "Now, please go. We're wasting time."

"Yes, yes. You're right."

Harriet took off down the path, her skirt and petticoat flying.

"No running, dear," Emma called after her.

Harriet, oblivious, pelted out to the street.

"Drat," Emma muttered.

Well, it was a very warm day, so she could only hope that the street would be quite deserted and that Harriet wouldn't bump into Miss Bates.

Miss Bates and her elderly mother lived in a small set of apartments overlooking the high street. And although she was a dear and kind woman, Miss Bates relished nothing so much as sharing news and gossip as widely as possible. If she were to get wind of this hideous situation, half the village would know of it within minutes and no doubt descend upon the church.

While she pondered that alarming thought, Emma stood in the doorway of the porch, keeping to her word to remain out of harm's way. But as the minutes crept by, she found it almost impossible to remain still. Too many questions troubled her.

Why had Mrs. Elton come to the church? How could she possibly slip and fatally injure herself? The chancel steps were shallow and covered in a sturdy red carpet. Mrs. Elton was not infirm to any degree, nor was she particularly clumsy. And how could a simple fall account for those marks on her neck?

As abhorrent as the idea might be, she had to acknowledge the likelihood that Mrs. Elton had met with foul play. But from whom and why? Had she arranged to meet someone and fallen into some sort of dispute? But, really, what sort of dispute could lead to her murder? While generally disliked by the locals, she *was* the vicar's wife. And while Emma had no patience for Mr. Elton—he had made an *exceedingly* forward marriage proposal to her the Christmas before last and had responded quite nastily when she'd refused him—the vicar was a well-regarded man. As far she knew, he had no enemies.

When she glanced toward the street, there was no sign of anyone. George was likely at his estate at this time of day, so no doubt it would take time to fetch him. But unless Dr. Hughes was out on a call, Harriet should be returning with him very soon.

Growing a trifle bored, which showed an unfortunate lack of sensibility on her part, Emma stepped back into the church. Surely there could be no harm in seeking respite from the hot sun. Even if Mrs. Elton *had* been murdered, the perpetrator was certainly long gone, leaving a mystery that George would be called upon to manage and help solve. Her husband already had so many responsibilities. Donwell Abbey, the Knightley family seat, greatly occupied his time, and there were also his duties as magistrate. George was so busy that sometimes Emma barely saw him until they sat down to dinner at Hartfield.

And now this murder in the church would cause a terrible uproar in their village. Vulgar speculation would abound, along with a degree of hysteria that would make life more difficult for Emma's already overworked husband.

When it came down to it, Mrs. Elton was proving to be just as difficult in death as in life.

Emma mentally winced, ashamed to entertain such an ugly thought. It wasn't Mrs. Elton's fault that she was now an undignified heap on the steps of the chancel. After she had suffered such a terrible death, to be left alone on a cold stone floor seemed an additional insult.

She squared her shoulders, refusing to lurk like a frightened rabbit at the back of the church. Although she and Mrs. Elton had cordially despised each other, the least she could do was keep watch over the unfortunate woman's corpse until George and the doctor arrived.

After marching up the aisle, she came to a halt by the body. Mrs. Elton's face had turned a mottled shade of gray, and her lips a ghastly shade of blue. As for her eyes . . .

Sinking down into the nearest pew, Emma struggled to catch her breath. Mrs. Elton's eyes seemed to bulge from their sockets in a fixed glare, as if she were tremendously offended. Since Mrs. Elton had been a woman who was frequently offended in life, Emma supposed it was only natural that she would feel equally put out to meet such an undignified end.

Still grappling with a sense of disbelief, she glanced around their pretty little church. Questions and secrets lingered in the air like dust motes in a sunbeam. Her gaze alighted on the stained-glass window on the south side of the church, with its commanding depiction of St. Michael, a sword of justice in one hand and the scales on which to weigh souls in the other. It was an ironic counterpoint to the scene in front of her, and she couldn't help thinking that the archangel looked almost as offended as poor Mrs. Elton.

*If only he could speak.*

Had Mrs. Elton simply been unlucky and encountered a thief? Yet nothing seemed to be missing. The large brass candlesticks were still on the altar, and the linens were undisturbed.

Of course, a thief could have gone into the vestry, where the cupboards contained some excellent silver, including an antique chalice and paten.

Emma rose and headed up the steps onto the chancel. She could at least take a quick peek into the vestry and ascertain if anything was missing.

She stopped when, from her left, there came the sound of quick footsteps and then a door clicking shut. It was the vestry door, the only other entrance to the church. She froze on the top step, trying to think over the pounding of her heart. Was her overwrought mind playing tricks on her? Because if not, it meant that someone had indeed been in the vestry, possibly for the entire time she'd been in the church.

Glancing behind her down the nave, she recalled her promise to Harriet. At the first sign of trouble, she was to leave the church immediately. Hesitating, though, she strained her ears. A deep silence once more settled over the church.

*Nothing ventured, Emma.*

Ignoring the warning voice in her head—which sounded remarkably like her husband's—she hurried up to the altar and grabbed one of the brass candlesticks. It was so heavy that she almost dropped it. Still, it might make for an effective weapon, if need be.

She fervently hoped it wouldn't come to that.

After creeping across the remaining distance to the vestry, she darted a look inside the room.

It was empty, and the door leading outside was half-open. The latch had obviously not caught. Mr. Elton had complained more than once about the faulty latch that needed to be repaired.

Emma hurried across to the door. It opened onto a gravel path that led around the back of the church to the lych-gate. That gate was now swinging in the gentle breeze. She rushed over to it, but there was no one in sight. The graveyard was deserted, as was the path that led out to the street.

After a brief internal debate, she decided it was pointless to attempt a pursuit. Whoever had been hiding had too great a start on her and had no doubt already disappeared. Besides, rushing down the street, brandishing a candlestick, would certainly attract just the sort of notice she was trying to avoid.

Turning back, she caught a flutter of white fabric in the grass by the gate. Frowning, she stooped to pick it up. It was a fine handkerchief made of cambric and edged with a particularly elegant stitch. It obviously belonged to a woman, and Emma had the feeling she'd seen the handkerchief before, or at least one with a similar sort of handiwork. She closed her eyes for a moment, pursuing the elusive wisp of memory that floated just beyond her grasp.

With a mental shrug, she finally opened her eyes and tucked the handkerchief into her sleeve. She'd give it a more thorough inspection later.

She returned to the vestry, where a quick check showed that nothing was disturbed and that the cupboards were intact and locked.

As Emma went into the chancel to replace the candlestick, her gaze fell on its partner. It was not in its usual place, appearing to have been shoved to the altar's edge, almost against the back wall. She reached out to move it back into position. Just as she was about to wrap her fingers around the stem, she jerked back, almost losing her balance. She caught herself and then leaned a steadying hand on the altar. Stretching up a bit, she peered at the sconce at the top of the stem.

And horror swept through her. She recoiled, breathing hard against the lurch of her stomach.

*Blood.*

Blood smeared, as if someone had hastily tried to wipe it off the candlestick. Any lingering doubts were now removed. Any question that Mrs. Elton had indeed been murdered was gone now that Emma had found what was obviously the murder weapon.

Sickened, she made her way back to the nave. For several moments, she concentrated on taking slow, steady breaths to bring her erratic heartbeat under control. Once more she forced herself to look at the crumpled body on the chancel steps. Beyond the terrible sadness in her breast, Emma felt a growing sense of outrage. To come to such a horrible end, and before the altar of her husband's church . . .

Mrs. Elton's murder cried out for justice.

"I'm sorry," she whispered. "You did not deserve such a cruel fate."

At the sudden sound of a quick, hard boot step, she nearly jumped out of her skin.

"Good God, what's happened?" Her husband's long stride ate up the length of the nave. "My Emma, are you all right?"

When George opened his arms, she flung herself into the safety of his encompassing embrace. Tears threatened, but she blinked them away. Her husband was here, and she was perfectly safe. Crying would only worry him. Worse yet, they would waste his time when there were far more important matters at hand.

Like finding a killer.

She pulled back but kept her hands braced on his forearms. His tall, masculine presence and his quiet strength chased away ghosts and fears, bringing reason and comfort in their wake. George would manage everything. Of that, Emma had no doubt.

"I'm perfectly fine," she said as calmly as she could manage. "You mustn't worry about me. But, George, Mrs. Elton . . . how positively dreadful."

He let her go, crouched down beside Mrs. Elton, and studied the body for several minutes while Emma impatiently waited. Then he rose and turned to her, his features grimly set.

"This cannot be simply an unfortunate accident," he said. "Far too much blood, among other things."

"Yes, the marks on her neck, too, as if someone tried to . . ."

*Throttle her*, Emma didn't say. It was the first time she'd formed that specific thought in her mind. To put one's hands around a woman's throat and squeeze hard enough to leave bruises? It was an image too horrifying to contemplate.

When George briefly cupped her cheek, the warmth of his palm brought her back to herself.

"Try not to think about it," he said. "At this point, we don't know what happened."

Emma did know, at least in part, but she simply nodded.

"Harriet was to join you today," he added. "Was she here when you discovered the body?"

"Yes. She was quite overcome."

"One would imagine so." A faint smile briefly lifted the corners of his mouth. "Not you, though."

"It would hardly help Mrs. Elton if both of us were to succumb to the vapors."

"I presume it was Harriet who sent that boy from the Crown to fetch me."

"Yes, and I also sent her to find Dr. Hughes. I cannot imagine what's keeping her, though. It was shortly after two by the tower clock when we found Mrs. Elton."

His dark eyebrows shot up. "You've been here by yourself for half an hour?"

"Not that long, because it took me some minutes to calm Harriet down and convey the proper instructions."

"It was wise to send for Dr. Hughes instead of Mr. Perry."

She shrugged. "There was nothing Mr. Perry could do, and Dr. Hughes is the coroner, after all."

"Yes, and as such, I would have been required to send for him immediately." George checked his pocket watch. "Hughes must be visiting a patient, or else he'd be here by now."

"And Harriet must have gone there after him."

Her husband looked dubious. "I trust you impressed upon her the need to be discreet and cautious."

"I did, although she was very rattled. But since neither Miss

Bates nor anyone else has descended upon us, we can assume that Harriet has so far managed to keep what she has seen to herself. You were at Donwell, I take it?"

"I was walking back to Hartfield when the boy found me."

She suddenly gasped and pressed a hand to his chest. "You didn't stop at Hartfield, did you? Please tell me the boy didn't stop there first."

Her father was a kind but fretful man who greatly depended on Emma for his daily comfort and peace. Any sort of upset or change, even a minor one, was enough to cut up his nerves and bring on a bout of ill health. George, unwilling to cause her father any distress, had therefore moved into Hartfield after their marriage. Since her father loved George like a son, he had gratefully welcomed him into their home rather than losing his daughter to Donwell.

Because her father remained fretful and easily overset, Emma dreaded the deleterious impact the murder of someone he knew would have on his health.

"The boy bypassed Hartfield and took the way to Donwell," her husband replied. "Your father knows nothing. Of course, it will be difficult breaking the news to him, but we cannot worry about that now."

She gathered herself. "You're right. We cannot leave Mrs. Elton here all day, and there is Mr. Elton to consider, as well."

"Hughes will take charge of the body and conduct a proper examination, and I'll break the news to Elton." Then he frowned. "Emma, why didn't you wait outside? I cannot be happy that you stayed in here by yourself."

She spread her hands wide. "I couldn't leave her alone, George. It just didn't seem right. Besides, I was perfectly safe."

*Or perhaps not.*

"I trust you saw or heard no one else the entire time?"

When she hesitated a second, alarm flared in his dark gaze, and he took a step closer. "Emma, what aren't you telling me?"

"I must show you something."

She led him to the altar and pointed to the blood-smeared candlestick. George leaned in to inspect it. Then he quickly pulled a handkerchief from an inside pocket, wrapped it around the base, and picked it up for a closer look.

"I think that must be . . ." Emma wriggled a hand.

"The murder weapon?" George starkly replied.

"That seems quite clear."

He carefully put the candlestick back down. "Did you hear or see anything else that gave you pause?"

"Besides the corpse lying on the chancel steps?"

Her husband sighed. Emma's sense of the absurd sometimes surfaced at inappropriate times, a habit she couldn't seem to break. Fortunately, George rarely held it against her.

"I did hear something," she admitted. "I believe there was someone in the vestry."

For a moment, he gaped at her. "While you were in the church?"

"Of course, George. How else could I have heard the noise?"

"Good God, Emma." He grimaced. "What did you do then?"

"I went to see who it was."

He took a hasty step forward, looking horrified. "Did it not occur to you that it was very likely the person who murdered Mrs. Elton?"

"Of course it did. That's why I took the other candlestick, in case I had to defend myself. A good thing, too, because when I put it back, I noticed the blood on the other one."

George was apparently struck speechless, an unusual state for him.

"Truly, dearest, I was perfectly safe," she earnestly added. "The sound I heard was someone *leaving* the vestry, which I thought quite odd. Why would a murderer hang about here instead of leaving right away?"

"I can think of one reason," he tersely replied.

"Which is?"

Instead of answering, he turned on his heel and stalked off to the vestry. Emma followed, unsurprised that he was upset. The lives of the Knightley and Woodhouse families had been intertwined for as long as she could remember, and George had been watching over her since she was a little girl. The notion that she might have been in danger would be bound to cause him dismay.

"I'm quite certain that nothing has been taken," she said as he prowled around the room. "And the cupboards are still locked. I thought at first Mrs. Elton might have surprised a thief, but that doesn't seem to be the case."

"It's too early to speculate." He took her by the elbow and steered her back to the chancel.

"I do wonder where Harriet is," she said. "She should have been—"

Harriet suddenly burst into the church. She was flustered and red faced, with her bonnet hanging by its ribbons from her neck.

"Mrs. Knightley, Dr. Hughes will come as soon as he can, but I just saw Mr. Elton on the street. He asked me if I was going to the church to attend to the flowers. I didn't know what to say. I . . . I just picked up my skirts and ran here to tell you. He was coming right behind me."

Emma led her to a pew. "Sit and rest, Harriet. Mr. Knightley will attend to Mr. Elton."

George was already striding down the nave to intercept the vicar. He stopped when Mr. Elton hurried into the church, looking both puzzled and harassed.

"Mr. Knightley," he exclaimed, "what are you doing here? I just saw Mrs. Martin in the street, and she was acting in a most irregular fashion."

"Oh, no," Harriet whimpered.

Both taller and more broad shouldered than the vicar,

George tried to block his view of the body. "Mr. Elton, why don't we step outside? There is something I must tell you."

"Why can you not tell me here?" Mr. Elton replied with a frown. He leaned left, and his gaze darted toward Emma and Harriet. "This is my church, and I insist—" He broke off, his eyes widening with horror and disbelief, as he spotted the body. "Augusta? Is that *my* Augusta?"

George placed his hands on the vicar's shoulders. "My dear Philip, if you would step out—"

Mr. Elton barged past him and almost tripped in his rush to the chancel steps. He stared down at his wife for a few seconds and then dropped to his knees.

"Augusta, Augusta," he moaned as he rocked back and forth. "What has happened to you?"

When he clutched at his wife's hands, looking like he would throw himself onto the body, George strode forward.

"Come, Mr. Elton." He took him by the arm and more or less hoisted him up. "It would be best to leave her until Dr. Hughes arrives."

"No, I will not! Not till I know how this could be!"

When George cast her a glance, Emma joined them.

"Come, Mr. Elton," she said, touching his arm. "Why don't you sit with me in one of the pews? Dr. Hughes should be here—"

Mr. Elton suddenly turned and threw himself upon her, exploding into sobs. Naturally, Emma wished to make allowances for the poor man's shock, but having a distraught vicar hanging about her neck was decidedly awkward.

Gingerly patting his back, Emma cast an imploring gaze at her husband, who was looking rather stunned.

"Help," she mouthed.

He sprang into action, gently pulling the vicar away from her. "Come, sir. Please sit down. Dr. Hughes will be here shortly to attend to your wife."

Mr. Elton subsided into a pew and pulled out his kerchief with trembling hands. He blotted his cheeks as he gave Emma a woebegone look.

"Dear Mrs. Knightley," he quavered. "Please forgive my outburst. But to see my poor Augusta like that . . . How can this possibly be?" He buried his face into his kerchief and wept.

"Dear sir, please think nothing of it." She straightened her mangled bodice and then sidled up to her husband. "Perhaps Mr. Elton should wait outside for Dr. Hughes. This is far too distressing a scene for him."

George nodded and again helped Mr. Elton to his feet. He guided him down the aisle, speaking in calm, comforting tone, and led the vicar outside.

Harriet gazed after them, looking quite woebegone herself. "Mrs. Knightley, I do not understand any of this. Who would wish Mrs. Elton dead?"

Emma pondered her friend's question for several moments. Mrs. Elton was possibly the most disliked person in Highbury. More than a few residents could barely stand to be in her presence—Emma being one of them.

So it seemed to her that Harriet was asking the wrong question. There were a number of people who might wish Mrs. Elton ill or even dead. The correct question therefore was, who would actually perform the foul deed of murder?

# CHAPTER 2

Sighing, Emma's father tucked the lap blanket around his legs. "Miss Bates was in such a state that I feared for her health. For her to walk home after suffering such a terrible shock was foolhardy, indeed. It would have been dreadful if she'd fainted or suffered a spell."

Emma poured him a small glass of ratafia. "But you had one of our footmen escort her home, Father. Miss Bates is perfectly safe."

"Quite right. I had forgotten. Still, I wish she had taken our carriage. It would have been no trouble for James to drive her."

That her father had been willing to call up the carriage indicated his degree of distress. Father hated to inconvenience their coachman—not to mention the horses, which were surely the most pampered beasts in all of Highbury.

Emma had just been breaking the news of Mrs. Elton's death to him when Miss Bates had unceremoniously burst into the drawing room. On learning of Mrs. Elton's demise, Miss Bates had immediately run for Hartfield, almost incoherent with shock. Emma had all but forced a glass of sherry down the poor woman's throat. Smelling salts had also been applied, and Miss Bates had eventually been persuaded to drink a cup of tea.

Having known the woman all her life, Emma was well aware of her tendency to respond to events, good or bad, in an excitable fashion. Still, she'd been surprised to see Miss Bates reduced to such a state. Although Miss Bates was the daughter of a vicar herself and thus had held Mrs. Elton in considerable esteem, they'd not been especially close. Mrs. Elton *had* been a friend to Miss Bates's niece, Jane Fairfax, if a dreadfully patronizing one. Mrs. Elton had even arranged for Jane to take a position as governess to a wealthy family in Bristol. That arrangement had come to naught, though, when it was revealed that Jane was secretly engaged to Frank Churchill, a man who stood to inherit a large estate from his maternal uncle.

Mrs. Elton had not been pleased to see her efforts summarily rejected. Emma, though, suspected she was aggrieved primarily because she'd not been privy to Jane's scandalous secret. Then again, neither had anyone else in Highbury, including Frank's father, Mr. Weston.

Although her friendship with Jane had eventually been repaired, the vicar's wife had subsequently been quite cool to Miss Bates. So, to see the little spinster so overwrought, especially in front of Emma's father, was surprising. Miss Bates was always mindful not to ruffle *dear Mr. Woodhouse*, but today she'd done more than ruffle him. Thankfully, Father had been so concerned for her welfare that he'd almost forgotten the state of his own nerves.

He now expelled a tremulous sigh. "What a dreadful day. Why, it was almost as bad as the day your dear mother died. I can barely stand to think of the horror of it all."

Emma's mouth dropped open. Her mother's untimely death had transformed her father into the anxious and fretful man that he was today.

"Father, I know you esteemed Mrs. Elton, and of course you

feel distressed for Mr. Elton. But I cannot allow you to think the two events are comparable."

He grimaced. "But, Emma, *you* discovered the body. To be exposed to such a thing . . . I cannot imagine anything worse."

"To be the victim would be quite a bit worse, I would think."

"You mustn't make light of this, my dear. I shouldn't be surprised if you fall dreadfully ill as a result of the shock. And the church can be so drafty at times. I hope you did not catch a chill."

If there was anything that struck mortal terror in her father's soul, it was the thought of catching a chill.

"I assure you, dearest, I was not a bit chilly this afternoon."

*Except when gazing at a throttled corpse.*

She pushed away the hideous thought. "It was very warm today, even in the church."

He flapped an alarmed hand. "To be overheated is just as bad. I think you should have a basin of Serle's gruel and then go straight to bed. Yes, that would be just the thing."

Their cook's gruel was the most appalling dish Emma had ever tasted and the bane of her childhood.

"Father, we've barely finished dinner. Besides, I wish to wait for George. You know he's been in the village all afternoon, helping Dr. Hughes and seeing to Mr. Elton. I should wonder if he's had even a bite to eat."

"I do hope George doesn't fall ill after spending the entire afternoon in that drafty church. It was very careless of Dr. Hughes to ask such a thing of him. Mr. Perry certainly will have something to say about it."

Emma had to swallow a smile, since her husband possessed a robust constitution and great energy. She had been the happy recipient of his vitality over the course of their marriage and could safely say she had no present fears for his health.

"As local magistrate, I'm afraid George's presence was necessary. Father, why don't you finish your ratafia and then retire for the night? Would you like to take the sleeping draught that Mr. Perry left for you? One of the footmen can bring it up."

"I shall certainly take it, else I'll not sleep a wink tonight. And I insist that you see Perry tomorrow, as well, Emma. We must make sure that you suffered no ill effects from today's distressing events."

"Of course, dear. If that will set your mind at ease."

The sound of footsteps in the hall and the murmur of masculine voices signaled that her overworked husband had finally returned home. Emma went to the door to greet him.

"Finally," she said. "I thought Dr. Hughes would never release you from your duties."

He slipped an arm about her waist and pressed a quick kiss to her cheek. "Yes, it's been a long day."

"You must be exhausted, George. Have you had anything to eat? I can ring for Serle to send up a tray. We had a lovely fricassee of veal as well as a splendid trifle."

Her father dramatically sighed. "And much more besides, but I could barely swallow a bite. Emma did her best to eat something—more for my sake, you understand. I know she did not wish me to worry after her terrible ordeal."

Truth be told, her terrible ordeal had left Emma terribly famished. She had demolished ample portions of the veal and the trifle and had finished dinner with an apple and cheese tart. Though rather insensitive of her, it hardly made sense to pretend she wasn't hungry.

And the veal *had* been excellent.

"That was very thoughtful of Emma," George wryly replied.

She smiled. "You know very well that nothing impairs my appetite, which is surely an unfortunate lack of sensibility on my part."

"Or a great deal of common sense. If we were to lose our appetites every time a tragic event occurred, the human race would starve in very short order."

"What an admirably practical view of things." Emma drew her husband to the settee on the other side of the fireplace. "But you have still not answered my question. Did you have anything to eat?"

"Yes. Once matters at the church were . . . sorted, Dr. Hughes and I needed to discuss the coroner's inquest. We stopped at the Crown for something to eat while attending to the details."

Emma went to the tea service on the mahogany sideboard. "You must have been pestered to death by the locals. I imagine there are very few in Highbury who've not heard the news by now."

"Mrs. Stokes put us in one of the private rooms, where we were able to enjoy our supper in relative peace."

She placed a few macaroons and a slice of the apple and cheese tart on a plate and carried it back with a cup of tea. "The Crown isn't known for its food, George. I hope you had enough to eat."

"One must hope the opposite," her father exclaimed. "Serle told me that Mrs. Stokes serves a great deal of cake. And I hope you didn't partake of any custard, George. One can never rely on the custards at coaching inns, you know."

Since they rarely left the environs of Highbury, coaching inns posed little danger to their general, not to mention culinary, welfare.

"We just had a cold repast of meats and cheese," he replied.

Father tsked. "I do hope the meat was not rancid, as it so often is at inns. Perhaps you should take a purgative."

George simply sighed. Normally well able to deal with her father, he was clearly feeling taxed this evening. Murder seemed like a dreadfully exhausting affair.

"Father," Emma said, "I think Mr. Perry would wish to see you in bed by now. He was quite emphatic that you have an early night."

"You are quite right, I'm sure. I shall retire immediately."

She helped him up and escorted him to the door, then handed him off there to a waiting footman.

"I'm sorry, dearest," she said, returning to her husband. "Father means well, but he is quite overset."

George stood and wrapped his arms about her. "And what about you, my Emma? Your father is not wrong to say it was a terrible shock."

She rested against his broad chest, feeling her tension drain away. In her husband's arms, she could almost imagine the horrors of the afternoon to be naught but an awful dream.

"You mustn't worry about me, George. You know I am rather unshockable."

"It grieves me that you were the first to find the body. But we must also be grateful for that, because you handled the situation with considerable aplomb." He pushed her back a bit to offer a stern look. "Excepting your investigation of noises in the vestry. I cannot be happy about that, Emma."

As they sat, she ignored his little criticism. After all, she'd had a lifetime of practice in doing so.

"Tell me about Mr. Elton. How does he fare?"

"Initially, as poorly as one would imagine. When I tried to persuade him to return to the vicarage with Dr. Hughes while I waited for the constable to arrive, he refused. He then insisted that the body be removed to the vicarage immediately, growing quite agitated about the matter. That, unfortunately, led to words with Constable Sharpe. Dr. Hughes was forced to intervene and acquiesce to his demand."

Emma waggled a hand. "I can understand Mr. Elton's objections, since one wouldn't wish to leave the poor woman on the floor like a heap of discarded clothing."

"As can I. But in the case of murder, the victim is usually kept at the scene of the crime until the coroner's jury has had a chance to view the body."

"How utterly ghastly."

"We would have placed Mrs. Elton on a table and covered her but would also have done our best to preserve the scene. Elton was passionate in his objections, however, stating that it would be a desecration to the church and to his wife's dignity. It was hard not to see his point."

Emma grimaced as she reached for a macaroon on her husband's plate. "Poor Mr. Elton. What a dreadful scene."

"Thankfully, once he convinced Dr. Hughes to have the body conveyed to the vicarage, he recovered somewhat. In fact, he supervised his own footmen in transporting Mrs. Elton home."

She thoughtfully chewed on her macaroon. "Mr. Elton was all but hysterical when Harriet and I were there. I didn't expect him to recover so quickly."

Her husband eyed her. "Unlike some who shall remain unnamed."

"George, if you were murdered, I'm sure I would lose my appetite."

He flashed her a wry smile before putting down his teacup and stretching out his legs, his booted feet almost brushing against her skirt. He fell into a brown study, as if mulling over an obscure point.

She nudged him. "What are you thinking?"

He glanced up. "I was pondering the Eltons' relationship. It was rather an odd one, you must admit."

"Really? I thought they were perfectly suited to each other. Both condescending and petty in exactly the same way."

When her husband raised his eyebrows, Emma wrinkled her nose. "And I am clearly a terrible person, given that poor Mrs. Elton was bashed over the head with a candlestick just hours ago."

"Yes, I am dreadfully shocked."

"I imagine you're used to me by now. But why would you be thinking about their relationship in the first place?"

"Sometimes I have wondered if there was any true affection between them."

Emma thought about that. "I think that cannot be true. They were always quite pleased with each other, you must admit. Mr. Elton took a great deal of pride in his wife."

"Indeed. Pride seemed to be at the center of their relationship—both in each other and in themselves."

"That's not surprising, given their respective temperaments."

George studied her with a rather inscrutable expression. "Sometimes I believe his previous affections for you were more genuine."

She scoffed. "Mr. Elton was in love with my position in society and my money. Once I refused him, any affection he felt was transformed into disdain."

"He certainly sought comfort from you this afternoon."

"Please don't remind me. George, that was so *terribly* awkward. But I'm sure he couldn't help himself, poor man."

"I suppose," he said before once more falling silent.

Emma nudged him again. "But truly, what is to be done? As magistrate, you must oversee this dreadful affair, on top of all your other responsibilities. I cannot think how you'll manage."

"I'll get to that in a minute. First, tell me about Miss Bates. How did she take the news?"

"Very poorly. We needed both smelling salts and sherry to produce any semblance of calm."

"I cannot imagine your father responded to that scene with equanimity."

"Miss Bates was so undone that it seemed to startle Father out of himself. I doubt he's ever seen her in such a state before."

George rubbed his chin. "It's rather odd, isn't it? While I accept that she is a sensitive soul, Miss Bates was not particularly close to Mrs. Elton."

"Perhaps it was simply encountering so heinous a crime against someone she knew."

"Still, one cannot help but wonder at so dramatic a reaction."

She waggled a hand. "How does one react appropriately to a murder, though? I hardly think there are standard expectations in that regard."

"I suppose you're right," George replied.

"I do not relish having the right of it in this situation, I assure you. So, what happens next?"

"The empaneling of the coroner's jury, in order to determine if Mrs. Elton was the victim of homicide."

Emma rolled her eyes. "George, I found the poor woman dead on the floor, with a bloody candlestick nearby. Surely there can be no doubt that it was murder."

"None, but the decision still rests with the coroner's jury. The law is particular in that regard."

"Did the good doctor arrive at any conclusions as to the cause of death?"

"The blow to the head seemed decisive to him."

She frowned. "What about the marks on Mrs. Elton's neck? The bruises were pronounced by the time I left the church."

"Dr. Hughes suspects those marks were left when a necklace was taken from her throat."

"I suppose that could be true. I wonder what necklace she was wearing?"

"Mr. Elton thought perhaps she was wearing her pearls."

Now *that* was surprising. "If it's the necklace I'm thinking of, it was a wedding gift from Mr. Elton."

And a valuable gift it was—a chandelier-style gold necklace decorated with pearls. Mrs. Elton had always taken great pride in it and would extol its value to anyone who would listen. It was, however, quite formal and not the sort of piece that one generally wore in the afternoon.

"Do you think it was taken before or after she was struck with the candlestick?" she asked.

"I cannot say."

If it was that particular necklace, it was certainly not prone to breakage. Ripping it from the throat of a struggling woman would be no easy task.

"And Dr. Hughes doesn't think the marks could have been caused by anything else?"

"He didn't say so."

Emma opened her eyes wide. "But, George, the bruises almost appeared as if she'd been—" The macaroon in her stomach suddenly curdled.

"Throttled?" he grimly finished.

"Yes. And surely that would have occurred before she was bashed over the head? What would be the point in..." She swallowed. "In performing such an act if she were already unconscious or dead?"

George shrugged. "No point at all."

Images of Mrs. Elton's last moments sprang to life in her mind. Outside the church, Highbury had gone about its business, its residents shopping at Ford's or at the bakery, quaffing an ale at the Crown, or making afternoon calls to friends. All while a desperate struggle played out in the peaceful setting of a church, where one should feel utterly safe.

Even now, on a warm summer's eve, while the sparrows twittered in the garden, it seemed impossible to imagine such a horror.

Yet no amount of pretending could wish it away.

"That poor woman," she quietly said.

Her husband rubbed a weary hand over his face. "There is much to be done these next several days, Emma. I will be out of the house a good part of the time."

"I know, dearest, and you're not to worry about that. I can manage whatever domestic affairs arise here or at Donwell."

"I will most likely need your assistance in making the funeral arrangements. I doubt Mr. Elton will be in a proper state to do so, and we must find a curate to conduct the service."

"Of course, George. But for tonight, you must try to get some rest. Surely you are now finished for the day."

He mustered a rueful smile. "I regret to inform you that Dr. Hughes will be stopping by shortly to give me a more detailed report. He will also take your statement while events are still fresh in your mind."

Emma sighed. "I suppose that's wise, although I don't stand in danger of forgetting anything about this dreadful experience."

Every detail was engraved on her mind, including Mrs. Elton's baleful glare of death. She suspected that expression would haunt her dreams for quite some time.

"You'll need to give testimony at the inquest," George added.

She stared at him, dismay welling up. The notion of reliving one of the worst days of her life in a public setting was appalling. "My written statement would not be sufficient?"

"I know testifying is an unpleasant prospect, but it cannot be helped. You and Harriet were the first witnesses, and you did discover the murder weapon. Your powers of observation are acute and will prove useful to the jury."

She sighed. "I wish they'd been less acute, then. And the mind reels to think of Harriet on the witness stand."

"You will help her through it."

Emma doubted that even she was up to the challenge of helping Harriet construct a coherent narrative. "Dearest, the poor girl spent a good part of the time with her head between her knees."

George huffed out a laugh and then rose to his feet when a quiet knock sounded on the door. "Enter."

Simon, their senior footman, came into the room. "Dr. Hughes to see you, sir."

"Please show him into my office. Mrs. Knightley and I will be along momentarily."

"Very good, sir."

Emma cocked her head. "Your office is rather small, George, and not particularly comfortable."

"Dr. Hughes tends to ramble on. If we make him too comfortable, he'll be inclined to linger. I have had quite enough of murder for one day and would like to spend at least part of the evening in quiet, with my wife."

"Then I will decline to offer any refreshments, although my reputation as a hostess is bound to suffer."

"I'm willing to take that risk." He offered her a hand. "Are you ready, my dear?"

"Yes, I do believe my loins are properly girded."

She came to her feet and paused only to shake out her skirts and straighten her collar.

"It's best not to jest with Dr. Hughes, Emma. He can be a trifle officious, and he takes his duties very seriously."

"George, even you cannot believe I would joke about murder."

He simply raised his eyebrows.

She held up a hand, as if taking an oath. "I promise to behave *and* to be the soul of brevity."

"Thank you. If you grow tired or find his questions too unpleasant, you must feel free to stop. I will not have you distressed by this, my darling. You have had enough of a shock for one day."

"For a year, more likely."

She took her husband's arm as she attempted to order her thoughts and chase away the niggling questions that circled the edges of her mind, refusing to be pinned down.

# CHAPTER 3

Dr. Hughes gave Emma a ponderous bow. "Mrs. Knightley, please excuse my calling at such a late hour. I will do my best to keep my inquiries short and to distress you as little as possible."

She smiled. "And I will do my best to help you, sir."

"Your magnanimity is greatly appreciated, madam. As a medical man, I can well surmise the degree of violence inflicted upon your nerves by the misfortune of stumbling upon such a shocking scene. It is most distressing for a woman of your character and standing. I sincerely regret your involvement."

She repressed the impulse to note that any sensible person would be distressed to stumble upon a bloody corpse.

"Fortunately, the shock was relatively short lived," she instead replied.

"Please sit, Doctor," George said. "I don't wish to impose upon my wife any longer than necessary."

Dr. Hughes rather officiously handed Emma to a walnut-framed chair but then planted himself in front of one of the inset bookcases that lined the walls of the study. George regarded him with an ironic eye before moving to sit behind his neatly ordered desk.

Dr. Hughes, a tall man, had a broad stomach and an imposing head of silver hair. A pair of too-small spectacles that perched halfway down his nose forced him to peer over them with a nearsighted squint. Emma wondered why he wore them. Perhaps he thought they imparted a learned air. For the rest, he was well but soberly dressed and gave the general impression of a serious man. She'd never heard complaints about his medical skills except from her father, who resented his existence on principle, since he was competition for his beloved Mr. Perry.

"Before we begin, Mrs. Knightley," Dr. Hughes started, "I would like to inform your husband of my latest discussion with Constable Sharpe. He imparted a few additional insights to me shortly after you left the Crown, Mr. Knightley. As I'm sure you can agree, time is imperative in these cases, and the constable did not wish to wait."

If George was irritated by his supercilious tone, he gave no indication. "Proceed, Doctor."

The doctor glanced at Emma. "I beg you to forgive me, madam, because some of the details may disturb you. Please believe that I have no wish to offend your delicate sensibilities."

"My sensibilities couldn't possibly be more offended than they were when I first saw Mrs. Elton's corpse," she replied. "Not to mention coming across the bloodstained murder weapon."

He raised a finger. "The ostensible murder weapon, Mrs. Knightley. We must not rush to conclusions."

She raised her eyebrows. "I would hate to rush to conclusions, sir. Nevertheless, it seems fairly evident that a heavy candlestick smeared with blood, only feet from a body with a significant blow to the skull, must have played some sort of role in the murder."

"Dr. Hughes, what additional observations did Constable Sharpe make after I left you?" George smoothly intervened.

The doctor eyed Emma suspiciously but then proceeded. "Mr. Sharpe now feels certain that robbery was the motive. Mrs. Elton's maid has confirmed that she was indeed wearing her pearl necklace when she left the house. The thief was apparently determined to get his hands on the necklace at any cost—including vile murder."

From what Emma knew of him, Constable Sharpe was a sober and diligent man. And far be it from her to jump to those pesky conclusions, but his report suggested a certain lack of imagination.

"If it was a thief," she asked, "then why didn't he take anything else? There are a number of valuable items in the church, including the candlesticks. In fact, he had one of those candlesticks right in his grasp."

Hughes gave her a rather pitying smile. "Clearly, Mrs. Elton surprised the thief in his criminal endeavors. And perhaps once he acquired the necklace, he felt no need to take anything else. As Mr. Elton has pointed out, the necklace is quite valuable."

"Yet one can't always tell these things at a glance. The pearls may have been artificial, and what appeared to be gold may have been brass. Real pearls are quite rare, whereas imitations are not."

Dr. Hughes began to look a trifle irritated. "The criminal classes aren't known for their wit, Mrs. Knightley. The villain obviously saw what looked to be an impressive necklace and took it."

George held up a hand. "So Constable Sharpe is saying that the thief went into the church, presumably with the intention of stealing the silver. When he was surprised by Mrs. Elton's appearance, he then decided to rob her instead and wound up killing her in the process."

"That is exactly what both Constable Sharpe *and* I are suggesting," Dr. Hughes replied with a degree of hauteur.

"I still fail to see why he didn't take the candlesticks," Emma argued. "They're also valuable, and they were *right* there."

The doctor scowled over the top of his spectacles. "Perhaps he ran out of time, or was alarmed by the outcome of his villainous actions. He was desperate to escape before anyone made the hideous discovery."

"But he had time to wipe down the murder weapon and put it quite carefully back on the altar. That doesn't suggest someone in a state of desperation or panic. It seems rather coldblooded to me."

"Constable Sharpe and I must disagree, Mrs. Knightley."

George leaned forward, deliberately catching her eye. "Perhaps the thief was rattled by the escalation of events. He obviously wanted the necklace, but I doubt he wished to kill Mrs. Elton in the process."

Emma had yet more questions, but her husband clearly did not want her quizzing Dr. Hughes.

Still . . .

"I wonder what Mrs. Elton was doing in the church in the first place?" she asked, more to herself.

Dr. Hughes nodded. "Ah, I have the answer to that. Mr. Elton was under the impression that his wife had a meeting with one of the villagers."

"I assume the vicar doesn't know who this person is," George said.

"He does not."

Emma looked at her husband. "Mrs. Elton rarely met with villagers on parish business, and certainly not in the church. She hardly stepped foot inside the building but for Sundays."

George hesitated for a moment. "It is odd, I'll grant you."

"Then you must also agree that the timing was also odd—or at least spectacularly unfortunate. Mrs. Elton just happened to have a meeting at the church at the same time as an unknown thief decided to rob the place?"

Dr. Hughes held up both hands. "Forgive me for stating that your observations are rather beside the point at this time. As I have already cautioned, we must refrain from jumping to conclusions. Constable Sharpe is on the case, and he will follow the appropriate lines of inquiry, including ascertaining who Mrs. Elton was meeting in the church and why."

"If anyone is jumping to conclusions . . . ," she began.

George hastily intervened. "We take your point, Dr. Hughes. Carry on."

"I wish to add only that since the cause of death is clear, there will be no need for an autopsy. Mr. Elton was adamantly opposed to another violation of his wife's dignity, and I see no reason to inflict further distress upon a grieving man."

Emma's stomach flip-flopped at the notion of Mrs. Elton sliced open like a specimen in an anatomical experiment. If she were ever to be murdered, she hoped George would be sensible enough to object to such a procedure.

"But," the doctor added, "as you know, the bereaved also insisted the body be removed to the vicarage. That will, unfortunately, complicate matters for the jury."

"One certainly sympathizes with Mr. Elton's feelings," Emma said. "And is keeping the body at the vicarage truly such a complication? The house is only a step from the church, after all."

"When the body is left at the scene, it does give the jury a more comprehensive picture of the crime," George replied. "However, in this case, I think the complications are minimal and will be easily dealt with. Mr. Elton made a strong case that it was inappropriate to leave a murdered corpse, much less his wife, in a sacred setting."

"Most irregular," Dr. Hughes muttered, obviously annoyed to see his authority overridden.

"Well," Emma said, "leaving it there would certainly put a damper on Sunday services."

When George breathed out a small sigh, she wrinkled her nose in apology. Really, though, the situation was so bizarre that one couldn't help blurting out the occasional odd comment.

"With your permission, Mr. Knightley," Dr. Hughes said in frigid tones, "I would like to take Mrs. Knightley's statement."

Emma mentally rolled her eyes. "You needn't ask my husband's permission, Dr. Hughes. I am perfectly happy to give you a statement."

Now the doctor looked scandalized. "I am simply trying to be polite, madam."

"Your courtesy is greatly appreciated, Dr. Hughes," George said. "I'm sure my wife is grateful, as well."

Emma glanced at her husband. When he narrowed his gaze, she was tempted to stick out her tongue just to tease him. Dr. Hughes would surely faint dead away at the sight.

"I am at your disposal, sir," she politely said.

"Then if you would please outline the events of this afternoon, beginning from the moment you entered the church until your husband arrived."

Emma gestured to the empty chair next to her. "Would you like to sit down, sir? My husband can provide paper and quill if you wish to take notes."

"That will not be necessary, Mrs. Knightley. I have excellent recall and a sharp mind."

*And a puffed-up ego.*

It struck her that relying on one's memory was hardly sound investigative practice. But since this was her first murder, she would reserve judgment.

"Mrs. Martin and I entered the church shortly after two in the afternoon. We were attending to our usual business of refreshing the flowers in the church prior to Sunday services."

"And you saw no one lurking about the premises or in the graveyard, behaving in a suspicious manner?"

*Like wiping off a bloody candlestick or digging a grave for the intended victim?*

"All was as it should be. The church caretaker, as usual, left the front door unlocked, and we proceeded inside."

With as much detail as she could recall—now wishing that she *had* written down some of those details—she recounted the sequence of events and her actions. When she began to describe the noises she'd heard emanating from the vestry, Dr. Hughes shot up a hand.

"Mrs. Knightley, are you suggesting that the killer was still in the church? In the vestry, to be precise?"

She shrugged. "How would I know who it was?"

He regarded her with frank disbelief. "You do realize that if there was someone in the vestry, it might very well have been the person who murdered Mrs. Elton."

Emma made a point of avoiding her husband's eye. "Of course. That is why I armed myself with one of the candlesticks before I went to investigate."

Dr. Hughes's eyes popped wide behind his tiny spectacles, making him look like a rather strange insect. "My word, Mrs. Knightley! I cannot believe your husband would approve of such reckless conduct."

Before she could bristle up, George intervened. "That is a matter between me and my wife, Dr. Hughes. Please carry on, since the hour grows late. I do not wish to fatigue Mrs. Knightley any more than necessary."

His tone, though calm, brooked no opposition. Emma decided that she would not be too fatigued to expend a little extra energy on her husband once they were alone.

"My apologies, sir," the doctor stiffly replied. "What happened next, madam, if I may be so bold as to ask?"

"I went into the vestry and found it empty. The door to the

churchyard was unlatched and partly open. I hurried outside to see if anyone was there, but both the churchyard and the path to the street were deserted."

Suddenly, her brain conjured up the image of the dainty white handkerchief lying by the lych-gate. In all the commotion it had slipped her mind, and she'd remembered only after returning home and changing her dress. Eager to speak with her father, she'd simply shoved the cloth in a box on her dressing table and promptly forgotten about it again.

"My dear?" George asked.

She looked at him. His gaze had grown suddenly sharp, as if he could see the wheels spinning in her head. One of those niggling questions, the ones that had dogged her for hours, was possibly coming into focus.

And the possible answer to that question gave her significant pause.

"Forgive me," she said. "I lost my train of thought for a moment."

"That is perfectly understandable," the doctor commented in an indulgent tone. "You were obviously quite rattled, so it is no wonder that your memory of events is vague or even a trifle faulty."

This time she didn't hide her irritation. "There is nothing faulty with my memory, Dr. Hughes. Nor was I so rattled that I could not think. Poor Mrs. Martin was overset for a time, but I never lost my ability to either observe or reason."

"Yes, I spoke with Mrs. Martin. She was quite overcome, which was certainly understandable." His attitude made it clear that he found Harriet's response to Mrs. Elton's demise more appropriately female.

"I, however, was not overcome, and I can relate with perfect clarity what I saw and heard," Emma retorted.

"My wife did discover the murder weapon," George pointed out.

"A lucky happenstance," Dr. Hughes replied.

Indignation surged in her breast. "There was nothing lucky about it. I noticed one of the candlesticks out of place. That then led me to observe that there was blood on it, which someone had clearly tried to—"

"In any event," the doctor said, talking over her, "you should leave these matters to the law. I am sure Constable Sharpe and I would have discovered the murder weapon soon enough. After all, it is our job as professionals to do so. Ladies—or even gentlemen—should never be required to undertake such unpleasant tasks."

Emma swallowed the impulse to snap at him. Unfortunately, the man was correct. She was simply a witness, while he was . . .

*Incredibly pompous and annoying.*

She also couldn't help but feel a strange sense of duty toward Mrs. Elton. As if in discovering the body, a certain obligation had been placed upon her, one she couldn't ignore.

"My dear?" George's gaze held both questions and concern.

She mustered a smile. "It's nothing. And of course I would never wish to interfere with any formal investigations."

Informal ones, however, might be another matter.

Dr. Hughes rewarded her with an avuncular smile. "No woman of taste or feeling—and of course you have a great deal of both—could wish to involve herself in such an ugly business. I sincerely regret that you and Mrs. Martin must be subjected to ongoing unpleasantness. It is indeed unfortunate that you had to discover the body."

"Better us than Mr. Elton, I suppose. The poor man was a complete wreck."

George stood, signaling the interview was ended. "I think we can all agree that my wife and Mrs. Martin comported themselves with commendable discretion and good sense. If not for them, we might have had half the village descending on the church."

Dr. Hughes held up his hands, as if conferring a benediction. "I do commend you on your forethought, Mrs. Knightley. As Highbury's physician, however, let me just note that because you have received such a terrible shock, I should be happy to prepare a calming draught for you or send round a tincture of laudanum to help you sleep."

"My nerves are perfectly fine, sir, but I thank you for your consideration."

"But surely—"

"That's enough for tonight, Dr. Hughes," George firmly said.

Hughes looked mildly offended but quickly regrouped. "As you wish, Mr. Knightley. That being the case, I will bid you—"

When Emma was struck by another one of those niggling questions, she couldn't help but interrupt him. "Dr. Hughes, do you think it within the realm of possibility that Mrs. Elton could have been killed by a woman?"

George shot her a startled look. "What?"

*Drat.*

Her tongue had unfortunately outrun her brain.

"I suppose I'm simply curious," she said, trying not to sound like a henwit. "I wonder if a woman—no one in particular, you understand—would have the strength to leave those marks on Mrs. Elton's throat. They were quite pronounced, which suggests a certain degree of strength, does it not?"

Both men stared at her as if she'd lost her mind, which was a trifle awkward. Still, she wanted the doctor's professional opinion. Even though the candlestick was heavy enough that she'd almost dropped it, Emma felt certain she could swing it with enough force to bash someone's head in. But to actually grapple with Mrs. Elton, seizing her by the throat and throttling her? That seemed beyond her.

"Well, Dr. Hughes?" she prompted after several moments of fraught silence.

"I suppose a strong woman could theoretically have done so," he reluctantly replied. "It's difficult, however, to imagine a lady having the fortitude to commit such a heinous act."

"I'm not talking about fortitude, sir. I'm talking about physical strength, enough to leave bruises on another person's neck."

"A woman who labored with her hands—a farm or kitchen worker, perhaps—might have the strength necessary to commit such a deed."

"So one engaged in physical labor," she said, needing to be sure.

He frowned. "Yes, but why would you even ask such a thing, madam? There is not a shred of evidence to suggest that Mrs. Elton was killed by a woman."

She waved an airy hand. "No, of course not. It was just a random thought on my part."

By now, George was regarding her with a marked degree of suspicion. Emma did her best to ignore him.

"Random thoughts are best left out of criminal investigations, Mrs. Knightley," Hughes intoned.

"Of course. Quite right, sir. Do forgive me."

"Is there anything else, my dear?" George asked.

She tendered what she hoped was a smile as innocent as a babe's. "No. We must let Dr. Hughes be on his way. I'm sure he still has much business to attend to."

George ushered the doctor out to the entrance hall. As the two men made their goodbyes, Emma sank down into her chair, mulling over everything she'd heard.

When her husband returned, she tilted her head. "That was quite something, wasn't it?"

He settled into his chair. "Vastly entertaining. I did warn you, though."

"I'm grateful you did. I must say, George, I cannot be impressed by Dr. Hughes. The general consensus seems to be that he is a competent enough physician, but what is your opinion of his skills as a coroner?"

"I have always found him to be perfectly adequate in terms of his medical assessments."

She scoffed. "That is a nonanswer, dearest."

His smile was wry. "Do I think he's a pompous ass? Yes, but he takes his duties seriously, and he is punctilious in meeting the legal obligations of the role."

"Don't you agree, though, that he was too ready to jump to conclusions? To assume that the killer must be a thief when several valuable pieces in the church were left untouched seems a rather hasty assumption to make."

"As he mentioned, perhaps Mrs. Elton frightened him off."

"He was so frightened that he murdered her," she dryly replied.

"Point taken. But it's also possible that matters simply got out of hand. Mrs. Elton may have challenged him or was about to cry out for help. And after he killed her, perhaps he was so rattled that he fled the scene rather than look for more items to steal."

"After taking her necklace, which is admittedly very valuable," she mused. "Still, he wasn't so rattled that he didn't fail to wipe down the murder weapon and put it back in its place on the altar."

George frowned at the ledger on his desk. "I admit it's a detail that troubles me."

"Because?"

He looked up, and their gazes locked.

"Because all of this might suggest that it was not a random theft or a crime of opportunity."

Emma sighed, hating his answer but unable to disagree. "And if it wasn't, then it means it had to be someone who knew her."

"Yes."

And that was precisely what her little niggles had been suggesting all along. "How utterly ghastly. But who could hate Mrs. Elton so much as to bash her over the head with a candlestick?" When her husband simply lifted a sardonic eyebrow, she threw him a mock glare. "Yes, very comical. But I'm serious, George."

His spark of humor vanished. "You're right, of course. And I am indeed grieved that the poor woman came to such a horrible end. She did not deserve such a fate."

"Nor does Mr. Elton deserve to be so shockingly served, either. I will be the first to admit that they were not a likable couple, but how utterly tragic her murder is. It's hard to imagine how Highbury will ever really recover."

As far as she knew, never in living memory had such a violent deed been committed in their heretofore peaceful village. To her, it felt like an essential innocence had been forever lost.

George studied her for several long moments. "Are you going to tell me? Or shall I guess?"

She sighed. "It's terribly annoying that you can read me so well."

"I've had many years of practice, Emma. I'm assuming it has something to do with your question regarding a woman's ability to commit murder."

She placed both her hands flat on his desk and studied her fingernails. Well, actually, she was avoiding his ability to see right through her.

*Coward.*

Looking up, she met his gaze. "I found something else at the church today. It might be nothing, but combined with the noises I heard in the vestry . . ."

*Oh dear.*

George was now regarding her with a marked degree of irritation. It was an expression she hadn't seen on his face since before their marriage, when they all too often argued over her behavior.

"In fairness," she hastily added, "I completely forgot about it until I was giving Dr. Hughes my statement. It seemed a little thing at the time, and it went clean out of my head."

"And what is this little thing?"

"When I went outside the church, I found something by the lych-gate."

He waited for a few moments. When she didn't immediately reply, his expression transformed from irritated to rueful. "Love, do you not trust me?"

She scrunched up her face by way of apology. "Of course I do."

Her curious reluctance to tell him what she had found stemmed from a sense that she would be opening Pandora's box. But opened it must be.

"I found a handkerchief in the grass by the lych-gate. Obviously, someone had dropped it there."

Understanding dawned in his expression. "A lady's handkerchief."

"Correct."

"But, Emma, there's no way of knowing who dropped it or when. It could have been Mrs. Elton or someone else passing through the churchyard in the past few days."

"But it rained yesterday, and the handkerchief was perfectly clean and dry. And I would recognize Mrs. Elton's handkerchiefs. She used to boast that hers were acquired from a fashionable linen draper in New Bond Street. They were stitched with her initials and always heavily scented, too."

"All right. What did you do with this mystery handkerchief?"

"Since I didn't wish to leave the body unattended, I simply shoved it up my sleeve. I forgot all about it until I was changing for dinner."

"Would you mind fetching it for me now?"

She went to retrieve the folded piece of cambric from the box on her dressing table. When she returned to the study, she gave it to George, who unfolded it and turned it over. Then he held it under the Argand lamp on his desk, inspecting it more closely.

"What is it?" she asked, leaning forward to look.

He pointed to one corner on the back side of the handkerchief.

Emma blinked. "Is that . . . ?"

"Blood? Yes, I believe it is."

Stunned, she sank back into her chair. "I was in such a hurry that I didn't notice that."

"It's just a small spot on one corner, so I'm not surprised you missed it."

Emma rubbed her forehead. The events of the day finally seemed to catch up with her, and she suddenly felt very weary.

"Good God," she whispered.

George carefully placed the handkerchief on his desk blotter and came round to take her hand. She clung to his fingers, comforted by his warmth.

"Emma, do you know to whom it belongs?" he asked.

She met his gaze. "The stitching seems familiar, but I can't place it."

He sighed. "We have to tell Dr. Hughes and Constable Sharpe. There's a very good chance it's evidence. And if you suspect whose it is, I'm afraid you'll have to reveal that, too."

"Yes, I know. It's just that it might mean . . ."

"That the person who committed the crime might be someone we know," he quietly answered for her.

Emma again rubbed her forehead, fighting the sensation that they were trapped in a spiraling nightmare. Murder had come to Highbury—and quite possibly close to home.

# CHAPTER 4

Emma set out immediately after breakfast. If there was one person who could answer the question that bedeviled her, it was her former governess, Mrs. Weston.

George had risen with the dawn to begin a day that would be full of the business of murder, and Emma's restless anxieties had compelled her to arise, as well. She'd dressed quickly and snatched a bite to eat before setting off to visit her dear friend, who, after George, was the person who knew her best.

In addition to sensible advice, Mrs. Weston would give her unstinting support. With the particular matter before her, Emma suspected she would need every bit of that support.

She turned into the graveled drive of Randalls, where the Westons resided with their little daughter, Anna, not yet one year of age. Emma loved the old Tudor mansion, a sprawling edifice of red brick with lovely casement windows and tall, fanciful chimneys. Enormous chestnut trees lined the drive, and ancient yew hedges intersected the lawns and flower beds. But for the modern fountain in the garden, one could well imagine a dashing knight in doublet and hose, a rapier by his side, trysting with his fair lady.

Come to think of it, a rapier might be particularly useful since there was still a killer on the loose. An image of the deceased Mrs. Elton sprang into her mind, and for the first time, Emma realized that taking a footman for escort might have been prudent.

Chastising her colorful imagination, she hurried to the front door. While it was early to be making calls, Emma had been given carte blanche to visit Randalls whenever she wished.

One of the maids opened the door and ushered her into the vaulted entrance hall.

"Good morning, Hannah. Is Mrs. Weston still at breakfast?"

"She's in the parlor with Miss Anna." Hannah cast a quick glance down the drive. "Begging your pardon, ma'am, but should you be walking by yourself all the way from Hartfield? I'm sure my father would have been happy to drive you, what with all these nasty villains running about."

Hannah's father, James, was Hartfield's coachman. Emma rarely felt the need for a coach, although loyal James was always ready to transport his charges the short distance it took to get anywhere in Highbury.

"Only one villain, most likely," Emma replied. "And I do hope he isn't lurking about the hedgerows in broad daylight, waiting for his next victim."

Hannah locked the door. "Poor Mrs. Elton was murdered in broad daylight, now, wasn't she? You just ring when you're ready to go, Mrs. Knightley, and I'll have the kitchen boy walk you home."

Once again, it struck Emma how the impacts of such a heinous deed could ripple outward, disturbing the peace of all those who lived within its dark pool. A new sort of danger seemed to hover over Highbury, bringing with it an unfamiliar vulnerability.

Hannah showed her into the parlor. With its low ceiling, wooden beams, and large fireplace, it imparted a sense of practical comfort. Mrs. Weston had added a number of feminine touches—chintz fabrics for the sofa and chairs and Chelsea porcelain vases filled with freshly cut flowers. Mr. Weston's contribution had been to modernize the chimney, an improvement greatly appreciated by resident and visitor alike.

Mrs. Weston was seated in a cozy nook by the window, attending to her needlework. She put aside her frame when she saw Emma, and hurried to meet her.

"Emma, dearest," she exclaimed, hugging her. "When we heard the dreadful news yesterday, Mr. Weston was ready to run all the way to Hartfield to see how you were. Only our fears that his presence would disturb your father held him back."

Emma was grateful for her friend's comforting hug. So many times as a child, when some little tragedy or mishap had struck, she'd found shelter in the affectionate embrace of her governess.

Of course, Miss Taylor, as she was then, had always been more than a governess. She'd ably filled the vacant role of mother in Emma's life. Endlessly patient, the young woman had nurtured both Emma and her sister, Isabella, with steadfast affection and gentle counsel.

The day Miss Taylor had married Mr. Weston had been one of mixed blessings. It had been a match Emma herself had promoted, and she'd been truly pleased to see her dear friend find contentment with an excellent man. Unfortunately, that also meant Miss Taylor was lost to Hartfield forever, replaced by Mrs. Weston, who took up new loves and concerns.

For a time, Emma had felt rather lost herself. But life—and a series of embarrassing mishaps—had taught her much since that fateful day. Now she found herself as contented as Mrs. Weston.

"I'm perfectly fine," she replied with a reassuring smile. "Father and I received your note before we went into dinner last night. Your words were a great comfort to him."

"What a dreadful experience for you, though." Mrs. Weston pressed her hand. "Do you think you could tell me a little about it? It might relieve your mind."

"Let me see sweet Anna first, as she always lifts my spirits. How is she this morning?"

They peeked into the cradle, set in front of the fireplace. Mrs. Weston touched a gentle hand to her daughter's head.

"She's sleeping, thank goodness. My little darling was awake very early, quite determined to have her father's attention. Naturally, Papa was happy to comply. He carried her all about the room, making the most ridiculous horsey noises. I thought I'd never get her back to sleep."

Emma gazed at the sweet girl, whose soft brunette locks curled out from under her cap and framed her rosy cheeks. Anna was the picture of peace and contentment. "She is the perfect antidote to yesterday's unpleasant events. I think I could look at her forever."

"*Unpleasant* seems an understatement." Mrs. Weston drew her to the sofa. "And poor Harriet! How did she react?"

Emma subsided onto the plump chintz cushions. "She was quite overset. Thankfully, she recovered and went off to find Dr. Hughes and George. I would have been in a terrible fix without her."

Mrs. Weston prepared a cup of tea, slipping in an extra lump of sugar as a treat. She'd done the same when Emma was a little girl, whenever she had fallen and skinned her knee or engaged in some other childish misadventure.

"Then I'm so glad that Harriet was there, so that you needn't face such an awful scene alone."

"I'm afraid the awfulness will continue for quite some time." She took the cup and gloomily stared into the brew as her mind's eye once more conjured up the hideous scene.

Mrs. Weston gently touched her shoulder. "I don't mean to press. If you'd rather not talk about it, I perfectly understand."

Emma mustered a smile. "I want to tell you, and I also need your advice. I'm in a stew, and I'm not quite sure how to proceed."

"I am always here for you, as is Mr. Weston."

"And that is a great comfort."

She plunged back into the events of yesterday, keeping her description as brief as possible. Still, Mrs. Weston went pale when Emma related how she'd checked the body.

"Heavens," she exclaimed. "I think I would have fainted dead away. However did you manage to keep your composure?"

"If Harriet hadn't been with me, I'm not sure I would have. Fortunately, she almost swooned, thus relieving me of the necessity to do it myself."

"Now, my dear, you can hardly blame the poor girl. She's been very sheltered, you know."

"It hasn't been my habit to stumble upon dead bodies, either."

"No, but you have never been prone to the vapors or irrational behavior. I shudder to think of your father or dear Isabella coming upon such a situation."

"Yes, they both have a great deal of sensibility. I seem, on the other hand, to have very little, and thank goodness for that, or we would be suffering the vapors at Hartfield every day."

Mrs. Weston smile was wry. "Not a likely scenario with Mr. Knightley in residence, I suspect."

"As you know, his influence on me started years ago. I learned early on that emotional flights of fancy impressed George very little. He either ignored me or gave me an improving book sure to bore me to tears. The latter was a very effective method of correction."

Mrs. Weston chuckled but then fleetingly pressed a hand to her lips. "How dreadful of me to laugh when poor Mrs. Elton is lying dead in the vicarage."

Emma shrugged. "I'm not sure how to act, to be frank. Part of me still refuses to believe it, and to believe that I'm involved in such a situation."

"Only as a witness. I assume you'll have to give testimony at the inquest—which naturally will be quite unpleasant—but that should be the end of it."

"Perhaps not quite," Emma replied after a moment's hesitation.

Mrs. Weston put down the teacup she'd just been raising to her lips. "Emma, what did you do?"

"It's not what I did so much as what I found."

Now that she'd come to it, she was again reluctant to share her suspicions.

"I will keep in the strictest confidence whatever you tell me, if that is what you wish," Mrs. Weston quietly said.

"Thank you, but it's bound to come out sooner or later. George knows of it already, if only in part."

That startled her former governess. "What can you tell me that you couldn't tell your husband?"

"First, you need to know that there was someone else in the church. I heard that person in the vestry after Harriet left."

"Good heavens! Emma, it could have been the . . ." Mrs. Weston obviously couldn't bring herself to say the word.

"Murderer? I doubt it, although I did have to steel myself before investigating."

Mrs. Weston stared at her in speechless horror.

"It was fine," Emma hastened to reassure her friend. "I heard that person leave by the vestry door. So it was perfectly safe."

"Emma Woodhouse, it was nothing of the sort," Mrs. Weston exclaimed, reverting to her governess ways. "You could have been killed!"

"As I said, the person had already fled the vestry. Nevertheless, I armed myself with a candlestick from the altar, just in case."

Mrs. Weston covered her eyes.

"And you needn't scold me," Emma added. "George has already made an adequate job of that."

Last night, after they'd gone to bed, he'd given her another lecture about the need to observe caution and to avoid meddling. It had taken a concerted effort to distract him, although distract him she had, and to their mutual satisfaction.

"I certainly cannot blame the poor man," Mrs. Weston said. "You must be more careful, Emma. Who knows what sort of madman could be about?"

"I'll be careful, I promise."

"And you're not to walk here alone, either, at least for the time being. If Mr. Weston has not returned by the time you leave, I will send the kitchen boy along with you."

Emma bit back a smile. "A very sensible precaution, to be sure."

Mrs. Weston brushed an invisible wrinkle from her skirts and made an effort to compose herself. "Now, you said there was something you wished to ask me. I will make a wild guess and assume it's about something you discovered in the church. Mr. Weston told me that the church was robbed, and that very likely poor Mrs. Elton surprised the thief during the act. Did you find something pertaining to the robbery?"

"Only Mrs. Elton was robbed and her necklace taken. The church's silver and plate remained untouched."

Mrs. Weston frowned. "How strange. If that was the case, why murder Mrs. Elton? Why not just take the necklace and flee?"

"That is a very pertinent question, although not one Dr. Hughes or Constable Sharpe seem particularly vexed about. Both assume that upon killing Mrs. Elton, the thief panicked and fled the scene. I suppose that's possible, but given the cold-blooded way Mrs. Elton was murdered, one would think the killer not inclined to panic."

Rather than panicking, the killer had taken the time to attempt to eliminate the evidence of his—or her—presence in the church.

Mrs. Weston studied her with consternation. "I hope you're not intending to meddle in the investigation, my dear."

Emma widened her eyes, trying to look innocent. "I cannot imagine why you would think I would. I'm merely curious, as any rational person would be. And . . . I'm also concerned."

"About someone in particular? Someone we know, perhaps?" Mrs. Weston shrewdly asked.

"Yes." She opened her reticule and drew out the mystery handkerchief. "I found this outside, by the lych-gate. Since it was clear to me that whoever was in the vestry had escaped using the side door, I went out to the churchyard to see if I could catch a glimpse of him. Or her."

Mrs. Weston's eyebrows shot up. "Her?"

Emma handed over the dainty piece of fabric. "This is what I found."

Her friend examined it. "Anyone could have dropped this in the past few days. How do you know . . . ?" Her voice trailed off. As she glanced up, a dawning alarm collected in her light brown eyes.

"Yes, that is a bloodstain," Emma confirmed.

Mrs. Weston held the piece of fabric gingerly, now looking slightly ill. "Mr. Knightley has seen this?"

"He wanted to take it to Dr. Hughes first thing this morning, but I told him I would do it."

"Would it not be more appropriate for him to do so? I hate to think of you so involved in this matter, Emma."

"I suggested that it made more sense if I took it. Dr. Hughes will wish to know why I didn't tell him last night." She shrugged. "It was because I simply forgot in all the excitement."

"How could you forget about a bloodstained handkerchief?"

"I didn't notice the blood at first." She circled a finger. "Dead body inside the church, remember? It was only later that George and I saw the stain. I think we can all agree it would be a stupendous coincidence if the blood did *not* belong to Mrs. Elton."

"Emma, what is it you wish to ask *me*?"

"I'd like you to take a close look at the stitching."

With a slight frown, Mrs. Weston held up the handkerchief to the light that was streaming through the casement windows. She studied the fabric for a long moment, and then a sharp breath hissed out from between her teeth.

Emma sighed. "You recognize the stitching."

"Of course. No one else in Highbury has such a delicate hand. Much better than mine, which is why I asked her to teach you and Isabella when you were girls."

Emma had been trying to convince herself that her anxieties were unfounded, but Mrs. Weston's answer put all doubts to rest.

"That's why I didn't wish to tell George until I was sure of it. But what it suggests defies belief. How is it possible to conclude that she could . . ."

The thought was both horrifying and ridiculous.

Mrs. Weston grasped her hand. "It doesn't mean that she had anything to do with the murder. It more likely means she was in the church shortly after the murder and was also the person hiding in the vestry."

"But why would she hide if she had nothing to do with it?"

"You know how easily flustered Miss Bates is. You truly cannot think her capable of murder."

"I fear Dr. Hughes and Constable Sharpe might not see it that way, given the evidence you hold in your other hand."

"No person of sense could believe her capable of killing anyone, much less Mrs. Elton."

From her experience, Emma was not entirely sure that Dr. Hughes was a sensible man. As for Constable Sharpe, it remained to be seen.

"True, but she hid in the vestry. That certainly seems suspicious by its nature."

"She was obviously very frightened."

"But she must have heard and recognized our voices. Why not then come out? Besides, how did she get blood on her handkerchief?"

Mrs. Weston looked puzzled. "You seem to be trying to convince yourself that Miss Bates is indeed responsible for Mrs. Elton's death."

"No, I'm trying to do the opposite—by making sense of her odd behavior. You didn't see her yesterday, when she visited Hartfield. She was so greatly upset that I almost called Mr. Perry."

"For all her excellent qualities, Miss Bates does not possess robust strength of temperament. And recall how Harriet first reacted. Is it so hard to believe that poor Miss Bates would wish for nothing more than to flee? That in a moment of panic, her desire to escape overrode her good sense?"

Since that had been Emma's initial reaction, she could not entirely disagree. "Still, feeling that impulse and acting upon it are two different things."

"I'm sure there's a perfectly reasonable explanation. But I do think it best if you let Mr. Knightley handle these matters. He will know exactly how to deal with Dr. Hughes *and* Miss Bates. He has such a gentle way with her."

"Yes, but—"

At that moment, Anna awoke with a wail. Mrs. Weston rose and went to her daughter, leaving Emma to her thoughts.

And what she thought was that she needed to talk to Miss Bates before George did. Her husband would always be a paragon of kindness to the poor woman, but he was also the local magistrate. That would put him into something of a bind, caught between his legal duties and his affections for an old friend.

No, Miss Bates needed to be prepared for what was to come. If there was a reasonable explanation for her presence in the church and the bloodstained handkerchief, Emma would be more likely to draw it out of her than any man, even one as kind as George.

She only prayed there *was* a reasonable explanation, because any other alternative was too disturbing to contemplate.

# CHAPTER 5

After bidding farewell to the kitchen boy at the gates of Hartfield, Emma continued into Highbury for the unwelcome task of confronting Miss Bates.

Mrs. Cole, one of Hartfield's neighbors, stood on the opposite side of the street, conversing with the baker's wife—likely gossiping about Mrs. Elton. Highbury's shock at her death was mixed with wild speculation.

One of the more ludicrous tales, told to her only this morning by her maid, proposed that Mrs. Elton had been slain by a vengeful ghost arisen from a church vault. When Emma had asked why a ghost would kill the vicar's wife, Betty had defensively replied that she was simply repeating what she'd heard from Mrs. Cole's footman, who'd heard it from a groom at the Crown, who'd heard it from persons unknown at the vicarage.

Flapping a hand, Mrs. Cole eagerly hailed her. Emma ducked her head and hurried along, praying that her neighbor—a good woman but greatly inclined to gossip—wouldn't follow.

As she made her way through the village square, several locals seemed more determined than usual to pay their respects.

A few even tried to stop her progress. Now feeling more than a trifle annoyed, Emma simply gave them a firm nod of the head and quickened her pace.

With relief, she finally reached the doorway that led up to the Bateses' modest set of rooms. Pausing for a moment to catch her breath, she glanced back at the street. Mr. Cox, the local solicitor, was now steaming in her direction, a purposeful gleam in his eye. Emma fled inside and slammed the door shut. It would seem she *did* need protection—not from deranged murderers, but from the local gossips.

She was not yet halfway up the stairs when the door at the top flew open and Miss Bates anxiously peered out, as if fearing callers. Normally, Miss Bates loved nothing more than visits, with long-winded chats and lengthy rereadings of the latest missive from her niece, Jane Churchill.

But not today, it would seem.

"Oh . . . oh, Mrs. Knightley," she exclaimed. "How . . . how kind of you to come calling when you must have so many other duties to attend to. Everyone in Highbury is telling such *dreadful* stories. I've not spoken to anyone myself, but I'm all atremble to hear such *terrible* things from Patty. Our maid, you know. So much gossip, she says. How terrible for poor Mrs. Elton. She would be appalled to hear such things said about her. And poor Mr. Elton! Mother is quite beside herself thinking about him."

"Yes, it's distressing," replied Emma in a sympathetic tone. "But I think it's best to ignore the tales as much as possible, as they are bound to be inaccurate."

Miss Bates ushered her into the parlor, then slammed the door shut so forcefully that Mrs. Bates, dozing by the fire, startled awake.

"Mother, it's Miss Woodhouse," Miss Bates loudly announced. "I mean Mrs. Knightley. So kind of her to call after yesterday's frightful experience at the church. Miss Woodhouse, I mean Mrs. Knightley . . . Dear me, I am such a scatterbrain today.

What would Mr. Knightley think to hear me call you Miss Wood-house? He would be quite shocked, I am sure."

Emma smiled. "It's not so surprising. After all, you knew Miss Woodhouse for a great deal longer than you have known Mrs. Knightley."

"Yes, yes, as you say. Look, Mother, it is Mrs. Knightley. To think that she would find the time to call on us is kindness itself. And what must Mr. Woodhouse think? He would not wish you to exert yourself on our behalf, Mrs. Knightley, especially in such hot weather."

Mrs. Bates, a tiny woman who was almost swallowed up by her ruffled mobcap and voluminous shawl, looked bemused. It was not an unusual response on her part, although she was obviously aware that her daughter was behaving more oddly than usual.

Emma stepped closer. "How are you this morning, Mrs. Bates? Well, I hope."

The elderly woman eyed her daughter for a few seconds before replying.

"I cannot complain, Mrs. Knightley," she said in voice reedy with advanced years. "How is Mr. Woodhouse this morning?"

"He is tolerably well, ma'am. Thank you for asking."

"Dear Mr. Woodhouse," exclaimed Miss Bates, fluttering like a demented moth between Emma and her mother. "So very kind yesterday. I was in such a state, Mrs. Knightley. I'm quite ashamed to think how I acted. But your father was such a comfort to me. And his insistence that James bring me home in the carriage!" She raised her voice. "Did you hear that, Mother? Mr. Woodhouse wished to call out the carriage for me. Of course, I refused. I know how Mr. Woodhouse hates to inconvenience poor James and the horses. But I was in such a state, you see. So very kind of him, don't you think, Mother?"

Mrs. Bates darted a perplexed glance at Emma. Having reached an age where she spent much of her time dozing by the fire, rousing only for a visit to Hartfield for tea and a game of quadrille, she must certainly now sense the anxiety churning through her daughter's waterfall of words.

Emma dreaded both the chore before her and the upset that was to come. Mrs. Bates was too old to manage the repercussions that would result from her daughter's involvement—however inadvertent—in Mrs. Elton's murder.

Miss Bates continued to stand in the center of the room, clenching her hands. Her gaze darted about, resting first here and then there, but never on Emma.

"Miss Bates, I hate to impose," Emma said. "But might we have a word? There is a particular matter I wish to discuss with you."

The spinster visibly startled. "How foolish of me to keep you standing. I cannot think how my manners have gone begging. And you have been so kind. No one could ask . . . ask for better friends." Her voice wavered as she sank down in her chair. Her face was bleached white as bone, and her eyes were red-rimmed behind her spectacles.

Miss Bates usually reminded Emma of a sparrow darting about in the hedgerows, her drab plumage offset by her cheerful—if occasionally irritating—chirping. The daughter of the former vicar, Hetty Bates had been raised in genteel and comfortable circumstances. But after the death of Reverend Bates, Hetty and her mother had descended to a state of near poverty. They had been forced to move from their former home to this small set of apartments and had to struggle to make ends meet. But so decent and kind were both women that they invoked in their friends and neighbors a true spirit of charity, which greatly ameliorated their reduced circumstances.

In recent months, those circumstances had improved even more, thanks to the marriage of their beloved niece, Jane, to Frank Churchill. Frank was Mr. Weston's only son and had been adopted at an early age by rich relations from Yorkshire after the tragic death of the first Mrs. Weston, thus becoming heir to a considerable fortune. Jane and Frank had wished to move their relatives to more genteel quarters, but Miss Bates had refused. She'd stated with her usual good cheer that she and her mother were perfectly content. They had everything necessary in their excellent family, cherished friends, and cozy life in their beloved Highbury.

Yet such was obviously no longer the case.

She sat across from Miss Bates, who had extracted a handkerchief from the pocket of her gown and was dabbing her cheek. Emma's heart sank as she noticed that the stitching matched that on the handkerchief she'd found in the graveyard.

Miss Bates met her gaze, and she then hastily shoved her handkerchief back into her pocket before mustering a travesty of a smile.

"Tea, Mrs. Knightley? We have an excellent apple cake from the bakery. No one makes apple cake as well as Mr. Wallis . . . oh, except for Hartfield's cook, naturally. No one makes an apple cake like Serle. I expect that's because she uses Mr. Knightley's apples. Everyone knows Donwell Abbey has the best apple orchard in the county. Just last week, I was speaking on that very subject with Mrs. Elton—" She broke off on a gasp. "Oh, Mrs. Elton! What is to be done, Mrs. Knightley? I cannot even think . . ."

"It's about Mrs. Elton that I wished to speak with you," Emma hastily interjected. "I do not wish to distress you, but I'm afraid I must ask you a question."

Miss Bates cast a fearful glance at her mother, who'd gone back to dozing by the fire. Her daughter breathed a sigh of relief and made a visible effort to compose herself.

"I cannot think what question you would need to ask, Mrs. Knightley. My mother and I live so quietly here. We cannot possibly know anything."

Emma opened her reticule and carefully pulled out the handkerchief. "I believe this is yours, is it not?"

Miss Bates stared for a moment, her eyes rounded in shock. "I . . . I . . . Where did you find that?"

"In the churchyard, by the lych-gate."

Miss Bates made a visible attempt to recover. "Oh . . . yes, that is mine. I must have dropped it the other day, when Mother and I went to put flowers on my father's grave. We try to do that every week, you know, if Mother feels up to it."

Emma sighed. Clearly, sterner measures were in order.

"Miss Bates, I truly hate to press you, but I think we must be honest with each other. I believe you dropped this yesterday, when you fled from the vestry."

For once, the spinster was struck dumb. Then, still silent, she shook her head in vigorous denial.

Emma turned over the piece of cambric and pointed to the bloodstain. "But, dear ma'am, how do you explain this?"

Miss Bates squeezed her eyes shut and again vigorously shook her head, as if in doing so, she would deny the very existence of yesterday's events. When Emma reached out and touched her arm, her eyes flew open.

"Please," Miss Bates pleaded in a thin, fear-laced voice. "Please don't make me talk about it."

Emma put aside the handkerchief and took her trembling hands. "Whatever happened, whatever you saw, you are not alone in this. Mr. Knightley and I will support you in every way possible, as will my father. Your friends will protect you, I promise."

But they could do nothing to help Miss Bates until she was persuaded to tell Emma what had happened. And that had to occur before the frightened woman was forced to confess to Dr. Hughes or Constable Sharpe, who would have little patience with her foibles and hesitations.

"Won't you please tell me what happened?" Emma coaxed. "Dear Miss Bates, please let me help you."

"You must think me very foolish," the spinster finally whispered. "But I simply wanted the whole thing to go away . . . to pretend I could forget I'd ever seen it."

"I wished to do the same. But we cannot forget it, can we?"

Miss Bates squeezed Emma's hands before letting go. "But you are so brave, Mrs. Knightley. My father always used to say I was too timid for my own good, and he was perfectly right. I have not the fortitude to deal with something as horrible as m-murder. Please don't make me do so."

*Timid* was not the word that Emma would have ever applied to Miss Bates, but she supposed it was apt in this situation.

"But you are also a vicar's daughter, and no one in Highbury has a greater sense of both morality and compassion than you do, Miss Bates."

The woman pulled out her handkerchief to dab her eyes and blew her nose. "You are too kind, Mrs. Knightley."

Sadly, Emma hadn't always been kind. But now she simply gave the poor dear an encouraging smile, silently willing her to talk. Never did she think she would actually *wish* for Miss Bates to talk, but murder produced strange, unintended effects.

"Do you remember what time it was when you came upon Mrs. Elton?" she finally asked.

"I . . . I'm not entirely sure. Only a few minutes before two o'clock, I believe."

That made sense to Emma, since she and Harriet had entered the church fifteen minutes after the hour at most.

"Did you know that Harriet and I were going to be in the church to do the flower arrangements?"

"I remembered when I heard you and Mrs. Martin out in the porch. That . . . that is when I hid in the vestry."

"Miss Bates, why *did* you hide?"

She seemed to crumple in her chair. "I . . . I was in such a terrible state. And then I heard your voices, and I couldn't bear for you to find me with . . . with Mrs. Elton . . . the way she looked. What would you think of me?"

Emma frowned. "We would think that you had stumbled upon the body, just as we had. Why would we assume anything different?"

Miss Bates flapped an agitated hand. "I don't know. But to discover me with Mrs. Elton like that . . . all alone and in such a state . . . someone might misconstrue . . ."

Emma forced herself to wait several seconds to see if she would continue. "Misconstrue what, Miss Bates?"

"Nothing, nothing at all. I'm just being foolish."

When Mrs. Bates gave a little snort, as if waking up, her daughter shot a fearful glance in her direction.

"Mother cannot know," she whispered. "Her heart. It's not strong."

There would be no way to avoid her mother finding out, since Miss Bates would be called to testify at the inquest. But mentioning that fact now would no doubt pitch her into full-blown hysterics.

Emma patted her knee. "You're not to worry about that. Just tell me what you saw when you entered the church."

Miss Bates drew in a trembling breath. "Well, at first, I saw nothing. But I was in the back, waiting, you know. So, I did not yet see the . . . Mrs. Elton."

"What were you waiting for?"

Miss Bates briefly rolled her lips inward, as if reluctant to answer. "I was to meet Mrs. Elton at two o'clock."

*Well, that is not good.*

Emma had to stifle any signs of dismay at such an unfortunate admission. God only knew what Dr. Hughes would make of it, though.

"And may I ask why you were meeting Mrs. Elton in the church instead of at your own apartments or the vicarage?"

Miss Bates lifted a trembling hand to her cheek. "Dear me, I can hardly remember. I swear it has all gone clean out of my head. But it was such a shock. Seeing her like that . . . so . . ."

"Yes, it was horrible, and it makes perfect sense that you would forget at the time. But surely you can recall now."

She looked everywhere but at Emma. "Now that I think about it, I believe it was to discuss new altar linens. Yes, indeed that was it. Because the old ones are terribly worn, you know. The last time Jane and Frank visited Highbury, Jane was quite shocked by the state of them. She offered to buy an entire new set for the church." She tried to smile. "So like Jane, isn't it? Only she would think to replace all the altar linens."

The altar linens were decidedly *not* worn, since Emma and her father had paid for a new set on Mr. Elton's arrival at the parish two years ago. Why would Miss Bates tell such a patently obvious lie?

"So you were waiting in the back of the church for Mrs. Elton. When did you finally go up to the chancel?"

"When I realized she was late. I like to go up to the front of the church and sit for a spell. It reminds me of the days when my father was vicar. But that's, that's when . . ."

"That's when you saw her." Emma recalled the scene to mind. "Miss Bates, did you touch the body?"

"Yes, but only because I didn't think she was dead, or else I would never have done such a thing," she blurted out. "I . . . I know I shouldn't have, but—"

Emma put out a reassuring hand. "It's fine. I did the same."

"I started to untie her bonnet," Miss Bates said in a wretched voice. "To give her some air. But that's when I saw the blood, and . . ." She covered her mouth.

"Yes, it was beyond horrific." Emma hesitated for a second. "Miss Bates, did you touch her collar or bodice?"

"Why would I do that?"

"Perhaps to give her some air?"

Miss Bates shook her head. "After I saw all the blood, I was too frightened to go near her again."

"Perfectly understandable. Did you notice if Mrs. Elton was wearing a necklace, by any chance?"

"I don't think she was. But it was all such a blur, especially after I realized she was dead. I cannot truly be sure what I saw."

"So, you don't recall if her collar was askew in any way or if the buttons at her throat were undone?" Emma didn't dare ask her if she'd noticed bruising on Mrs. Elton's throat.

Miss Bates's eyes went as wide as a startled rabbit's. "Why would I notice something like that, Mrs. Knightley, especially when she was already dead? Besides, I couldn't bear to look at her for fear of becoming sick."

Emma sighed. "Yes, quite."

Miss Bates would make a dreadful witness at the inquest. She could only hope Dr. Hughes would take into account the poor woman's excitable nature.

"Just a few more questions, if I may. Do you recall how your handkerchief became stained with Mrs. Elton's blood?"

She looked rather green at the memory. "I already had it in my hand when I went to untie her bonnet. It must have brushed against some of her hair. Her hair, it was quite . . ."

"Yes, I saw. Try not to think about it."

"But how can one not think about it?" she burst out. "I will see that horrible sight before me for the rest of my days. If only Mrs. Elton and I hadn't—"

When she broke off with a little gasp, a ripple of alarm skittered through Emma. "If only you hadn't what, Miss Bates?"

When the woman shrank back, Emma grimaced. "Forgive me, ma'am. I don't mean to be sharp with you. But please finish what you were going to say. You and Mrs. Elton hadn't . . . what?"

"That is to say . . . nothing, nothing at all, really. But some might misconstrue it. It was just a silly thing, really. Mrs. Elton was a trifle annoyed with me, which is not to be wondered at. In her kindness, she overlooked my failings and eccentricities. Always so generous, so ready to forgive."

"But why would Mrs. Elton be annoyed with you?"

The spinster seemed to struggle to find the words. "She . . . she has always been such a good friend to us, especially to dear Jane. Such kindness, such condescension she showed to Jane during that difficult time. You remember how Mrs. Elton arranged for her to become a governess to one of her friends in Bristol, and with such generous terms, too. You might also re-call—"

Emma's impatience finally got the better of her. "Yes, I re-call. But what does this have to do with you and Mrs. Elton and what happened yesterday?"

"Poor Jane. She will be so distressed by all of this," Miss Bates said, now fully off on her tangent. "And in her condition, too. Frank will never forgive me."

Emma frowned. "And what condition is that?"

Miss Bates seemed to brighten. "Jane is in the family way. It's still early days, so we are quite secret about it. She was to write to Mrs. Weston this week. But Jane's health has never been good, you know, and when she hears this dreadful news, I fear it will affect her."

"Frank will take care of her, you may be sure."

"Very true. Thank goodness for Frank. He and Jane are so very generous to us, but we cannot be a burden to them, espe-cially now. With friends like you and Mr. Knightley, we want for nothing. And Mrs. Elton's generosity! It was beyond any-thing. If only—" She suddenly pressed her lips together, look-ing . . . frightened?

Yes, Miss Bates was indeed frightened. Of Mrs. Elton, if Emma didn't miss her guess.

She tried to phrase her next question as delicately as she could. "Did Mrs. Elton perform a particular service for you, one that left you feeling indebted to her?"

"I . . . I . . . Well, she was always so generous, you know."

*Generous* was not a term Emma would have applied to

Mrs. Elton, at least when it came to others. To herself, however, the vicar's wife was more than generous.

"Then can you tell me why you and Mrs. Elton fell out?" she gently asked.

Miss Bates was now visibly trembling. "It was just a trifling thing, I promise, and the fault was all mine. And now she is dead. Dead! I cannot bear it."

She burst into tears, taking refuge behind her hands. Dismayed, Emma snatched up her reticule and began digging through it for smelling salts.

"Hetty, what's wrong?" came a quavering voice from the chair by the fireplace.

Startled, Emma glanced over. She'd all but forgotten that Mrs. Bates was in the room. But the elderly woman was now wide awake and staring at her daughter, her wrinkled features doubly wrinkled in concern.

Emma dredged up a smile. "Miss Bates is simply upset about Mrs. Elton. She'll be fine momentarily."

Miss Bates blew her nose and tried to compose herself. "Everything is fine, Mother. Mrs. Knightley is right, as always. We are all grieved by Mrs. Elton's death. So terribly upsetting."

By this point, Emma was finding Mrs. Elton's death more aggravating than not, since the woman was proving just as difficult in death as she was in life. As the next bit of news she needed to impart would surely illustrate.

"Miss Bates, while I am loathe to distress you any further, we must tell Mr. Knightley that you were at the church and that you discovered the body before Harriet and I did."

Miss Bates moaned. "Must we?"

"I'm afraid so."

"Yes . . . yes, you are right, as always. So silly of me to run away, but I was so frightened and did not know what to do."

"I can speak to Mr. Knightley on your behalf, if you like. I can explain why you left the church so suddenly."

Miss Bates clutched at Emma's hands, as if clutching a life-line in a stormy sea. "Would you? I cannot bear the idea of talking about this again."

Emma steeled herself. "I'm afraid you will have to talk about it again, Miss Bates. Dr. Hughes and Constable Sharpe will both wish to speak to you, since you discovered the body. But Mr. Knightley and I will do everything to support you in any way we can. I promise."

Miss Bates stared at her, utterly horrified. Then she collapsed in her chair, her body shaking with sobs.

"Hetty, Hetty, what is the matter?" cried her mother, struggling to stand.

Emma jumped to her feet. "Everything is fine, Mrs. Bates. You're not to worry. I will take care of this."

The old woman gaped at her, clearly thinking her a ninny. A moment later, rapid footsteps sounded on the stairs. The door flew open to reveal Patty, laden with a basket of foodstuffs.

"Patty, thank goodness," Emma exclaimed. "Do you have any smelling salts?"

The competent young woman dumped her basket on the floor and hurried to Miss Bates. "Smelling salts won't work, ma'am. I'll put her to bed and then run to fetch Mr. Perry."

"No, you stay with Miss Bates," Emma replied. "I'll fetch Mr. Perry."

Patty nodded before hoisting Miss Bates up from the chair. She wrapped her arm around the weeping spinster's waist and all but carried her from the room.

With a weary sigh, Emma dropped back into her chair.

"Mrs. Knightley," Mrs. Bates said in a tremulous voice. "Please tell me what's wrong."

*Everything*, she was tempted to reply. And she feared that was no exaggeration.

# CHAPTER 6

Emma smiled at her husband as he ushered her out Hartfield's front door. Sadly, the beloved of her soul did not smile back.

"I cannot be happy about this, Emma," George said. "You should have spoken to me before confronting Miss Bates."

Over the years, she'd learned that although George mostly had the right of things, he wasn't *always* right. This was one of those times.

"In all fairness, George, you went out very early this morning to see Dr. Hughes and then Constable Sharpe."

"You could have waited until I returned home for luncheon," he dryly replied.

"Dearest, did you truly wish to be the first to confront Miss Bates about her extremely odd behavior? As gentle as I was, the poor woman was still overcome with hysterics. I had to fetch Mr. Perry to attend to her." She breathed out a dramatic sigh. "But if you believe you could have managed the situation more adroitly, I sincerely apologize for overstepping."

His mouth twitched only slightly, but she caught it. "Ha. Admit it, George. You loathe feminine vapors."

"I concede your point," he said as they walked down the drive. "Still, I do not relish explaining to Dr. Hughes or Constable Sharpe that you spoke to Miss Bates first. It is hardly proper procedure, Emma."

"You're the magistrate, George. Simply act"—she waved an airy hand—"magisterial."

"Perhaps you could explain that to Dr. Hughes. He seems markedly unimpressed by my *magisterial* qualities."

"How dreadfully unhelpful of him. I suspect he believes that he should be magistrate, not you."

"The good doctor does seem to have an excellent regard for his own opinion."

When Emma laughed, he finally cracked a smile.

"My poor George," she said, "all this is a great deal of fuss and bother for you."

"What truly matters is obtaining justice for Mrs. Elton. Everything else pales in comparison."

Her amusement faded at the truth of that sobering reflection. "I hope Dr. Hughes and Constable Sharpe are up to the task. You're too busy to catch the killer by yourself."

"I'm sure they will do everything necessary."

Though Emma doubted that, George didn't need her pestering him with concerns beyond his control.

"Did you have the opportunity to write to Jane Churchill?" he asked.

"By the time I had explained the situation to Mrs. Bates and then fetched Mr. Perry, I was barely able to arrive home before luncheon. In any case, after thinking on it, I believe it would be best if Mrs. Weston wrote to Jane. She will know just what to say. The Westons are stopping by for tea later this afternoon, so I will speak with her then."

George shook his head. "This is a great deal of trouble for you, too. I am sorry for it."

"I am happy to help, especially if it relieves you of some of your burdens."

"It cannot have been easy to explain this unfortunate situation to Mrs. Bates," he said as they entered Highbury.

The dear old lady had been dreadfully distressed as Emma explained the situation to her. It had been Mrs. Bates who'd asked her to write to Jane, since she and her daughter would need the support of the Churchills to see them through this ordeal.

"She was so upset, especially when I told her that Miss Bates might be required to give testimony at the coroner's inquest."

"You can be sure she will," he replied rather grimly. "First, though, she will need to give her statement to Dr. Hughes. I suspect Constable Sharpe will wish to question her, as well."

They paused as Mr. Cox rode by on his new filly, which, according to Harriet, was his current pride and joy. One would think his children would qualify as such, but knowing Mr. Cox's impertinent daughters, Emma couldn't blame the man for preferring his horse.

"Good morning, Mr. Knightley, Mrs. Knightley," he called, preening a bit.

They returned his greeting before resuming their discussion.

"I hope you intend to prepare both men for the likely outcome of such questioning," Emma said. "Constable Sharpe in particular seems the sort of person who will provoke Miss Bates into a bout of the vapors."

"A hideous prospect, to be sure. I might even be forced to employ some smelling salts for myself."

Emma choked back a laugh. "It's quite wicked of you to make me laugh when we are talking of such dreadful things."

He cast her an ironic glance as they turned into Vicarage Lane. "Forgive me. I find that since our marriage, my sense of what is appropriate has become somewhat impaired."

"Truly? Then, well done me."

He snorted.

"But in all seriousness, George," she continued, "Miss Bates's manner of speech is so confused, especially when she's perturbed, that I'm afraid she will completely befuddle Dr. Hughes *and* annoy Mr. Sharpe."

"Dr. Hughes is already aware of her foibles. As for Constable Sharpe, he's convinced that Mrs. Elton was murdered for her necklace. It would take a great deal of imagination for anyone to envision Miss Bates engaging in such a brazen act of thievery, and our constable is not a man of imagination."

"From what I've observed of him in the past, his wits certainly do not live up to his name."

"Now, Emma," said her husband, gently chiding. "Constable Sharpe takes his duties very seriously. While the parish vestry was generous in paying him a small salary, it is hardly adequate for a task of this nature. He is a farmer as well as a constable, as you know, and I'm sure he'd rather be minding his own business than tracking down poachers or keeping order in taverns. It's a thankless job which very few men wish to take on."

George was an advocate of a more professional policing, of the type that had recently been introduced in London and other large cities. But customs in the country were hard to change—as was the attitude that stouthearted Englishmen could manage their own affairs without the law breathing down their necks.

"True, but Mr. Sharpe seems to be leaping to conclusions. I think I could do a better job of investigating, quite frankly," she replied.

"Then I suppose you should submit your application for the position of constable to the vestry council forthwith—if not directly to the Crown."

Before she could scold him, a little girl in a smock pelted out of one of the small cottages that fronted Vicarage Lane.

Lucy Peters was a sweet child who helped her widowed

mother take care of her younger siblings. Mrs. Peters had been ill of late, unable to attend her job as a seamstress. Emma had visited the family just a few days ago with a basket of nourishing provisions, and she'd spent some time there with the children.

She smiled at the girl. "Good afternoon, Lucy. How is your mother today?"

"Ever so much better, Mrs. Knightley, since you sent Mr. Perry. Mama said to thank you for the broth and fruit. And all them nice pastries." She favored them with a gap-toothed grin. "Me and my brothers liked them orange scones a lot, so I'm to be sure to say thank you for them, too."

Emma gently tapped the little girl on the nose. "Shall I bring some more scones? I feel sure that our cook is making a fresh batch today."

Lucy gave a vigorous nod. "Yes, please. Me and my brothers would be ever so grateful, Mrs. Knightley."

"Then I shall see you tomorrow. Give your mother our regards."

As the little girl skipped back to the cottage, Emma reached for her husband's arm, intending to walk on. Instead, George cast a swift glance around the lane and then tipped up her chin to press a kiss to her lips. She happily received it, although she couldn't help laughing as he pulled back.

"And what was that for, George?"

"A token of my appreciation. You're a good woman, Emma Knightley, and I consider myself a fortunate man to call you wife."

She took his arm. "If I really am a good woman, I suspect it's more a credit to you than to me. You certainly schooled me often enough for my impertinent behavior when I was growing up."

"Then I can only say I had a very apt pupil."

"I am obviously a credit to us both. But I do hope I'm past

the point of schooling, and certainly scolding. I recall that you delivered some rather spectacular scolds on occasion."

"I will endeavor to refrain from future scolds if you endeavor to refrain from giving me reasons for them."

Emma suspected that George might soon have a few opportunities to scold her, since he wished her to be involved in the murder investigation as little as possible. Naturally, she wouldn't dream of interfering in an unhelpful way, but she *had* made two important discoveries—the murder weapon itself and the fact that Miss Bates had been the first person to stumble across the scene. Given that, she saw no harm in keeping her hand in.

In a minor way, of course.

They approached the vicarage, an old and not especially good house, although the present occupant—and his unfortunate wife—had smartened it up considerably. While it inconveniently stood only steps from the lane, Mrs. Elton had seen the door painted a handsome green and installed a shiny brass knocker in the shape of a lion's head. She had purchased new curtains and rugs throughout and had also expanded the flower gardens and shrubbery right up to the edge of the churchyard, which backed up against the vicarage grounds.

Even with all her changes, it was still an old-fashioned house, with reception rooms so small, according to Mrs. Elton, as to be barely respectable. She'd talked of plans to add a new wing that would hold a dining parlor and a modern kitchen with a new stove. Alas, those plans would now be unrealized. After the death of his wife, Emma couldn't imagine that Mr. Elton would care very much about smart dining parlors or new stoves.

A liveried footman, another of Mrs. Elton's innovations, admitted them. Mrs. Elton had claimed that one couldn't possibly live with any degree of elegance without liveried footmen. She clearly modeled herself on her sister, the fashionable Mrs. Suckling of Maple Grove, who apparently had three.

Despite several planned excursions, Mrs. Elton's sister and brother-in-law had yet to make the trip to Highbury. Still, Mrs. Elton had always talked about the Sucklings and Maple Grove at such length that Emma felt she knew them quite well — and quite well enough, indeed. She supposed, however, that she would meet them soon, since the Sucklings would no doubt wish to attend the funeral.

"Good afternoon, sir," the footman said. "Mr. Elton is with Mr. Suckling, but he asked me to fetch him as soon as you and Mrs. Knightley arrived."

Emma exchanged a quick glance with her husband. Mr. Suckling had certainly made a quick journey from Bristol.

The footman led them across the entrance hall, recently painted a rather bold shade of green. Only last year, Mr. Elton had all the public rooms freshly painted in shades of cream and dove gray in anticipation of the arrival of the new Mrs. Elton. Apparently, however, the husband's choice of color had not met with approval, as a peek into the dining room also seemed to suggest. It had been papered rather than painted, and with expensive silk, if Emma didn't miss her guess.

The double doors to the drawing room were firmly closed, and the presence of a black wreath above the frame signaled that the body rested within.

They were shown to a small parlor toward the back of the house and left to wait there.

Emma took a seat on the sofa. "I wonder if Mrs. Suckling accompanied her husband."

"I doubt it," George replied as he wandered to the window that overlooked the garden. "Mr. Suckling must have traveled very quickly to arrive in such good time."

"Surely Mrs. Suckling will come to Highbury, though. She and her sister were so close."

"Perhaps Mr. Suckling intends to take the body back to Maple Grove."

Emma frowned. "I shouldn't think so. Given that Mr. Elton is a vicar, one would expect his wife to be buried in his church. Besides, transporting a body in the middle of the summer hardly seems sensible, George."

A spark of amusement lit his eyes. "How practical of you to note that, my dear."

The very wealthy often transported bodies back to their estates if their loved ones inconveniently died in London or some other far-flung place. Only they could afford to do so, since it required packing the body in ice to preserve it on the journey.

"I do seem to have become rather comfortable in discussing dead bodies," she admitted.

"Only rather?" he wryly replied.

"George, this is a very inappropriate conversation. Imagine what Mr. Elton would say if he heard us."

He cocked his head to listen. "I don't hear anything. He must still be closeted away with his brother-in-law."

Emma found that odd. Mr. Elton was always obsequious in his attentions to George—and to her, now that she was married to the master of Donwell Abbey.

George went back to staring out the window, while Emma fidgeted and looked around the room. She'd been in this parlor only a few times, but she couldn't help noticing that it now boasted a new and expensive escritoire in the French style.

"I do hope nothing is wrong," she said after a bit. "It's not like Mr. Elton to keep you waiting."

George turned from the window and came to sit beside her. "It is not, but perhaps Mr. Suckling only just arrived. It would be natural that he and Elton would have much to discuss."

That made sense. Both Mr. and Mrs. Elton had always been very conscious of the importance of their relationship with the Sucklings. Even in the midst of his own grief, Mr. Elton wouldn't wish to slight his brother-in-law in any way.

A quick step in the hall brought Emma and George to their feet. The door opened, and the vicar, looking harassed, hurried into the room.

"Mr. Knightley, do accept my profound apologies. Unpardonable of me to keep you waiting."

When George replied that they'd not been waiting long at all, Mr. Elton protested.

"No, you are both too polite." Then he grasped Emma's gloved hand, gazing earnestly into her eyes. "Mrs. Knightley, this terrible tragedy must still be a great shock to you. I cannot bear to think of your distress at finding my poor Augusta, or how upset poor Mr. Woodhouse must have been at the news. Be assured that I will call on your esteemed father as soon as I can, and please extend my apologies for such a gross assault on your delicate sensibilities."

Emma thought the assault on poor Mrs. Elton was of far more note than any damage inflicted on her sensibilities. "I'm perfectly fine, Mr. Elton. You are not to worry about me."

"You are too noble, dear lady, but I'm sure Mr. Knightley must also be very aggrieved." He cast an imploring glance at George. "Do forgive me, sir. I would have given anything for poor Mrs. Knightley to be spared the horrific scene at our church."

"I think you'll find that Mrs. Knightley is quite resilient. She has suffered no lasting ill effects from that most sad day," George reassured him.

Mr. Elton gazed at Emma with a soulful expression. "How brave you are, Mrs. Knightley. An inspiration to all of us."

Brave Mrs. Knightley was now trying to retrieve her hand from Mr. Elton's grasp.

"Mr. Elton," she said, "I'm in perfectly good health and have suffered no ill effects from the discovery of your wife's body."

When he dropped her hand, she realized her assurances were a trifle *too* robust.

"Of course, I am excessively grieved at poor Mrs. Elton's tragic demise," she hastily added. "We are all of us terribly distressed for you, my father especially. He asked me to convey his condolences, and he hopes to have a proper visit with you after the funeral. You are to come spend the afternoon at Hartfield when you are able."

Her father had an absolute horror of funerals, convinced they were breeding grounds for hideous ailments.

When Mr. Elton again reached for her hand, Emma forestalled him by rummaging inside her reticule for a handkerchief. Foiled in his attempt, the vicar took refuge in a lugubrious sigh.

"I cannot yet comprehend that my dear Augusta is gone. I half expect her to rise from her lonely bier and come into the parlor to greet you, like Lazarus called forth from the grave."

Emma could scarcely think of anything more appalling than Mrs. Elton rising from her coffin. Fortunately, the door opened, and a man came into the room, sparing her the need of a reply.

Elton mustered a smile for the new arrival. "Ah, Horace, allow me to introduce you to Mr. and Mrs. Knightley, of whom you have heard so much." He glanced at George. "May I present to you my brother-in-law, Mr. Suckling of Maple Grove?"

"Please accept our condolences," George said, exchanging bows. "It is a terrible blow to your wife, no doubt."

"Yes, she is exceedingly distraught." Mr. Suckling paused to give Emma a barely there nod. "Ma'am."

His brusque manner bordered on rudeness, but she, of course, made allowances for the unusual circumstances. Still, the next few moments suggested that Mr. Suckling was a brusque sort of person, as he made no further attempt to engage in conversation. He simply stood in the middle of the room, glowering at the floor.

After a few awkward minutes, Mr. Elton waved a hand toward the sofa. "Mrs. Knightley, please sit. Shall I ring for tea?"

Emma resumed her seat on the sofa. "No, thank you. George and I do not wish to trouble you."

"It is no trouble at all, Mrs. Knightley. I will just step out—"

"For God's sake, Philip," Mr. Suckling impatiently cut in. "I'm sure the Knightleys have better things to do than dawdle around here with tea and biscuits. As do you and I."

The vicar gaped at his brother-in-law with offended astonishment.

George smoothly stepped in. "Thank you, Mr. Elton, but there is no need to entertain us. Mrs. Knightley and I simply wished you to know that we are happy to lend any necessary assistance."

"And I am deeply grateful, sir," he replied. "Please do sit."

George sat down next to Emma, while Mr. Elton took the needlepointed wing chair opposite the sofa. Mr. Suckling remained standing, apparently impatient for them to be gone.

While Mr. Elton and George discussed funeral details, Emma observed Mr. Suckling. He was a tall man of middle years, with blunt features and a high forehead that seemed creased in a permanent frown, which suggested a general state of disapproval with the world. His coat was well cut and expensive, and his boots were in the latest style. He wore a black silk armband but made no other concession to the mourning state, instead sporting a pale yellow waistcoat, an elaborately tied cravat, and a number of fobs.

True, he must have had to rush from Bristol without the chance to acquire proper clothing, but there was something odd about the man and his attitude. Rather than giving the appearance of grief, he seemed almost . . . angry.

Then again, anger at a loved one's murder was undoubtedly a natural response.

George touched her arm. "Mr. Elton has just been telling me

of the arrangements for the funeral. It's to be held the day after the coroner's inquest."

She blinked. "Of course. So, Mrs. Elton will be buried in Highbury, after all."

The vicar nodded. "Her family has quite a fine vault at St. Mary Redcliffe Church in Bristol, and there was some idea that she should be interred there. But I couldn't bear to have my dear Augusta anywhere but in my little churchyard, always near me. Besides, her abhorrence of finery would reject anything elaborate, you know. The arrangements shall all be quite simple and quiet, just as she would have wished."

Mr. Suckling made a distinctly derisive snort. Mr. Elton, however, ignored him.

Emma decided it best to ignore him, too. "Then with those matters decided, we would ask you to allow us to hold the funeral reception at Donwell Abbey. We will be happy to host those who attend the service, as well as any other Highbury residents who wish to stop by to pay their respects."

The vicar pressed a feeling hand to his heart. "I will happily take you up on your generous offer. I find myself quite unable to play a proper host on such a dread day."

"Hell and damnation, Philip," Mr. Suckling suddenly barked. "Augusta was murdered! The funeral should be private, not an opportunity for gossips and village idiots to stand about and gawk at us."

Mr. Elton turned to stare at his brother-in-law. Mr. Suckling stared right back, his expression a virtual challenge.

When Emma poked George in the thigh, he cleared his throat to capture the attention of the glaring brothers-in-law.

"There will be a good number of people who wish to pay their respects to Mrs. Elton's memory," George said. "Especially among the ladies. As many of them will not attend the funeral service, as is customary, they can offer their condolences to Mr. Elton at Donwell Abbey."

Mr. Elton turned to him with relief. "Exactly so, Mr. Knightley. Even in her short time here, my dear wife commanded *great* affection among the locals. Is that not so, Mrs. Knightley?"

"Indeed, your wife made quite an impression on all of us," she replied.

*Of one sort or another.*

When Mr. Suckling muttered something uncomplimentary, she decided it was best to forge ahead. "Mr. Elton, will other friends and family of Mrs. Elton be attending? They are welcome to stay at Donwell, if that is more convenient for you. I can assure you that the accommodations are far more comfortable than at the Crown."

Mrs. Hodges, Donwell's housekeeper, would probably string her up for making such an offer, but it seemed the charitable thing to do.

Mr. Elton sighed. "Such generosity! But with the exception of my brother-in-law, I believe only locals will be in attendance."

"Mrs. Suckling will not be coming to Highbury?" asked Emma, surprised.

Mr. Suckling scowled at her. "My wife is too distressed by Augusta's murder. She will remain in London, where she will be safe."

Emma was about to point out that murderers were hardly running about Highbury in broad daylight until she realized that at least one murderer might, in fact, be doing just that.

"I didn't realize you were staying in London, sir," she replied with an apologetic smile. "That, at least, is more convenient, since it is only sixteen miles from Highbury."

"There's nothing convenient about running back and forth between London and Highbury, I assure you."

*Good God.* The man was rudeness personified.

"Mr. Suckling, we had no prior knowledge of your travel

arrangements," George said in austere tones. "Or what is convenient for you and Mrs. Suckling."

Mr. Elton looked vaguely alarmed. "Of course not. Horace and Selina traveled to London only a week ago, to avail themselves of some shopping. Then they intended to travel here for their long-awaited visit." His face crumpled a bit. "Augusta was so looking forward to showing Highbury to her dear sister. She particularly wished to introduce Selina to you, Mrs. Knightley."

Emma grimaced in sympathy. "How very sad, sir. I have heard Mrs. Elton speak many times of the anticipated pleasures of her sister's visit."

"Yes," Mr. Suckling brusquely put in. "Selina is very cut up about it."

Unlike her husband, it seemed.

"Now," he continued, "may we turn to more pressing matters? I must away to London this afternoon, and I was hoping to hear a report on the investigation before I leave. Knightley, I understand that you're the local magistrate. What can you tell me thus far?"

*Knightley?*

Really, he was even ruder than Mrs. Elton had been.

Her husband coolly nodded. "I shall be happy to do so, if Mr. Elton desires it."

"I don't know why he should object. Selina will wish for a report, and God knows I took care of Augusta for years before her marriage. There should be no question that I am entitled to hear the report."

Emma was caught by his turn of phrase. What did he mean by *took care* of Mrs. Elton? And why was he so combative?

"I have no objection, Horace," the vicar replied in a mild tone.

"Splendid. Then let's get on with it."

"As you must surely surmise," George said, "we are in the

early stages of the investigation. The coroner and the constable are questioning witnesses, and arrangements are being made for the inquest, which begins tomorrow."

With an admirable economy of words, he related the relevant details and the arrangements for the inquest. After Mr. Suckling brusquely interrupted several times, Emma wished that for once her husband would respond in kind—or at least call him Suckling instead of Mr. Suckling.

"The killer was obviously after Augusta's necklace and didn't care how he got it," said Mr. Suckling. "Bad luck, Philip. I know how much you spent on the piece."

"Good God, Horace!" Mr. Elton exclaimed. "I would gladly give up a hundred necklaces to have my beloved wife back."

His brother-in-law rolled his eyes. "Knightley, are there any leads on this thief, or is my sister-in-law likely to be denied justice?"

"We should refrain from making any assumptions at this point."

"So you have no leads," Mr. Suckling dismissively replied.

Emma couldn't help but bristle. "In point of fact, sir, we don't even know if the murderer *was* a random thief or if theft was the original motive in the case."

George shot her a warning glance. "My dear, perhaps it might be—"

"What the devil can you mean, Mrs. Knightley?" Mr. Suckling demanded.

"Horace, such language in the presence of a lady is hardly fitting," Mr. Elton admonished.

"What isn't *fitting* is Augusta's murder. And I would still like an answer, if I may."

"Of course," Emma crisply replied. "Aside from Mrs. Elton's necklace, nothing else was stolen. Since the church is in possession of some very fine silver and brass, it seems odd that any thief would ignore at least those items on the altar."

Mr. Suckling frowned. "That is odd."

"Mrs. Elton might have surprised the thief before he had the chance to rob the church," George said, sounding a trifle annoyed.

"But the killer used the brass candlestick to . . ." She trailed off, reluctant to state matters so bluntly.

"Bludgeon my sister-in-law," Mr. Suckling finished, suffering no such qualms.

Emma nodded. "It's a very fine piece, as is its mate. They were right there for the taking."

Mr. Elton frowned. "Mrs. Knightley, what are you suggesting?"

When she glanced at George, he simply lifted an ironic eyebrow.

*You're in it now, Emma.*

"I can't help wondering if there wasn't a different reason for her murder," she said. "Or one in addition to the theft of the necklace."

"Such as?" Mr. Suckling rapped out.

George finally intervened. "Mr. Elton, had your wife been troubled by anything or anyone of late? I did not wish to distress you in the immediate aftermath of the crime, but it is a question that now must be asked."

The vicar frowned, as if thinking.

Mr. Suckling made an impatient noise. "It's not a complicated question, Philip. Was there anything that was troubling Augusta in the weeks before her death?"

"Yes, if you must know," Mr. Elton replied with some reluctance. "She'd fallen into a dispute with Miss Bates. I believe it led to an argument with her only a few days before Augusta's death."

*Drat and double drat.*

Mr. Suckling looked startled. "Bates. You mean the Fairfax girl's aunt?"

"Yes, although Jane is now Mrs. Churchill," the vicar replied. "She married Frank Churchill last year."

"Why was Augusta quarreling with Miss Bates?" his brother-in-law asked.

"She neglected to provide me with any details. At the time, it didn't seem very serious. Then again, Augusta never wished me to think ill of my parishioners, kind soul that she was."

"Fortunately, I don't suffer from the same scruples," Mr. Suckling replied. "Knightley, given this information, I take it that you'll be questioning Miss Bates. If you believe she's a suspect, I will want to know about it."

Emma could keep silent no longer. "She is *not* a suspect. It's ridiculous to imagine poor Miss Bates bashing *anyone* over the head with a candlestick."

George let out an exasperated sigh. "Emma, you will distress Mr. Elton."

She winced. "Forgive me, Mr. Elton. But you must admit that it's entirely far-fetched to believe Miss Bates to have committed such an act."

"I completely agree," he earnestly replied. "And please do not worry on my account, Mrs. Knightley. You could never offend me."

That was patently untrue, but apparently, old resentments had been forgotten under the weight of Mrs. Elton's demise.

"This Miss Bates character sounds rather fishy to me," Mr. Suckling opined.

Emma glared at him. "Well, she is not."

"Mr. Suckling," George hastily said, "Dr. Hughes and I will keep you and Mr. Elton apprised of any developments. In the meantime, everyone should avoid arriving at unfounded conclusions. The coroner's inquest will be informative, and you will be able to ask any questions of Dr. Hughes at that time. I take it you will be there?"

"I will ride from London first thing in the morning."

"Excellent. Then we will be on our way," George said as he came to his feet. "We will see you tomorrow, Mr. Suckling."

Mr. Elton escorted them to the front hall, mingling profuse apologies with profound thanks. When the vicarage door finally shut behind them, Emma leaned against it and breathed out an exasperated sigh.

Her husband gazed at her with a sardonic eye. "Well, my dear, that didn't go quite as expected, did it?"

# CHAPTER 7

Emma pushed away from the vicarage door. "I certainly didn't expect Mr. Elton to blurt out that his wife and Miss Bates had been quarreling. From what Miss Bates told me this morning, it was distressing but not of great import, so I'm surprised he mentioned it."

Now, though, it seemed that there might have been a serious falling-out, and that could cast Miss Bates in a suspicious light.

"Mr. Elton seemed to take a similar view of the matter," he replied.

"Not Mr. Suckling," she gloomily said as she took his arm and started down the lane.

"Anyone who knows Miss Bates will realize it would be ridiculous to suspect her of any sort of crime, much less murder."

"I suppose it was rather reckless of me to raise the issue. I'm sorry, George."

"You raised an issue that needed to be addressed. Certainly, Constable Sharpe will ask Mr. Elton if his wife had enemies. And he'll be asking others about that, too, no doubt."

"He might be surprised to discover she had a few."

He scoffed. "Surely not enemies. Rather, people who just didn't like her."

"That would be a fairly long list. George, if suspicion points to Miss Bates, I cannot think what will happen. She is incapable of defending herself against any sort of charge. I do hope you'll be present when she is questioned. You'll need to help her, because she seems incapable of constructing a coherent narrative of her actions."

*Perhaps she doesn't have one.*

That alarming thought almost had her tripping over her feet.

"Miss Bates was simply an unfortunate bystander, and that will become clear soon enough," he replied.

They set a leisurely pace along the lane. It was a beautiful afternoon, and to rush toward the next fraught encounter seemed a sacrilege. Larks twittered in the hedgerows, and the summery smell of mown hay competed with the scent of wild roses edging the lane. Emma wished she could wind up time like a ball of yarn and move back to the day before the murder. Then she could pretend that the greatest crisis she faced was a cow wandering into the kitchen garden or her father's dismay over Mrs. Goddard eating a second piece of cake.

"I'm curious to hear your thoughts on Mr. Suckling," George said, breaking the fragile tranquility.

Emma grimaced. "Frankly, I found him dreadfully rude and hard-hearted. By the way, you were splendid in putting him in his place."

"If you hadn't been present, I would have used stronger language."

"If I hadn't been present, there likely would have been no need to employ such measures. Mr. Suckling doesn't appear to like women—or, at least, one woman in particular."

No doubt Mrs. Elton had shared her low opinion of Emma with the Sucklings.

"His behavior toward you was certainly inappropriate, but it was his reaction to his brother-in-law that I found most surprising."

"Yes, his rudeness toward poor Mr. Elton was very awkward." She frowned. "It's rather mystifying, because I'd never sensed that there was anything but excellent relations between the families."

"Perhaps Mr. Suckling is rattled by circumstances and grieving the death of his sister-in-law."

"He didn't seem grief-stricken to me. Rather, I sensed a marked impatience with the entire situation."

"True," George admitted. "Certainly, Mr. Elton was displeased with his attitude."

As they reached the end of Vicarage Lane, her mind landed on another aspect of the discussion that had troubled her.

"Did it strike you as strange that Mr. Suckling wished for a private funeral?" she asked. "Even Mr. Elton seems to want something very simple. Yet I cannot imagine Mrs. Elton would have approved of such spare arrangements."

If Mrs. Elton were able to plan her own funeral, Emma was certain it would include an elaborate cortège, a lengthy service, and as many mourners as possible.

George nodded. "It did. Considering that the poor woman is the vicar's wife, one would think Mr. Elton would display a nicer attention to detail. But I suppose there is bound to be some natural discomfort. Death at such a young age would be distressing under any circumstance—and doubly so in this case."

"All the more reason to honor her passing. Mr. Elton did seem genuinely grateful, though, that we offered to hold the reception at Donwell."

"Thus saving him a significant cost, something which should win the approval of Mr. Suckling. We must also ensure that the reception is as plain as possible, although naturally in the best of taste."

When Emma couldn't hold back a laugh, it shocked Farmer

Mitchell, who happened to be passing by. He cast her a startled glance before politely tipping his hat.

"That was positively wicked of you, George," she said after they'd acknowledged the farmer's greeting. "To make me laugh in the middle of the street when everyone is so upset about Mrs. Elton's dreadful demise."

"I'm sure Highbury will return to normal once the inquest and funeral are over. What does not directly affect us fades quickly from our minds."

She looked askance at him. "That's a rather cynical view of things, George."

"But true, nonetheless. Now, I must be away to meet with Dr. Hughes. We need to go over the jury lists for the inquest. Are you returning to Hartfield?"

"I must stop at Ford's. Father is in dire need of gloves, so I thought to pick them up and then return home in time for tea with the Westons."

"Then allow me the pleasure of serving as your escort."

He ushered her along the street, exchanging pleasantries with various locals. Emma was pleased to note the respect accorded to her husband. It was based, she knew, not on *what* he was, but on *who* he was. Once again, she congratulated herself for having the good sense to fall in love with so kind and generous a man.

They had just passed the Crown Inn when Harriet came rushing toward them, her bonnet ribbons flapping behind her.

"Mrs. Knightley," she puffed. "I was just coming to find you."

"Goodness, Harriet, whatever can be the matter?"

Her friend bobbed George a little curtsy. "Forgive me, Mr. Knightley. But I need to speak with Mrs. Knightley *quite* urgently."

Emma stifled a sigh. *What now?*

"Then I'll be on my way," George said. "That is, unless you think you need me, Emma."

"Thank you, but I will manage."

"I'll see you back at Hartfield, then, but not before dinner. Dr. Hughes might wish to address the issue you and I talked about as soon as possible, and that might take some time."

Interrogating Miss Bates, in other words.

After tipping his hat to Harriet, he set off at a brisk pace.

"Harriet, what has put you all in a fever?" Emma asked. "Is everyone well at Abbey Mill Farm?"

"Yes, Mrs. Knightley. I didn't mean to alarm you." She flashed a happy smile. "In fact, one of Robert's heifers calved this morning. He bought the cow on Mr. Knightley's recommendation, so as you can imagine, the calf is splendid. And it's ever so much nicer to think about that sweet calf than poor Mrs. Elton lying dead in the church."

Emma blinked at Harriet's artless reply. "Er, that's very nice, dear. But why are you in such a bother?"

"I was going to Ford's to pick up some cambric when I ran into Miss Anne Cox. She was going to Ford's, too, so I could hardly avoid her." She grimaced. "I don't think she likes me. She'll make cutting remarks but then says she's only joking."

Emma patted her arm. "She's jealous because you married Robert. Don't forget that she once expressed interest in him. I dare say she cannot forgive you for snatching him up from under her rather long nose."

Harriet's eyes rounded with shock. "But Robert was never interested in Miss Cox! He told me so himself."

Emma truly loved her friend, but sometimes conducting a sensible conversation with her was a trifle challenging. "It was simply a figure of speech, dear. You must put Miss Cox in her place, Harriet. There is no need to tolerate her pert comments."

"But I can never think of anything to say in the moment. I tried writing cutting remarks in my scrapbook, but when I see Miss Cox, I always forget them."

"Never mind. I'm going to Ford's, so come with me. If Miss Cox is still there, I will make any necessary cutting remarks."

Harriet flapped a hand. "That's not really what I wanted to

tell you. Miss Cox also said some awful things about poor Miss Bates. She said Miss Bates had something to do with Mrs. Elton's murder."

If Emma were inclined to salty oaths, she would be employing one right now. "What exactly did she say?"

"That her mother saw Miss Bates running away from the church on the afternoon of the murder. She was in a terrible fluster and acting very suspicious—like she'd seen a ghost, Mrs. Cox said."

"Not a ghost, but a dead body."

Harriet gasped. "Mrs. Knightley, whatever do you mean?"

"Where is Miss Cox now?"

"Still at Ford's. We saw Mrs. Cole and Mrs. Gilbert through the window, and she was very eager to speak with them. I didn't know what to do, so I was running to Hartfield to find you."

Emma started to march her in the direction of Ford's. "That was very quick thinking, Harriet."

"But whatever did you mean about Miss Bates?"

"She was indeed at the church. In fact, she discovered Mrs. Elton's body a few minutes before we did."

Harriet practically skidded to a halt in the middle of the square. "What?"

"I'll explain later. That dreadful Anne Cox will undoubtedly spread very unhelpful rumors if we don't stop her."

They hurried along until they reached Ford's, where Emma paused to catch her breath. She must be calm and act as if she and Harriet had simply happened upon whatever conversation was taking place there.

As casually as she could, she gazed into the wide bow windows of Highbury's principal millinery shop, pretending to inspect the display of bonnets. What she saw inside was alarming—Anne and her sister, Susan, in close conversation with Mrs. Cole and Mrs. Gilbert. Mrs. Ford hovered on the edges of the conversation, unnecessarily rearranging a pile of gloves.

"Blast," she muttered.

"Mrs. Knightley!" Harriet exclaimed.

"Now, Harriet, when we go in, we must pretend that nothing is wrong. We must not inflame scurrilous gossip."

"But how will we do that?"

"Leave it to me. Just act as if we were going about our business and happened to stumble upon the conversation. Understand?"

Harriet looked dubious. But she always trusted Emma, so she squared her shoulders as if going into battle. "Lead on, Mrs. Knightley."

Emma swept into the shop, Harriet in her wake. Anne and Susan spun around, their eyes bulging like those of sheep startled by a loud bang. Mrs. Cole and Mrs. Gilbert also looked rather, well, sheepish, which confirmed Emma's suspicions.

"Good morning," she said with a bright smile.

Mrs. Cole came to her, concern marking her pleasant features. "Mrs. Knightley, such a dreadful business, and such a shock for you and poor Harriet. We have just been talking about it, and we are all quite worried on your behalf."

"We are both perfectly well, Mrs. Cole, thank you," Emma replied. "And how are your daughters? I hear from Mrs. Weston that they are making great strides on the pianoforte."

Mrs. Cole looked a trifle daunted by such an ordinary reply, but she managed a smile and replied that her daughters were developing into regular prodigies.

Mr. Cole had been successful in trade, and he and his family lived in a style second only to that of Hartfield. Since they had a great love of society, they were forever hosting dinners, card parties, and musical evenings. Emma and her father had eventually been drawn into their social set through the intervention of Frank Churchill and the Westons. And although Mrs. Cole had a marked tendency to gossip—a flaw Emma had to admit she also possessed on occasion—she was a genuinely kind and charitable person, as was her husband.

"And how is Mr. Cole?" Emma asked after Mrs. Cole had finally run out of things to say about her daughters.

That proved to be a disastrous inquiry. "Very disturbed, I'm sorry to say. Dr. Hughes has issued his jury summons for the inquest, and Mr. Cole is on the list. We are all of us very upset by Mrs. Elton's murder, of course, but Mr. Cole is particularly engaged with business at this time of year. A jury summons is quite inconvenient, Mrs. Knightley."

*Not as inconvenient as having one's head bashed in.*

Emma mustered a consoling smile. "It's a distressing business, but the inquest should go quickly, since only a determination of murder must be made. There is no doubt of that."

"I should hope so, for Mr. Elton's sake," Susan chimed in. "It cannot be very nice to have poor Mrs. Elton lying in the vicarage drawing room in all this heat while they wait for the burial."

"Hideous," Anne commented with a certain degree of relish.

Both Mrs. Cole and Mrs. Gilbert looked aghast, and Harriet turned rather green.

Susan, however, was oblivious to the effect of her unfortunate remark. And why she must wear *that* particular shade of puce with her freckled complexion was an enduring mystery. Then again, neither of the sisters had ever suffered from an excess of good taste.

"I should think it would be very exciting to sit on the coroner's jury," Anne said. "You get to hear all the gory details *and* see the body. It's so *horribly* thrilling, just like one of Mrs. Radcliffe novels."

"There is nothing thrilling about it," Emma replied in blighting tones.

"I shouldn't wish it on my worst enemy," Harriet quietly said.

Anne flipped a dangling curl over her shoulder. "La, Harriet,

I didn't take you for such a chicken heart. I'm sure I should have been very brave in your situation."

Emma had to resist the urge to box the girl's ears. "Mrs. Martin acted with commendable courage in a dreadful situation. And I can only hope that everyone in Highbury will behave with the same sensitivity she has also displayed in the aftermath."

Anne bristled. "I'm sure Susan and I would have done everything proper if we'd discovered the body. You may be sure of that, Mrs. Knightley."

Emma turned her back on her to address Mrs. Ford. "My father is in need of a new pair of gloves, ma'am. Nothing too heavy, but a nice, soft kid that would be suitable for summer wear."

The woman sprang into action. "If you'll step over to the shelves, I can show you a lovely selection that's come in just this week from London."

Emma took her time perusing the gloves, hoping the Cox girls would vacate the premises. But they continued to linger by a collection of plumed bonnets, carelessly trying them on and exchanging whispers. Mrs. Cole and Mrs. Gilbert, meanwhile, had fallen into a fairly innocuous conversation about the upcoming funeral.

Emma inspected a pair of dove-gray gloves. "What do you think of these, Harriet?"

Harriet gave the question her full consideration. "They're very nice, but do you think—"

"La, how can you think about gloves when there's a desperate killer running about Highbury," Anne loudly exclaimed. "It makes my blood quiver like icicles just thinking about it."

Emma raised her eyebrows. "Miss Cox, icicles do not quiver. As to your other point, I hardly think you are correct."

Susan imitated her sister's defiant stance. "But Miss Bates was running all about the village around the time of the murder. Acting very oddly, according to Mama."

"Surely you cannot be suggesting that Miss Bates had anything to do with the murder," Mrs. Cole exclaimed, clearly shocked.

"Why couldn't she?" Anne boldly stated. "She's poor, and everyone knows that poor people will do anything to survive."

There were gasps all around.

Emma looked down her nose at Anne. "What a decidedly uncharitable thing to say."

"Well, Mama *did* see Miss Bates run down the street around the time of the murder," Susan said in a defensive tone.

"Acting *very* suspiciously," Anne added.

Before Emma could respond, Mrs. Ford dismayingly entered the fray.

"I'm afraid Miss Cox is correct," she said. "I also saw Miss Bates that day—twice, in fact. She passed by on the way to the church just before two. She seemed very distracted."

"Miss Bates is often distracted," Emma pointed out.

"True, Mrs. Knightley. But I stepped outside to speak to her. She had ordered yarn to knit some gloves for her mother. But when I called to say it was in, she pretended not to hear me."

"Perhaps she didn't actually hear you."

"But some thirty minutes later, she returned this way, actually running. She seemed . . ." Mrs. Ford grimaced. "Distraught."

Emma tried not to grit her teeth. "Mrs. Ford, surely you are not suggesting that Miss Bates had anything to do with Mrs. Elton's demise. Miss Bates and Mrs. Elton were very friendly with each other."

*At least until recently.*

"Pish," Anne tossed off. "Everyone knows that's not true, especially after Jane married Frank Churchill. Jane and Miss Bates made a fool out of Mrs. Elton. And Miss Bates acting so high and mighty about Jane and Frank, when it was really quite scandalous what they did."

Susan nodded. "A secret engagement. I remember Mama

said she would die with shame if her daughters ever acted like that. She also said Mrs. Elton was—"

Emma interrupted her. "Perhaps your mother should consider saying less on the matter. Nor can I believe that your father, a solicitor, would be pleased to hear that you were spreading unpleasant gossip about Miss Bates."

Anne looked defensive. "It's not as if anyone would actually *blame* Miss Bates or anyone else for murdering Mrs. Elton. She was always lording it over the rest of us, as if she were too good for Highbury."

"That is quite enough, Anne," Mrs. Cole said with heavy disapproval. "Mrs. Knightley is correct to say that your father would be most displeased with this foolish conversation."

"Thank you, Mrs. Cole." Emma turned to Harriet. "Dearest, have you found everything you were looking for?"

"Er . . . ," her friend replied, caught off guard.

"Excellent. Then we shall be on our way."

She took Harriet by the arm and marched her out of the shop. The door slammed shut behind them, with the little shop bell jingling frantically.

"Oh, Mrs. Knightley," Harriet said as she hurried to keep pace with Emma. "You were splendid. I was so upset that I could hardly string two thoughts together."

"It was an utterly stupid conversation."

And one that could potentially do a great deal of damage to Miss Bates, especially once it became known that she *had* been present at the scene of the crime.

"But you gave Anne such a splendid set-down."

"I was tempted to box her ears. Only the knowledge that I might be charged with assault prevented me from doing so. It would be very embarrassing for Mr. Knightley if I were to land in prison."

Harriet giggled.

Emma slowed her pace as the flames of her anger died down. "What a trial those two girls must be to their parents."

Harriet cast her a troubled glance. "But Miss Bates *is* involved, isn't she? You said so yourself, Mrs. Knightley. Can you tell me how?"

She nodded. "Come to Hartfield and have a cup of tea. I'll explain everything there. It was all an unfortunate misunderstanding, of course, but it's still worrisome."

And it was also worrisome that despite her best efforts to nip the ugly gossip in the bud, it would surely continue to spread.

Miss Bates, Emma feared, was in rather serious trouble.

# CHAPTER 8

The former ballroom at the Crown Inn was already crowded with Highbury residents. A few rows of chairs at the front of the room were set aside for witnesses, while another twelve against the east wall were reserved for the men who sat on the coroner's jury.

Emma thought the inquest an unnecessary distraction, but the law was the law. So they must all be jammed into a stuffy room to rehash distressing details, only to arrive hours later at a foregone conclusion.

She glanced at her father, who looked remarkably out of place in an elegant greatcoat and his best hat and gloves. Behind them hovered a footman, cashmere shawl at the ready in case his master encountered an errant draft. There was little chance of that, given the warm summer weather.

"Father, it's so crowded in here," she said. "I promise to look after Miss Bates if you wish to return home."

"Is Miss Bates here?" he anxiously replied. "Do you see her?"

An elderly gentleman seated off to the side let out a violent sneeze—sans handkerchief.

Father looked aghast. "Emma, this crowd is quite dreadful. Dr. Hughes was most remiss in allowing it."

That Mrs. Elton's inquest was being seen as something of an entertainment was unfortunately obvious. An excited buzz filled the room, and a number of villagers had brought along bundles of food, as if attending a sporting event. The scent of meat pies and a strong odor of onions wafted through the air, curdling her stomach.

"It is certainly not ideal, but you needn't stay, dearest. I'm sure Miss Bates will be fine."

*Or not.*

Miss Bates would be the first witness to testify. Given how poorly she'd dealt with Emma's sympathetic questioning, it was hard to imagine that she would perform any better under the present circumstances.

Her father adopted a look of dogged determination. "No, my dear. I will not shrink from my duty. Miss Bates is my very dear friend, and I have every intention of supporting her in her time of trial."

When heads whipped around at this pronouncement, Emma mentally winced. *Trial* and *Miss Bates* were an unfortunate combination in this particular situation.

Constable Sharpe startled her by suddenly looming by her side. The man reminded her of a terrier, darting about and appearing when least expected.

"Mrs. Knightley, can I be of assistance?" he asked, his bristly eyebrows snapping together in an almost comical glower.

Rail thin and of middling height, Mr. Sharpe gave the impression of narrowness, both in form and temperament. His spare features and plain black garb suggested the air of a disgruntled cleric.

"Thank you, but we're fine," she replied.

He tipped his hat to her father before directing his scowl back at her. "You're blocking the doorway, Mrs. Knightley.

Best take your seat, before you jam the place up. The whole town is fit to squeeze in here, as if they have nothing better to do."

Father looked over his shoulder and then grasped her elbow with some urgency. "Emma, there is a family standing behind us, with three children. Children!"

"Yes, it's quite shocking for them to be exposed to such a scene."

"But they might be infectious, Emma. You know how infectious children can be."

She repressed an entirely inappropriate urge to laugh as she gently nudged him forward.

As they processed up the center aisle, her father was oblivious to the stares and comments that followed in their wake. He so rarely ventured past the gates of Hartfield that to see him in person—at the local inn, no less—was a novelty.

There were many faces in the crowd that she didn't recognize. More than just the locals had come to witness the spectacle, which was to be expected. The murder of a vicar's wife was bound to have caused a commotion throughout the surrounding countryside.

Mrs. Weston and Harriet, seated in the front row, stood to greet them.

"Mr. Woodhouse!" exclaimed Mrs. Weston. "What a surprise."

Emma could well understand her reaction, since a volcano spewing forth in the middle of the town square was almost more likely than her father's appearance at such a public event.

"I couldn't countenance the thought of Miss Bates going through this ordeal without my support," he replied. "But if she can bear it, I certainly must steel myself to do the same."

When foolish titters erupted behind them, Emma turned to encounter the unwelcome sight of the Cox sisters, sitting in the second row with their mother.

Anne smirked at her. "La, Mrs. Knightley, your father does

say the quaintest things. What a dear old fellow to be so kind to Miss Bates."

Mrs. Cox rapped the girl's hand with a small fan. "Anne, mind what you say. Mrs. Knightley will be shocked to hear you speak of her father that way."

Anne looked surly but held her tongue. Not for the first time, Emma wondered how such a respectable woman could have raised such an unappealing child.

"Good afternoon, Mrs. Cox," she said. "I hope you're well."

The woman stood and bobbed a curtsy. "As well as can be expected, Mrs. Knightley. To be called on to speak about such things in front of all these people . . . why, it makes my heart quail just to think of it."

"Yes, it's very distressing."

"For some more than others," Susan Cox said, casting a meaningful gaze at Miss Bates.

Father had moved down the row to speak to Miss Bates, who stood and clutched at his hands, words tumbling from her lips. Emma exchanged a worried glance with Mrs. Weston before joining them.

"Oh, Mrs. Knightley," Miss Bates exclaimed. "I cannot tell you how much it heartens me that dear Mr. Woodhouse has ventured from Hartfield to support me today. But such a shocking thing, to have his peace all cut up." She gazed earnestly at Emma's father. "I cannot think this can be good for your health, sir. I truly think you should return home."

"For you to suffer through this alone was a prospect I could not bear," he replied. "My health cannot be thought of, not at a time like this."

Emma felt her jaw sag open like an old dresser drawer. There was hardly a moment in her father's life that his health—or the health of his loved ones—failed to be his primary concern. That he would so boldly throw caution to the winds was now beyond astonishing.

Miss Bates pressed his hands. "I know I'm terribly selfish, Mr. Woodhouse, but your presence will be of such a great comfort to me, especially when I must—" She broke off, her mild blue eyes filling with tears.

"Miss Bates, perhaps you should sit down," Emma said, very aware of the interest they were attracting.

"Oh, you are quite right," Miss Bates replied with a weak smile. "To keep your father standing is very shocking of me. Now, where should Mr. Woodhouse sit, Mrs. Knightley? You would know best how to arrange things."

"My father can sit right here beside you, Miss Bates, and perhaps Harriet can sit on your other side. If you need anything, such as a glass of lemonade or a cup of tea, I'm sure Harriet will be happy to fetch it for you."

"Of course," said Harriet. "And Robert should be along at any moment. He's very good at fetching things. He would be here already, but he was detained because one of our other heifers calved this morning. I told Robert that Elsie's timing was very inconvenient, but he said heifers don't give a fig for inquests, or anything else but their dinner."

Miss Bates seemed much struck by that comment. "Very true, Mrs. Martin. Dear me, a new calf just this morning. Mr. Martin must be very pleased."

"He is, and she is the sweetest little calf, Miss Bates. We are all quite excited and wondering what to name her."

While Miss Bates was properly diverted by Harriet's cheerful prattle, Emma settled her father into his seat.

"Would you like to take off your coat or hat, dearest? Simon can hold them for you, if you like. He'll stand just off to the side there."

Emma's father regarded her with horror. "To remove my coat would be madness in this environment. In fact, please have Simon help me with the shawl. I can drape it over my knees. I feel sure there is a draft on the floor, Emma. I wish we had thought to bring another shawl for you."

"I'm perfectly fine, Father."

While Simon helped her father with his shawl, Emma took the seat next to Mrs. Weston.

"I am greatly surprised that Mr. Woodhouse came with you," her friend said. "I would not have thought such a thing possible."

"He insisted. I told him there would likely be people here with head colds, but even that didn't frighten him off."

Mrs. Weston frowned. "I've never known him to exert himself in such a fashion. What did Mr. Knightley have to say about it?"

Emma pulled a face. "He doesn't know yet, since he left the house early. But he won't be pleased. Dr. Hughes intended to summon Father to sit on the jury, but George convinced him that his health wouldn't allow for it. I cannot wait to see the good doctor's expression when he sees Father sitting in the front row."

"It's all so dreadful. If Mr. Weston wasn't sitting on the jury, I'm sure I would not have come at all."

"Speaking of the jury, I thought they would have returned by now. How long can it take to look at the crime scene?"

"I believe they have gone to view the body, as well."

Emma blinked in surprise. "Truly? I thought Mr. Elton was adamantly opposed to that."

It was a normal, if rather gruesome, procedure for a coroner's jury to view the body of the victim. According to George, however, Mr. Elton had raised a vociferous objection, deeming it a violation of his wife's dignity.

Mrs. Weston leaned in a bit closer. "Dr. Hughes was apparently equally adamant that the jury be allowed to see her."

"I find myself much in agreement with Mr. Elton," Emma replied.

When Anne Cox leaned forward and rested a hand on the back of Mrs. Weston's chair, Emma jumped. She'd forgotten the dratted girl was behind her.

"It's dreadfully horrible, isn't it?" Anne said with an exaggerated shudder. "With Mrs. Elton just lying there in her coffin, her skull all bashed in. Don't you think—"

"I think you should refrain from tasteless speculation," Emma interrupted.

Mrs. Cox, who'd been talking to Susan, turned to Anne. "Why are you pestering Mrs. Knightley? Sit back, now, like a good girl, and be quiet."

Anne subsided into her seat but not before casting Emma a disgruntled scowl.

"Miss Cox seems to have taken a dislike of you, Emma," Mrs. Weston murmured. "Do you know why?"

"I gave her a set-down the other day at Ford's because she was gossiping about Miss Bates."

"That is most unfortunate." Mrs. Weston flipped open the small watch pinned to her dark green spencer. "At least the jury should be returning soon. I hate to think of them standing about in all this heat."

"It cannot be worse than sitting in here."

She leaned out to check on her father, who now seemed perfectly comfortable. He was in close conversation with Miss Bates, even sharing his cashmere shawl with her. The sight of him in such intimate conversation with the spinster—admittedly an old friend—was more than slightly disconcerting, and Emma had to shrug away the odd sensation that something had just shifted under her feet.

Impatient for matters to be underway, she glanced behind her, hoping to see some sign of the jury's return. Instead, she spotted Robert Martin making his way toward them.

"Good afternoon, Mrs. Knightley, Mrs. Weston," he said, doffing his cap. "Can I fetch you anything? Something cool to drink, perhaps?"

Emma glanced at Mrs. Weston, who shook her head. "No, we're fine, Robert. Did you see any sign of the jury on your way here?"

"I did. They were just coming out of the church. It looked like Mr. Knightley was trying to move them along, but Dr. Hughes was still jawing at them."

Emma affected surprise. "Dr. Hughes still talking? How shocking."

Robert raised a hand to smother a grin before moving over to sit with Harriet.

Over the past nine months, Emma had gotten to know Robert quite well. He was a trifle rough around the edges but possessed both a good heart and excellent common sense—just as George had told her all those months ago, when the young man first proposed to Harriet.

It was a rather lowering thought, but George had proved to be a better matchmaker than she was.

For a few minutes, Emma sat in silence, recalling the last time she'd been in this very room. It was for the Westons' ball given in honor of Frank Churchill. The space had been transformed into a graceful assembly hall, its flaws hidden by the glow of candlelight and festoons of flowers and greenery. In Miss Bates's inimitable words, the Crown Inn had been transformed into a fairyland conjured up by Aladdin's lamp.

That magic had long since faded, along with the dingy gray wallpaper and the tired-looking wainscoting. Now it was the perfect setting for a murder inquiry, sure to lower one's spirits to match the occasion.

With something of a commotion, the jury arrived and made their way to their designated seats. Emma recognized some of the faces, but several were unfamiliar, because they were drawn from the surrounding villages, as was required by law.

Dr. Hughes and a young man—his son, she believed—followed the jury in. Behind them came Mr. Elton and George. The vicar gave Emma and Mrs. Weston a wan smile as he passed along to the end of the row.

"Aren't you going to sit with Dr. Hughes?" Emma whispered as George slipped into the empty seat next to her.

"My duties are finished for the moment. Like you, I will now be called as a witness."

Mrs. Weston leaned forward. "Is Mr. Suckling not here to support his brother?"

George glanced over his shoulder. "He's by the door. Like Mr. Elton, he opposed the viewing of the body. Dr. Hughes was forced to overrule them, so Suckling is in a temper. I suggested he remain at the back of the room in case he should feel the need to step out for some fresh air."

"Very adroitly done," Emma wryly replied.

"Sadly, our coroner is also in a rather unfortunate mood."

Emma glanced at Dr. Hughes, who was indeed looking thunderous as he organized his papers on a small table. "Is he ever in a fortunate mood?"

George was staring down the front row. "Emma, why is your father here?"

"He insisted on coming to support Miss Bates. I couldn't talk him out of it, George. Not even the threat of drafts could deter him."

Her husband sighed. "Dr. Hughes will not be pleased."

Just then, the coroner looked up, and his gaze landed on Emma's father. His expression transformed into one of disbelief. Then he glared, first at poor Father, who remained blissfully unaware of the ire directed his way, and then at George, as if he were personally responsible for this unwelcome state of affairs.

George simply returned a bland smile. Dr. Hughes fumed a bit but went back to arranging his papers.

"I believe you've fallen out of favor with Dr. Hughes," Emma said.

"I don't believe I've ever been *in* favor, but he'll simply have to put up with me."

"More like *you* have to put up with him."

He tapped a finger to his lips. "Hush, my dear. He's about to begin."

A murmur of excitement rippled through the room as Dr. Hughes stepped forward. "Ladies and gentlemen, as you can see, the jury is now present. They were sworn in earlier this morning, and Mr. Weston was selected as foreman. The scene of the crime has been viewed by the jury, as has the victim's body."

"My poor Augusta," Mr. Elton uttered in a broken voice, loud enough to be heard by the jury and everyone in the first several rows. "Such an affront to her dignity."

That triggered a round of sympathetic murmurs. Dr. Hughes glared the room into relative silence.

"Having fulfilled those requirements under the law," he continued, "we will now proceed to call witnesses to give testimony regarding the death of Mrs. Elton, such that will assist the jury in reaching a conclusion regarding a charge of murder."

When he paused for dramatic effect, with one hand pressed to his waistcoat, Emma was hard put not to roll her eyes. Could the pompous fellow not just get on with it?

"I now call the coroner's first witness," Dr. Hughes announced in stentorian tones. "Miss Henrietta Bates, will you please step forward."

# CHAPTER 9

When Miss Bates swayed in her seat, Emma prayed she wouldn't keel over in a dead faint.

George swiftly rose. "Come, Miss Bates. Let me help you."

She managed a trembling smile as she took his hand. "Oh, Mr. Knightley. You are too kind. But then you are always so kind. And I'm acting quite foolishly. I am among friends, after all. What is there to be afraid of?"

Emma's father gave an encouraging nod. "Yes, go with Mr. Knightley. He will see you settled, as well as one can be in such a drafty room. I am shocked to see so many open windows. Mr. Perry would not allow such a thing, I am sure."

When a ripple of laughter moved through the crowd, Emma could practically hear Dr. Hughes grinding his molars to dust.

"But I feel certain that Dr. Hughes will have the good sense not to pester you," her father added. "So do not worry, dear Miss Bates."

"Cryin' shame," came a voice from the crowd. "Pesterin' a gentle lady like Miss Bates."

Mutters of agreement followed, including some from the jury.

Dr. Hughes scowled like thunder. "There will be silence in the courtroom!"

"This ain't a courtroom," a wag yelled back.

"Hold your tongue, now," barked Constable Sharpe from the back, "or I'll be arresting you for disturbing the peace."

George, ignoring it all, escorted Miss Bates to the chair next to the coroner's table and returned to his seat next to Emma.

Dr. Hughes walked around to stand in front of Miss Bates, peering at her over his ill-fitting spectacles. "Please state your name, ma'am."

Miss Bates looked perplexed. "But you already know my name."

"For the record," he gritted out.

Emma whispered to Mrs. Weston, "Is it my imagination, or does the good doctor seem a trifle out of sorts?"

Her friend choked back a laugh. "Hush, Emma. It is too bad of you."

After Miss Bates stated her full name, the coroner swore her in and began his questions.

"Miss Bates, as far as we know, you were the first person to enter the church on the afternoon in question. Can you—"

She interrupted him. "I don't know if that's truly the case, sir. The church was open, you see. I walked right in, so I imagine anyone else might have done so, as well." She paused, as if struck by a thought. "Especially the murderer, of course, since he was there before I was."

"Unless *you* were the murderer, Miss Bates, that is obviously the case," Dr. Hughes replied, clearly annoyed.

When Miss Bates visibly flinched, Emma's heart sank. She could sense the poor woman inching closer to the edge of a cliff.

"Ma'am," said Dr. Hughes, "can you tell me what time you entered the church?"

She made an effort to compose herself. "It was just before two o'clock, as I recall."

"And why were you going to the church?"

She fussed with her reticule, extracting a handkerchief.

"Miss Bates, would you please answer the question?"

"Of course. I do apologize. I . . . I was to . . . to meet Mrs. Elton," she stammered, ending on close to a whisper.

"I am not sure the jury heard you. You were to meet Mrs. Elton there, is that correct?"

"Yes."

"And what was the purpose of this meeting?"

That elicited a lengthy, garbled reply about altar linens, vestry cabinets, and mice. By the end of her recital, even Dr. Hughes looked daunted.

"Er, thank you," he said. "Now, please relate to the jury what you witnessed upon entering the church."

What little color that remained leached from the spinster's face. "I . . . I saw the body of Mrs. Elton lying on the steps of the chancel. The most dreadful thing I have ever seen in my life."

Mr. Elton let out an anguished moan and covered his face with his hands, as if overcome.

A startled Dr. Hughes took a moment to recover, apparently, his train of thought. "Indeed a distressing sight, Miss Bates. So, when you entered the church, did you immediately realize that Mrs. Elton was dead?"

"Oh, no. Or, at least, I don't think I did. I was so shocked to see her lying in . . . in so awkward a position. Mrs. Elton was always so graceful, you know. Quite the most elegant woman in Highbury—but for Mrs. Knightley, of course, and my niece, Jane, Jane Churchill, that is. Jane is so terribly elegant. Mrs. Elton herself said so on many an occasion."

Dr. Hughes manfully waded back in. "After spotting the body, what did you do next?"

"I rushed to Mrs. Elton. I thought perhaps she had fainted and was in need of smelling salts. It was a warm day, and I thought perhaps she was overcome by the heat."

"And when did you conclude that she was not overcome but deceased?"

"When I . . . I knelt down to untie her bonnet, hoping to give her air. That's when I saw all the . . . the blood."

"How utterly ghastly," Anne Cox loudly whispered. "Only think, Susan—"

Emma turned around and glared her into submission.

Dr. Hughes continued to question Miss Bates, extracting her testimony in fits and starts. It more or less matched what she'd told Emma, with occasional meanderings into inartful commentary, which clearly frustrated the coroner. She couldn't truly blame him. With Miss Bates, one often became lost in her welter of words, with the risk of never finding one's way back to sensible discourse.

Emma tensed, though, after Dr. Hughes obliged the spinster to explain why she'd run away.

"It was foolish of me," she tearfully said. "But I was so frightened. When I heard voices from outside the church, I became even more frightened, and so . . . and so I ran and hid. I . . . I couldn't even begin to think. All I could see was poor Mrs. Elton and all the blood. And that was . . ." Her frail composure broke, and she dabbed her handkerchief under her spectacles, wiping away tears.

Emma's father flapped a hand to catch her eye. "Emma, Dr. Hughes is badgering Miss Bates. Mr. Knightley must make him stop."

"I think Father is right," she murmured to George. "She'll become hysterical if this continues."

*Or, much worse, blurt out something incriminating.* Miss Bates was behaving as if she had something to hide—which Emma was quite certain she did.

George leaned forward to address the coroner in a low voice. "Dr. Hughes, might I suggest that you conclude your questions now? You have already recorded Miss Bates's testimony from your interview the other day."

Dr. Hughes looked disgruntled. "I have only one more question for Miss Bates, sir."

George narrowed his gaze in warning before giving a nod.

By now, Miss Bates had recovered somewhat. When Dr. Hughes turned back to address her, she even managed a semblance of a smile.

"Madam, we have your written testimony," he said, "but there is one additional point that has not been adequately addressed."

"Yes, Dr. Hughes?" she faintly replied.

"Have you recently had a quarrel or a falling-out with Mrs. Elton?"

Miss Bates stifled a gasp and had to struggle to reply. "Mrs. Elton has always been such a dear friend to us—to me and, of course, to our dear Jane. I have never forgotten her kindness to Jane. Such attentions she gave to her, such . . . such consideration. It was beyond anything. I never saw anything like it before in my life." She turned pleading eyes on Mr. Elton. "Such a good, generous woman, your wife. One can hardly imagine quarreling with her. Dear Mr. Elton, you cannot imagine that we would be anything but grateful to your dear wife. She was the most magnanimous soul . . . always so generous—"

"Miss Bates, you will address me or the jury," Dr. Hughes interrupted.

When the poor woman shrank back in her chair, Emma was hard put not to rush forward and box the pompous man's ears.

"Emma, Emma," her father exclaimed. "This harassment must stop. Mr. Knightley, you must make it stop!"

This set the room into something of an uproar. One fellow, dressed in the humble garb of a farmworker, jumped to his feet.

"You leave the poor lady alone, Dr. Grumbleguts," he yelled. "It ain't right to treat her like that."

"Sit down, you fool," snapped a fellow sitting behind him. "The doctor is just doing his job."

The room now threatened to dissolve into complete disorder. Dr. Hughes and Constable Sharpe commenced shouting at the crowd, which only increased the din.

With an exasperated sigh, George rose.

"Ladies and gentlemen," he called out. "I would ask that you please come to order, so that this business may proceed to its conclusion. The sooner we finish, the sooner Miss Bates may step down, which is something we all wish."

The hubbub subsided as he scanned the room with a stern gaze. As the largest landowner and the local magistrate, George would always command respect. But the true source of his influence was his sterling character. When he spoke, people listened, because he spoke only when he had something worthwhile to say, and only when he could say it with absolute truth.

Within a few moments, order was restored.

"Dr. Hughes," George said, turning to the coroner. "Are you now finished with Miss Bates?"

"The jury must have the opportunity to pose questions now," replied the doctor. "As per proper procedure."

George blew out an exasperated breath before resuming his seat.

"Is the jury truly allowed to do that?" Emma murmured.

"Unfortunately, yes."

"Gentlemen, do you have any questions for the witness?" Dr. Hughes asked the jury.

One man, whom Emma didn't recognize, raised a hand. "I do, Your Honor."

Dr. Hughes was clearly pleased to be addressed with such a flattering honorific. "Go ahead, my good man."

"I don't fathom why Miss Bates ran when she heard the voices of the other ladies. She knew them, didn't she?"

"That is correct," the coroner replied.

"Then why run? I don't mean to be rude to the lady, but it makes no sense."

Dr. Hughes turned back to Miss Bates. "Ma'am?"

"But I already explained that," she burst out. "I . . . I simply couldn't think clearly. All the blood . . . poor Mrs. Elton . . . I simply couldn't bear it a moment longer. I had to get away!"

The cadaverous fellow shook his head. "I'm sorry, miss. It still makes no sense to me."

"Well, I can't explain it any better than that," she exclaimed.

Then her brief show of defiance collapsed, and she buried her face in her handkerchief and burst into tears.

Emma's father threw off his shawl and rose with surprising alacrity. "Dr. Hughes, I insist you cease this monstrous display. If you do not, you will have *me* to answer to."

It took a few moments for Emma to recover from the astonishment that her father had leapt into the role of knight-errant. She elbowed her husband. "Do something, George."

Her husband, apparently also suffering a paralysis of astonishment, shook it off and came to his feet. "That is enough, Dr. Hughes. Miss Bates is clearly not well."

"The jury has the right to question the—"

Mr. Weston jumped up. "No more questions for Miss Bates."

Quickly, George stepped forward and helped the spinster to stand. Robert Martin took her other arm, and the two men escorted her out of the room.

"I am seeing Miss Bates home, and I will remain with her there until Perry can be called," Emma's father said to her.

Emma also came to her feet, followed by Mrs. Weston. "Are you sure, Father? I can go with Miss Bates and send our footman for Mr. Perry."

Dr. Hughes clucked his tongue. "Mrs. Knightley, you are the next witness to testify."

When Emma grimaced, her father patted her shoulder. "I

will be fine, my dear, but you must take my shawl. I do not want you catching a chill."

He then marched off, leaving Emma and Mrs. Weston to stare after him.

"Whatever has come over your father?" Mrs. Weston finally asked as they resumed their seats.

Before Emma could answer, George returned.

"My father has apparently been transformed into Sir Galahad," she said.

"Indeed," replied her husband. "He insisted on taking Miss Bates home. Has he ever done such a thing before?"

"Never. He was always afraid their rooms were too drafty."

Dr. Hughes loudly cleared his throat. "I will now call the next witness."

George took her hand. "Are you ready, my Emma?"

"I can hardly do worse than Miss Bates, I would think."

"You'll be fine. But please refrain from any impulse to tease Dr. Hughes."

Emma smiled. "I shall be the soul of discretion, I promise."

Dr. Hughes was evidently annoyed. "I will repeat the question, Mrs. Knightley. Did you, at that point, observe anything out of the ordinary?"

*Besides dead Mrs. Elton in a pool of blood?*

How could he ask such a silly question?

Emma's gaze flickered to George. Clearly knowing what she was thinking, he narrowed his gaze in warning.

She adopted a solemn expression. "No, Dr. Hughes. After I sent Mrs. Martin to fetch you, I saw nothing outside of the ordinary."

"To be clear, you went back inside the church to keep watch over the scene?"

"Yes. I was aware that the church should remain undisturbed until you and my husband could arrive. I was also concerned for Mr. Elton. I did not wish him to enter unprepared for such a terrible scene."

Seated in front of her, Mr. Elton rested a soulful hand on his chest. "Such kindness," he said in a tremulous voice. "Even in such a moment, that Mrs. Knightley should think of my feelings."

Dr. Hughes sighed. "I would ask that the other witnesses refrain from commenting."

"Of course, my dear sir," the vicar replied. "Do forgive me."

"Thank you. Now, Mrs. Knightley, why did you choose to go back into the church? You promised Mrs. Martin that you would remain outside, and yet you did not."

The doctor's tone suggested there was something suspicious about *her* behavior, which was most annoying of him.

"It was a very warm day, and I grew hot outside."

"I imagine you were worried about your complexion in all that sun," he said in a condescending tone.

"I was wearing a bonnet," she dryly replied.

Laughter rippled through the crowd.

"Order, please," the doctor huffed. "Mrs. Knightley, what did you do next?"

"I thought to have a look around, to see if anything *was* out of place."

"And what were the results of your . . . investigations?"

"It occurred to me that perhaps a thief had been in the church."

"And that Mrs. Elton had surprised the thief in the middle of his criminal act?"

"Yes."

The doctor addressed the jury. "As you will hear from later testimony, this is a very likely scenario. Do continue, Mrs. Knightley."

"At first glance, I failed to see anything out of place. But I feared that a thief might have broken into the cupboards in the vestry—to go after the silver."

"So you went into the vestry to look."

She hesitated. "Not immediately."

"And why was that?"

"Because I heard footsteps, and then the sound of the vestry door closing."

Dr. Hughes held up a finger. "In fact, you heard Miss Bates fleeing the church."

"As it so happened, I heard Miss Bates *leaving* the vestry. Although, of course, I didn't realize it was her at the time."

"What did you do next?

"After a few moments, I went into the vestry."

He raised incredulous eyebrows. "But it had already occurred to you that a murderer might have entered the church. Did that fact not give you pause or a sensible degree of caution?"

"As I already mentioned, whoever had been in the vestry had departed, so I did not consider myself to be in any danger."

The coroner scoffed. "One might suggest you acted rather recklessly, madam."

Why was the dratted man treating her like an adversary instead of a witness?

"I thought it important to catch a glimpse of whoever had been hiding in the vestry. And I did arm myself with a brass candlestick for protection."

"That's the ticket, Mrs. Knightley," called an admiring voice from the crowd.

Mr. Elton raised his hands in a prayerful attitude. "Such courage in the face of danger . . . a true heroine."

Emma caught George's sigh.

Dr. Hughes continued to question her, and they had a bit of a brangle over the discovery of the handkerchief.

"Why did you not think to give it to me as soon as I arrived at the church? You should have done so," he said.

"Forgive me, sir. I was distracted by the death of Mrs. Elton."

He blustered a bit. "We will return to that question. What then transpired?"

"I went to return the candlestick to the altar. That's when I noticed that its mate was out of position."

"Was there anything unusual about that other candlestick?"

"Yes. It appeared to have blood on it."

There were gasps from the assemblage. Apparently, that detail was not widely known.

"And did you notice anything else about this apparent blood?"

"It was smeared, as if someone had tried to wipe it clean."

Dr. Hughes reached down to pluck something from a basket on the floor by the table. He unwrapped the candlestick, bundled in a white cloth. "Is this the candlestick in question?"

Emma nodded. "It appears to be."

He turned it on its side and brought it closer for her to inspect. "And is this the smear of blood, Mrs. Knightley?"

The blood had now dried almost to black on the sconce, with a small dark smear on the stem below. Seeing it again made her feel queasy, and she had to swallow before she could answer.

"Yes."

Dr. Hughes showed the candlestick to the jury, walking slowly down the line so they could inspect it. A thrill of horror enveloped the crowd like an invisible mist. Mr. Elton covered his face with a large handkerchief, clearly overcome.

The doctor returned to the front of the room. "Mrs. Knightley, what conclusion did you draw when you saw the blood on the candlestick?"

Emma carefully chose her words. "It seemed likely that it had been used to injure Mrs. Elton."

"Fatally so," Dr. Hughes commented.

The man certainly had a penchant for stating the obvious. She didn't bother responding.

"What did you do after this discovery?" he asked.

"I thought it best to simply wait for you and my husband."

"A wise course of action, Mrs. Knightley."

His tone suggested that it was the first sensible thing she'd done during the entire episode.

Emma spent the next few minutes recounting the rest of what had transpired—sans the detail of Mr. Elton throwing himself into her arms. There was no need to embarrass the poor man.

"Thank you, Mrs. Knightley," Dr. Hughes said. "Your testimony has been most clarifying."

Assuming he was finished, and grateful for the opportunity to escape, she had begun to rise when he held up a restraining hand.

"Not quite yet, madam," he said.

*Rats.* He was going to ask her about that wretched handkerchief, after all.

"I would like to return to the matter of the handkerchief," he confirmed.

Emma fixed a placid expression to her face. In order to help Miss Bates, she had to remain calm.

The doctor raised a finger. "You stated that you put the handkerchief away and did not remember it until later that evening."

"Correct."

Then he spread his hands wide. "Mrs. Knightley, how could you forget something that turned out to be so vitally important?"

"Dr. Hughes, people go through the lych-gate into the churchyard all the time. Anyone could have dropped it."

"Really?" he replied with blatant skepticism.

She gave him a sweet smile. "Many of Highbury's residents

like to visit the resting places of their departed loved ones. For instance, I visit the grave of my own dear mother on a regular basis."

Her answer flustered him, forcing him to take a moment to recover his composure. "So, when did you discover that it was, in fact, a *vital* clue in the investigation?"

"Since it belongs to Miss Bates, I hardly think it's a vital clue, sir. She simply dropped it when hurrying from the church in her quite understandable fright."

"I will be the judge of what is and is not a vital clue, Mrs. Knightley. Now, please answer the question."

She had to repress a scowl. "When my husband and I noticed the small stain of blood on it, we realized the handkerchief could have some relevance to the circumstances."

Mr. Elton's head jerked up, and he peered at her, as if perplexed or even befuddled.

"Mrs. Knightley, did you recognize whom the item belonged to?" asked Dr. Hughes.

Emma drew her attention away from Mr. Elton and back to the doctor. "Not immediately."

"But you did conclude that the handkerchief with the bloodstain belongs to Miss Bates, did you not?"

"Eventually, yes," she reluctantly replied.

When excited buzz went through the crowd, her heart sank further.

"And why did you not bring this to my attention first thing the next morning?" Dr. Hughes asked in a stern tone.

"Simply because I wasn't sure at that point if it did belong to Miss Bates. I wished to ascertain that for myself before approaching you with the matter."

He let out an indignant little huff. "A most irregular course of action, Mrs. Knightley. As I am sure your husband will agree."

"And you will certainly have the opportunity to ask him that yourself."

George cleared his throat—covering up a laugh, she had no doubt.

"In any event," she added, "I did not wish to risk presenting you with false or misleading evidence."

"So you took it upon yourself to question Miss Bates."

"Only to ascertain that she was the owner of the handkerchief. After doing so, I immediately relayed that information to my husband, who then took it to you."

He peered suspiciously over his spectacles. "So, you were not attempting to warn Miss Bates in any way or to influence the outcome of my investigations?"

Emma adopted a wide-eyed expression. "Why would I wish to do that?"

Dr. Hughes glared at her a moment longer before turning to the jury. "Do you have any questions for the witness?"

"We do not," Mr. Weston firmly said, apparently wishing to forestall any additional questioning.

"Very well," said the coroner. "You may step down, Mrs. Knightley."

Emma breathed a mental sigh of relief and held out a hand, all but obliging Dr. Hughes to assist her back to her seat.

After she was settled, George leaned over. "One of your better efforts, my dear."

"I thought so," she whispered back.

After a short break for luncheon, Dr. Hughes called Harriet to the stand. She gave a rather confused but mostly accurate accounting of what she had seen. Then George gave his testimony. With unflappable calm, he related his role that day, both as witness and magistrate. His testimony was clear and to the point and concluded in short order.

Mr. Elton's testimony took longer, since he was overcome with emotion throughout, even though he had very little to add. He confirmed that his wife had been wearing her pearls that day, and that the necklace was missing when he arrived at the scene. The vicar also indicated that he believed a thief had robbed his wife and then murdered her.

Thankfully, that drew some of the attention away from questions about Miss Bates's suspicious behavior. But when Mrs. Ford was sworn in, Emma mentally grimaced. Her testimony could undo all that.

"Mrs. Ford, you reported seeing Miss Bates passing your shop on the way to the church. Did you, perchance, speak to her?"

"I tried, but Miss Bates failed to hear me."

"Was she too far away for her to hear you?"

Mrs. Ford wavered for a few seconds. "No, she simply didn't seem to hear me."

Dr. Hughes adopted a tremendously solemn expression. "And why do you think that was?"

"She seemed distracted. Or, perhaps, in a hurry."

"And was she not also in a hurry when she came back down the street approximately thirty minutes later?"

"I suppose you could say that," she reluctantly replied.

Dr. Hughes stared over his spectacles. "According to Mrs. Cox's written statement, Miss Bates was all but racing down the street in a very flustered manner. Would you say that is an accurate description?"

"I suppose so," came the terse reply.

Obviously, Emma wasn't the only witness who was worried about Miss Bates.

After Mrs. Ford stepped down, Dr. Hughes declined to call additional witnesses. He did note that Mrs. Cox's statement supported previous testimonies, and that everything had been duly entered into the record.

"Such a shame not to call Mama," Anne loudly whispered to her sister. "She wore her new bonnet especially for the inquest."

"It's just plain mean," Susan replied. "Mama would have been a splendid witness."

Emma repressed the impulse to turn around and whack them both with her reticule.

In excruciating detail, Dr. Hughes then summed up the witness testimony and his own findings. The room grew stuffier and *quite* odiferous, since someone seated nearby had consumed onions for lunch. Finally, however, the doctor concluded his summation and sent the jury off to a private room to begin their deliberations.

With sighs of relief, Emma and Mrs. Weston stood, thankful to stretch cramped limbs.

"I can hardly think it will take the jury very long to reach their conclusion," Emma said.

Her husband extracted his pocket watch. "No, I imagine we'll be at Hartfield well in time for dinner."

Mr. Elton hurried over to join them. "My dear Mrs. Knightley, I wish to thank you for your tremendous courage in giving testimony. I must also commend our dear Mrs. Martin. She has been most kind to me during this dreadful ordeal."

Emma gave him a reassuring smile. "How are you bearing up, Mr. Elton? Can we be of any service to you?"

"I am extremely unnerved, but I must be strong for my brother-in-law's sake." He glanced toward the back. "I see that Mr. Suckling is waving to me. We must finish preparations for the funeral, you know."

The vicar heaved a sigh and stood there, making no effort to leave.

Emma and George exchanged a glance.

"Don't let us keep you, Mr. Elton," George finally said. "But do send a note around to Hartfield if you need me."

He gave a little start. "Oh, yes, of course. Forgive me, sir. I am easily distracted these days. Mrs. Knightley, I will see you tomorrow. You, as well, Mrs. Weston."

Another bow and he hurried down the aisle to join Mr. Suckling.

When George regarded her thoughtfully, Emma raised her eyebrows. "What?"

He hesitated but then shook his head. "It's nothing. I must have a word with Dr. Hughes, but I'll only be a moment."

When he stepped away, Harriet rushed up to take his place.

"Mrs. Knightley, you were wonderful on the witness stand. I'm afraid I found Dr. Hughes so very intimidating. I hope I didn't appear too foolish."

"You did very well, dear. As for our coroner, that man should be included in Dr. Johnson's dictionary, under the definition of *pompous ass.*"

"Emma, there is no need for vulgar language," Mrs. Weston gently reprimanded. "Thankfully, this gruesome business is now over but for the jury's verdict. We may all rest easy."

Emma shook her head. "It won't be over until we discover Mrs. Elton's killer."

Mrs. Weston looked startled. "We? I do hope your investigating days are over, my dear."

"Now you sound just like George."

"Then I suggest you listen to him. Such things are best left to the men in charge."

"But it was Mrs. Knightley who discovered the murder weapon," Harriet pointed out. "*And* found out that Miss Bates had been hiding in the vestry. Although that hasn't turned out very well, has it?"

"Which is exactly why one cannot leave the matter solely to men like Dr. Hughes and Constable Sharpe," Emma replied.

Neither man impressed her with either their acumen or their manner.

And then there was Miss Bates. Something must be done to help the poor woman, not only for her sake but also for that of

Emma's father. As long as his dear friend labored under suspicion, Father's peace would be entirely cut up.

"You must promise me that you won't interfere, Emma," Mrs. Weston said. "We must leave the matter with Mr. Knightley. I am sure that is what he would wish you to do."

Emma pressed a hand to her bodice. "Me, interfere? You must be thinking of some other Emma."

Mrs. Weston's only response was a resigned sigh.

# CHAPTER 10

A thunderous crash echoed through Donwell Abbey's cavernous kitchen. Emma and Mrs. Hodges, the abbey's housekeeper, spun around to confront a catastrophe of shattered dishware and scattered pastries. Donwell's lone footman stood in the center of the mess, his breeches and stockings liberally splashed with pastry cream.

"I'm right sorry, Mrs. Knightley," Harry plaintively said. "The dish started to slip out of my hands, and I couldn't stop it."

"Goodness, you are the clumsiest man I've ever known," Mrs. Hodges exclaimed. "All those pastries ruined. What will the master say about that?"

Harry's face blanched as white as the cream that had once filled the pastries, and he stared at Emma with a pleading gaze.

"It will be our secret, Harry," she said, knowing George wouldn't give a fig. "Now, please clean yourself up and then go help with the arriving carriages."

The poor fellow bobbed his head and scurried away, clearly grateful to escape the housekeeper's wrath.

"Why the master keeps that clumsy oaf about the place is a

mystery," groused Mrs. Hodges. "Wasting Serle's best pastries, and with so many mouths to feed."

"We have plenty of food, thanks to you and Serle planning everything so splendidly," Emma soothingly replied. "I am quite in admiration of you both."

The housekeeper looked slightly mollified. "We've done our best, ma'am, but it's been years since the abbey served so many guests. I can't say that we're used to it."

The old-fashioned kitchen now bustled with servants, most imported from Hartfield and even a few from Randalls. But for Mrs. Hodges, Harry, and a few maids, George currently kept no other house servants on Donwell's staff. Since his move to Hartfield, many of the rooms had been closed up. Some parts of the abbey, like the kitchen, stood in dire need of updating.

The combined staff had thus far done a splendid job. Who could have foreseen that a funeral reception would turn into the principal event on Highbury's social calendar? It seemed almost everyone from the village and surrounding parishes had crammed into Donwell's noble halls, ostensibly to pay their respects.

"I think most everyone is here by now," Emma said. "Some of the men will be arriving a bit later, because they stayed behind for the graveside committal."

Mrs. Hodges looked vaguely alarmed. "How many more are expected, madam?"

"I shouldn't think more than a dozen or so. I do hope there is plenty of cider on tap, though. It seems to be very popular."

Donwell's orchards produced excellent cider, which was obviously a major draw for many of their guests.

Mrs. Hodges nodded. "We should have enough. Mr. Knightley instructed Mr. Larkins to bring in several casks of ale from the Crown to supplement the cider."

"And where is Larkins?"

"In the stables. Trying to sort out the horses and vehicles."

Emma sighed. "What a bother for all of you. When he does come in, could you ask him to—"

The door from the stable yard swung open, admitting both Larkins and George.

She smiled at her husband. "Hiding out from the guests in the stables already, are we?"

"It seemed the sensible thing to do. Emma, did we really need to invite half the inhabitants of the county? I doubt many of them even knew Mrs. Elton or set foot in Highbury's church."

"I'm sorry, dearest. They just showed up."

Mrs. Hodges muttered her dissatisfaction before bustling off to confer with Serle, who was preparing a large pot of chocolate on the abbey's lamentably old-fashioned stove.

"And how goes the battle, Mr. Larkins?" asked Emma. "Have you managed to properly sort out the stables?"

"Aye, missus. The lads from Randalls have been a great help, and James is lending a hand," he replied, his blunt speech faintly tinged with a brogue. "It's naught we cannot handle."

Larkins was the very definition of dependable, and his skillful management of Donwell's lands had greatly eased the burden on George. There had apparently been some unfortunate mutterings around the village when he'd first been hired, because he was an Irish immigrant—although he'd lived in England since he was a boy—and a Catholic to boot. But the man's plainspoken honesty and his dedication to all things Donwell, including its tenants, had finally won over the suspicious locals.

"Thankfully, the commotion is only for one afternoon," George said. "So peace and quiet should return by sundown."

"I wouldn't be so sure," Emma teased. "I suspect many of our guests have every intention of staying for dinner."

Mrs. Hodges and Serle, who were arranging trays of tea biscuits and meringues, jerked their heads up. They wore equal expressions of alarm.

Emma waved her hands. "I'm joking."

She hoped.

"George, how is Mr. Elton?" she asked. "The poor man. Such a dreadful experience, having to oversee the funeral of his own wife."

"The curate from St. Albans has fortunately relieved him of the necessary duties. In fact, Mr. Elton and Mr. Suckling should be here momentarily. They both wished to spend some time at the graveside."

"Then we should go up," Emma said. "Mr. Larkins, could you see that extra chairs are placed on the lawn? I'm trying to encourage some of the young people to go outside. The great hall is terribly crowded."

"Aye, Mrs. Knightley."

Emma made one more check with Mrs. Hodges and then allowed George to escort her upstairs.

"What a great deal of trouble for you, my dear," her husband said as they climbed the shallow set of stairs that led to the service corridor.

"Much more so for the staff. They are all to be commended for pulling this increasingly absurd affair together so quickly. And Larkins is an absolute treasure."

He stopped her partway down the old stone corridor. "You're the treasure, my love," he said before pressing a lingering kiss to her lips.

When footsteps sounded at the other end of the passage, they parted. A Randalls footman hurried by with an empty tray of sherry glasses, giving them a harried nod.

"Really, George, how scandalous," she said. "Kissing in front of the servants. Whatever will they think?"

"I suspect they're too busy to notice," he replied as they began to make their way toward the front of the house.

"How was the funeral? It sounds like all went as well as could be expected."

"It did. The church was quite crowded."

Emma, naturally, did not attend, nor did Mrs. Weston. Ladies did not participate in funerals, although in the country it wasn't unusual for the local folk, both men and women, to go to the church service.

She touched the black silk scarf tied around her husband's arm. "You're still wearing your own scarf. I take it you left Mr. Elton's funeral memento in the carriage?"

"He did not distribute any funeral mementos."

"To no one?" she asked, amazed.

"No."

"What about Mr. Suckling?"

"As far as I know, neither man gave funeral mementos to anyone."

It was customary to give mementos to family and friends of the deceased. Depending on the financial standing of the family—and Mr. Elton was quite plump in the pocket, thanks to Mrs. Elton—black silk scarfs or armbands were often given out, as well as black or white gloves. Black silk hatbands were sometimes distributed, as well. Gifts and items of clothing were also provided to the family's servants, who were expected to observe mourning along with their master.

Emma frowned. "Mr. Elton is generally very punctilious about funeral etiquette."

"Perhaps he feared he would not have enough for all those who attended. Death by murder was all but certain to draw a crowd. Most coming for the wrong reasons," he dryly finished.

"I cannot believe Mrs. Elton would approve of so frugal a state of affairs. She is no doubt looking down—or up—from wherever she is, mortified at such cheeseparing ways."

"Emma," he replied in a long-suffering tone.

She crinkled her nose in silent apology. "What about the procession? I know the vicarage is but a few steps from the church, but they could easily bring the casket in a proper procession by the lane to the lych-gate."

"No procession, either, I'm afraid."

Emma began to feel more than simply astonished. Although she and the vicar's wife had little appreciation for each other—well, no appreciation, if one were honest—the poor woman deserved better than such an unceremonious exit from life.

"I cannot believe it, George. How do you account for it?"

"I cannot."

"Mrs. Elton would have hated it. You know how much she liked to make a show of things, and this was her final opportunity to do so."

His mouth twitched. "Indeed."

"You may laugh at me all you like, but I cannot help but wonder what Mrs. Suckling thought of it. Did she remain at the vicarage? Do you know if she's coming to Donwell with Mr. Elton and Mr. Suckling?"

"Mrs. Suckling did not make the journey from London."

Emma came to a halt. "Mrs. Elton's own sister didn't come?"

He took her elbow and walked. "If you wish for more details, I suggest you speak to Harriet or the Cox sisters. They were conversing at some length after the service. I'm sure they can provide you with a much more detailed account than I could."

"That makes no sense. Harriet and the Cox sisters do not get on."

Nothing seemed to be making any sense.

George steered her into the long gallery. "Mr. Elton and Mr. Suckling will be arriving very soon. We should be there to receive them."

"Of course."

Still, she intended to speak to Harriet as soon as possible.

Her husband had a legion of estimable qualities, but the ability to describe interesting events was not one of them.

A few guests had wandered into the long gallery, escaping the crush in the great hall. With its splendid view of the gardens, the gallery was a peaceful retreat in the oldest part of the abbey.

When they passed through the old stone doorcase of the great hall, Emma gasped in dismay.

The most impressive room in the house, the great hall was a reminder of Donwell's antique origins, boasting a timbered ceiling and an intricately carved ancient wooden screen. The magnificent space was normally imbued with a noble silence and the weight of history.

Today, though, its quiet nobility had been shattered by the mighty din of a crowd that had grown larger in the short time she'd been belowstairs.

"Oh, dear," was all she managed.

Even George looked stunned.

Apparently, Mrs. Elton's funeral was now akin to a national holiday. A gaggle of children were playing hide-and-seek among the trestle tables, and there were even a few infants in their mothers' arms and toddlers in leading strings.

She grabbed her husband's arm. "George, whatever will Mr. Elton think of such an unseemly commotion?"

"We can only hope he'll be pleased that so many of his parishioners have come to pay their respects."

She eyed the guests jostling about the refreshment tables. "That is indeed an optimistic view," she said as she watched young Arthur Otway weave an unsteady path through the crowd. She could only assume he'd already enjoyed copious amounts of the Crown's ale.

They made their way through the expansive space. Emma was rather amused, if unsurprised, by how many people she didn't recognize. Her life, even after marriage, was still confined to a small circle of friends and acquaintances, and she rarely moved beyond the confines of the village. Her father objected to travel of any sort and had once claimed that he'd barely survived Emma's wedding trip to the seaside, even though Isabella and John had come down from London to stay with him.

George took her arm. "Elton has arrived."

Through the tall windows that overlooked the drive, she could see a handsome town carriage pulling up to the portico— Mr. Suckling's, no doubt.

By the time she and George reached the front entrance, Mr. Elton had disembarked. To Emma's surprise, he turned to hand down Harriet, who was followed by Robert and Mr. Suckling.

While George greeted the men, Emma took her friend by the hand. "Harriet, you are looking quite flushed. It's so dreadfully warm today, is it not? Are you well?"

Harriet was indeed looking out of sorts, which was unusual. Unless encountering an upsetting circumstance—like a corpse in the church—she was a remarkably even-tempered girl. Yet today she seemed positively flustered.

"It's just rather warm, as you say." She turned to Mr. Elton and dredged up a smile. "It was so kind of you to take us up in Mr. Suckling's carriage. And kind of Mr. Suckling, as well."

"It wasn't my idea," Mr. Suckling replied, "so your thanks are not necessary."

Harriet flushed an even brighter red, while poor Robert went stiff as a plank.

Mr. Elton shook his head in disapproval. "Horace, one could hardly expect Mr. and Mrs. Martin to walk all the way to Donwell in this heat. Especially when they have been so kind to us."

"I'm sure they do it every day. It's the country, after all."

"We didn't mean to put you out, Mr. Suckling," Robert said in a stiff tone. "And we appreciate the kindness."

"Mr. Martin, it is you and your wife who have been so kind,"

Mr. Elton earnestly replied before turning to Emma. "Your dear friend has been such a blessing and a support to me through this entire ordeal, Mrs. Knightley, especially during that dreadful inquest."

Given the unfortunate history between Harriet and Mr. Elton, it was more than slightly ironic that he was now turning to the young woman for comfort. Emma could only imagine what his dearly departed would have had to say about such a development.

"You have had a very difficult day," Emma replied, "and you should not be standing out in this heat. And you are most welcome, too, Mr. Suckling."

"Much obliged," Mr. Suckling tersely replied. "Can't imagine why we're standing about and gabbing in the first place."

George quickly led the dratted man into the hall. The rest of them followed, although Robert immediately excused himself and disappeared into the crowd.

Mr. Suckling took off his hat—one banded with a very handsome piece of black satin, Emma noticed—and handed it to a footman.

"Well," he said to George. "This is quite the pile you have here. The Knightleys have obviously done splendidly for themselves over the years."

Emma blinked. Mr. Elton looked pained, while Harriet . . . wasn't paying attention. She was craning up, as if searching for someone in the general melee.

"Horace, what a thing to say," Mr. Elton admonished. "You will embarrass Mr. Knightley."

"I'm simply expressing my admiration. Smallridge would like this place, you know. Puts me in mind of his estate, although Pomphrey Manor is certainly more modern."

"The Smallridges are good friends of Mr. and Mrs. Suckling," Mr. Elton said. "You may recall."

"Yes, I do recall," replied Emma.

It would be impossible to forget, since Mrs. Elton had talked incessantly about the Smallridges and her other wealthy acquaintances.

"I would be happy to show you about the abbey," George tactfully said to Mr. Suckling. "Despite Mr. Elton's protestations, you cannot offend me by admiring my family's home."

Mr. Suckling jabbed the vicar in the arm. "There, Philip, you are much too nice about these things. Knightley knows what I am about. Gentlemen of our standing always do."

"Then I shall be happy to give you a tour after you and Mr. Elton have something to eat and drink," George said, glancing at Emma.

Recalled to her duties, she glanced about the hall. Unfortunately, every seat was taken.

"Mr. Elton, I'm afraid it's rather hideously crowded in here," she said. "Might I suggest that you join my father and Mrs. and Miss Bates in the east drawing room? They are well set up there, and the room is both quiet and cool. Mrs. Weston is with them, too."

The arrangement served both her father and Miss Bates. The poor woman was still in a fragile state, unable to converse with any degree of coherence. Keeping her away from the other guests seemed both necessary and wise.

"My father is eager to speak with you, Mr. Elton," she added. "He very much wished to attend the funeral but did not feel quite up to it."

Mr. Elton seized her hand. "Your father is a great friend to all of us. And so charitable to Miss Bates in her time of need."

Mr. Suckling scoffed. "That bloody woman. Mark my words. She may play the henwit, but she had something to do with Augusta's death."

Emma's patience with the man ran out. "That is a *ridiculous* assertion."

"This is not the best place to conduct a conversation of this nature," George said in austere tones. "Or conduct it at all."

Especially since Miss Prince and Miss Richardson, teachers at Mrs. Goddard's school, stood only feet away, straining to overhear.

The vicar grimaced. "Quite right, Mr. Knightley. Our dear Miss Bates is the kindest woman one could ever hope to find. It is, of course, utter nonsense to imagine that she could ever hurt anyone."

When Mr. Suckling started to argue, George took him by the elbow. "Allow me to escort you to the refreshment table. We have some excellent cider from Donwell's own apple orchard. Very refreshing in all this heat."

"Very well," Mr. Suckling grumbled. "Are you coming, Philip?"

"I must pay my respects to Mr. Woodhouse first. I will find you later."

"Have it your way. Ah, I see Weston, so I'll have a chat with him. He seems a sensible man, unlike so many in this benighted village." He smirked rather unpleasantly. "Present company excepted, of course," he added to George.

With a bland smile, George led Mr. Suckling away. Emma breathed a sigh of relief, but only after she had directed an admonishing frown at Miss Prince and Miss Richardson, who finally took the hint and moved off.

Mr. Elton sighed. "You must forgive my brother-in-law, Mrs. Knightley. He is very worried about Selina. She's in a delicate condition, you know."

"I did not know," she replied. "And, of course, that perfectly explains Mr. Suckling's . . . fretfulness."

Emma didn't think there was any excuse for the man's bad behavior, but pregnancy certainly explained why Mrs. Suckling had not made the trip to Highbury.

She smiled at Harriet, who'd not said a word since entering

the house. "Will you come to the east drawing room with us, dear? It will be much more pleasant than this crush."

The girl gave a visible start. "Ah, I think not, Mrs. Knightley. I . . . I believe I must find Robert." She then disappeared into the crowd.

"Poor Mrs. Martin," said the vicar. "She is very affected by my dear Augusta's death. The loss is a terrible blow—mostly for me, of course, but also for Highbury. How will we ever recover from the loss of such a magnificent woman, Mrs. Knightley?"

Since Emma felt quite beyond making an appropriate response to his observation, she took refuge in sympathetic murmurs as she led him away.

# CHAPTER 11

The yellow drawing room was Emma's favorite. The walls were hung with striped silk wallpaper in the loveliest shade of pale lemon, and the settees were covered in matching shades as they flanked either side of the handsome Adam fireplace. Comfortable overstuffed chairs were arranged in cozy groupings, better to view the contents of the curio cabinets and bookcases, which held various family collections—medals, antique books, rare seashells, vibrant corals, and other curiosities carefully gathered over the generations.

Even better was the lovely view out the tall windows, which overlooked the lush green lawns and the fine orchards stretching down to a rippling stream in the distance. In her many visits to Donwell over the years, Emma had come to love its quiet excellences—just as she'd come to love its master. The abbey was as much a reflection of George and his character as it was a great house that had stood the test of time with quiet dignity.

Today, however, the room was anything but quiet, but rather a scene of stormy emotions and a flood of tears from Miss Bates.

"Ma'am, do not cry so," Emma said, crouching in front of her. "You'll make yourself sick."

Emma's father had joined Miss Bates on the settee. "You must take care, dear lady. I heard children coughing when we arrived. Emma, what was Mr. Knightley thinking to invite so many people?"

"He didn't invite all of them, Father. They simply appeared here."

A distressed Mr. Elton hovered nearby. "I am to blame. I allowed myself to impose on Mr. Knightley's generosity in hosting the reception."

This particular crisis *was* actually the vicar's fault, having been precipitated by an unfortunate question to Miss Bates.

Initially, the conversation had proved uneventful. There had been a brief discussion of the funeral service, but also much talk of the weather and various people's health. Mrs. Bates had snoozed peacefully in her chair, and even Miss Bates had seemed calm as the men weighted the merits of appropriate comestibles at a funeral reception.

But then Mr. Elton had made the fatal error. "Ma'am," he said to Miss Bates, "I have been meaning to ask you a question, if I may."

"Indeed, of course. A question. Whatever can it be? I wonder."

"Before my wife departed the house on that final, tragic day, she made a slight mention of something she wished to discuss with you—something beyond the arrangements for the altar linens. While it seemed a topic of some import, she rushed away so as not to keep you waiting. I don't wish to pry, but can you tell me what you were to discuss? It would give me great comfort if I could fulfill any of Augusta's last wishes."

During his little speech Miss Bates had gone terribly pale and tense. "I . . . I cannot . . . I mean, that is to say, I do not know whatever you can be referring to, sir. I . . . I do not know what she may have wished to discuss."

"I do not wish to cause you distress," Mr. Elton had hastily replied. "But I was so struck by Augusta's manner that day. And since you were the last person she was to meet, I thought—"

At that point, Miss Bates had burst into tears, and Emma had now spent five minutes trying to calm her. A flustered Mr. Elton had offered—helpfully or unhelpfully, depending on one's view—to speak with her at another time. That had only made Miss Bates weep harder.

Growing exasperated, Emma retrieved her father's smelling salts and employed them. Miss Bates gasped, hiccuping, as she tried to catch her breath. Clearly, this was no simple case of overwrought nerves. What was this unknown issue, and why did it upset Miss Bates so greatly? Once again, it struck her as decidedly odd that the two ladies had decided to meet in so furtive a manner in the church.

"Please, Miss Bates," she said. "Your mother will be worried if she sees you in such a state."

Mrs. Bates, thankfully, had snoozed through the commotion. Still, her daughter made a visible effort to control herself, although tears continued to flow through incoherent apologies.

Mr. Elton touched Emma's shoulder. "Perhaps I should go. I have no wish to cause dear Miss Bates any further distress, and I regret that I asked her such an indelicate question in the first place."

Sighing, Emma rose to her feet. "That might be best. If you could perhaps find Mr. Perry, I would be forever in your debt."

He grasped her free hand. "I will search for him with the greatest of diligence. And if there is any other way I can serve, you have simply to ask."

"Just Mr. Perry, sir. And please get yourself something to eat. I'm sure you're quite worn out."

"You are too kind, madam. You think only of others and not of yourself."

"Yes, yes," Emma's father cut in before she could reply. "But please do hurry, Mr. Elton. It is vital that you find Perry immediately."

The vicar beat a hasty retreat.

"I thought he would never go," her father said with an indignant huff.

"It's been a very difficult day for him," Emma replied in a soothing tone. "He is not himself."

"He was very insensitive to Miss Bates."

Miss Bates wiped her nose and drew in a shuddering breath. "You mustn't worry about me, Mr. Woodhouse. For me to act in such a way . . . quite shocking . . . really. I feel terrible for Mr. Elton. To distress you all . . . I am qui-quite ashamed of myself."

"Emma, pour Miss Bates a sherry, just a small one to steady her nerves," Father ordered. "And check on Mrs. Bates, as well, to see if she is in need of something to calm her nerves."

She eyed her father, still amazed by his newly decisive manner.

"Don't dawdle, my dear," he added.

After fetching a glass of sherry from the sideboard, Emma tiptoed up to Mrs. Bates, who was still asleep.

*Lucky her.*

When Mr. Perry hurried into the room, Emma expelled a sigh of relief. "Thank you for coming so promptly."

"Mr. Elton said it was an emergency."

The poor man looked harried, which was not to be wondered at. Even on a solemn occasion such as a funeral reception, her father kept him hopping.

"Perry, you must attend to Miss Bates," Father exclaimed. "Her nerves are in tatters, and she will fall ill."

"Surely not. Miss Bates is always so healthy. In fact, Mr. Woodhouse, I was certain I'd been called to attend you."

"I'm perfectly well, but you must see to Miss Bates."

Emma and Mr. Perry exchanged a startled glance. The words

*perfectly* and *well* were not ones that normally existed side by side in her parent's lexicon.

"Father, I must attend to the other guests," she said as the apothecary began to speak to Miss Bates. "I'll return as soon as I can."

He gave her a distracted wave. "As you wish, my dear."

After slipping from the room—and breathing a massive sigh of relief—Emma decided to search for her husband and Harriet. She was a trifle worried about her friend. It was clear that something had distressed her, beyond the natural emotions generated by the occasion.

When she reached the great hall, she couldn't help wincing at the din. She'd been to Christmas parties more solemn than this occasion—although, to be fair, the lugubrious note at some of their holiday festivities was usually due to the behavior of her own relations.

Going up on her toes, she searched for George and Harriet in the throng, but neither seemed to be present.

A peal of laughter from a nearby table caught her attention. *Drat.*

Anne Cox was holding forth with her sister, along with the Otway girls and Miss Bickerton. They were clearly gossiping like mad and having *too* much fun. Enough was enough.

When she marched over to their table, Miss Bickerton scrambled to her feet. The others looked rather shamefaced, except for the unrepentant Anne.

"Thank you for joining us this afternoon, ladies," Emma said. "I'm sure Mr. Elton and Mr. Suckling are grateful that you came to pay your respects in their time of *profound grief.*"

"Thank you, Mrs. Knightley," Susan rushed to say. "It was ever so kind of you to have us, and of course, we wished to pay our respects to poor Mr. Elton."

The others bobbed their heads, looking rather like a bevy of quails, as they expressed a garbled mix of thanks and sympathies.

Anne interrupted them with an affected laugh. "La, girls. There's no need to babble. I'm sure Mrs. Knightley can hardly make out a word."

Miss Bickerton, a parlor boarder at Mrs. Goddard's school, cast Emma a tentative smile. "I do apologize, Mrs. Knightley. We don't mean to kick up a fuss."

"You seemed to be having quite a lively conversation," Emma replied. "May I enquire as to the topic?"

"It was nothing, Mrs. Knightley. Just a bit of silly gossip," Miss Bickerton replied.

"Perhaps this is not the best occasion for silly gossip."

They all looked decidedly uncomfortable—except for Anne, who was her usual smug self.

"It wasn't totally silly gossip, Mrs. Knightley," Anne said. "It's *tremendously* frightening, in fact."

Emma crossed her arms. "How so?"

Miss Bickerton cast a wary glance around and then leaned forward, as if not wishing to be overheard. "It's just that some people are saying that Mrs. Elton was murdered by a vengeful spirit. It happened in a church, after all. Right on top of one of the burial vaults."

*Not this again.*

"And why would a vengeful spirit wish to rise up and murder the vicar's wife?" When Caroline Otway started to answer, Emma shot up a hand. "Never mind. I do not wish to hear it. Who is spreading this tale?"

Anne shrugged. "Just people."

"Which people?"

"Lots of people, I suppose," Anne replied in a chippy tone. "You know how everyone likes to gossip."

"I don't think anyone meant any harm, Mrs. Knightley,"

Susan hastened to say. "It's just so very odd that poor Mrs. Elton was killed in the church in the middle of the day, and yet no one saw or heard a thing. It does sound like something a ghost would do."

"It's very strange, you must admit," added Caroline.

"I admit nothing of the sort. And let me assure you that Mrs. Elton was *not* killed by a vengeful ghost," Emma replied in a cool tone. "If I hear one more word of this ridiculous tale from any of you, I will be speaking to your mothers and to Mrs. Goddard. Do I make myself clear?"

That pronouncement caused widespread alarm.

"None of us will say another word, we promise!" exclaimed Miss Bickerton, flapping a hand.

"Thank you."

Emma turned on her heel and marched off. Annoyed that she'd been drawn into the deranged discussion in the first place, she weighed the merits of quaffing a fortifying glass of wine versus escaping the reception altogether. But the latter would mean abandoning her poor husband, so the former it was to be.

As she was forging her way to the refreshment table, a hand gripped her arm. Emma jumped—her nerves were clearly on edge, as well—and turned to find Harriet, teary-eyed and mussed.

"Good God, Harriet, whatever is the matter?"

"Something dreadful," her friend dramatically stated. "And I don't know what to do."

Repressing a sigh, Emma took her hand and led her from the hall. At this rate, she'd need to keep smelling salts in every room in the house.

# Chapter 12

Emma led Harriet to a wrought-iron bench at one end of Donwell's gardens, underneath a majestic oak. They sat in silence, absorbing the peaceful vista. Below the formal gardens were the meadows, bound by avenues of the noble oaks and beeches that had been planted long ago. Some of the younger folk walked along the shaded avenues or strolled toward the strawberry beds and the lime walk beyond that. Still, not many had ventured out into the bright sunlight, leaving Emma and her friend with much-needed quiet and privacy.

When Harriet let out a melancholy sigh, Emma stirred.

"Dearest, whatever is the matter?"

"I don't think Robert loves me anymore," Harriet blurted out. "And it's just the most horrible thing I could ever imagine."

This was *not* what Emma had been expecting. It took her a moment to collect her thoughts.

"Harriet, I have never met a man more in love than Robert Martin is with you. Have you forgotten that he waited for you for almost a year while you fell in love with two other men?"

"But I fell in love with those other men only because you encouraged me."

While that was true—although she'd certainly never encouraged Harriet to fall in love with George—Emma refused to go off track. "Everyone knows how much Robert loves you. How could you arrive at such an odd conclusion?"

"Because he's been flirting with Anne Cox. He even did it right in front of me!"

Then she buried her face in her hands and wept.

Emma sighed. Robert Martin was a good man of common sense, but no one would ever accuse him of an excess of imagination. The poor fellow likely wouldn't have any idea if Anne was flirting with him or merely discussing the state of his crops.

"Now, Harriet, let us be sensible. Although I do not doubt that Anne *tried* to flirt with Robert, I'm sure that he was simply being polite."

"But you didn't see them. It was so . . . so blatant."

Emma found herself once more longing for that glass of wine. "When did this supposed flirtation take place?"

"They had a very long chat before the funeral. Then, after the service, when I stopped to talk to Mrs. Goddard, they began flirting again. Anne even asked to borrow his handkerchief, because she'd forgotten hers at home." Harriet suddenly scowled. "She wasn't crying or even the least bit upset. I'm sure she wanted it as a love token."

Emma had to repress an impulse to laugh at the notion of Robert Martin's handkerchief serving as a love token for anyone. "If you were talking to Mrs. Goddard, how do you know she asked to borrow his handkerchief?"

"Because when I joined them, Anne made a point of using it to wipe her eyes. Then, when she tried to give it back to Robert, he insisted she keep it."

"Very sensible of him. I certainly wouldn't want my handkerchief back after a vulgar person like Anne Cox had used it."

That gave Harriet pause. "But that's just the sort of thing I used to do when I fancied myself in love with Mr. Elton."

In the throes of young love, the girl had filched a few souvenirs from Mr. Elton, including a bit of leftover sticking plaster. Such an item had struck Emma as decidedly unromantic, but tastes obviously varied.

"I remember. Still, you didn't make a show of it, which Anne was obviously doing to annoy you."

"When we were waiting for Mr. Elton and Mr. Suckling, Robert told me that he felt sorry for Anne because she was so distressed, and that she was too tenderhearted for such sad scenes." Harriet gave a defiant little sniff. "Which suggests that I don't have a tender heart."

Emma marveled, and not for the first time, at how utterly dimwitted men could be when it came to women. "I would wager that it was Anne who made a point of speaking such drivel. It certainly doesn't sound like the sort of thing Robert would say."

"I . . . I suppose you're right."

"Anne was simply playing on Robert's good nature, dear. It has absolutely nothing to do with you or his feelings for you."

"Are you sure?"

"Of course. And might I just point out that you are the prettiest and the nicest girl in all of Highbury. You can be sure Robert is well aware of that."

Her friend grimaced. "But later he talked to her for the longest time, when he was supposed to be fetching me a cider—which he forgot to do."

Emma studied her for a few moments. "Harriet, did you say something to Robert about this?"

"I . . . I might have."

"What, exactly, did you say?"

"I simply asked him why he was flirting with Anne."

"And how did he respond?"

"He just stared at me."

"I'm sure he was stunned by the question."

"Then I asked him if he still loved me, and he just told me not to be silly."

Once more, Emma pondered the idiocy of men. "Harriet, I

am dead certain he meant that you were silly to even ask the question, since of course he loves you. Still, I can understand why you were upset. Men are quite dreadful at expressing their emotions, you know."

"I suppose that's true."

"How then did this regrettable discussion with Robert conclude?"

"Well . . . I suppose I ran away from him and came to find you."

"Dearest, this really is just a tempest in a teapot. Anne is jealous because she fancied Robert for herself, so she's trying to cause trouble. It's truly no more complicated than that."

Harriet rubbed the tip of her nose. "Truly?"

"I promise," Emma firmly said. "And you are understandably worn down by the travails of the past few days, as well as by the funeral service."

"Yes, it was terribly sad today. I don't know how Mr. Elton is able to bear it."

That was exactly the transition Emma had been looking for. "How was he during the service?"

"He seemed terribly cut up. But very dignified, too."

"And was Mr. Suckling equally cut up?"

"No, although I suppose he wouldn't be, since he was only her brother-in-law. In fact, he seemed irritated and was quite snappish when Mr. Cox and Mr. Gilbert offered their condolences."

Emma frowned. "How odd. I always thought Mrs. Elton and her brother-in-law were close. And what of the arrangements themselves? From what Mr. Knightley tells me, they were rather simple."

Harriet pursed her lips. "I don't really know, since I've been to only one other funeral in my life. Mrs. Gilbert did say she was surprised to see such a plain affair, though, especially because Mrs. Elton was the wife of the vicar."

"Yes, that is odd."

"Mr. Suckling wore a silk armband and a silk hatband, but Mr. Elton's servants had only black cotton armbands. Mrs. Cole was quite struck by that."

"What about the female servants?"

"The housekeeper had a black dress. The maids did not have proper mourning clothes, and so were not to come, according to Mrs. Cole."

Another mystery. There should have been plenty of time to acquire the appropriate mourning clothes for the servants.

"Who else attended from the staff?"

Harriet shook her head. "Only the two footmen. I didn't see the coachman or groom."

"Good heavens."

"Perhaps Mr. Elton was too overcome with grief to manage anything better."

Perhaps, but the fact that *both* the deceased's husband and brother-in-law put on such a poor showing defied feeling and custom.

Emma pondered the odd lack of decorum that seemed to have afflicted so many in their little village. It was as if the intrusion of violence into their orderly lives had set Highbury and its residents all askew.

When Harriet let out a wistful sigh, Emma recalled herself. Her friend was clearly wishing to be with her husband—or, at least, to keep him away from Anne.

She stood and pulled the girl to her feet. "Harriet, go find Robert and ask him to take you home. The past several days have been very trying for you, and you should get some rest."

Harriet looked torn. "I think I should stay, in case you need help."

"Everything is perfectly under control. You've paid your respects to Mr. Elton, and there is certainly no need to spend more time around the Cox sisters. I cannot imagine how their mother puts up with them. If I were that poor woman, I'd be compelled to run away from home."

As intended, that produced a giggle from Harriet.

Emma gave her friend a little push. "Off with you, dear."

"Aren't you coming back to the house?"

"I must find Mr. Knightley. I believe he's in one of the gardens with guests."

Even if she didn't find George, a quiet stroll and a little think would be most welcome.

After hugging Harriet farewell, Emma set off for the lime walk. George may have taken some of the male guests for an excursion around the grounds, and that particular view was one of the best.

As she passed the strawberry beds, she exchanged greetings with Mrs. Goddard and a few of her teachers, who were strolling between the rows. Thankfully, no children were out trampling William Larkins's beloved strawberry plants.

Emma shaded her eyes and peered ahead to the lime walk.

*Drat.*

There was no sign of George, so she supposed she should return to the great hall.

Suddenly, she heard angry voices rising from behind a stand of oak trees beyond the walk. One belonged to Mr. Elton. The other voice was belligerent and easily recognized.

Mr. Suckling.

She hesitated. While George would certainly counsel her to leave the men to their private discussion, Mr. Suckling struck her as the sort of man who could stoop to berating a grieving widower. She found the man's bullying ways infuriating.

After stepping onto the grass, she sidled between the trees, where she could ascertain that Mr. Suckling was indeed upbraiding poor Mr. Elton.

"This is all your fault," he barked. "Thank God Selina stayed in London, so she didn't have to see how poorly you've managed things. Not one blasted funeral memento, not even for Knightley or Weston."

"May I remind you that I was in the unenviable position of overseeing my own wife's funeral service and committal?" Mr. Elton replied with dignity. "Be assured that I will see to the appropriate mementos in due course. And I fail to see why you should blame me for anything about this dreadful situation."

"Because you were responsible for her, you fool. What Augusta saw in this ridiculous place—or you—is beyond me."

Righteous anger almost propelled Emma from her hiding place, but burgeoning curiosity held her back.

She crept forward and peered around the trunk of a large oak. The men stood several feet away, their backs half-turned to her. Still, she could see their faces. Mr. Suckling's beefy features were flushed and shiny from heat and an anger that all but shimmered in the air. Mr. Elton, by contrast, stood quietly, his face cast in shadow by his wide cleric's hat.

"Augusta and I loved each other," the vicar said in a flat tone. "We had a very happy marriage, and I doubt I will ever recover from this blow."

"For a man who's so devastated, you've made a bloody poor showing of her funeral. As you just pointed out, you're the blasted vicar! And now you tell me you're not going to place a commemorative monument inside the church? Why the bloody hell not?"

"Because it's an old church, Horace, and there is no room left for a proper monument. And while you may be cavalier with my wife's money, I will not spend it on a shabby memorial in a forgotten corner of the church."

Mr. Suckling chopped a sharp hand. "Stop blithering nonsense. You need to honor Augusta's memory in the proper fashion. Selina and I insist on it."

"Augusta's resting place is in the best part of the churchyard, under that beautiful beech tree. She was very fond of that tree. She said it was quite the best beech in all of Highbury."

"She didn't give a damn about trees."

"Perhaps you didn't know your sister-in-law as well as you think."

Mr. Suckling's only reply was a derisive snort.

"As well," the vicar continued, "I have every intention of erecting a handsome memorial over her grave—with your help, of course. I would think that you and dear Selina would be happy to contribute to a fine monument to honor Augusta. An angel, perhaps, one in mourning for . . ."

When he choked off his words, Emma couldn't help but feel pity. She also felt a wee bit of shame that she—and George, too, in all fairness—had been so dismissive of the Eltons' marital relationship.

"I have no intention of helping you with Augusta's memorial," Mr. Suckling retorted. "That is your responsibility."

Mr. Elton seemed to steady himself. "I cannot imagine Selina will agree with you. But if you choose not to honor your sister-in-law, then I will select something not quite so grand. I'm sure Augusta would have preferred that, anyway. She had quite a horror of excessive displays of finery, you know."

Emma had indeed heard Mrs. Elton express a horror of finery—while wearing more finery than any other woman in the village.

Mr. Suckling snorted. "That's ridiculous. Have it your way, but know that Selina will not be pleased."

"Selina could not even be bothered to make the short trip to Highbury," Mr. Elton angrily replied, finally showing some temper. "So, please, no lectures on what Augusta preferred. As her spouse, I cherished her more than anyone."

"Then why in blazes did you let her go traipsing all over Highbury, wearing her most valuable piece of jewelry? No wonder she found herself set upon by a thief. I've no doubt this scabby place is full of them."

*Well, really.*

If there was anyone acting in a scabby fashion, it was Mr. Suckling.

"If Augusta wished to wear her jewelry somewhere, it was no business of mine to tell her otherwise. Besides, I hardly notice such things. I am not a man of fashion, Horace. I am a simple country vicar."

Now, that was a bit much. Mr. Elton was well aware of the finer things in life. He was also ambitious—which Emma discovered in a most unpleasant manner when he'd proposed to her.

"I don't care what she might have wished," Suckling retorted. "It was damned careless to allow her to wear the blasted thing so freely. And I'll wager you could use such a valuable piece right now—to buy a fine headstone, for instance."

Mr. Elton bristled. "If you are suggesting that I would sell those pearls, you are much mistaken. That necklace was my wedding present to her. I would never dispose of something that meant a great deal to both of us."

"You'd be a fool not to if you're strapped for funds."

"If there is any question of that, it rests on you. Not on Augusta, and certainly not on me."

By now, Emma's mind was reeling from the variety of accusations being tossed about. None of it made sense.

"I have had enough of this ridiculous conversation," Mr. Suckling said in a haughty tone. "I must be off to London. Selina will be waiting for me."

"Your presence will, of course, be missed," Mr. Elton replied, equally haughtily.

"I'll return for the reading of Augusta's will, so you won't have to miss me for long."

A tense silence ensued.

"There is no will," the vicar finally replied.

His brother-in-law reared back, startled. "Of course she had a will. Augusta told me that she intended to draw one up once the marriage settlements had been agreed to."

"Well, she didn't."

Mr. Suckling looked flummoxed. "But that makes no sense. She had assets at her disposal that must be accounted for. Her jewelry, for one thing, and family heirlooms that I know to be of value."

"All I can tell you is that Augusta managed her own affairs as she saw fit. I trusted her completely to do so."

"What does the coroner have to say? By law, he's responsible for her effects."

"The issue hasn't come up. As you might have noticed, he and I both had other matters to attend to—including a murder inquest."

His brother-in-law stared at him, clearly incredulous. "Philip, you are a fool. And do not think we are finished with this subject. When I return, I will want clear answers about Augusta's estate."

"As for that, *you* should be the one providing answers to *me* in that regard."

"I have better things to do than stand here and listen to foolish innuendos. I will speak with you upon my return."

As quietly as she could, Emma scrambled back to the graveled path. She pinned a smile on her face and did her best to give the impression that she had just this moment arrived at the lime walk.

Mr. Suckling stormed out from the trees, then pulled up short with an oath when he saw her. It was thankfully rude enough that it could explain her no doubt flustered appearance.

"Sir! You gave me a shock. I had no idea you were out here."

The man glared at her. "Why would you?"

She didn't have to pretend to be offended, since he was really *quite* rude.

"I'm looking for my husband," she replied. "Have you seen him? I think he must have come this way with Mr. Elton."

The vicar emerged from the trees. "Here I am, Mrs. Knightley. Horace and I were simply having a quiet stroll. I thought to show him the lime walk and the abbey's beautiful vistas."

"How kind of you." She smiled at Mr. Suckling. "I hope you found it refreshing. It was rather stifling in the hall."

"It's stifling out here, too. If you'll excuse me, ma'am, I must be on my way back to town. My wife is expecting me."

"Of course, sir. Please give her our condolences."

Mr. Suckling turned on his heel and stalked off.

"Please forgive my brother-in-law," Mr. Elton said, looking embarrassed. "He naturally found this a difficult day."

"Think nothing of it. But this is an even more difficult day for you." She took in his pasty features and worn look. "You should not be out in his heat, sir. It's too much."

He clasped his hands in a prayerful gesture. "You are wise, as always, madam. I have perhaps spent too much time in the sun. I'm afraid the press of people in the great hall became too overwhelming in my present state."

"Then we will find you a quiet place to sit, where no one will bother you."

They turned to walk toward the house.

"You, Mrs. Knightley, are never a bother," he said. "In fact, I would consider it an honor if you sat with me. Your friendship—and that of your husband—is more than consolation. I do not know how I should survive without it."

Emma tried to hide her surprise at his effusive praise. While she felt a great deal of sympathy for him, they were not friends. Still, one was bound to be emotional at such a time, when pushed beyond the limits of one's ordinary life.

"We are happy to be of help in any small way."

The vicar sighed. "You are so modest, Mrs. Knightley. Just like my dear Augusta."

Emma didn't quite know how to take that. "Er, thank you, sir."

He pressed a hand to his chest. "Please call me Philip, Mrs. Knightley. We are such old friends, are we not?"

She began to wonder if he *had* been out in the sun too long. "We all need friends at a time like this, Mr. Elton. And speaking of friends, perhaps you might enjoy having a quiet chat with Mrs. Cole. I know she's very worried for you."

"Ah, dear Mrs. Cole. She and Augusta were such bosom friends. Mrs. Cole will miss her greatly."

"As will many others in Highbury, sir. Mrs. Goddard, for instance."

"Very true, Mrs. Knightley. My Augusta took a great interest in the school, you know. Always so ready with advice and help whenever it was needed. I do not know how Mrs. Goddard will get on without her wise counsel."

Nodding and encouraging this innocent—if fantastical—discourse as best she could, Emma led the vicar back to the house.

# CHAPTER 13

At the dressing table, Emma braided her hair in preparation for bed. After supervising the restoration of order after the lengthy reception, she and George had decided to spend the night at Donwell.

"I do hope Father is all right. He worries when I'm not home with him."

George, reading by the fireplace, glanced up with a reassuring smile. "Other than telling you to be sure to avoid drafts in the corridors, he raised no objection."

"I suppose his mind was full of Miss Bates. He insisted on taking her and her mother home in our carriage."

"He is remarkably protective of Miss Bates."

"They have been friends for a very long time, after all."

"Miss Bates has many dear friends, including Mrs. Cole and Mrs. Goddard."

Emma recognized *that* particular tone. "George, what are you suggesting?"

He put down his novel. "I find it interesting that Miss Bates has come to rely so heavily on your father. He is not a person one would generally turn to in a crisis."

"I'll admit Father has been managing this entire murder business quite well. I thought he would be afraid to let me out of his sight."

"One can only assume that your father accepts Constable Sharpe's conclusion that Mrs. Elton's killer is long gone."

Emma finished off her braid and tied it with a ribbon. "It's rather unsettling to see him acting so . . . decisively. I hardly recognize him."

"We have all been upended by Mrs. Elton's murder, as I'm sure you observed in the odd behavior of some of our guests today."

"The circumstances didn't disturb anyone's appetite," she wryly replied.

George chuckled before returning to his book.

After studying her husband for a few moments—always an enjoyable pastime—she rose and donned the cambric wrapper draped over the corner of the enormous four-poster bed. Despite her father's admonitions, it was a lovely evening. A warm breeze wafted through the windows, barely ruffling the brocaded curtains.

Unable to resist the call of the summer-soft air, she wandered over to gaze out at the night-shrouded garden. The scents of roses and lilacs drifted up from below. In the distance, at the base of the meadow, she could hear the rippling stream merrily dancing in the darkness. Only the knowledge that a cold-blooded killer was at large shadowed the serene peace after so fraught a day.

"What is it, my Emma?" George quietly asked.

She smiled. "Do you always know what I'm thinking?"

"One doesn't need to be a mind reader, given the events of the past few days."

Joining him, she made to sit in the matching wingback chair, but he snagged her wrist and drew her onto his lap. She went with a contented sigh.

"I was thinking about a very odd conversation I had with Mr. Elton this afternoon," she said.

"Given your mutual history, surely that is not a unique event."

She rolled her eyes. "True."

"What was so odd about this particular conversation?"

When she began to fiddle with a button on his waistcoat, he stilled her hand. "Emma, what aren't you telling me?"

The dear, dratted man knew her too well. "I didn't precisely *have* a conversation with Mr. Elton so much as overhear a conversation."

His sigh ruffled her hair. "You were eavesdropping."

"It would seem that I was."

"Emma . . ."

She sat up to meet his gaze. "George, I didn't intend to eavesdrop. It just rather happened."

"Such things seem to happen to you on a regular basis," he dryly replied.

"I was actually looking for you. I thought perhaps you'd taken some of the guests down the lime walk. And I also had the *most* disconcerting conversation with Harriet. But Mr. Elton takes precedence."

"I await both reports with bated breath."

She poked his chest. "None of your sarcasm, sir. When I was looking for you, I chanced to hear a very unpleasant argument between Mr. Elton and Mr. Suckling. At one point, I feared they might even come to blows."

George frowned. "Mr. Suckling is not the most convivial person, but I always assumed they had a good relationship."

"Apparently, no longer. And the subject of the argument was Mrs. Elton."

He studied her for a few moments. "As loathe as I am to violate Elton's privacy, I suppose you'd best tell me."

"You *are* the magistrate, George. You should know everything that might be of relevance to the investigation."

Although he now rolled his eyes, he didn't dispute the point.

But when she related the details of the tense discussion, he frowned. "Emma, are you suggesting that Elton cannot afford a proper memorial?"

"I had the sense that such might be the case. Although Mr. Elton claimed the lack of room in the church as the reason for declining such an expense."

"I'll admit the church has a substantive number of memorials, but I'm sure room could be found to give Mrs. Elton a proper memorial stone, at the very least."

"Then why would he make such a claim?"

He shook his head. "I don't know. Mrs. Elton brought a substantial sum of money to the marriage, and Elton already had his own independence. Although not large, it was perfectly sufficient for his needs."

"True, but they were inclined to spend rather freely."

"Unless one or both had become addicted to cards, it's hard to imagine how they could run through her fortune in less than a year. And although Mrs. Elton could be a spendthrift, Elton is not. The man is very aware of the value of money."

"Yes, as I discovered, to my misfortune."

"My love, I am certain that Elton's marriage proposal to you had nothing to do with your fortune and everything to do with your beauty and wit."

Emma didn't fail to notice the gleam of amusement in his gaze. "Nicely done, Mr. Knightley."

"I do try. Now, what was Suckling's response to his brother-in-law's parsimony?"

"He was adamant that the cost of a proper memorial was Mr. Elton's responsibility. Our vicar then tried to make the case that Mrs. Elton would not have wished for anything grand—given her well-known abhorrence of finery, you understand."

MURDER IN HIGHBURY   165

George snorted. "No doubt Suckling wasn't convinced by that line of argument."

"He was not."

"And I cannot but agree with him that it's Elton's responsibility."

"True, but Mr. Elton seemed to suggest Mr. Suckling was somehow responsible for his—or Mrs. Elton's—financial problems." She twirled a hand. "That's assuming they actually had problems. Mr. Suckling seemed very insulted by the suggestion and said Mr. Elton was talking nonsense. He refused to discuss it any further, which was most annoying."

"What a shame you didn't think to ask the gentlemen to clarify their remarks."

She eyed him with severity. "Be serious, George."

"Very well. As fascinating as this is, I'm not sure what it has to do with Mrs. Elton's murder. Are you suggesting that either her husband or brother-in-law was somehow involved?"

She shrugged. "Not Mr. Elton, who has been rendered genuinely distraught by her death. Besides, he's hardly the murdering type."

"And what is the murdering type?"

"Certainly not our vicar. He's much too obsequious to be a murderer."

"That is undoubtedly a unique perspective on the character of murderers. Still, I must agree with you in this case."

Emma held up a finger. "Now, as for Mr. Suckling . . . he is a thoroughly dislikable man with a bad temper."

"But what motive would he have? For one thing, why would he steal her necklace? He's a wealthy man, after all. And by all accounts, he was fond of his sister-in-law. Do not forget that Mrs. Elton spent a great deal of time at Maple Grove. I doubt she would have done so if they disliked each other."

She sighed. "I must admit that your logic is sound. How frustrating. I wonder if we will ever discover who murdered her."

"We must hope so, but there is little to be gained by useless speculation." He raised an eyebrow. "Or by intruding on the private affairs of others," he pointedly added.

"I didn't actually intrude, George."

"I understand. But please remember that it is not your place to investigate this crime."

She poked a finger at his chest. "No, it's yours. I'm simply telling you what I heard."

"And I appreciate that, but the actual business of investigation belongs to Constable Sharpe and, to a small extent, Dr. Hughes. I will convey any pertinent information to them. I'm not sure, however, that a quarrel between Elton and Suckling meets that standard."

"I suppose you're right," she reluctantly replied.

Still, she couldn't imagine quarreling over mundane matters like memorial plaques and funeral mementos after such a traumatic day. Everything about that unpleasant scene between the brothers-in-law struck her as odd. However, as George had pointed out, many in Highbury were not acting their usual selves, either.

"I'm glad you agree," he said. "Now, is there anything else that needs my attention, or can we go to bed?"

Another detail did occur. "Mrs. Elton didn't leave a will. Is that not very strange?"

George's dark eyebrows ticked up. "Are you certain?"

"Absolutely. Mr. Suckling was quite upset. He made a point of saying that his sister-in-law had intended to draw up a will before her marriage, but Mr. Elton insisted that she had not done so. He also claimed that Mr. Suckling would know more about her estate than he did. I must say I found that strange."

He looked thoughtful for a few moments. "Perhaps Suckling and his solicitor drew up the marriage settlements on Mrs. Elton's behalf. If so, he would know a great deal about her financial standing. What I find strange, however, is that Dr. Hughes never mentioned the lack of a will to me."

"Why would he?"

"The coroner is responsible for assessing the value of the deceased's belongings. He would also know whether she had a will or not."

"Then I have given you something of use, after all," she commented.

"You have, and I will be raising the issue with Dr. Hughes tomorrow."

Given the suddenly austere tone of her husband's voice, Emma might be prompted to feel some sympathy for the coroner. But since Dr. Hughes was not a sympathetic man, that would be a waste of her time.

"Is there anything else?" he asked.

"Not unless you wish to hear about my conversation with Harriet. It was almost as gruesome as the argument between Mr. Suckling and Mr. Elton."

George gently tipped her off his lap and rose. "Then I would beg you to spare me. Besides, I can think of better ways to spend our time, especially after a trying day."

Emma wrapped her arms around his neck. "Do tell, husband."

"I find that I would much rather show you."

And with that, he led her off to bed.

# CHAPTER 14

"Are you sure Mr. Elton will wish to see us?" Harriet asked as they left Hartfield. "The funeral was but yesterday."

Emma shifted the basket of puddings to her other arm. "We are making a very proper condolence call, and you know how much Mr. Elton enjoys our cook's puddings. They will cheer him up."

While it was true that she wanted to see how the vicar was managing, she remained curious about yesterday's scene behind the lime walk. Despite George's admonitions to leave well enough alone, Emma couldn't help but be curious—especially about the state of the Eltons' finances.

"I'm also hoping to ask Mr. Elton a few questions," she added.

Harriet looked askance. "What sort of questions?"

"About the funeral and Mrs. Elton's memorial." Emma again shifted the basket.

Harriet reached for it as they turned into Vicarage Lane. "Let me take that. I'm sure it's too heavy for you."

Emma happily relinquished it. "Thank you, dear."

"Why are you going to ask Mr. Elton about the funeral?"

"Because I find it odd that it was so plain. Mr. Knightley and I would have been happy to help him with the arrangements if he'd felt too overwhelmed."

That sounded entirely reasonable, to her ears.

"But what if that makes him think he didn't do it properly?" Harriet replied. "Won't he be offended?"

"I will be very sensitive, naturally. Pay particular attention to his answer if I have the opportunity to question why Mrs. Elton did not write a will."

Harriet shot her a surprised glance. "She did not? But even I have a will. Robert insisted I write one when we married."

"Apparently, Mrs. Elton did not do the same."

"Perhaps she just forgot."

"It's still odd, though. Harriet, it's imperative that we specifically note anything that touches on the murder, including any information we might, er, stumble across."

Her friend stopped dead in the middle of the lane. "Isn't that what Constable Sharpe and Dr. Hughes are already doing?"

"That is what they *should* be doing, but I have little confidence in their talents or acumen."

"Surely Mr. Knightley will know what to do, though."

"Mr. Knightley is extremely busy, and I worry that he cannot depend on either Dr. Hughes or Constable Sharpe to investigate properly. Besides, it's our duty as residents of Highbury to assist the law in any way we can."

Especially since the law seemed to be haring off in the wrong direction.

"I don't think Robert will like me getting involved, Mrs. Knightley," Harriet dubiously replied.

"We're not truly getting involved, dear. We're simply collecting information, like you did with your scrapbooks, remember?"

"But they were just silly collections of riddles and poems."

"Your scrapbooks are elegant and well organized. You have

a talent for such things, dear. If we should discover anything—
and I'm not saying we will—you can help me present the findings to Mr. Knightley in an accurate manner, which he will
appreciate."

She mentally crossed her fingers, since her beloved had made
his thoughts on the matter of amateur investigating very clear.
But this was *murder*, and one possibly committed by someone
they knew, despite theories of random thieves or even vengeful
ghosts. There was also the added complication of Miss Bates.
She'd been cast under a shadow of suspicion, which had cut up
her peace and the peace of all her friends, including Emma's father.

No matter what George said, she found it impossible to do
nothing.

"I suppose, if you think it proper," Harriet conceded.

"I think it our moral duty as stouthearted Englishwomen."

Her friend clasped the basket to her chest, almost tipping a
cloth-covered pudding into the dirt. "Mrs. Knightley, you
make it sound so romantic! It's almost as if we're in an adven-
ture like one of Mrs. Radcliffe's stories."

"Nothing so vulgar, I hope."

Mrs. Elton's murder was ghastly enough without deranged
monks or dim-witted virgins running about the place.

When they arrived at the vicarage, a soberly dressed footman
sporting a black armband opened the door.

"Good afternoon," Emma said. "Is Mr. Elton at home?"

"No, Mrs. Knightley. If you'd like me to take—"

The housekeeper appeared from the back of the hall. "That
will be all, Joseph. I will attend to the ladies."

"Yes, Mrs. Wright."

Attired in a black gown and a cap with matching black ribbons, Mrs. Wright curtsied. "Good afternoon, Mrs. Knightley.
Mr. Elton has just stepped out for a moment. Would you care
to wait?"

"If it is no inconvenience."

"Mr. Elton left instructions that if you or Mr. Knightley were to call, I should please ask you to wait."

She took the basket from Harriet, barely looking at her, and then showed them to the back parlor. "If you will have a seat, Mrs. Knightley, I will bring up the tea tray."

Emma frowned, annoyed by the woman's insistence on ignoring Harriet. "Thank you. Mrs. Martin and I would *both* appreciate a cup of tea."

Although the housekeeper seemed inclined to bristle, she stiffly nodded and retreated from the room. Thankfully, Harriet was too busy looking about to notice anything amiss.

"I've been in Mr. Elton's house only once. Do you remember, Mrs. Knightley? You broke your shoelace, and we stepped inside so you could repair it."

That was an uncomfortable reminder for Emma, since that manufactured incident had occurred when she was convinced that Mr. Elton was in love with Harriet. "Did I? You have the most remarkable memory, dear."

"We sat in the front drawing room then, but this room is very pretty. Mrs. Elton had such excellent taste."

"I find Abbey Mill Farm very pretty. And your second drawing room is larger, too."

Harriet peeked through a half-open door into another room. "This must be Mr. Elton's study."

"Do come away, Harriet. Anyone would think you were . . ."

*Snooping.*

"Robert needs a new desk," her friend explained. "I know very little about desks, but Mr. Elton is sure to have a fine one."

Emma wandered over to the door and casually cast a gaze at the desktop. It was covered with a haphazard pile of books, letters, ledgers, and scraps of paper—a treasure trove of information. She leaned forward, trying to get a better view of—

The parlor door opened, and Emma spun around, almost

tripping over her feet. Mrs. Wright entered the room, bearing a tea tray.

"How delightful," Emma enthused, a trifle too enthusiastically. "Tea!"

Harriet cast her a sideways glance but gave the housekeeper a warm smile. "Do you need help, Mrs. Wright? That tray looks quite heavy."

"I'm well able to handle it," the housekeeper frostily replied as she thumped the tray down on the table in front of the chaise. Teacups rattled alarmingly.

That Mrs. Wright obviously didn't approve of Harriet was likely because her mistress hadn't approved of her, either.

"You may go, Mrs. Wright," Emma said. "I'm sure you have much to attend to."

"Thank you, madam. We are in something of a state, as you can imagine." For a moment, her face crumpled into unhappy lines. "One hardly knows what to make of it."

"It's a terrible shock for the entire household," Emma replied with a twinge of guilt. "I'm sure Mr. Elton would be lost without you."

"Thank you, madam. I endeavor to do my best." The housekeeper then stalked from the room.

Emma sighed. "Goodness, that wasn't the least bit awkward."

"I'm not sure what I did to offend her," Harriet ruefully said.

"Nothing, dear. Mrs. Wright was apparently very close to her mistress and no doubt feels a great deal of loyalty to her."

"And since Mrs. Elton didn't like me . . ."

"It's silly. One might think servants didn't have minds of their own."

"I wish Mrs. Elton hadn't disliked me so much."

"The fault rested entirely with her. But Mr. Elton has been very appreciative of your support, which is certainly cheering."

And all it took was his wife getting murdered.

Harriet brightened. "I do hope Mr. Elton and I can be friends again. Both Robert and I would like to help him through this terrible time."

Emma suspected that Robert wanted nothing to do with his former rival for Harriet's affections. "I'm going to pour you a cup of tea, and then I want you to sit by the window and keep an eye on the lane."

"Why?" Harriet asked.

"I want you to keep watch for Mr. Elton."

"Won't we hear him come in?"

"I'm going to take a quick look at his desk."

Harriet's mouth dropped open. "What if Mr. Elton returns and catches you?"

Emma hastily prepared a cup and thrust it at her friend, the liquid sloshing into the saucer. "That's why I need you to keep watch."

Her friend sighed before trudging over to the needlepointed armchair by the window.

Emma slipped into the study. The vicar's desk was indeed a fine piece of furniture. It was also a fine mess.

"Where to start?" she muttered.

Not with the ledgers—too detailed. Instead, she began to quickly sift through the correspondence. Most of it seemed to be from his family or other clergymen, although there were quite a few bills. Some were already opened, and the amounts she saw made her blink. One from a millinery shop in London demonstrated that Mrs. Elton had spent extravagantly on her gowns. Bills that detailed household expenses and food were mixed. While some were entirely reasonable, a few suggested a definite penchant for luxury. That was no surprise, since Mrs. Elton had frequently spoken of modeling her housekeeping on that of Mr. Suckling's residence, Maple Grove.

Were the Eltons living beyond their means? And could it be

that a desperate tradesman was trying to collect what was owed to him? Unlucky tradesmen were sometimes forced into bankruptcy because their genteel customers simply refused to pay bills. Still, it was hard to imagine an irate milliner or wine merchant storming down from London to murder Mrs. Elton over an outstanding invoice or two.

Harriet jumped up. "Mrs. Knightley, I can see Mr. Elton coming down the lane!"

"I'm almost finished."

Hurriedly, she scanned the rest of the desk, lifting papers and searching quickly for anything that shed light on the Eltons' financial standing.

"Mrs. Knightley, he's at the front door," Harriet hissed.

A piece of crumpled paper half-thrust inside a book caught her attention. Emma flipped the book open, careful not to disturb the positioning of the note.

The note was short, poorly written, and . . . chilling.

Harriet rushed over. "Mrs. Knightley, I can *hear* Mr. Elton."

Emma slammed the book shut and scampered with Harriet to the sofa. They both plopped down as steps sounded in the hall. She schooled her face into a composed expression, trying to pretend she had *not* just read a threat of violence against Mr. Elton.

The vicar entered, all smiles. "Dear ladies, forgive me for making you wait. If I had known you were coming, I never would have left the house. No, no, do not get up."

They both stood, anyway, and Harriet bobbed a curtsy.

Emma extended a hand. "There is no need to apologize, dear sir."

He took her hand. "You are kindness itself, madam. I just now was calling on Mrs. Saunders. She is doing poorly, and her husband is quite worried. As you can imagine, I greatly sympathize and wished to give Mr. Saunders any words of comfort I could provide."

Harriet looked much struck. "How very kind to think of others in your time of trial. You are so brave, sir."

His smile now turned wan. "Thank you, Mrs. Martin. I cannot allow my grief to stand in the way of my duty to my parishioners."

"Mr. Elton, surely you must be allowed some relief from your work," Emma said. "You will tire yourself out."

"It's what Augusta would have wanted. For me to care for the parish and the people she came to love so greatly."

Emma distinctly remembered Mrs. Elton referring to Highbury as the most troublesome parish she'd ever seen. "Indeed. Sir, may I pour you some tea?"

"Thank you, Mrs. Knightley. I find myself quite parched."

"Then sit and rest," she said as she prepared him a cup. "We cannot have you falling ill."

"Your wishes, dear madam, are always of great importance to me, so I will do my best to remain in good health."

Emma mentally blinked at the effusive statement. They were hardly bosom beaus. It was the opposite, in fact, until their very recent rapprochement. Still, Mr. Elton had always had a penchant for flowery and slightly absurd speech, especially when moved.

"How is Mr. Woodhouse today?" he asked. "I was sorry to see him and Miss Bates so distressed after the funeral."

"My father is well and sends his regards."

The less said about yesterday's events, the better, especially when it came to Miss Bates.

There then ensued an extended pause while they sipped their tea. Emma racked her brain for a way to raise a number of awkward issues, including the ugly threat currently sitting on the vicar's desk.

"Mr. Elton," Harriet eventually said, "I wanted to say how moving the service was yesterday. I found the curate's sermon very affecting."

He smiled. "I helped Mr. Johnson write it, you know. I couldn't bear for my dear wife to receive short shrift."

Emma blessed her friend for raising the exact issue she wished to discuss. "Harriet was telling me all about the service. She said it was very dignified and . . . simple."

"Just as Augusta would have wished." He sighed. "And to be frank, I did not have the heart for anything else."

"Perfectly understandable," she replied.

"I do not know how I shall go on without her. Augusta took care of all matters domestic and financial, you know. Now I find myself quite overwhelmed."

*Ah, an opening.*

"Surely Mr. and Mrs. Suckling will be able to help you," Emma said. "Dealing with Mrs. Elton's personal effects, for instance."

He took a sip of tea before answering. "The matter is a trifle complicated, I'm afraid."

She hesitated only a moment. "I understand Mrs. Elton did not leave a will?"

The vicar looked taken aback.

"My husband mentioned it, just in passing," she hastily added.

She could only hope that George and the vicar never had a discussion regarding said will. That would be a *decidedly* awkward conversation.

"Ah, of course. As magistrate, Mr. Knightley would know all about such things. As I explained to Dr. Hughes, Augusta meant to write a will, but she was always too busy. And who could anticipate that her life would be so cruelly cut short?"

"I hope you don't encounter additional difficulties in that regard," Emma replied.

"Who is to say? Augusta managed everything, as I said. She had quite a fine head for financial matters, while I'm a simple man of the cloth."

As George had noted, there was nothing simple about Mr. Elton and money.

Harriet suddenly piped up. "Since Mrs. Elton didn't leave a will, that means you'll inherit everything, including her lovely jewelry and beautiful clothes."

Emma mentally winced at her friend's blunt approach. "Harriet, you'll embarrass poor Mr. Elton."

"But, Mrs. Knightley, you mentioned it first," she replied, looking perplexed.

"I simply wished to relay to Mr. Elton that I would be happy to assist him in any small matters—for instance, going through Mrs. Elton's personal effects. That is a difficult task." She gave Mr. Elton an apologetic smile. "I know that my father struggled with it when my mother passed."

Mr. Elton grimaced. "Dear Mr. Woodhouse. Such a sad bond we now share."

"Be assured that I am happy to provide any necessary assistance."

"I am most grateful, dear madam. But my housekeeper has already taken on that task. She was devoted to my wife and will certainly know what she would have wished."

*Drat.*

She'd rather been hoping for the opportunity to snoop around Mrs. Elton's bedroom, although she hardly knew what she expected to find.

"It must be a comfort to be able to rely on Mrs. Wright during such a difficult time. And everyone else in Highbury, of course," she said instead.

*Except for one particular person who wishes you dead.*

"And all wish to help *you*, Mr. Elton," she meaningfully added. "*Every* last person in the village, I'm sure."

She carefully watched for his reaction, but he simply nodded.

"I am indeed fortunate to have friends such as yourself and

Mr. Knightley." Then he bestowed a warm smile on Harriet. "And you, too, Mrs. Martin. You have been *such* a comfort."

When Harriet gazed soulfully back at him, Emma decided — with some alarm — that their visit was best concluded. Mr. Elton escorted them to the door, assuring Emma that he would soon call on *dear Mr. Woodhouse.*

As they walked along Vicarage Lane, Emma listened to Harriet's sympathetic observations about *poor Mr. Elton* with only half an ear, because she was fixed on her startling discovery. Their vicar seemed to have acquired a true and possibly dangerous enemy. And that begged the question, had the danger extended to Mrs. Elton, as well?

# CHAPTER 15

Emma found her husband in the study. "There you are. When did you get back from Donwell?"

George glanced up from his ledgers with a smile. "About a half hour ago. I'm sorry I didn't join you and your father for tea. I needed to check some figures for William Larkins regarding the sale of some sheep."

She subsided into a chair. "Goodness, I don't know how you can bear the excitement."

"A welcome change from my discussions with Dr. Hughes and Constable Sharpe, I assure you. The former insists on laboriously reviewing every detail of the investigation, and the latter vacillates between wishing to interrogate Miss Bates and arresting any vagrant within a mile of Highbury. Compared to that, discussing sheep with Larkins is positively restful."

"Constable Sharpe is truly a dreary man," she replied. "And fatally lacking in imagination if that is the best he can do."

"Perhaps you can share that assessment with our good constable when next you see him. Then he can be annoyed with you instead of me for advising him against wholesale arrests."

She widened her eyes. "Why, George, I am simply an innocent bystander, remember?"

He pushed his ledger aside and folded his hands on the desk. "What aren't you telling me?"

"You are the most irritatingly perceptive man I have ever met," she wryly replied.

He sighed. "Emma, what have you been doing?"

"Nothing terrible, dearest. I just happened to stumble across an interesting piece of information that may or may not have anything to do with Mrs. Elton's murder."

He narrowed his dark gaze. "How, exactly, did you *stumble* across that information?"

"Harriet and I paid a condolence call to Mr. Elton this afternoon." She frowned, momentarily diverted. "George, I'm worried about Harriet and Robert. Robert is jealous of Mr. Elton. That's ridiculous, but for the fact that Harriet *does* seem to be feeling sentimental about Mr. Elton, which is rather alarming."

"I confess to little interest in the Martins' domestic affairs and advise you to show a similar disinterest. As you recall, your judgment in that regard has been somewhat faulty in the past."

"But Harriet came right out and told me they were having problems. How can I ignore that?"

"Most couples, on occasion, do rub up against each other."

"We don't."

"That remains to be seen," he sardonically replied.

She ignored that. "I think you should talk to Robert. Give him some advice on his dealings with Harriet, one married man to another."

"That would simply embarrass the poor fellow, and he would certainly guess *why* I was speaking to him."

She crinkled her nose. "I suppose you're right. In that case, I will do my best to emulate Mr. Knightley levels of disinterest."

"Mr. Knightley would be grateful. Now, may we return to the discussion of the information you stumbled across?"

"Would you like to finish your work first? I don't mind waiting."

He smiled. "It will take only a few minutes longer, and then I can give you my full attention."

Emma rested her elbows on his desk and propped her chin in her hands. It was silly of her, but she enjoyed watching him work. George was such a remarkable man, in his own understated way. He handled the details of their rather complicated life without the least bit of fuss. More importantly, he loved her with a steadfast love that she still found entirely remarkable.

After a few minutes, he closed his ledger and glanced up with a quizzical smile. "Emma?"

"I was thinking that I must be the most fortunate woman in Surrey."

"And why is that?"

"Because you married me."

"The good fortune is all mine. I still marvel that you could love me after listening to so many lectures over the years."

She sat up straight. "Then I hope you will remember your good fortune when I tell you what I found out today."

Or, rather, about *how* she had found it.

"I'm not going to like this, am I?"

She waggled a hand. "I'm not sure. What do you know about Dick Curtis?"

His frown indicated he was a bit thrown by the question. "Why?"

"I'll tell you momentarily. Do you know him?"

"I know that the past several years have been difficult for him. He's a farm laborer—a steady worker until he injured his hand a few years ago. Shortly thereafter, his father died, and Dick lost the cottage they resided in. He currently lives in one of the poor cottages past the vicarage. Farmer Mitchell tries to employ Dick as much as he is able, usually working in the dairy."

"So he's obviously struggling."

"That is a fair assessment. Why does it matter?"

"Because he made a quite vile threat against Mr. Elton. One might even call it a death threat."

George's eyebrows practically shot up to his hairline. "And how do you know this?"

She rubbed her finger over a slight imperfection in the wood of his desk.

"Emma?"

"Well, I just happened to see the note in which he made the threat."

Her husband scoffed. "You just happened to see it."

"Yes."

"Where?"

"On Mr. Elton's desk. But, George, it was *so* crude. I cannot think Dick Curtis is very educated."

That comment failed to deflect him. "And was Mr. Elton also in his office at the time you saw this note?"

"Well . . . no."

"Emma—"

She held up a hand. "Mr. Elton has no idea that I saw it. He had stepped out for a few minutes when we called, so we decided to wait. The door to his office was open. I thought it made sense to . . . to look around a bit."

"You mean go through his private papers." He looked severe. "And what if he had discovered you snooping? Did you think of that?"

"Certainly. I set Harriet to keep a lookout. Mr. Elton never suspected a thing."

He stared at her in disbelief. "You enlisted Harriet? I cannot imagine Robert would be very pleased about that."

While that was undoubtedly true, she rather thought he was missing the point. "George, don't you want to know what was in the note? I think it could be germane to the investigation."

"Emma, I already warned you about this. You are not to interfere."

"I'm not interfering. I'm finding potential clues, which is certainly more than one can say for Constable Sharpe."

"Or me?"

She scoffed. "Dearest, I would never say such a thing. Now, do you want to know what I found, or would you rather just scowl at me?"

"Since my scowls have little effect, you'd best get on with it."

"Thank you. As I said, it was a very threatening note. Dick Curtis called Mr. Elton a *right bastard*. He said that he wanted to rip Mr. Elton's head off and shove it up his . . ." She wrinkled her nose. "Well, Mr. Elton's posterior."

George grimaced. "I'm sorry you had to read such a thing."

"It's no matter."

"I do not want you or any other woman subjected to such crude and frightening language."

"After discovering Mrs. Elton's bloodstained corpse, it's hard to get fussed about a spot of vulgar language. It was the intent of the note I found disturbing."

"Indeed. I wonder why Curtis was threatening our vicar."

"Curtis mentioned something about being denied a place on the parish poor roll. That surprised me, because I thought such matters were decided by the vestry council."

George absently tapped his finger on the edge of his desk. "Generally, they are, although Elton is still empowered to make decisions on his own. I did miss a vestry meeting last month. Perhaps the decision was made then."

"But Mr. Weston also sits on the council. I can hardly see him turning down someone clearly in need of aid."

"True. I will have to speak to Elton about this."

*Oh dear.*

"I hope you can find a way to do so without . . ."

"Mentioning you? Alas, the wages of sin, my dear."

She narrowed her gaze. "George—"

He flashed a quick smile. "I will find a way to raise the subject without implicating you or Harriet."

"Thank you. What do you think about the threat itself?"

"Disturbing, but it was made against Mr. Elton, not his wife."

"Perhaps she advised him to turn Curtis down. More often than not, she seemed to think the impoverished were to blame for their sad condition."

"But would Curtis know that? I cannot imagine Mrs. Elton sitting in on meetings with her husband's parishioners."

That was indisputably true. "Perhaps he sought to exact revenge against Mr. Elton through his wife?"

A frown marked George's brow. "As far as I know, Curtis has never caused any sort of trouble, and Farmer Mitchell thinks highly of the man. The note was certainly ill-judged, but it seems more likely the result of frustration than any intent to hurt Mr. Elton."

She heaved a sigh of frustration. "Drat. I thought it might be of use to you."

"There's another possibility, of course."

Emma perked up. "Yes?"

"Curtis might have decided to exact his revenge by robbing the church. And that way he could get valuable items to pawn."

"So, Mrs. Elton happened to come across him committing the act, possibly with his hands already on the candlestick." She clapped her hands together. "George, it makes perfect sense. In his desperation, Curtis would feel like he had no other choice but to kill her, because she could identify him. He then took her necklace and ran."

"But as you have pointed out several times, why did he not also steal other valuable items in the church, including the candlestick?"

She tried to work through this vexing question. "Perhaps he

feared that Mr. Elton would direct the finger of suspicion at him. He would find it difficult to hide the larger items, unlike the necklace."

George slowly nodded. "That's possible, though it would require a certain degree of forethought. Were you able to ascertain when Curtis wrote this note?"

"No. And I do realize that assuming he is the killer doesn't account for every detail of the crime. But you must admit it makes more sense for it to be Curtis than Miss Bates."

"It does."

"So you'll pursue it?"

"I will, but carefully. I don't wish to accuse an innocent man or to drag you into it. I will simply tell Elton that it's come to my attention that he rejected the man's addition to the poor roll, and ask him why he did so."

"But what if Mr. Elton doesn't mention the note?"

"Since he hasn't mentioned it yet, I suspect he doesn't see it as a very credible threat. Thus, the need to not overreact."

Emma conceded the point. "Then I'll leave the matter in your capable hands."

"Thank you. Now, are there any other secrets you'd like to reveal at this time?"

She rose and headed for the door. "Only that Mrs. Goddard and the Bates ladies are joining us for dinner. Father sent round a note to invite them this afternoon."

Her beleaguered husband simply sighed.

"Not to worry," she said. "I'll seat you next to Mrs. Bates. With any luck, you can both have a refreshing nap during the dessert course."

His snort of laughter followed her out of the room.

They were sitting in the drawing room after dinner when a footman entered and murmured in George's ear. His eyebrows ticked up as he listened.

"Mrs. Goddard needs another glass of sherry, my dear," Emma's father said, pulling her attention away from George.

"Of course. Forgive me."

Father and the ladies were at the card table, engaged in a round of whist. For this evening, at least, Miss Bates could forget about dead bodies and pestering constables and enjoy the company of friends.

George came over and drew Emma away from the group. "My dear, Mr. Elton has come to call."

She cast a worried glance at Miss Bates. "I suppose we cannot have him standing out in the hall. You'd best invite him in for tea."

"He wishes to speak to us privately. I told Simon to put him in the library."

*Now what?*

"You go ahead, George. I'll replenish the refreshments and then join you."

After he left, she quickly refilled glass and cups and dished out scones and jam. Then she touched her father's shoulder.

"Dearest, I must step out for a moment. Ring for Simon if you need anything."

Her father, intent on his cards, nodded. "Whatever you wish, my dear."

Breathing a sigh of relief to have escaped questioning, Emma slipped out.

"Mrs. Knightley, a thousand pardons for disturbing you," Mr. Elton said as she entered the library. "But this truly couldn't wait."

More problems.

"It is no matter, sir. Would you like a cup of tea or perhaps a sherry?"

"You are too kind, but I have no wish to disturb your evening more than necessary."

She ushered him to a club chair, while she and George sat

opposite on the chaise. Instead of getting straight to the point, however, the vicar breathed out a sigh and fell into a melancholic study.

"Mr. Elton," George said after several long moments. "I'm assuming the matter you wish to discuss touches on the murder investigation?"

"What?" He winced. "Forgive me, my mind tends to wander. Yes, it does touch on that, although it may be nothing at all."

*Perhaps the note from Dick Curtis?*

"If it can be construed as evidence," George replied, "you should take it directly to Constable Sharpe."

The vicar hesitated. "I'm not entirely sure what to make of it, sir. I must also admit that I find Constable Sharpe's manner unhelpful at times, so I thought it best to consult you first."

"A wise decision, Mr. Elton," Emma said with an encouraging smile.

George threw her an ironic glance before refocusing on their guest. "May I ask why you feel the need for my wife to be present?"

"Because the issue in question regards Miss Bates," he replied. "I'm afraid it might cast the poor woman in an unfortunate light. That being the case, I thought it sensible to speak with Mrs. Knightley, as well, since Miss Bates obviously relies on her and Mr. Woodhouse for support and comfort."

*Drat, and double drat.*

"I do hope we can keep this matter away from my father," she said more sharply than she intended.

Mr. Elton's eyes popped wide. "I wouldn't upset your father for the world, dear madam. Indeed, I debated long and hard as to whether I should even share this information."

"Perhaps you can allow us to judge its relevance," George said.

"Of course." The vicar extracted a folded sheet of paper from his coat and gave it to George.

Emma tried to read over her husband's shoulder. "What does it say?"

With his face set like stone, George handed it over.

In the few moments it took her to read, her heart plummeted to the root cellar. Part of her denied what she was seeing, because it simply didn't make sense.

"This is a promissory note between Miss Bates and Mrs. Elton for fifty pounds," she flatly stated.

"Mr. Elton, are you sure that your wife loaned Miss Bates this entire sum?" George asked.

"I think so. My wife managed her own financial matters. She did often consult with Mr. Suckling but generally did as she wished with her money."

"This is a great deal of money," Emma exclaimed. "Especially for Miss Bates."

The vicar sighed—again. "That was Augusta's way. She was always so openhearted and generous."

Having known Mrs. Elton, Emma would bet a bob that the loan had nothing to do with selfless generosity. Why, then?

George retrieved the note from her. "So, we can assume that this was the source of the awkwardness between the two ladies."

"I believe so," Mr. Elton replied.

"Are you also suggesting that Miss Bates could not or would not repay the loan?"

The vicar spread his hands wide. "I cannot answer that, Mr. Knightley. But I do know that Augusta was unhappy with Miss Bates."

Emma fought a rising sense of dread. "Do you truly think that Miss Bates would murder Mrs. Elton because of a debt, sir?"

"Of course one does not wish to even *think* such a thing. That is why I thought to ask both your opinions first."

"My opinion is that it's ridiculous," she retorted. "I'm quite amazed you would even consider it."

"My dear," George said in a warning voice.

She rounded on her husband. "If Miss Bates needed money, she only had to ask Jane, or even my father or Mr. Weston. Why in heaven's name would she go to Mrs. Elton?"

"I cannot answer that," he calmly replied. "But Miss Bates can."

"George, she has only just begun to recover her equanimity. This will throw her into a complete stew."

"I'm sure there must be a reasonable explanation, and only Miss Bates can supply it."

"I concede the point," she grudgingly admitted. "But must we ask her tonight?"

"Better to ask while she is here, with friends."

Mr. Elton half rose from his chair. "Gracious! I had no idea Miss Bates was here tonight. Forgive me, Mr. Knightley. This can surely wait until tomorrow."

"I think it's best to attend to the matter now," he replied. "Then we can best decide what is to be done."

Emma stared at him, aghast. "Surely you're not thinking of giving the note to Constable Sharpe."

"I hope that won't be necessary."

That was *not* a reassuring answer.

"Miss Bates will obviously not wish to discuss this in front of her mother," she warned.

Mr. Elton sighed for the third time. "Poor Mrs. Bates. Such a trial for her."

Really, must he be *so* tiresome? Emma had sympathy for his loss, but this was an unnecessary distraction. If Miss Bates could not provide a satisfactory answer—an all too likely scenario regardless of her innocence—then George would feel obligated to notify Constable Sharpe.

And Mr. Elton had yet to even allude to the note from Dick Curtis, which was *very* odd.

George stood. "I will ask Mrs. Goddard and your father to distract Mrs. Bates while I speak to Miss Bates."

"But how, George? They're playing cards."

"I will manage."

Disturbed and wanting to protest, she gazed up at him. His eyes held infinite kindness, but she also knew he would stand firm. In his decisive mind, waiting would serve no purpose. He was, unfortunately, correct.

She managed a smile. "Very well. Whatever you think is best."

He briefly pressed her shoulder before quitting the room.

"Madam, I apologize for bringing this trouble upon you," Mr. Elton said. "It was not my intention—"

"Sir, surely you cannot believe Miss Bates guilty of so heinous a crime," Emma interrupted. "If she had borrowed a thousand pounds, she still wouldn't commit such a vile act."

He grimaced. "I agree that the mind revolts against any such idea. As Miss Bates has said time and again, she was always deeply grateful for any little attentions Augusta paid her."

Rather like a poor relation grateful for any notice from her betters. As far as Emma was concerned, Miss Bates had shown the finer character by so graciously tolerating Mrs. Elton's irritating condescension.

"Then knowing that, why did you bring this note forward?"

"I would not have done so if the matter had not been raised at the inquest. It was an unanswered question that clearly troubled Dr. Hughes, and I now have in my possession the possible answer. I truly felt I had no choice, Mrs. Knightley, else I would have gladly spared Miss Bates further distress."

Emma grudgingly admitted the justice of his claim. Trying to shield a friend was one thing. Withholding information from the law was quite another.

They sat for a few moments in uncomfortable silence before she recalled her duties as a hostess.

"Mr. Elton, would you like—"

"Mrs. Knightley, may I just say—"

They exchanged an awkward smile.

"Dear madam, forgive me for interrupting you," continued Mr. Elton. "Please go ahead."

"Are you sure I cannot offer you something to drink?"

"You are kindness itself, but I am perfectly fine."

"Then what were you going to say, sir?"

"I was simply going to note your exemplary kindness toward me in these dreadful days. You are a treasure, Mrs. Knightley, a veritable treasure. I do hope my dear friend Mr. Knightley realizes his great fortune in having the honor to be your husband."

She blinked. His thanks were understandable, but his praise seemed rather exaggerated.

*Best to make light of it.*

"Mr. Knightley is well aware of his good fortune," she said with a smile. "And if he is ever in danger of forgetting, I will be sure to remind him."

He inclined his head. "No man could ever forget you, Mrs. Knightley."

"Er, thank you."

"Just as I will never forget my dear Augusta," he added, heaving a sigh. "Her image is imprinted on my memory like a blazing comet. How could one ever forget such a woman, Mrs. Knightley? Despite the pain, does one even *wish* to forget? I do not!"

She struggled to find a sensible yet sympathetic reply. "Mr. Elton, are you *sure* you do not wish for a sherry?"

He managed a weak smile. "I have let my emotions run away with me again. I assure you that I *will* recover my equanimity with such friends as you and Mr. Knightley to support me. And dear, dear Harriet—I mean, Mrs. Martin. Your friend is a true angel, Mrs. Knightley. I am *quite* overcome by her generosity of spirit in these dark days."

Emma could barely muster a response to this alarmingly warm paean to Harriet. "Indeed. She is an excellent friend."

*George, where are you?*

Thankfully, he reentered the room in the next moment.

"There you are at last," she said with relief.

He looked surprised. "I've been gone only a few minutes, my dear."

She glanced at the bronze clock on the mantel. He'd been gone less than ten minutes, even though it had felt like an age.

"Of course. It's just that we're eager to hear how you got on with Miss Bates."

George resumed his seat. "Not terribly well. As you predicted, she was reluctant to speak in the presence of her mother."

She sighed. "Oh dear."

"Indeed, Mrs. Knightley," exclaimed the vicar. "Her reluctance to speak with Mr. Knightley is concerning."

Emma had to repress a flare of irritation. "One cannot blame her for not wishing to disturb her mother. That is hardly a crime."

"Just as you say, madam," he quickly replied. "But as the Good Book says, one must bring what is hidden in darkness into the light."

"The only darkness is the confusion in Miss Bates's mind," she retorted. "I'm sure there's a perfectly reasonable explanation for all of this."

George held up a restraining hand. "Which I expect to hear tomorrow. Mrs. Bates generally takes a nap in the early afternoon, so Miss Bates has asked me to stop by then to speak with her."

"She gave no hint about the note whatsoever?" Mr. Elton asked.

"I'm afraid not."

The vicar seemed to steel himself. "Sir, I think you *must* relay the contents of this note to Dr. Hughes. He specifically raised the issue of a dispute between my wife and Miss Bates during the inquest. I am most uncomfortable with the idea of withholding this information from him."

Emma frowned. "Sir, I thought we agreed that Miss Bates had nothing to do with your wife's murder."

"And I am sure you are correct, Mrs. Knightley. Still, it would seem remiss of me not to hand this evidence over to Dr. Hughes— if for no other reason than to clear Miss Bates of any suspicion. She will provide a sensible explanation, and that will be the end of it."

"But—"

George took her hand. "I'm afraid Mr. Elton is correct. The note must be turned over to Dr. Hughes. It will then be up to him whether to include it in the records of the inquest."

He held her gaze, silently asking her to trust him. And what else could she do in front of their dratted vicar? She would never contradict George publicly.

*Privately . . .*

"I'm sure you know best," she finally replied.

Mr. Elton stood. "Then I shall take my leave. Again, my apologies for disturbing you."

George also rose. "If you will allow me to hold on to the note, I will show it to Dr. Hughes tomorrow."

Mr. Elton nodded. "No doubt Dr. Hughes will wish to be part of the discussion with Miss Bates."

Emma almost choked. The pompous coroner would frighten Miss Bates half to death.

When Mr. Elton grasped Emma's hand to bow over it, she was hard pressed not to give him a good box on the ear.

"I'll be right back," George said, then cast a significant look at Emma before following Mr. Elton out of the room.

She stood and began to pace. When he returned, she marched up to him.

"How could you agree to show that benighted note to Dr. Hughes? Surely you cannot believe that making it public will clear Miss Bates of suspicion. It will do exactly the opposite!"

He gathered her hands and held them against his chest.

"His logic in that regard is erroneous. What is not in error, unfortunately, is the fact that Miss Bates has been engaging in some very odd behavior. No matter my personal feelings, as magistrate, I cannot ignore that."

She blew out an exasperated sigh. "All right, but it's ridiculous to suspect Miss Bates. She wouldn't kill Mrs. Elton over a debt when any number of us could have repaid it for her."

George looked thoughtful. "Very true. Nevertheless, I cannot help but wonder if Elton is planning to pursue some sort of repayment from Miss Bates—if not now, then later."

That gave her pause. Again, she recalled the strange discussion about finances between Mr. Elton and Mr. Suckling after the funeral. "He could have written directly to Jane or Frank, if such is the case."

"Also true. I cannot account for his behavior in that respect."

"And why must Dr. Hughes go with you tomorrow? You'll not get a coherent word out of poor Miss Bates if he's there."

"I don't believe I made any such promise regarding Dr. Hughes."

She stared at him. "But you said—"

His smile was wry. "My dear, please give me more credit than that. I will speak to Miss Bates alone and then share with Dr. Hughes both the note and the information she provides. That will allow me at least some measure of control over this situation."

Her anxiety receded a notch. "Mr. Elton won't like that, I suspect."

"Which is why I didn't tell him. Emma, I will do my best to protect Miss Bates and her mother. But the truth must come out, whatever it is."

"Miss Bates is *not* a murderer."

"Agreed. But I believe there is something in this situation that might provide clues as to why Mrs. Elton was murdered."

The light dawned. "So, you agree with me that the killer probably knew Mrs. Elton."

He shrugged. "I don't know, but there are too many unanswered questions, and that disturbs me."

Emma had been feeling the same almost from the moment she'd discovered the body.

"For now, however," he added, "we should keep our suspicions to ourselves."

"Of course. Thank goodness Frank and Jane will be arriving in a few days. I'm sure they will be a great comfort to Miss Bates and will afford a measure of protection against all this nonsense."

"Let us hope. In the meantime, we should return to our guests and do what we can to reassure Miss Bates before sending her home."

Emma steeled herself for the coming encounter—and for the days ahead. They would be difficult, and who knew how they would end?

# CHAPTER 16

"Emma," her father said, catching her in the entrance hall as she donned her bonnet. "Why don't you invite Miss Bates and her mother to come for dinner and spend the evening here? Hartfield is a healthier environment for them than their drafty apartment. I must speak to Perry about such unhealthful conditions when next I see him."

She mentally sighed. At this rate, she might was well move the Bates ladies into Hartfield and be done with it.

"Shall I also ask Mrs. Goddard to come by to make up a card table?"

"No, I think it best if we have a quiet evening. Perhaps you could play the pianoforte. Miss Bates would enjoy that. She misses Jane's playing very much, and I know she would be happy for a little music."

"I am not a stitch on Jane, but I will do my best."

"Nonsense, my dear. You play exceedingly well. But I do hope Jane and Frank will be here soon. Their presence will give Miss Bates such comfort."

"Don't forget they are coming from Yorkshire. With Jane in

a delicate condition, they must travel with that consideration in mind."

Her father tut-tutted. "I am most perturbed with Dr. Hughes for creating such a disturbance and endangering everyone's health. Perry would never do so, I feel sure."

"Dr. Hughes is only doing his duty. And he is certainly not responsible for poor Mrs. Elton's death."

"Perhaps not, but Mr. Elton should have known better. He should not have allowed his wife to go off and get murdered in the first place. It is a very bad business, Emma. I do not approve."

It took her a moment to wrestle an inappropriate laugh back down her throat. "I don't think anyone approves, Father, including Mr. Elton."

He sighed. "I suppose you're right. But poor Miss Bates. Does Mr. Elton ever think of the strain on her?"

"I'm sure he regrets this entire horrible situation."

Her father still looked disapproving, which Emma found odd. Mr. Elton had always been such a favorite of his.

"Why don't you take your turn around the garden?" she suggested. "It's such a mild afternoon. I think it will do you good."

"Very well, my dear. I will see you when you get back."

She escaped from the house and set off in a hurry, feverish to discover the outcome of the interview with Miss Bates. After sleeping on the issue, George had decided to send a brief note to Dr. Hughes, informing him that he would be asking Miss Bates a few additional questions this morning.

"Must you, George?" Emma had asked with dismay. "Dr. Hughes is so utterly pompous that I wouldn't be surprised if he barged in on your discussion and tried to take over. That would pitch Miss Bates into a terrible flutter."

"I will make it clear that I wish to speak with her alone but afterward will call on him with any relevant information."

"But why does he need to know about it *before* the meeting?"

"The man hates surprises, Emma. I am hopeful there's a perfectly reasonable explanation regarding the promissory note. If there is not, however, Dr. Hughes will respond better to this new information with some forewarning."

When she'd started to argue, he'd taken her hand. "Please remember that although I oversee this investigation, I cannot appear to be protecting Miss Bates from lawful scrutiny, no matter how much I might wish to."

His logic, unfortunately, was sound. George was in a difficult position and was doing what was necessary to avoid accusations of favoritism. Still, she'd anxiously counted the minutes until she could reasonably call on Miss Bates.

She hurried through the village and arrived at Miss Bates's apartment in short order. But when she started up the stairs, she was startled to hear raised voices. One of those voices belonged to her husband.

The door to the apartment flew open, and Patty rushed out, cramming a lopsided bonnet on her head.

"Mrs. Knightley," she cried. "Thank goodness you're here!"

They met halfway up the stairs. "Patty, whatever is going on?"

"It's that Constable Sharpe fellow. He's been awfully mean to Miss Bates. Mr. Knightley had to yell at him to make him stop. I'm going to Mr. Perry to fetch some calming powders."

The notion of George yelling at anyone was both astonishing and alarming. Matters must be dire.

"Patty, I think you should bring Mr. Perry, if he's available. I'll stay with Miss Bates until you return."

"I'll be quick."

Emma hurried up the rest of the staircase. The quarreling voices had subsided somewhat, although she could still hear George, and he was clearly annoyed.

She marched in and all but skidded to a halt at the scene before her.

George and the constable stood on opposite sides of the small parlor, engaged in a glaring contest. Seated by the fireplace, Miss Bates was perched on a stool next to her mother's chair, clutching her aged parent's hand. Mrs. Bates was wide awake and scowling at Constable Sharpe with an astounding degree of ferocity. If a pistol were close at hand, Emma had little doubt that Mrs. Bates would happily rid the world of a certain officer of the law.

"Good God," Emma exclaimed. "What is happening here?"

George looked relieved. "Ah, thank—"

"The prevention of my sworn duty is what's happening," barked Constable Sharpe. "And I'll not be having it, nor will Dr. Hughes. Not from Mr. Knightley—or from you, for that matter."

"You forget yourself, sir," George said in a cold voice.

Emma put on her most imperious air. "Indeed. It would seem that *Mr.* Sharpe has also forgotten that the magistrate is the King's chief representative in this parish. I am astonished that you and Dr. Hughes are so deficient in your understanding of the law."

The constable bristled. "It's not the magistrate's job to investigate crime, missus. It's mine."

"And does this investigation include harassing ladies to the point of tears?" she retorted. "May I remind you that Mrs. Bates is in frail health? I can only hope Dr. Hughes, as a physician, does not advocate such cruel behavior."

At the moment, Mrs. Bates looked ready to leap from her chair and brain Constable Sharpe with her cane.

"If Miss Bates had simply answered my questions, we wouldn't be having such problems," he shot back.

"And if you had waited for my arrival, we could have avoided this problem entirely," George pointed out. "I specifically asked Dr. Hughes to delay any questioning until after I spoke to Miss Bates."

"Well, he didn't tell *me* that, now did he?"

"An unfortunate oversight I will certainly address," George tersely replied.

"Dear ma'am," Emma said, going to Miss Bates, "come sit with me on the sofa. We will have a quiet chat and get everything sorted."

"Mrs. Knightley," she quavered, "my mind is in such a muddle!"

"And no wonder, with such a dreadful scene."

When Mr. Sharpe began to bluster, George glared him into silence.

Emma and Miss Bates settled on the sofa, while Constable Sharpe moved to stand in front of the fireplace, his legs akimbo and with a thunderous scowl on his face. But he'd ceased barking, which was an improvement.

"Can I get you a cup of tea, Miss Bates?" Emma asked.

The spinster forced a trembling smile. "No, thank you. I . . . I would like to answer Mr. Knightley's question, so as not to disturb my mother any longer than necessary."

"Perhaps your mother would be more comfortable in her bedroom," George suggested.

"I am fine where I am," Mrs. Bates firmly replied.

George nodded before directing a hard look at the constable. "Mr. Sharpe, I understand you had raised the matter of the promissory note shortly before my arrival this morning."

"That I had, Mr. Knightley, and the lady started pitching a fit instead of answering a simple question. Carrying on in a very suspicious manner, if you ask me."

Miss Bates turned pleading eyes on George. "That is not true, sir. The constable hardly gave me a chance to speak, and my mother was becoming upset."

Emma's anger stirred again. "Really, Mr. Sharpe, frightening two helpless women. I cannot imagine what you were thinking."

"I'm thinking that I'm trying to catch a murderer," he retorted.

"You're not going to find him here!"

"Thank you, my dear," George dryly put in. "Now, Miss Bates, can you tell us why you signed the promissory note with Mrs. Elton?"

"I'll . . . I'll try, Mr. Knightley, but everything has been so confusing. I can barely put two thoughts together."

"I understand. So, let us start at the beginning. You signed the note approximately two months ago, for fifty pounds. Is that correct?"

"Yes. I thought it too much money, but Mrs. Elton insisted. She said that for her, it was just a trifle."

It was anything but, unless one was either very rich or very careless.

"Miss Bates," Emma said, "if you needed money, why didn't you simply ask Jane or me? We are always happy to help you."

The spinster looked woeful. "I didn't truly need the money. That's what I tried to tell Mrs. Elton, but she wouldn't take no for an answer."

Emma and George exchanged a startled glance. Even Mr. Sharpe looked rather blank.

"Then why agree to borrow it?" George asked.

"But I didn't borrow anything. In fact, I *gave* Mrs. Elton money, and then she insisted on loaning me the rest."

Emma frowned. "Forgive me, ma'am. Why would *you* give Mrs. Elton money, only to have her then turn about and loan you funds?"

Miss Bates fluttered a hand. "I'm afraid I don't entirely understand it myself."

"Can you tell me what prompted the discussion of money with Mrs. Elton in the first place?" George asked. "That would be most helpful."

She made an effort to compose herself. "Mrs. Elton had come

to visit because she knew we were expecting a letter from Jane. So very kind, you know, always interested to hear about Jane and Frank. Of course, I no longer need to read Jane's letters to you, Mrs. Knightley, because you correspond with her quite regularly."

After many months of misunderstandings and ill feelings, and once all secrets had been revealed, Emma and Jane had finally been able to strike up a true friendship. They wrote to each other twice a month, thus sparing Emma the obligation of listening to Miss Bates parse letters from her niece. She had truly come to value her friendship with Jane, but there could still be too much of a good thing.

"So, Mrs. Elton stopped by to hear you read Jane's letter," Emma prompted.

"Yes. And somehow . . . I'm not really sure . . . but somehow, we began to talk about money. I still cannot understand how the subject even arose. But Mrs. Elton was so easy to talk to, you know. There was never any lack of subjects to discuss."

"What led to Mrs. Elton's offer to loan you funds?" George asked.

"Let me think . . . Yes, it started with the letter. Jane always makes a point of asking if we need anything, perhaps a little extra money for Mother's medicine, or if I might need a new pair of spectacles. That sort of thing."

"Perfectly appropriate," Emma said.

Miss Bates grimaced. "We hate that Jane and Frank feel they must take care of us, as if we are poor dependents. They give us more than we could possibly need."

"What does that have to do with Mrs. Elton?" Constable Sharpe interjected.

Though George gave him a baleful glare, Miss Bates reacted calmly enough.

"I mentioned to her that I wished Jane didn't feel so responsible for us. Mother and I have everything we need. So much so that I have ... I *had* ten pounds that I was able to put away over the past few years. I was determined not to spend it, so we'd have it for emergencies."

Emma was surprised to hear Miss Bates was so adept at handling her money. For a woman in her position, ten pounds was a considerable sum.

"Then how did you find yourself accepting a loan from Mrs. Elton?" George gently asked.

"She was very sympathetic to my discomfort in feeling obligated to Frank and Jane and said that every woman should strive as much as possible for independence. And that the best way to do so was by investing one's money in a good bank."

Emma couldn't help gaping at her. "Mrs. Elton gave you investment advice?"

Miss Bates nodded.

George held up a hand. "I think I understand now. Mrs. Elton didn't give you monies directly. She took your ten pounds, added her fifty, and invested the total on your behalf."

Miss Bates flashed him a relieved smile. "Yes, that's it. She said it was very safe and that I should realize a tidy sum on my investment. Because she said ten pounds wasn't nearly enough to invest, she loaned me the additional funds."

Mrs. Bates, quiet through the entire discussion, let out a weary sigh. "Oh, Hetty."

Her daughter's face crumpled. "I see now that it was very foolish. But it was Mrs. Elton, and she was quite insistent. I ... I thought it would be ... Well, I don't know what I thought. She just seemed to sweep me away, and ... and it seemed a sensible and correct thing to do at the time."

"Investing one's money is generally a sensible thing to do," George assured her.

But apparently not in this case, and why in heaven's name would Mrs. Elton give a fig about investing money for Miss Bates?

"Miss Bates," she asked, "if Mrs. Elton was so willing, what then was the cause of your quarrel?"

"She needed the money back, apparently, and was quite insistent that I repay her. I told her that I couldn't. I'd never had it, because it was her money to begin with." She anxiously twined her fingers together. "She was very unhappy with that answer."

"When did this particular conversation occur?" George asked.

"The Monday prior to her death."

Constable Sharpe let out a derisive snort, earning another glare from George.

Emma laid a hand on the spinster's arm. "Did Mrs. Elton mention why she needed the money so urgently?"

Miss Bates shook her head.

"Did she upbraid you in any way for refusing?"

"She said that I should not have encouraged her." The little spinster looked terribly sad. "I thought that such an odd comment, Mrs. Knightley, because Mrs. Elton had been so insistent that I allow her to invest on my behalf."

"What did she do after you told her that you couldn't repay the funds?" asked George.

"She said that I must repay the funds within the month. When I said that I couldn't, she got up rather hastily and said she had other business to attend to." She grimaced. "Before she left, she insisted that I meet with her on that . . . that Saturday, at the church, to discuss the matter further. I . . . I was so rattled by then that I agreed to do so, even though I couldn't imagine how anything might be different."

"So you arranged to meet with the victim on the day of the murder," interjected Constable Sharpe with typical bluntness. "Did you tell your mother or anyone else you were meeting her?"

Miss Bates cringed. "No."

"Why not?"

"I . . . I suppose I was embarrassed."

The constable huffed out a breath. "And is that the real reason, or were you planning on *confronting* poor Mrs. Elton?"

Miss Bates started to tremble. "I . . . I don't know what you mean."

"I mean—"

"That's enough, Constable," George sharply interjected.

Emma drew her attention. "Miss Bates, do know why she wished to meet at the church, rather than at your apartment or the vicarage?"

"I wondered about that, too, Mrs. Knightley. At the time, I thought she was trying to spare Mother's feelings—and shield me from Mr. Elton's disapproval, if he were to come upon our discussion. So I agreed that the church would be more appropriate."

Emma could think of an alternative explanation—Mrs. Elton didn't wish for her *caro sposo* to overhear the conversation.

"That makes perfect sense," she said instead.

Constable Sharpe suddenly jabbed a finger at Miss Bates. "If someone was planning on murder, a deserted church on Saturday afternoon would be just the place."

Mrs. Bates suddenly thumped her cane on the floor. "Idiot!" she cried, shocking them all into silence.

George recovered first. "Constable, you will refrain from making such dramatic—and baseless—accusations, or we will be having words again."

"Begging your pardon, Mr. Knightley, but it's my job to conduct the investigation *and* arrest any suspects as I see fit. To my way of thinking, there's more than enough evidence to arrest Miss Bates for the murder of Mrs. Elton."

Mrs. Bates let out a horrified cry, while Miss Bates shrank against the sofa cushions, clearly terrified.

Outraged, Emma jumped to her feet. "You are much mistaken, sir, if you think Miss Bates is guilty of this crime."

Constable Sharpe now jabbed an angry finger at her. "And you're not to be interfering with my duties, missus."

"George," she exclaimed. "Do some . . ."

The words died on her lips. Only rarely had she ever seen her husband truly angry. Now, however, his eyes glittered with fury. He stepped forward, crowding the constable back against the fireplace mantel.

"You will do nothing of the sort," he all but growled. "The evidence against Miss Bates is, in fact, extremely thin and easily explained."

Clearly startled by George's ferocious response, the constable blinked. But then his chin went up. "I disagree, sir. Miss Bates certainly had reason to hate Mrs. Elton—"

"But I didn't!" the spinster cried.

"And she fled the scene and then lied about it. To my way of thinking, there's more than enough evidence to arrest her, and that's what I intend to do."

"That is beyond ridiculous," Emma snapped. "Miss Bates is completely incapable of hurting anyone. In addition, she had no reason to."

"Fifty pounds says otherwise," the constable countered.

"My husband and I could have repaid that amount on a moment's notice. So could my father, Mr. Weston, and Jane Churchill. And as Miss Bates pointed out, she never received any actual funds from Mrs. Elton in the first place."

"The promissory note is legally binding. Miss Bates owed that money to Mrs. Elton whether she wants to admit it or not."

Frustrated, Emma turned to her husband. "George, do something!"

"I should be happy to, if given the chance," he replied in an exasperated tone. "Constable, I do not agree with your assessment of the situation. At a minimum, it requires further investigation. Therefore, you will not be arresting Miss Bates, and I enjoin you to refrain from discussing this matter with anyone but Dr. Hughes or myself. I will meet with you and the doctor later this afternoon to determine the next steps."

Sharpe bristled. "But—"

George held up a magisterial hand. "Do I make myself clear?"

"You do, but I object to your interference, Mr. Knightley. I *greatly* object."

"Duly noted. Now, I suggest you take your leave, since you have caused the ladies enough upset for one day."

The constable slapped his short-brimmed hat on his head. "Very well, but the suspect had best not try to abscond."

When Miss Bates whimpered, Emma plopped down on the sofa and put her arm around the poor dear's trembling shoulders.

"It is no more likely that Miss Bates would leave Highbury than I would fly to the moon, you silly man," she exclaimed. "You are completely ridiculous."

After directing a fiery glare her way, the constable stormed out of the room and slammed the door behind him.

George sighed. "Emma—"

"Yes, I know. Bad Emma." She hugged Miss Bates. "But, really, it's utter nonsense."

Sadly, Miss Bates did not seem to agree it was just nonsense, since she collapsed, weeping, into Emma's arms.

Mrs. Bates started to struggle up from her seat. "Hetty, you'll make yourself sick!"

George hastened to her. "Please sit, dear ma'am. Emma will take care of Miss Bates, and Mr. Perry will be here shortly."

Hasty footfalls thankfully sounded just moments later. Patty burst into the room, followed by the rather winded apothecary.

"Sorry to be so long," Patty gasped. "I had to run all the way to Abbey Mill Farm to fetch him."

"And we all but ran back," he gasped.

"Thank you, sir," Emma said. "As you can see, Miss Bates is in a rather bad way."

"What has caused her such distress?"

"Constable Sharpe threatened to arrest her."

"That varlet will touch her over my dead body," Mrs. Bates exclaimed.

They all blinked, stunned by such a vigorous defense. Even Miss Bates paused mid-hiccup to stare at her mother.

"Er, quite, Mrs. Bates," said George. "But it will not come to that."

The apothecary looked much concerned. "Miss Bates will need to lie down, and then I will attend to Mrs. Bates."

The old woman waved a hand. "Do not worry about me, Mr. Perry. Just see to Hetty."

Mr. Perry then helped Miss Bates to her feet and led her off, with Patty tut-tutting behind them.

Mrs. Bates breathed out a weary sigh. "Mr. Knightley, what is going to happen? What are we to do?"

In a calm, comforting voice, George assured her that no harm would come to her daughter.

"We all know Miss Bates had nothing to do with the murder, ma'am," Emma added. "And Jane and Frank will be here very soon, and then you and Miss Bates will be comfortable again."

She and George kept up their reassurances until Mr. Perry returned to inform them that Miss Bates was now resting comfortably and should be able to sleep. As his attention turned to Mrs. Bates, Emma and George took their leave. On their way out, they instructed Patty to send a note to Hartfield if either of the ladies needed assistance.

"Good God," Emma said once down in the street. "I would like to *kill* that awful constable."

"I would suggest you not bandy about that particular sentiment, my dear. You might find yourself behind bars."

"Along with Miss Bates. George, you simply cannot allow that to happen."

"I won't. As you so adroitly pointed out, there was obviously no need for Miss Bates to resort to murder over the loan. It was a superficial and ill-conceived conclusion on the constable's part."

"I do hope Dr. Hughes doesn't behave as idiotically."

"I suspect I can convince him to disregard Sharpe's flawed reasoning. But I can certainly prevent either of them from doing anything rash."

They walked in silence, deep in thought, as they turned their steps toward Hartfield.

"But what a strange story it is," she finally said. "Mrs. Elton volunteering to invest her own money on Miss Bates's behalf, only to then insist that she repay the loan a scant two months later. I cannot fathom it."

"I could be in error, but I suspect that Mrs. Elton lost her investment in some failed scheme, along with the monies she put in on behalf of Miss Bates."

Emma cast him a startled glance. "But Miss Bates said it was to be invested in a bank, not in any risky sort of undertaking."

"Banks have been known to fail. It's not an unusual occurrence."

"But why did Mrs. Elton persuade Miss Bates to do such a thing in the first place? She's hardly the sort of person one would think to partner with in an investment scheme."

"I have no credible answer to that question yet."

Unbidden, the unsettling argument between Mr. Elton and Mr. Suckling on the day of the funeral came into her thoughts. She turned the details of that fraught conversation over in her mind, dissecting it for clues to Mrs. Elton's strange behavior.

When they reached the iron gates of Hartfield, Emma voiced her ruminations. "George, could it be that the Eltons were— are—having financial difficulties? I think you must question Mr. Elton about it. Because if they were . . ."

"It might be germane to the case," he finished for her. "I know, but that doesn't necessarily help Miss Bates."

"Blast," she muttered.

When her husband chuckled, she cut him a sheepish grin. "How vulgar of me. I do apologize."

He bent and kissed the tip of her nose. "You captured my feelings precisely. Now, if you will excuse me, I must be off to speak with Dr. Hughes. Constable Sharpe is no doubt already detailing my legalistic failings to him, and I must mitigate any damage."

"And keep Miss Bates out of the gaol."

"That too."

"I must tell Father why the Bates ladies will not be joining us for dinner," she said, making a face. "He will not be happy with this development."

"Then it would appear we both have our work cut out for us."

Emma could not disagree. Nor could she deny that finding the true killer was now a more pressing task than ever.

# CHAPTER 17

Emma put down her needlework and rose as Harriet entered the drawing room. "I thought you were busy in the village with Mrs. Martin today."

"We finished our shopping, so I thought to run over to Hartfield. I have something I particularly wanted to tell you. And Mama said to be sure to give you her best wishes."

Emma found it heartwarming that Harriet had developed such a loving relationship with her mother-in-law. For the young woman, it was a true gift. She'd never known her natural mother, and Emma understood better than most how that absence could wound the soul.

"Please give Mrs. Martin my best wishes. Now, what was so important that you had to run over?" Emma frowned. "Has that dreadful Anne Cox been pestering you again?"

"I haven't seen her since the funeral, nor has Robert."

"Thank goodness."

Slowly, the normal rhythms of life had reasserted themselves, and a sense of everyday order had been restored to most in their little village. There were some notable exceptions, starting with—

"Dear me, I forgot to ask," said Harriet, interrupting Emma's thought. "How is Mr. Woodhouse? Has he recovered from his upset?"

"He is still very distressed for Miss Bates and very angry with Mr. Elton, whom Father blames entirely for the current state of affairs."

"How sad. They have always been such good friends."

"It's very awkward. Father will not allow Mr. Elton to visit Hartfield, and Miss Bates feels terribly guilty to be the cause of the rupture in their relationship."

She had to admit that it was getting tiresome. Father was insistent that Mr. Elton had no business showing the promissory note to anyone, much less raising it as a matter of suspicion against Miss Bates, who blamed herself for the misunderstanding in the first place. Unfortunately, the matter had become a topic of endless discussion every time Miss Bates and her mother came for dinner or tea.

Even George, whose patience was vast, was beginning to show signs of desperation. He'd taken to excusing himself immediately after dinner, citing a pressing amount of business. Emma didn't blame him, wishing *she* had pressing business, as well.

"How uncomfortable," Harriet said. "However do you manage it?"

"Most uneasily. For one thing, we have to keep reminding Father and Miss Bates to refrain from discussing the issue in front of the servants. We don't wish it to be widely known that Constable Sharpe tried to arrest her."

Thankfully, Dr. Hughes had chosen to support George rather than the constable. Although still disturbed by Miss Bates's actions on the day of the murder, the coroner was old-fashioned enough to be repelled by the notion of placing a gentlewoman under arrest. He'd also agreed that the existence of the promissory note should be repressed for now in order to keep gossip about the case to a minimum.

"Speaking of Mr. Elton," Harriet said with some hesitation, "I ran into him at the top of Vicarage Lane. He guessed that I was coming to Hartfield, and asked that I convey his best wishes to you, along with his hopes that everyone at Hartfield was in good health."

Emma sighed. "How did he seem?"

"Very cast down. I wish I could have been more of a comfort to him, but he wasn't inclined to talk."

"Breaking the news to him about Hartfield was the most awkward conversation I've ever had. And that, as you know, is saying quite a lot."

After hearing that Constable Sharpe had tried to arrest Miss Bates, Emma's father had lost his temper with quite astonishing vigor. He'd insisted that she write to Mr. Elton immediately and forbid him to step foot onto Hartfield's grounds. No amount of persuasion had been sufficient to change Father's mind, and Emma supposed she couldn't blame him.

She'd known immediately that Mr. Elton would be upset by the prohibition. He had always valued his connection with Hartfield—regardless of any past feelings toward its mistress— and would be sensitive to its loss.

Instead of writing, she'd summoned the courage to deliver the unpleasant news in person. Although she'd known he'd be distressed, she hadn't anticipated how deeply the vicar would be affected. So downcast was he that she'd feared he would burst into tears and once more fall upon her bosom, as he'd done that hideous day in the church. As greatly as she pitied the poor man, she had no desire to reprise *that* particular episode.

Needless to say, she'd fled the vicarage as soon as she could.

"Poor Mrs. Knightley," Harriet said with ready sympathy. "I wish I could help, either with Mr. Elton or dear Mr. Wood-house."

"I'm hopeful that the situation will improve when Jane and Frank arrive. Their presence will give Mrs. and Miss Bates a great deal of comfort and serve as a welcome distraction for everyone."

"When are they expected?"

"They should arrive at Randalls tomorrow afternoon. Frank insisted that Jane rest for a few days at Leamington Spa, but she is now feeling stronger. There should be no more delays."

"That is good news indeed."

"Yes. Now, let's sit and be comfortable, and you can tell me why you needed to rush over here."

"Oh, yes!" Harriet exclaimed as she took a seat. "I'd almost forgotten, but I think it could be *terribly* important. To the investigation, I mean."

Emma perked up. "Do tell."

"While Mama and I were at Ford's, Miss Nash stepped in. We fell to talking, and she told me the strangest thing. And you know Miss Nash is not inclined to gossip, so I think we must take it seriously."

Miss Nash, the head teacher at Mrs. Goddard's, had been a good friend to Harriet when she was a parlor boarder at the school. But as far as Emma could ascertain, the young woman delighted in gossip as much as the next person. After all, she had once told Harriet that Anne Cox would have been happy to marry Robert Martin.

Although, in that case, her idle chatter had proved accurate.

"What did she tell you?"

Harriet leaned closer, almost whispering. "A few days before her murder, Mrs. Elton visited the school to speak to Mrs. Goddard. Miss Nash overheard Mrs. Elton say to the maid that she needed to speak to Mrs. Goddard on an urgent matter." She paused dramatically and cast a glance over her shoulder. Apparently, all this murder business had created a burgeoning sense of the dramatic in Emma's friend.

"We are quite alone, dear," Emma said. "No one can hear us."

Harriet looked slightly abashed. "Sorry. Anyway, Miss Nash said that Mrs. Elton and Mrs. Goddard had a *terrible* argument, which could be heard out in the hall. Mrs. Elton was doing the yelling, and she sounded *very* angry."

Now that *was* interesting. "I take it Miss Nash was out in the hall?"

Harriet nodded.

"Did she have any idea what the argument was about?" Emma asked.

"She couldn't make that out."

"Did Miss Nash have anything else to report?"

"Yes. After a few minutes, Mrs. Elton came storming out of Mrs. Goddard's office. She marched right past Miss Nash and was very snappy with the maid as she opened the door for her."

"And were Miss Nash and the maid the only ones present in the hall?"

"She didn't mention anyone else."

Emma fell to ruminating. What business was there between Mrs. Elton and Mrs. Goddard? Mrs. Goddard was a very sensible, good sort of woman. More than once, Emma had suspected that Mrs. Elton's fine airs occasionally annoyed the headmistress, which made this encounter all the more interesting.

"So, do you think it has something to do with the murder?" Harriet prompted.

"Given the timing, it would seem a remarkable coincidence if it did not. It's hard to imagine Mrs. Goddard as a murderer, though." Emma cocked an eyebrow. "I presume Miss Nash was not suggesting any nefarious activities on her employer's part?"

Harriet shook her head. "Miss Nash has the greatest admiration for Mrs. Goddard. But she thought the argument very strange, coming just before Mrs. Elton's murder."

Emma's instincts were telling her that the incident must indeed be connected to the murder, at least in a tangential way. "Did Miss Nash tell anyone else about this?"

"No, but she did ask Mrs. Goddard about it. Mrs. Goddard apologized and said that Mrs. Elton was upset about a private matter. She also asked Miss Nash not to mention it to the other teachers."

"Then why did she tell you?"

Harriet grimaced. "She says Mrs. Goddard is not herself. She seems very upset about something, and Miss Nash is worried for her."

"Am I correct in assuming that Miss Nash wanted you to share this information with me?" Emma asked.

"Yes, because she doesn't know what to do. Apparently, Mrs. Goddard snapped at some of the girls the other day, when they were simply running about the lawn. And she even forgot about one of her classes, which left the girls sitting in the classroom for a half hour."

Emma raised her eyebrows. "But she is always so punctual, and she never loses her temper with the girls. She is patience itself with my father."

Harriet hesitated. "Do you think this really could have something to do with Mrs. Elton's death?"

Emma stood. "There's only one way to find out. We're going to call on Mrs. Goddard and ask her."

"Now?"

"Of course now. When it comes to murder, one mustn't let a promising clue go to waste."

Mrs. Goddard ushered Emma and Harriet to a chintz-covered sofa in the drawing room. Through an open window, they could hear schoolgirls playing an enthusiastic and noisy game of shuttlecock.

"Goodness, what a ruckus," Mrs. Goddard exclaimed. "Mrs. Knightley, would you like me to close the window?"

"Not at all. It's such a lovely day that I was tempted to join in with the girls."

"We always had a great deal of fun in the summer," said Harriet to her former headmistress. "You let us spend plenty of time outside."

"I want my pupils to be strong and healthy, not die-away maidens who swoon at the slightest exertion," Mrs. Goddard replied with a smile.

"They are very lucky girls," said Emma.

That Mrs. Goddard genuinely cared for her pupils was beyond doubt. Her school deserved its fine reputation, and the good woman had worked hard over the years to achieve and preserve it.

The headmistress sat opposite them and began to prepare tea. "We have been fortunate to have the patronage of so many kind people like yourselves and dear Mr. Woodhouse. And I have been blessed to teach wonderful girls like Harriet."

For a few minutes, they chatted amicably about school matters while they sipped tea and nibbled macaroons. Emma had to do a little schooling of her own—in patience, because she was eager to skip the formalities and get to the bottom of yet another mysterious chapter in the increasingly murky tale of Mrs. Elton.

And she sensed that underneath Mrs. Goddard's affable façade lurked uneasiness.

As Harriet and Mrs. Goddard talked, Emma glanced around. It had been some months since she'd been in the drawing room, which was generally employed to receive parents and guardians. It was quietly tasteful, and stylish enough to reassure anxious mothers that their darlings would be properly cared for and taught their manners.

"Mrs. Goddard," she said. "Are those new curtains?"

They were quite smart, glazed calico in a rich hunter green that matched the sturdy but tasteful rug over polished floorboards. The curtains were tied back with black velvet cords, which added a discreetly fashionable touch.

"Why, yes, they are," the headmistress replied. "How clever of you to notice."

Emma got the distinct impression that Mrs. Goddard wished she hadn't noticed.

"And that's a new writing desk in the corner," Harriet exclaimed. "It fits so nicely in that spot, as if it was made for it."

It was indeed handsome and likely ordered from London, since there would be no one in Highbury who could make such a fine piece.

Mrs. Goddard turned around to look, as if surprised to find it there. "Yes, it is rather new, I suppose. Miss Nash was in desperate need of a writing desk, since hers was quite falling to pieces. So, she took my old desk—not that it was *that* old—and I replaced it with this one."

That was rather a lot of words from Mrs. Goddard, who was beginning to sound almost like Miss Bates.

"A perfectly neat solution," Emma said.

When an awkward silence followed that observation, she decided it was time to get to the heart of the matter.

"As delightful as it is to see you, ma'am," she said, "this is not entirely a social call."

Uncertainty flashed for a moment across Mrs. Goddard's face before her expression smoothed into its usual placid lines.

"Of course, I am always happy to be of assistance, Mrs. Knightley. What can I do for you?"

"It's rather a delicate matter. I have no wish to cause you distress, but—"

"Miss Nash overhead you arguing with Mrs. Elton," Harriet burst out. "She said Mrs. Elton sounded very angry and that you were upset. And that you're *still* upset."

Harriet had many wonderful qualities. Subtlety was not one of them.

Mrs. Goddard went very still as her gaze darted between Emma and Harriet.

"I don't know what to say," she finally replied. "Except to note that those discussions were private, and I would prefer they remain that way."

"Please don't be mad at Miss Nash," Harriet pleaded. "She was worried about you."

"She *is* worried about you," Emma smoothly interjected. "Miss Nash spoke with Harriet because of her concern for your well-being."

"Then why are *you* here, Mrs. Knightley?" the headmistress sharply asked.

That tone was decidedly unusual for her. Clearly, Mrs. Goddard was rattled.

"Harriet came to me because she knows my father and I greatly value your friendship," she calmly replied. "We would wish to be of assistance if necessary."

"It's not."

Emma refused to retreat, because every instinct clamored that something was wrong. "Are you quite sure, Mrs. Goddard? Whatever you and Mrs. Elton discussed has surely affected you."

The headmistress glanced down at her lap, as if unable to meet Emma's gaze. When she smoothed her skirts with trembling fingers, Emma knew she'd hit the mark.

"Ma'am," she gently said, "as you know, Miss Bates has come under a degree of suspicion in this dreadful affair. We only wish to help her—and you, if need be. If you can impart any information that might shed light on Mrs. Elton's odd behavior, it could prove to be very useful."

Mrs. Goddard breathed out a weary sigh, her shoulders slumping a bit. "You needn't dance around the situation any longer, Mrs. Knightley. Miss Bates told me that Constable

Sharpe tried to arrest her. That's why I've been in such a state, and I'm utterly unsure what to do about it."

It was Emma's turn to sigh. "We've been trying to keep that information private."

"You mustn't blame poor Miss Bates. She told me quite by accident. She certainly didn't intend to blurt it out."

Unfortunately, blurting things out was rather a specialty for Miss Bates.

"You've told no one else?"

"Of course not." The headmistress suddenly scowled. "Really, Mrs. Knightley, Constable Sharpe is quite a dreadful man to treat our dear Miss Bates so cruelly."

"I cannot disagree," Emma dryly replied. "Fortunately, Dr. Hughes does not support the charge."

She wasn't convinced, however, that the odious Mr. Sharpe wouldn't make a concerted effort to sway the coroner to his way of thinking.

"Everyone is upset about Miss Bates," said Harriet. "But why have you been in such a state?"

Mrs. Goddard grimaced. "I have been concerned not just for Miss Bates but also . . . for myself."

Emma put down her teacup. "Ma'am, there is no delicate way to ask this, so I will be direct. Did Mrs. Elton lend you money?"

The headmistress blinked. "No, she did not. Nor did I ever ask her for money."

Emma frowned. "Are you aware that Mrs. Elton loaned Miss Bates a considerable sum?"

"Yes, although I cannot imagine why she would agree to such a thing."

That was a discussion for another time.

"If Mrs. Elton didn't lend you money, then why are you concerned for yourself?"

"She didn't lend me money, Mrs. Knightley. She *gave* me

money—or, rather, she made a donation to the school. As did her sister, although, of course, that money came through Mrs. Elton. I've never met Mrs. Suckling."

Emma was now thoroughly confused. "I don't understand."

"I think I do," Harriet said. "They wished to become patronesses of the school, didn't they? I overheard Mrs. Elton talking about it a few months ago at Mrs. Cole's dinner party."

Mrs. Goddard nodded. "Exactly so. Both Mrs. Elton and her sister were interested in becoming more charitably engaged, and they felt my school was a worthy venture in that respect."

Emma couldn't help feeling slightly annoyed, which was admittedly an irrational response.

"I didn't realize you were looking for patrons. Mr. Knightley and I would have been happy to contribute, as would my father."

Mrs. Goddard shook her head. "You have all been so generous over the years that I could never ask you to do more than you already have. And, truly, all our basic needs are met by the school fees."

"But you did wish to make improvements," Harriet doggedly said. "Some new furniture and also repairs to the roof."

Emma glanced at the new curtains. "Did Mrs. Elton hear you speak of these improvements?"

Mrs. Goddard's cheeks flushed pink. "I believe I might have mentioned it to her."

She'd obviously done more than mention it. And given Mrs. Elton's prideful nature, she would have enjoyed playing the role of noble patroness.

"But, then, why the argument?"

Mrs. Goddard shifted in her seat. "I assure you, it was one-sided."

"Undoubtedly. I have never heard you raise your voice to anyone."

"That is very true," Harriet stoutly added.

"Thank you," Mrs. Goddard said quietly.

"I will also hazard a guess that Mrs. Elton wished you to return the donation," said Emma.

Mrs. Goddard nodded. "She came to call a few days before her murder. She demanded I return the money, both her and her sister's donations. I told her, of course, that I could not, since the money had already been spent."

Emma grimaced. "That must have gone down a treat."

"I assure you that she did not hold back from expressing her great displeasure. I did offer to try to sell my new writing desk—or give it to her—but she grew very annoyed at that suggestion."

"Did she tell you why she needed the money?"

"No, and I cannot understand why she was so displeased. Mrs. Elton has always taken such a kind interest in the school, and I have always considered her a friend. It was a shocking encounter, Mrs. Knightley."

A rude Mrs. Elton was not the least bit shocking, in Emma's opinion. But it was becoming ever more apparent that the Eltons, or at least Mrs. Elton, had money troubles.

"You did not speak to her again before her death?"

"I did not."

Emma fell silent, pondering this new wrinkle in the fabric.

"I know I should have mentioned it," Mrs. Goddard unhappily said, "but it seemed clear that Mrs. Elton was killed by a passing thief. Then, when Miss Bates told me about the promissory note and how Constable Sharpe tried to arrest her . . ."

"You were afraid you might come under suspicion, as well," Emma gently finished.

She looked ashamed. "Yes."

"Mrs. Goddard, no one could possibly suspect you," Harriet exclaimed. "You are always so kind to everyone, even to Mrs. Elton—who was not a very nice person."

Mrs. Goddard regarded her former pupil with a misty smile. "Thank you, dear child."

Emma nodded. "Harriet is correct. It's nonsense to think you could have had anything to do with Mrs. Elton's murder."

"I'm not sure Constable Sharpe would agree."

"I hold no stock in any opinion held by Constable Sharpe, I assure you."

In fact, Emma was convinced that she and Harriet were making a better job of the investigation than either the constable or the coroner.

"Mrs. Goddard, would you be comfortable if I shared this discussion with my husband?"

The woman's eyes popped wide with alarm. "I don't know. After what happened to Miss Bates . . ."

"It will not happen to you," Emma firmly replied. "I highly doubt that Mr. Knightley will need to share this information with either Dr. Hughes or Constable Sharpe. The money was a freely given donation, not a loan. But it does point to a pattern of strange behavior on Mrs. Elton's part."

When Mrs. Goddard still hesitated, Emma leaned forward and pressed her hand. "Please trust me, ma'am. My husband will be very discreet, and this information could be useful to his investigation."

The headmistress finally nodded her consent. "I suppose one must. And I do hope the murderer is soon caught, Mrs. Knightley. My girls are afraid to step outside the grounds of the school without a teacher and are even afraid to go to church."

Harriet cocked her head. "The vengeful ghost?"

"Yes."

"I thought I put an end to that nonsensical tale," Emma said, exasperation flaring. "Please assure the girls there is no murderous ghost lurking about the church."

Mrs. Goddard sighed again. "Better for a ghost to be blamed than Miss Bates."

# CHAPTER 18

Feeling wilted after trudging home from Donwell in the heat, Emma handed her bonnet to the waiting footman.

"Mr. Woodhouse is waiting for you in the drawing room, ma'am," he said.

"Thank you, Simon."

She was desperate for a relaxing cup of tea, especially since she and George had not had a relaxing conversation.

After parting ways with Harriet, she'd set off for Donwell. George had been in his study, trying to catch up on his work. Initially, he'd been surprised and rather annoyed to hear of her discussion with Mrs. Goddard. He'd bluntly expressed the opinion that Emma should have come to him first before marching off to interrogate potential witnesses.

Emma stuck to her guns. As had been the case with Miss Bates, she remained convinced that Mrs. Goddard had been more forthcoming with her than she would have been with George. After a few tart remarks about interfering in official investigations, he eventually agreed. Thankfully, he also agreed that there was no immediate need to further question Mrs. Goddard or relay what Emma had discovered to Constable Sharpe. Instead, George deemed it necessary to acquire additional information before proceeding further.

"Will that require a closer look at the Eltons' finances?" Emma asked.

"Yes, and I'd like more information about Suckling's finances, as well. There are too many unanswered questions to continue ignoring that line of enquiry."

Emma thoroughly approved, since Mr. Suckling had become her favorite candidate as the murderer. There was clearly trouble between the in-laws, and money seemed to be at the heart of it.

After a brief discussion on how to go about such an enquiry, George decided to write to his brother, John, who resided in London. Married to Isabella, Emma's older sister, John was an accomplished barrister with a thriving practice. If anyone could unearth the necessary information about Mr. Suckling's finances, it would be he.

As for discovering the truth of Mr. Elton's financial situation, George insisted she leave the matter with him. A bit reluctantly, she agreed—mostly because she couldn't imagine the circumstances in which the subject would naturally arise.

Now she had nothing to do but enjoy a cup of tea with her father before retiring for a bath before dinner.

"Has my father had tea, Simon?" she asked.

"Mr. Woodhouse insisted on waiting for you and so would not allow me to prepare him a cup."

The footman's carefully blank expression made her sigh. "Is he upset about something?"

"I believe so, Mrs. Knightley."

When she lifted her eyebrows in silent enquiry, he gave a slight grimace.

"Mr. Elton stopped by this afternoon," he said. "To call on Mr. Woodhouse."

*Drat.*

"I take it my father did not respond well."

"Mr. Woodhouse instructed me to eject Mr. Elton from the premises," he woodenly replied.

She gaped at him. "You mean literally eject him?"

"I believe the phrase employed was *toss the bounder out of my house.*"

It took Emma a few moments to collect her wits. "I take it Miss Bates was visiting at the time."

"Yes, madam."

"I'm going to assume you did *not* physically eject Mr. Elton from the house."

"No. I explained to Mr. Elton that Mr. Woodhouse was not receiving guests at present."

She eyed him. "Is there something else, Simon?"

Again, he grimaced. "I'm afraid Mr. Elton might have heard the order for his removal. Mr. Woodhouse was quite, er, forceful."

*Double drat.*

Apparently, it *was* asking too much to have a quiet cup of tea and a bath.

"Is Miss Bates still here?"

"She left a short time ago."

"In a fit of the vapors, no doubt."

The footman's left eyelid twitched.

"Thank you, Simon. The situation must have been hideous, but I'm sure you managed it as well as it could be."

As she headed for the drawing room, Emma realized that until the true killer was caught, they'd be forever subjected to bouts of the vapors and her father's alarming changes in temperament.

As soon as she entered, Father threw off his lap blanket and all but sprang to his feet. "Emma, Mr. Elton had the temerity to call, and it upset Miss Bates terribly. I have never been so astounded in my life."

She gently pressed him back into the chair. "I know it was up-setting, but I'm not sure we needed to threaten poor Mr. Elton. Simply saying that one is not receiving calls would have done quite nicely."

He flapped an agitated hand. "But I thought you made it clear to Mr. Elton that he was not to call."

"I did, but I cannot control his every movement. Perhaps he was coming to apologize."

"I do not want his apologies, and I do not want him in my house again. To accuse Miss Bates of murder—it's simply out-rageous! In fact, I will write to the bishop and insist he send us a new vicar. I will not step foot in that church, and neither will you, until this issue is addressed."

Emma forced herself not to grit her teeth. "Father, it was Constable Sharpe who accused Miss Bates, not Mr. Elton."

"That would not have happened if he'd kept that foolish note to himself. And Mrs. Elton had no business pestering Miss Bates in the first place. The Eltons have caused a great deal of trouble, and I do not approve of trouble, Emma."

At this point, she found it hard to disagree with him. "I know, Father, but don't forget that poor Mrs. Elton is dead."

He drew his lap blanket up to his chest and glared at her. "Miss Bates had nothing to do with that."

She sighed with resignation. "What would you have me do?"

"Tell Mr. Elton that he is no longer welcome at Hartfield."

"I already did that."

"Then please tell him again."

"Very well, dear. Let me pour you a cup of tea, and then I'll take care of it."

By the time she got him settled with his tea, it occurred to her that delivering the message in person—as unpleasant as it would surely be—might give her the opportunity to discreetly probe the vicar about his financial situation. George would dis-approve, but Mr. Elton might find it more comfortable to speak with her than with the man for whom he had so much respect. Mr. Elton greatly admired George, and admitting his difficulties to him would be embarrassing. If she could spare the vicar's blushes, she was willing to endure another awkward visit.

After retrieving her bonnet, she set off and soon arrived at the vicarage. Since its master was home, she was ushered into the formal drawing room, now absent signs of mourning.

Mr. Elton hurried in a few minutes later. "Mrs. Knightley, do forgive me. As soon as the footman informed me of your arrival, I hastened to the kitchen and asked Mrs. Wright to prepare tea."

"That's very kind, but you needn't put yourself to so much trouble."

"I can think of nothing more elevating than a visit from you, Mrs. Knightley—although certainly Mrs. Martin is always a true ray of light in a bleak landscape. Your friend is not with you today, I see."

"She is busy at home."

He sighed. "Dear, dear Mrs. Martin."

*Oh . . . dear.*

"But I am forgetting my manners," he said. "Please do sit."

Rather surprisingly, he sat next to her on the red velvet settee. In his sober clerical garb, he looked out of place in the excessively stylish room, with its emphasis on red velvet, along with much gold fringe on the curtains and cushions. As well, there was bright yellow wallpaper and several large brass wall sconces. In totality, the decor was hardly what one expected in the home of a country vicar.

"Will Mr. Knightley also be dropping by?" he asked in a hopeful voice.

"I'm afraid not. Donwell keeps him so busy at this time of year."

He pulled a sad face. "I have no doubt that his duties regarding Augusta's investigation have greatly burdened him. I am truly sorry, Mrs. Knightley. You have both been so kind."

"There is no need to apologize, sir. We are happy to help."

"What would Highbury do without you, dear madam? How fortunate we are to have such models of compassion at Hartfield and Donwell Abbey."

She mentally winced, since one of those models of compassion had been on the verge of ejecting him out the front door less than an hour ago.

"And how are you, sir? Have you been able to find a bit of peace and quiet these past few days?"

His shoulders slumped. "That's just it, Mrs. Knightley. It's *too* quiet. Augusta had such a dynamic personality. Always busy, always bringing energy to everything she did."

While Emma had always found Mrs. Elton exhausting, of course Mr. Elton would feel differently. The vicarage no doubt echoed with her absence. Emma had experienced that same emptiness after her mother died—her laughter fading to silence, the scent of her perfume drifting away to nothing.

Still, Mr. Elton was a young man, so it was likely he would eventually recover and go on to lead a happy and productive life. And it would be with a less annoying woman than the first Mrs. Elton, one could hope.

She touched his sleeve. "I hope you can take comfort in the concern of your friends."

He tentatively put out a hand. "Indeed I do, madam. In fact—"

When the door opened, he sprang to his feet with startling alacrity. Goodness, but the man's behavior was changeable. Not for the first time, she wondered if grief had slightly unhinged him.

"Ah, Mrs. Wright with tea," he exclaimed as the housekeeper entered, followed by a footman holding the tray.

Mrs. Wright gave a stiff nod. "Good afternoon, Mrs. Knightley. Sir, do you wish me to pour?"

"I think we can impose on Mrs. Knightley to perform that duty, can we not?" he said, smiling at Emma.

"I should be happy to."

After another stiff nod, the housekeeper retreated, the footman in her wake.

As Emma prepared tea, she asked the vicar a few innocuous questions about church matters. He soon seemed to unbend and cast off some of his morose demeanor. After a few more minutes, however, he shifted a bit, suddenly looking awkward.

"How is your father?" he asked. "I called earlier today, hoping he would agree to see me, but he was not receiving visitors. I do hope Mr. Woodhouse isn't suffering from poor health. I should be most distressed to hear so."

Emma mentally prepared to deliver the blow. "It is my father that I wish to speak with you about, sir."

He perked up. "I stand ready to serve Mr. Woodhouse in any way I can."

"Unfortunately, I must again ask you to refrain from visiting Hartfield. I truly regret making this request, but it is necessary for my father's well-being."

He sighed. "I feared he was still displeased with me."

She was surprised by his mild response. It seemed Mr. Elton had not heard Father yelling, after all.

"Let me just say that he remains perturbed about certain matters pertaining to the investigation. While I'm sure this is only a temporary situation, I must beg your understanding for the time being, Mr. Elton."

He briefly closed his eyes, shaking his head. "Madam, please know that I now *deeply* regret ever raising the issue. I had no idea that Constable Sharpe would act in so ungentlemanly a fashion toward poor Miss Bates."

Emma blinked in surprise. "You know about that?"

"I spoke to Dr. Hughes this morning. The constable was also present and was quite insistent that I be informed of his conclusions regarding Miss Bates—and his regrettable actions. Naturally, I was devastated to hear that you were all subjected to such an unpleasant scene. That is why I went to call upon Mr. Woodhouse to offer my sincere apologies."

*Too late, I'm afraid.*

"I appreciate that, Mr. Elton, but I fear my father will continue to remain disturbed until his friend is fully cleared of suspicion."

"Which he blames on me," he morosely said.

Emma gave him an apologetic grimace.

He made an attempt to rally. "Ah, well, as vicar, I am called upon to be understanding. 'Judge not, that ye be not judged,' as the Good Book says. I know Mr. Woodhouse to be a good and loyal man who suffers for his friend. I only hope that someday he can find a way to forgive me."

That was a surprisingly charitable view from a person who had often displayed a certain meanness of character.

In the aftermath of his wife's death, Emma had found Mr. Elton's behavior erratic, even strange. But perhaps grief was transforming him into a man more perceptive of the sensibilities of others, a man with a greater understanding of the natural foibles of his neighbors and friends.

"I appreciate your kindness, Mr. Elton. As I mentioned, I'm sure the situation is temporary."

"I truly do understand, though I must admit that your steadfast friendship has been a great source of consolation. To be deprived of it—no matter how justly—is indeed a cruel blow."

That seemed a bit much.

"Mr. Knightley and I are always at your disposal, and of course, you are welcome at Donwell. May I pour you another cup of tea?"

He smiled. "You and Mr. Knightley are both so kind."

Congratulating herself for getting over rough ground with relative ease, she decided it was time to venture into more rocky terrain.

"And how is Mr. Suckling?" she casually asked as she refilled his cup. "Will he be returning to Highbury? You must find his help a *great* comfort."

There. That was certainly a leading question.

Mr. Elton took the cup before answering. "My brother-in-law will be returning in a few days to assist me with some outstanding financial matters. I have little head for business, which is why I depend so much on Horace. He is an excellent man."

She mentally blinked at this blatant reframing of their relationship. "Well, you are fortunate to have his assistance, then. I hope those financial matters will not prove too troubling."

"I shouldn't think so."

He alternately sipped his tea and smiled at her, apparently having nothing further to say. Clearly, he needed a nudge.

"My husband would be happy to assist you, as well, Mr. Elton. As you know, he is quite adept in financial and legal matters."

The vicar looked surprised. "Of course, but I wouldn't dream of imposing on him. He's much too busy to worry about my little problems."

Emma mentally regrouped.

"And how are you faring when it comes to managing your household, sir? Because I know you relied greatly on your wife, I should be happy to help until you find your footing." She gave him an encouraging smile. "I have been managing Hartfield for several years, so I have quite a bit of experience in that regard."

He seemed to consider her offer. Emma held her breath, willing him to say yes.

Alas, the vicar regretfully shook his head. "I can no more impose on you than I can on your husband, dear madam. Mrs. Wright and I will muddle along, never fear. And I always have Horace to fall back upon."

As much as it annoyed her, Emma now had to admit defeat. Mr. Elton was a closed book in regard to his finances.

"Of course. Still, if you encounter any difficulties or wish to make changes in your style of housekeeping, please don't hesitate to ask for my help."

He issued a melancholy sigh. "I imagine my housekeeping will be much reduced, now that I am a widower. My sole focus will henceforth be the well-being of my parishioners, Mrs. Knightley."

"Very proper, I'm sure." She put down her cup. "Thank you for the tea, Mr. Elton."

With profuse expressions of gratitude for her support, he escorted her to the door. As she was making her farewells, he hesitantly touched her arm.

"Mrs. Knightley, may I ask a great favor of you?"

"Of course."

"I would be grateful if you could again convey my apologies to your father. At the time, it seemed that coming forward with the promissory note was both a matter of conscience and a sacred duty I owed to my wife."

That took Emma by surprise. Revealing the promissory note had ultimately led to nothing but embarrassing questions about his wife and her fraught relations with her neighbors.

"Mr. Elton, surely you never believed Miss Bates capable of murder."

He grimaced. "No, which is why I now regret it. I simply wished to explain why I acted as I did, in the hope that Mr. Woodhouse might come to understand my reasoning—no matter how faulty it may have been."

Emma suspected that no amount of reasoning would sway her father. Yet saying so would simply make the vicar feel worse.

"I cannot promise anything, but I will do my best," she replied.

He gave her a grateful smile. "Of course you will, Mrs. Knightley. You never do anything less."

# CHAPTER 19

"Dear Mrs. Knightley, you're looking splendid," Frank Churchill enthused, rising to greet Emma as she entered the Westons' drawing room.

Frank was as handsome and charming as ever. For a brief spell, she'd once fancied herself in love with him, only to find that his attentions were simply a ruse to distract from his secret engagement to Jane. Like all his friends and family, Emma had been initially outraged by such ungentlemanly behavior. And like everyone else—with the possible exception of George—she'd forgiven him.

"How are you feeling, Jane?" she asked as the young woman also rose to greet her. "Better, I hope."

"I'm still fatigued," Jane admitted. "But that is to be expected after such a long journey. Thankfully, Highbury is so delightful at this time of year. I am sure I will benefit from the fine weather."

"It's also quite hot," Mrs. Weston said as they took their seats. "You must be careful not to overexert yourself."

Emma felt a twinge of anxiety. Jane's normally lovely complexion was more sallow than ivory, and her eyes bore shadows underneath. "That's very true, Jane. In your condition you must be particularly careful."

At the allusion to her pregnancy, the young woman blushed, which at least had the benefit of bringing some color to her cheeks.

Frank took his wife's hand. "You must recover your strength before you rush off to slay dragons, dear girl."

"It's that blasted constable who's causing all the trouble," Mr. Weston complained. "I'd like to give him a piece of my mind, but Mrs. Weston absolutely forbids me."

"Because you would only make things worse, my dear," his wife replied.

Emma sighed. "Yes, unfortunately. Both Dr. Hughes and Constable Sharpe resent what they perceive as any interference in their duties. And although the constable has been dreadful in his treatment of poor Miss Bates, I will grudgingly acknowledge that he does take those duties very seriously. Sadly, he's completely lacking in imagination and acumen, and that is a fatal combination when charged with investigating a murder."

His gaze acute, Frank studied her for a few moments. "Then I suppose we'll have to investigate it ourselves. I imagine you've already made a start of it."

"Goodness," Emma exclaimed, adopting what she hoped was an innocent expression. "Whatever can you be talking about?"

"Ha! I knew it. You *have* been investigating. Tell all, Mrs. Knightley. What have you discovered so far?"

For all his occasionally feckless ways, Frank was far from stupid. He had a keen eye and a quick wit—talents developed out of necessity, no doubt, when he and Jane had been secretly engaged. He'd fooled them all, which certainly took some skill.

"I'm sure Mr. Knightley has the investigation well in hand," Mrs. Weston said in an admonishing tone. "Is that not right, Emma?"

"Naturally, he has it in hand. With my help, of course."

Mrs. Weston sighed, but Frank simply grinned.

"And where have your investigations taken you?" he asked again.

"For one thing, they've led to some very interesting information about Mrs. Elton."

Emma explained her discussion with Mrs. Goddard, leaving out any details that might embarrass the headmistress or Miss Nash.

"Good heavens, Emma," Mrs. Weston exclaimed. "What an extraordinary story."

"What does Mr. Knightley make of it?" asked Mr. Weston.

Emma hesitated, aware that George would not wish her to discuss the case too freely. In fact, he would probably prefer her not to discuss it at all.

"He is looking into the matter from every angle," she finally said.

Mr. Weston tapped the side of his nose. "Keeping it close to his vest, eh? Don't want to start any rumors, do we?"

Too late, Emma remembered that Mr. Weston was rather a champion at starting rumors—or, at least, someone fatally incapable of keeping secrets.

"Let me just say that it would be wise to discuss such delicate matters only among ourselves," she said.

Mrs. Weston gazed pointedly at her husband. "She means you, my dear."

He had the grace to look sheepish.

"I'm grateful, though, to know as much as possible," Jane said. "I've found it most distressing to be so in the dark. It makes one feel quite powerless."

Frank was looking thoughtful. "This information doesn't exactly clear Aunt Hetty, though, does it?"

"Not decisively," Emma admitted.

"Then please know that I stand ready to help you and Mr.

Knightley in any way I can," he said in a determined tone. "We must clear Aunt Hetty's name as soon as possible, not just for her sake but for Jane and Mrs. Bates, as well. Their health and peace of mind depend on it."

Mrs. Weston began to look alarmed. "I'm sure Mr. Knightley is perfectly capable of handling matters on his own. There is no need for you—or Emma—to get involved."

Jane touched her husband's hand. "I have to agree, Frank. I'm not sure it's wise to interfere."

Mr. Weston scoffed. "Nonsense. Between the two of them, Frank and Emma have more brains than the rest of us put together. And since Emma knows everything that goes on in Highbury, how could she not be a tremendous help?"

Because both women were now frowning at their husbands, Emma felt it best to change the subject. "Well, we shall see. And before I forget, my father has charged me to invite you all to come to Hartfield for dinner tomorrow. He would love to see you, and it will be just the thing for Mrs. and Miss Bates."

There were the usual hesitations and reluctances to inconvenience dear Mr. Woodhouse, but Emma stood firm. With the invitation finally accepted, she rose to take her leave.

"I'll see you out," said Mr. Weston. "Oh, the devil. I almost forgot to tell you, but you'll certainly wish to know before Mr. Woodhouse finds out."

Emma sighed. More trouble, apparently.

"It's the poultry thief," he explained. "The blighter is back, I'm afraid."

Last year Highbury had experienced a rash of poultry thefts that had gone on for some weeks. Even Hartfield had not been left unscathed, which had greatly upset her father.

"He stole my best rooster and two of my hens," complained Mrs. Weston. "We certainly do not need that scoundrel running about on top of everything else."

"Maybe we can accuse him of Mrs. Elton's murder, instead of Aunt Hetty," Frank wryly suggested.

Jane sighed. "That is not in the least bit amusing, Frank."

"Perhaps not, but it would certainly make life easier," he replied.

If only it were that simple, Emma thought as Mr. Weston escorted her from the room.

Emma took a seat opposite her father in the drawing room, resigned to the fact that all her efforts to distract him over dinner had come to naught.

"I am *quite* upset," he exclaimed once again. "First, Mrs. Elton's murder, and now that dreadful poultry thief has returned."

She crinkled her nose to resist the urge to laugh. "I know, dearest, but you must admit that the two are quite distinct in both degree and kind."

"It was a thief who killed Mrs. Elton, Emma. Who's to say that it's not this same villain? We could all be murdered in our beds!"

"The poultry thief breaks into only chicken coops. Besides, we have George to protect us, and James and the footmen, as well. We're perfectly safe."

"I'm not sure I will ever feel safe again. Who could have imagined Highbury becoming such a den of criminality? We grow as bad as the stews of London!"

Her father, despite Emma's best efforts, had clearly fallen into one of his fretful episodes. When he had Miss Bates to worry about, he thought less about himself. But the return of the poultry thief was obviously a threat too close to home.

He sighed. "And poor George. He is so busy that he couldn't even join us for dinner, and now he is late for tea. What was Mr. Elton thinking to allow his wife to be murdered? It has put everyone in an uproar."

Clearly, Father was far from ready to forgive their vicar. Mr. Elton would simply have to do without the comforts of Hartfield for the present.

As she replenished her father's teacup, the drawing room door opened, and her husband entered.

"Father and I were quite ready to give up on you, George," she said with a smile. "I hope you're finished with your work for the evening."

"I apologize for keeping you waiting, but I am now at your disposal."

She studied him, taking in the weariness in his gaze and the tense set of his shoulders. "Would you prefer a brandy to a cup of tea?"

That won her a wry look. "That bad, is it?"

"You simply look a bit pulled around the edges. The brandy will help you sleep."

George glanced at her father, who was arranging his lap blanket, and then leaned in to murmur in her ear. "I can think of something else that would surely aid my sleep."

Emma choked. "Behave yourself, sir."

"George, what is to be done about this poultry thief?" her father asked as Emma fetched the brandy. "Surely the constable will now turn his attentions to the villain instead of pestering Miss Bates."

"I'm afraid the poultry thief is unlikely to be top of mind for Constable Sharpe," George replied.

"Highbury has become infested with criminals. I do not approve."

"Neither does Mrs. Weston, since the varlet made off with her prize rooster and two hens," Emma wryly said.

Her father grimaced. "Poor Mrs. Weston. She should never have left Hartfield, you know. She was much safer here than at Randalls."

"Mrs. Weston is perfectly safe, Father," Emma said as she brought George his drink. "And I'm sure the thief will eventually go away. That's what he did last year."

"I refuse to believe the poultry thief's return is coincidental to Mrs. Elton's murder."

When George cast her a startled glance, Emma simply shrugged. Only her father could surmise that Mrs. Elton's killer and the poultry thief would be one and the same.

"I'm looking forward to the Westons and the Churchills coming for dinner tomorrow night," she said, trying for a happy distraction. "Mrs. and Miss Bates will be so happy to spend time with them."

Father held up a hand. "There must not be cake, Emma, or any rich foods. Mrs. Churchill must be careful, in her present condition."

"Yes, dear."

"How did Jane seem to you?" George asked as she settled next to him on the settee.

"Tired, but determined to be of service to her aunt and grandmother."

"I cannot help wondering if this visit will be too much for her. It was perhaps unwise of Frank to allow her to make the journey."

George had always taken a great interest in Jane's well-being, something that had caused Emma more than one pang of jealousy before their marriage. Of course, such an emotion would now be entirely ridiculous.

"I'm sure Frank will take excellent care of her." She hesitated for a moment before continuing. "Frank also wished me to tell you that he is happy to assist you in any way he can, and that you should not hesitate to ask for his help."

Frowning, George put down his glass. "Help with what?"

"With the investigation, of course. Frank is very worried about the impact of this dreadful situation on both Miss Bates and Jane and wishes to help in any way he can."

"Emma, as I have previously noted, we do not need civilians interfering in this investigation—much less Frank Churchill."

"Yes, I recall. But in this case, the civilians seem to be doing a better job of it than Constable Sharpe, certainly."

"I take it you're referring to yourself," he dryly replied.

"You must admit that Harriet and I have supplied you with some very valuable information."

"And I'm grateful. Still, there is quite a difference between overhearing something and actively investigating. This investigation is also not without a potential risk, my dear. I will not have you putting yourself in harm's way."

"I assure you, I have no desire to do so. But we're not talking about me, dearest. We're talking about Frank."

He began to look irritated. "I hope you didn't encourage him to think he had any role to play in this investigation, because that would be highly inappropriate."

"Of course not," she replied, trying not to bristle. "It was Mr. Weston who did that."

He sighed. "Emma, what did you tell them?"

"Very little, really. Well, perhaps more than a little, but only what I thought they had a right to know."

"It's not up to you to make that decision."

She cast a quick glance in her father's direction. Thankfully, he had fallen into a peaceful doze and would not overhear their *slight* disagreement.

"I simply gave them a few basic facts. They surely have the right to know, given that Miss Bates is Jane's aunt. And they only wish to help, George."

"I sympathize, but you should not be encouraging them. Especially not Frank."

"I didn't encourage him!"

When her father snorted, Emma froze, as did George. Fortunately, Father subsided back into his doze.

"I didn't encourage anyone," she forcefully whispered. "And Frank is only trying to be helpful."

"I don't need his help," George whispered back. "And you are *not* to go haring off with him, searching for clues and interrogating innocent people. In fact, I think it best if you spend as little time with Frank Churchill as possible."

"But he's coming to dinner tomorrow!"

"Regrettable, since the man does nothing but tow trouble in his wake. I have precious little time to waste these days, Emma, particularly on foolish dinner parties. Nor do I wish to spend an evening with Frank Churchill."

She stared at him, astonished by his words and by the scowl marking his handsome features. "George, you're being quite unreasonable. One might even conclude that you're jealous of Frank."

Her husband went as stiff as a fireplace poker. Then he picked up his glass and tossed back the last of his brandy before coming to his feet.

"If you'll excuse me, I believe I have some work to finish in my study."

Her husband turned on his heel and stalked from the room, leaving Emma with her mouth hanging open. Much too late, she realized that George's disapproval of Frank Churchill had not abated one jot.

# CHAPTER 20

Emma gloomily buttered her toast. She'd woken up with a headache, no appetite, and the conviction that she'd been very foolish.

She and George had rarely exchanged a cross word since their wedding day. They'd had the occasional brangle—some habits were a bit *too* hard to break—but they'd never truly argued. That is, until she'd brought up the one person who annoyed him more than any other—Frank Churchill.

Not that she entirely disagreed with George's assessment of Frank's character. Nevertheless, taken in full measure, she thought Frank to be a good man, if not quite worthy of Jane. Unfortunately, Emma's beloved failed to share that view, a point made clear when he did not return to the drawing room. George had eventually joined her in bed, but very late and in an exceedingly annoying way, falling asleep the instant his head hit the pillow. And he was already gone when she awoke, out for an early morning ride.

At the other end of the dining room table, her father glanced up from his gazette. "Emma, you've barely touched your toast. Are you feeling unwell?"

She forced a bright smile. "Indeed no, Father. You know I am never unwell."

He perused her with anxiety. "You are too pale, my dear. Perhaps you should retire back to bed."

Emma reached for the orange marmalade, slathered it on her toast, and then bit it with a show of enthusiasm.

"I was simply thinking about what we should serve for dinner tonight," she replied after managing to choke the toast down. "We must make it a bit of a celebration, now that Frank and Jane have arrived. Miss Bates will enjoy that."

Her father continued to eye her before finally turning to address the footman. "Simon, please ask Serle to prepare a bowl of gruel for Miss Emma."

Simon cast her a sympathetic glance before exiting the room. No one in Hartfield, except her father, willingly consumed Serle's gruel. Apparently, quarreling with one's husband left one looking so pulled that drastic measures were seen to be necessary.

When she heard a step in the hall a few minutes later, she grimaced. Serle must have had a pot of gruel on the hob, ready and waiting to torture her. Well, she supposed it was a fitting punishment for allowing the sun to set without attempting to make peace with her loved one.

The door opened, and her loved one himself entered the room. When George paused for a moment, his expression inscrutable, Emma had the horrible sense that he was about to beat a hasty retreat. Instead, he quietly greeted her father before coming to join her.

She forced a bright smile. "Good morning, dearest. I hope you enjoyed your ride."

"I did, and it had the added benefit of giving me a chance to think."

*Drat.* He was obviously still annoyed with her.

She affected a light tone. "May I ask what you were thinking about?"

His expression finally broke, and he gave her a charmingly rueful smile. Emma felt the oddest sensation in the middle of her chest, like a ray of sunlight had just pierced her heart.

"My idiotic behavior last night." He leaned down, dropping his voice to a murmur. "Forgive me, Emma. I was a jealous fool."

When he kissed her cheek, that little ray turned into a bright beam of light.

"I was silly, too," she admitted. "And I'm sorry if I said anything at Randalls that I shouldn't have."

"Is everything all right, Emma?" her father asked.

"Everything is fine. George is telling me what a splendid ride he had."

The door opened, and Simon reentered, carrying a steaming bowl on a platter. "Your gruel, Mrs. Knightley."

George cocked an eyebrow at her.

"Father thinks I look a trifle peaked," she explained. "He thought a bowl of gruel would be helpful."

"My poor darling," he said, trying not to laugh.

"Well, I'm feeling much better now," she said. "You may put it on the sideboard, Simon."

"Emma, it would do you good," her father exclaimed. "Please try to eat some."

"It's odd," said George as he took his seat. "As I was riding, I thought I would like nothing better than a bowl of Serle's excellent gruel. You may put it at my place, Simon."

"Are you sure, sir?" the footman asked, sounding slightly incredulous.

"Quite."

Emma suddenly felt rather misty. Very little could prove a husband's love more than throwing himself on the altar of Serle's hideous gruel.

Fortunately, another interruption spared them both. Thomas, the junior footman, entered the room.

"Mr. Knightley, Constable Sharpe has come to call," he said.

She and George exchanged surprised glances at such an early visit.

Her husband stood. "I'll come immediately."

When he moved to pull back her chair, Emma lifted her eyebrows. "You want me to go with you?"

"If you have questions, you'll be able to ask Sharpe directly."

"He'll not be pleased by my presence, I'm sure."

"Since I trust your judgment considerably more than his, I find myself unmoved by that consideration."

"George, if you don't stop being so kind, I will surely burst into tears," she said as he showed her into the corridor.

"My dear, you will alarm Constable Sharpe if you do so."

She smothered a laugh.

The constable, waiting in the entrance hall, predictably looked unhappy to see her.

"Mrs. Knightley," he tersely said. "Mr. Knightley, if I may have a moment of your time."

"My wife and I will see you in the study," George calmly replied.

The constable fell in behind them, muttering under his breath.

George ushered them into his office and seated Emma. The constable, however, remained standing.

"This news must be of some import to bring you out so early in the day," George said.

"Indeed, sir. Mr. Elton came knocking on my door first thing." The constable paused with great significance.

"And?"

"We've finally got him, Mr. Knightley, dead to rights," Mr. Sharpe triumphantly stated.

Emma sucked in a startled breath. "Him?"

"You have a suspect in custody?" her husband asked.

"I have the *murderer* in custody. It's Dick Curtis, a farm laborer."

Emma opened her eyes wide at George, but he shot her a warning glance. Clearly, he didn't wish her to reveal that she'd seen the incriminating note.

"Are you sure it was Dick Curtis who killed Mrs. Elton?" she asked.

The constable bristled. "Of course. As I said, we have him dead to rights."

George held up a restraining hand. "Why would Dick Curtis murder Mrs. Elton? Do you have any evidence?"

"All that I need, Mr. Knightley. As for motive, it was filthy revenge."

"I would be grateful for a *full* explanation, Constable. Not just some cryptic remarks," George said, growing a trifle exasperated.

Mr. Sharpe tugged on his vest, looking self-satisfied. "Curtis had a grudge against Mr. Elton. Even sent him a threatening note—nasty one, too. I told Mr. Elton he should have shown it to me as soon as he got it, but he said he didn't want to get Dick in trouble. I said, 'You've got a kind heart, Vicar. But *this* is murder.'"

Emma almost rolled her eyes at his theatrics. "The threatening note was made against Mr. Elton, correct?"

He nodded. "I just said so."

"Then why murder *Mrs.* Elton?"

"As I stated, ma'am, filthy rev—"

George cut him off. "Why did Mr. Elton specifically call your attention to the note this morning?"

"He heard what happened last night at the Crown," Sharpe replied, as if that explained everything.

George looked severe. "Mr. Sharpe, I would be grateful if you would clearly and completely detail the sequence of events—from the beginning."

"Yes, it all seems rather muddled," said Emma.

Mr. Sharpe gave a stiff little bow. "My apologies. I don't mean to muddle Mrs. Knightley."

This time, Emma did roll her eyes. Thankfully, she supposed, the constable failed to notice.

"A few weeks back," he said, "Mr. Elton received a nasty note from Dick Curtis, all but threatening to kill him."

When George shot her a quick glance, Emma gave a tiny nod of confirmation. The crude note could be read, if one were so inclined, as a death threat. Certainly, it contained ill intent.

"Do you know why Dick threatened the vicar?" George asked.

"Because he'd applied to be put on the parish poor roll, and Mr. Elton had turned him down."

"Did Mr. Elton show the note to anyone else?"

"No, sir. He didn't wish to embarrass Curtis." The constable shook his head. "Poor Mr. Elton now realizes what a fatal mistake that was, given recent events."

To Emma, it still seemed rather a longbow to draw. Ugly notes were a far cry from murder, especially for a man who'd never caused any trouble before. "Do you have any other evidence against Curtis?"

"I do," he triumphantly said. "Dick was at the Crown last night, and in his cups. He was railing and carrying on something bad, full of inflammatory remarks about Mr. Elton. Mrs. Stokes finally kicked him and his mates out into the street."

"Remarks about Mr. Elton not putting him on the poor roll?" asked George.

"Indeed, and he was using some very ugly language."

George shook his head. "But that is hardly definitive, I'm afraid."

"Ah, but then Dick said clear as day in front of everyone that he was glad Mrs. Elton was dead. That she was just as nasty and mean as her husband, and she had got everything she deserved." He shook his head. "The villain didn't even care that everyone in the taproom heard him, including Mr. Elton's groom and Mr. Cole's coachman."

As greatly as Emma wished for Miss Bates to be cleared, she

couldn't help but feel skeptical about Sharpe's conclusion. If Dick Curtis was indeed the murderer, his actions struck her as incredibly foolish.

"Do you know if Dick ever had dealings with Mrs. Elton?" she asked.

Mr. Sharpe addressed his answer to George, which was *quite* annoying. "I asked Mr. Elton that very same question when he brought me the note this morning. He said he couldn't be sure."

"Is Mr. Elton also of the opinion that Dick Curtis murdered his wife?" asked George.

"He is, sir. When Mr. Elton refused to put him on the roll, Dick turned . . ." He paused, as if searching for the right word. "Menacing. Yes, that was what he said. Then he got the note a few days later."

George tapped a finger to his lips. "Why did Mr. Elton turn him down in the first place?"

"I didn't ask, but everyone knows Dick's a layabout."

"Perhaps, but Mrs. Elton had nothing to do with parish business," Emma objected. "Why murder her and not Mr. Elton?"

"It was clearly a crime of opportunity," Sharpe replied in a condescending tone. "Dick must have seen Mrs. Elton go into the church and followed her. Maybe he tried to get her to change the vicar's mind. But when she wouldn't, he decided to steal her necklace. She fought back, and he killed her."

Emma had seen Dick Curtis in the village on more the one occasion. Despite his disability, he was a burly and fit man. "Why, then, the need to use the candlestick to kill her? As a farmhand, he was naturally quite strong."

The constable's expression suggested the very question itself was offensive. "Mayhap he was injured in the tussle for the necklace. Or he wanted to throw us off the scent by using a weapon, like he didn't have the strength to kill her." He tugged on his vest again. "Like a woman had done it," he pointedly added.

Emma scoffed. "But that would require a degree of fore-thought. Which suggests it was *not* a crime of opportunity."

"Now, see here, Mrs. Knightley—"

When George loudly cleared his throat, the constable subsided with a grumble.

"I think the more likely scenario, *if* one accepts that Curtis did indeed murder Mrs. Elton—" George started.

"He did it, Mr. Knightley," Mr. Sharpe interrupted.

George ignored him, looking at Emma instead. "If he did it, then I think it possible that his damaged hand forced him to use the candlestick to strike the final blow."

An image of Mrs. Elton sprang into her mind, the ugly marks on the woman's throat in high relief. Would a man with such an injury have the strength to do such a thing or do it with one hand?

"Perhaps," she admitted. "But then why would he make such incriminating statements in public? It would be incredibly foolhardy."

"Criminals aren't generally known for their brains, Mrs. Knightley," Mr. Sharpe said. "And he *was* in his cups."

"Very much into his cups if he were to all but confess to a murder in a public setting," she sarcastically replied.

"Where is Curtis now?" George asked.

"Locked up in the cellar at the Crown. But as soon as we're finished, I'll be transporting him to the gaol in Guildford."

"Surely that's premature," Emma exclaimed.

"Mr. Elton disagrees, ma'am. He's very perturbed that the villain has been allowed to roam about Highbury, a danger to everyone."

"I would like to speak to Curtis before you move him," said George.

Constable Sharpe gave a vigorous shake of the head. "Begging your pardon, Mr. Knightley, but if you wish to speak to Dick, you can do so at the county gaol. The arrangements for transport have already been made."

"Good heavens," Emma said. "What's the rush? If the magistrate wishes to speak to the accused, I cannot imagine any justifiable impediment to that."

"Mr. Knightley can speak to him as much as he wants after he's safely stowed away," the constable huffily replied. "Dr. Hughes agrees with an immediate removal, for the safety of all in Highbury."

She frowned. "This is ridiculous. How can Dick be a danger if he's already locked up in the cellar?"

George's gaze flickered her way, containing a clear warning. *Let me handle this.*

"So you spoke to Dr. Hughes before coming to Hartfield?" he asked the constable in a bland voice.

Mr. Sharpe lifted his chin with pugnacious disdain. "It seemed the proper order of things. He *is* the coroner."

"And I am the magistrate."

"Indeed, sir, so you are surely aware that the poultry thief has struck again. The sooner I have Dick safely stowed away, the sooner I can go after that blighter."

Emma found herself unable to hold her tongue. "One would almost think you believe the theft of chickens to be equal to murder."

Mr. Sharpe glowered at her. "This thief is becoming bolder, ma'am. Why, he even raided the doctor's chicken coop night before last."

She sighed. "I suppose that explains our coroner's eagerness to dispose of Dick Curtis."

The doctor was a devoted fancier of several rare breeds of hens. When not attending to his patients—or dead bodies—he was often to be found out in his gardens, cooing over his hens with paternal affection.

The constable turned his shoulder on her to address George. "I've got reports from some neighboring farms, as well, including one in your parish, sir. Donwell, that is."

"I am aware that Donwell is my parish," George dryly replied.

"Well, who knows what will happen next if that fellow is not brought to heel?"

"A shortage of eggs, I would imagine," Emma commented.

Her husband studiously avoided looking at her, although she saw his mouth twitch. "Very well, Constable. You may transport the prisoner. Please make the necessary arrangements for me to speak with Curtis tomorrow morning."

Mr. Sharpe threw Emma a triumphant glance. "I will be happy to do so. Now, if that will be all, sir, I'll be on my way."

George stayed seated, simply giving him a cool nod.

The constable looked slightly disconcerted but mustered an awkward bow. "Mrs. Knightley."

Emma gave him a smile that was mostly teeth. "I'm sure you can find your way out, Mr. Sharpe."

When he'd departed, she blew out an exasperated sigh. "I don't know how you can be so calm, George. That dreadful man has gone behind your back from the beginning."

"Yes, I did notice that," he said with a trace of sarcasm. "You may be sure I will be speaking with Dr. Hughes about proper procedure, as well as the inappropriateness of civilians interfering in policing matters."

She widened her eyes. "I hope you're not speaking of me."

"This time, I'm referring to Mr. Elton."

"I can understand Mr. Elton's feelings, but one would think that the theft of Dr. Hughes's chickens—no matter how excellent they may be—is of less import than finding Mrs. Elton's real killer."

George tilted his head to study her. "How can we be certain Dick isn't the killer?"

"We cannot, but it doesn't make sense. And I would bet a bob that Mrs. Elton never exchanged one word with the man."

"Revenge is always a motive, and killing a loved one—not to

mention stealing an expensive necklace—is about as much revenge as one can get."

"About that necklace, George. It has yet to be found, or connected to Dick."

"There will need to be a search, and I intend to do that myself."

Emma perked up. "Do you need help?"

"I will take one of the grooms. I think it best you remain here to protect Hartfield from the poultry thief."

"Now you're being ridiculous. And I still think Dick is lacking a motive. Yes, Mr. Elton turned him down, but the poor fellow simply could have come to you instead. Or he could have applied to the full vestry council when next it met, could he not?"

"I will be raising that very issue with him tomorrow, I assure you. But it's not entirely outside the realm of possibility that Dick was the killer. He clearly hates our vicar and obviously had no great love for Mrs. Elton. It may be, as Sharpe says, that an opportunity presented itself and he stumbled into the rest."

"But to then make such blatantly incriminating statements to others? I don't know the man, but is he truly that foolish?"

"He's not ever struck me as such, but poverty and despair can drive one to do desperate things."

That was an undeniable truth. "I can't help but feel sorry for him, even though it would make life easier if he were the guilty party. Miss Bates would no longer be under suspicion."

"And life could begin to return to normal." He rose from his desk. "As much as I esteem Miss Bates, the notion that she will be spending most evenings at Hartfield for the foreseeable future does give me pause."

Emma adopted a puzzled expression. "Whatever can you mean, dearest?"

He laughed and then came round his desk to give her a parting kiss.

"When may we expect to see you again?" she asked after returning his embrace.

"After I conduct a search of Dick's quarters and likely hiding places, I intend to stop and have a word with Dr. Hughes."

Emma held up a hand. "He may have taken to his bed. His beloved chickens, you know. I suggest you take smelling salts."

"Now who's being ridiculous?"

She pointed to herself.

He briefly cupped her cheek. "Stay out of trouble, will you?"

"Always."

A masculine snort was her only reply.

# CHAPTER 21

After seeing George off to Guildford the next morning, Emma accompanied her father on his daily turn about the gardens. He set a leisurely pace, giving her ample opportunity to ponder yesterday's revelations.

"I cannot like this Constable Sharpe, Emma," her father suddenly exclaimed, breaking into her thoughts. "He seems to go about arresting people without a care for anyone's feelings."

She glanced at him, surprised. "I would have thought you relieved that Miss Bates is no longer a suspect. You must admit our dinner party last night was all the better for it."

Everyone had been thrilled to hear that Miss Bates was no longer a suspect, and the gathering had indeed taken on a celebratory nature. George, the dear man, had even made an extra effort to be polite to Frank, which had pleased Jane.

"Of course I am greatly relieved for my dear friend," Emma's father replied. "But Dick Curtis seems such a decent fellow. Whenever we passed him in the carriage, he was always so polite as to stop and raise his hat. For a common laborer, he has very nice manners."

"George will get to the bottom of it, never fear."

Her observation evoked a grimace from him. "But, Emma, to be forced to ride all the way to Guildford! Prisons are always so dreadfully damp, too. I fear poor George will catch a chill."

"I'm sure he'll take every precaution, dearest."

"This is all Mr. Elton's fault. He set Constable Sharpe on poor Miss Bates and now has done the same with Curtis. No wonder the fellow sent Mr. Elton a nasty note. I tell you, Emma, once George has seen that unfortunate man released from prison, I will be raising these issues with the vestry council."

"George cannot . . . oh, never mind."

She saw little point in trying to correct her father's wildly askew understanding of the situation.

"Remember what Mr. Perry said," she added. "You're not to be upsetting your nerves. I promise you that George will take care of everything."

"If anything is upsetting my nerves, it's Mr. Elton. Everything was perfectly fine in Highbury until he became vicar and began to interfere in the affairs of others."

Emma found that she couldn't entirely disagree with her father, but voicing such would hardly be helpful. "But that's rather the job of a vicar—interfering in the lives of parishioners in the hope of bettering them."

"Then he has made a very bad job of it. And he has a very obsequious manner, which I have always found quite annoying."

She almost gaped at him. "And yet he was always such a great favorite of yours, as was Mrs. Elton."

"That is exactly my point, Emma. If Mr. Elton had attended more to his own business instead of interfering in the affairs of others, Mrs. Elton might still be alive."

A hail from the house interrupted their bizarre conversation. With relief, she saw Frank Churchill coming out into the gardens.

"Good morning, Mr. Woodhouse, Mrs. Knightley," Frank said as he joined them. "I hope I find you both well."

"You do," she replied. "How is everyone at Randalls? Has Jane recovered from last night's exertions?"

"She has, and I am to thank you for a splendid evening. It was a most welcome occasion."

"But you must be more careful, Frank," Father said. "Jane is in a delicate state. I was quite dismayed to see her eat a piece of cake."

Frank winked at Emma. "Do you hear that, Mrs. Knightley? No more cakes for Jane."

"Very sensible, although I'm not sure Jane will agree. Now, are you simply passing by, or would you like to join us for tea?"

"I'm going into Highbury to run an errand, so I thought to see if you had any need to go into the village. I should be happy to escort you."

His offer was accompanied by a significant look she could easily decipher. Frank wished to speak with her privately.

Hiding her surprise behind a smile, she agreed. "Let me fetch my hat."

It took but a few minutes to settle her father in the drawing room and then retrieve her hat. But by the time she rejoined Frank, he was clearly in a fever of impatience.

He took her arm and began to march her down the graveled drive.

"Goodness, Frank," she exclaimed. "Why all the rush?"

He smiled sheepishly and slowed his pace. "Jane frequently scolds me for rushing about like a madman. Can't think how she puts up with me."

"I expect it has something to do with your large fortune."

He burst into laughter. "Dear Emma, please never change."

"Why would I? Now, what has you in such a fever?"

"It's about Dick Curtis," he said as they passed between Hartfield's gates. "He's been falsely accused."

She shot him a sharp glance. "Truly? I rather suspected as much, but why do *you* think that?"

"Because of Sally Linden, a housemaid at Randalls. Do you know her?"

"Yes. I believe Mrs. Weston thinks very well of her."

"She also happens to be Dick Curtis's niece."

When Emma came to a startled halt, Frank walked on a few paces before noticing and coming about.

"I didn't know that," she exclaimed.

He nodded. "Yes, and Sally swears that her uncle was nowhere near the church at the time of the murder, and there is a witness to prove it."

He took her arm and began to walk her into the village high street.

"I assume we're going to see that person now," she wryly said.

"Yes. I intended to alert Mr. Knightley, but your footman says he's away for the day."

"He's riding to Guildford to speak with Dick Curtis in the county gaol."

Frank snorted. "Constable Sharpe strikes again."

"Unfortunately."

"Poor Sally is in tatters over it, so I thought if we could verify Dick's whereabouts at the time of the murder, you could tell Mr. Knightley when he returns to Hartfield."

"Why not go to Constable Sharpe with this information?"

"Sally went straight to the blasted man first thing this morning, but he's convinced Dick is the killer. Wouldn't even listen to the poor girl."

Emma shook her head. "That man is *such* a nuisance. But what about Dr. Hughes?"

"He was apparently indisposed this morning and not taking callers."

"How inconvenient. Perhaps he is still in mourning for his chickens."

Frank laughed again.

They came abreast of the linen-draper's shop. Mrs. Ford was out front, watering her geraniums in a clay pot by the door.

"Good morning, Mrs. Knightley, Mr. Churchill. A fine morning for a walk, is it not?" she called, inspecting them with a great deal of curiosity.

Frank tipped his hat. "Indeed it is."

"Don't slow down," Emma warned, "or she'll pepper us with a thousand questions."

"At least we've given her something to gossip about. The two of us rushing through the village so early in the day."

And wouldn't George just love hearing about that?

Ignoring the prospect that her husband would likely disapprove of this excursion, she turned back to Frank.

"May I ask where we're going?"

"To see Farmer Mitchell. Sally claims that Dick was working at Mitchell's farm that day and was there well past the time when Mrs. Elton was murdered."

"Mr. Mitchell would certainly prove a credible witness, if he can verify Dick's whereabouts."

"That's what I intend to find out."

A few minutes' brisk walk brought them to the turn into Mr. Mitchell's prosperous and tidy farmstead. Although not large, Riverwatch Farm possessed excellent pastureland and produced some of the finest cheeses in the whole district. More to the point, the farmer was a good and honest man whose word was unimpeachable.

As they approached the rambling whitewashed farmhouse, Mr. Mitchell issued forth from his barn.

"Mrs. Knightley, you wait right there," he called. "Or you'll be getting them shoes of yours dirty in the muck."

He strode over to meet them, then pulled his cap to Emma and gave Frank a genial nod.

"It's a pleasure to see you, Mr. Churchill," he said. "Miss Bates will be all the more comfortable for having you and Mrs. Churchill here in Highbury. Poor lady's been going through an awful time, God love her."

"The murder is why we've come to speak with you," said Emma.

He nodded, perhaps as if he'd been expecting them. "Would you like to step inside? The missus can fix you a cup of tea in no time."

She smiled at him. "Thank you, but we don't wish to keep you. I would be grateful, though, if you could send a wheel of your cheddar around to Hartfield. Serle raved about your last batch."

"I'll have one of the lads bring it over this afternoon. Now, how can I help?"

"I'm not sure if you know this," she replied, "but Constable Sharpe has arrested Dick Curtis for Mrs. Elton's murder."

He let out a disgusted snort. "I heard. Sharpe's got the wrong end of it, I reckon."

"Sally Linden claims that Dick was working here the day of the murder," Frank said. "Is that true?"

"Aye. Dick was here all day, doing odd jobs and helping the missus clean out the cellar. I know he's a bit of a rough one, but he's a good man, and he's been dealt a hard blow with that hand of his. I try to give him as much work as I can."

Emma and Frank exchanged a glance.

"Was Dick here that entire afternoon?" she asked.

"That's what I told Constable Sharpe. He came sniffing around here after Dick was flapping his gums at the Crown. Now, I'm not claiming old Dick should have said those things or written that silly note, but he would never hurt no one, especially a lady. I've known him all my life, and he's never lifted a hand to anyone."

"Sharpe obviously didn't believe you," Frank said.

"No. I told Sharpe that Dick was working down in the cellar most of the afternoon, and my missus was in the kitchen or down with him the whole time. But Sharpe says Dick must have snuck out when my missus wasn't looking, then went and robbed and killed Mrs. Elton. I asked him, 'Well, where's the bloody necklace, then?' " He grimaced. "Begging your pardon, Mrs. Knightley."

"I share your opinion, sir. No apology is necessary."

"I surely hope you can help Dick," he earnestly said. "He's a good man, even if he sometimes can't get himself out of his own way."

"Mr. Knightley will do everything he can to help him," Emma assured him. "Thank you, sir, and please give my best to Mrs. Mitchell."

"I will, ma'am, and I'll have that cheddar sent round by the end of the afternoon."

As they set off down the lane, Frank looked thoughtful. "So, Dick Curtis should be in the clear. Unfortunately, poor Aunt Hetty may now again fall under suspicion."

Emma sighed. "Yes, I have little doubt that Mr. Sharpe will now pester Miss Bates again."

Frank made a small growling noise. "I think it's time the constable and I have a word about this harassment of Aunt Hetty."

"Given his temperament, that will not help. But George and Dr. Hughes will manage him, never fear."

"For now," he grimly replied.

She pulled him to a halt. "No one in Highbury believes that Miss Bates is responsible for Mrs. Elton's murder except for silly Constable Sharpe. Surely you know that?"

"And are you entirely sure that's so?" he challenged.

It took her a moment to understand. "Mr. Elton? No, he doesn't believe it, either. He simply thought he was doing the right thing by bringing the promissory note to George's attention."

"Always so dutiful, our vicar," Frank sarcastically replied. "In this case, I wish he'd exercised more judgment than duty."

"Yes, but he truly regrets it now."

"No doubt because he is exiled from both Hartfield and Randalls. My father is furious with Mr. Elton, which is an unusual state for him, as you know. He won't let the bounder set foot on the grounds."

"My father feels the same. I've never seen him so vexed about anything."

"Bless the dear fellow. He's been quite the champion on Aunt Hetty's behalf."

"Well, I look forward to the day when this dreadful mess is behind us. Then Father can go back to insisting that we all eat Serle's hideous gruel, and Miss Bates can fuss about Jane's letters or her mother's spectacles."

He flashed a quick smile that bordered on a smirk. "Spectacles. I'm very good at repairing them, as you know."

Despite her worries, Emma couldn't help but laugh. Whilst secretly betrothed to Jane, Frank had used every excuse to spend time with her, but in a seemingly innocent fashion. He had offered to sit with Mrs. Bates and even once had repaired her spectacles.

"It was too bad of you, Frank. I'm sure you were laughing at all of us behind our backs."

As they turned into the high street, his features fell into serious lines. "Sometimes, but I also caused my dearest Jane a great deal of distress. And now to see her in distress again . . ." He struck a fist against his palm. "We must put an end to this. The true killer must be run to ground."

"Please know that George truly is doing everything possible.

We all are, Frank. You must be patient and reassure Jane as best you can. It would be a terrible thing if her health were to take an adverse turn because of this."

"If there's more of this, I can assure you that Sharpe's health will be adversely affected, too."

Alarmed by his tone, Emma did her best to turn his thoughts toward more cheerful channels. She enquired after his uncle and the estate in Yorkshire and wondered if he and Jane would be visiting London. Such harmless chitchat, along with a few encounters with locals as they walked through the village, seemed to restore his peace of mind.

"Will you come in for tea?" she asked when they reached Hartfield. "Father would be so pleased to see you."

"Gladly, although I don't imagine Mr. Knightley will have returned yet."

"Not for another hour or so, I would imagine."

She couldn't help thinking it might be better if Frank was safely returned to Randalls before George returned to Hartfield. While her husband had been the soul of courtesy last night, she had no wish to try his patience further.

Her father, ensconced in the drawing room, hailed their appearance with relief. "Thank goodness you've returned. It's much too hot for all this walking about. Where did you go?"

"We went to see Farmer Mitchell," Frank replied.

She mentally sighed, since she'd already told her father they were simply attending to errands in the village.

Father reacted with perturbation. "Emma, farms are very dirty. Why in Heaven's name would you go to a farm?"

"Mr. Mitchell's farm is very clean, dearest. And Serle always says they have the best cheese in the entire district."

"Not to worry, Mr. Woodhouse," Frank reassured him. "We stood in the drive while we talked, and stayed only a few minutes. It was perfectly safe."

"But why go in the first place?"

Resigned, Emma decided to tell him the truth. "Mr. Mitchell was able to vouch for Dick Curtis. Dick was working at the farm during the time that Mrs. Elton was murdered."

Her father went very still. She held her breath, waiting for him to arrive at the unwelcome conclusion.

"Emma, you should not have done such a thing," he finally exclaimed. "Now Constable Sharpe will try to arrest poor Miss Bates again."

She sat on the ottoman by his chair and took his hand. "George will not allow that to happen. Besides, you said yourself that Dick was innocent. We cannot wish to see him charged for a crime he didn't commit."

His thin face wrinkled with concern. "But Miss Bates is innocent, too."

"And everyone knows that."

"Constable Sharpe certainly does not." He flapped his other hand in the air. "This is all Mr. Elton's fault, Emma. *He* is responsible for this terrible predicament."

When Simon entered the room with the tea service, Emma welcomed the distraction. "I promise you that George will take care of everything. Now, shall we—"

"We must certainly hope for that," Frank interrupted. "But I think we can also agree that Elton's actions have caused a great deal of trouble. How can Aunt Hetty—or any of us—ever be comfortable with him again?"

Emma regarded him with exasperation. "The man's wife was murdered, Frank. You cannot blame him for wanting to see justice done."

"I can when he points the finger at innocent people."

She sighed.

Simon gently cleared his throat. "Mrs. Knightley, would you like me to prepare the tea?"

Dredging up a smile, she shook her head. "I'll do it. You may go, Simon."

"Very good, madam."

He'd barely exited the room before George walked in.

"I see we have a visitor for tea," he said in a tone as dry as chalk.

*Drat, drat, drat.*

She jumped to her feet. "George, I didn't expect you so early."

"Mr. Knightley, just the man I wish to see," Frank said.

George's eyebrows went up with polite incredulity. "And why is that?"

"Dearest, let me prepare you a cup of tea," Emma said, all but shoving him onto the settee. "You must be parched from your long ride."

"It wasn't so long, my dear. And my errand was over rather quickly."

"That's exactly what I wished to speak with you about," Frank said. "Emma—that is, Mrs. Knightley—and I discovered evidence that vindicates Dick Curtis."

"Did you now?"

Emma winced. She had heard that deceptively bland tone before and knew what it meant.

"We didn't really discover it, George," she said, handing him a teacup. "I mean, *I* didn't discover it. Frank, er, Mr. Churchill, did. I had very little to do with it."

Frank held up a hand. "Now, don't count yourself short, Mrs. Knightley. From what I can tell, nothing escapes your sharp notice."

"Although you must stop going to farms and other dirty places, Emma," her father put in. "You might catch a fever."

She grimaced a silent apology to her husband, who now regarded her with a sardonic eye.

While she served tea and kept her father distracted, Frank recounted their discoveries to George.

"That perfectly corroborates what Curtis told me," he said when Frank had finished.

"So you'll be able to get him released from the gaol?" Emma asked.

"On my way home, I left a message with Mrs. Hughes, asking the doctor to call on me as soon as possible to discuss the matter." George rose to his feet. "Thank you for this information, Mr. Churchill. I'm sure you must be wishing to return to Randalls."

"I am, but if you wish me to stay to speak with Dr. Hughes—"

George bluntly cut him off. "Not necessary."

Frank took the summary dismissal with his usual good grace, even winking at Emma on his way out.

When he'd departed, she rounded on her husband. "Really, George, that was quite rude. Frank was only trying to help."

"I assure you, Dr. Hughes would appreciate Frank's presence as little as I do."

"Frank agrees with me about Mr. Elton," Father said. "Which is very sensible of him."

"*Sensible* is not a word one normally applies to Frank Churchill," George replied. "And what were you agreeing with him about?"

"I'll tell you later," Emma hastily interjected. "Father, why don't you go upstairs and have a little rest before dinner?"

He nodded. "An excellent suggestion, especially if Dr. Hughes is to be calling. George, I do not approve of him. He drones on quite dreadfully."

"I think none of us approve of him, sir, but we must forebear."

Once George had escorted her father from the room, he returned to sit with Emma. "Now, what are your father and Frank in agreement about?"

"Father thinks Mr. Elton is to blame for much of the trouble in Highbury since Mrs. Elton's murder. Frank agrees with him."

"One can hardly blame either of them for that opinion, I suppose."

"Dearest, the poor man's wife was brutally murdered. I think we must make allowances."

"Very true. Just as I will make allowances for you going off with Frank to investigate that murder."

She quickly reached for the teapot. "Would you like another cup of tea?"

"A game attempt at diversion, my love. We *will* resume this conversation later, but I believe I just heard the door. That should be Dr. Hughes."

For once, Emma was grateful that the coroner was about to descend upon them. "Shall we offer him tea?"

"No. I've already had to put up with a great deal today, including a prison visit and an insolent pup winking at my wife."

She choked out a laugh. "For shame, George. Those two events cannot possibly be of equal concern."

Her husband looked about to retort when Dr. Hughes was ushered in.

"Thank you for your promptness," George said, going to meet him. "I promise we won't keep you long."

"When Mr. Knightley calls, I spring to action," he replied with a ponderous attempt at humor. "Now, sir, how can I be of help?"

"Dick Curtis is not guilty of Mrs. Elton's murder and must be released from the gaol."

Dr. Hughes peered at him over the top of his tiny spectacles. "And what is the proof of this?"

With an admirable economy of words—and declining to mention Emma's involvement—George outlined the evidence acquired from Farmer Mitchell. The doctor was soon nodding in agreement.

"That certainly seems definitive, Mr. Knightley, since Farmer Mitchell and his wife are most trustworthy people."

"So Dick will be released?" Emma asked.

"If Mr. Knightley will be so kind as to send a letter to the warden, I will inform Constable Sharpe that he is to turn the investigation in another direction."

She couldn't refrain from narrowing her gaze at him. "I hope that direction is not toward Miss Bates. That would be outside of enough."

While Dr. Hughes looked mildly affronted by her remark, he did not disagree. "Although it's true that her behavior was initially suspicious, Miss Bates does not possess the strength or temperament to carry out such a heinous crime."

Emma quietly breathed a sigh of relief. "Thank you, sir. I worried that the constable was fixed on the promissory note as sufficient motive for murdering Mrs. Elton."

"I believe the issues surrounding the note have been adequately addressed. I might also add that ladies, in general, are incapable of violent criminal acts. They are delicate creatures, easily overset by such things as the sight of blood."

Emma found his analysis both silly and irritating. Motivated by the greater good, however, she declined to debate with him.

"I don't imagine Constable Sharpe will be pleased to be told that he now has no viable suspects," she said instead.

Dr. Hughes shot up a dramatic finger. "But I think we do, Mrs. Knightley."

Emma exchanged a startled glance with her husband.

"This is news to me," said George. "Who is this suspect?"

"Why, the poultry thief, of course. He is back and has grown excessively bold. He is clearly a dangerous man and a vile thief."

Emma felt her jaw sag like an ill-fitting drawer, while George regarded the doctor with an astonished expression.

She found her voice. "Sir, I don't wish to be rude, but how does one go from raiding a chicken coop to murdering the vicar's wife?"

"Mrs. Knightley, I assure you that a man capable of stealing a much-prized Speckled Sussex hen is capable of anything."

*Good God.* Their coroner was a complete idiot.

"Doctor, I must admit that your theory seems a trifle unusual," George diplomatically commented.

Exasperated, Emma shook her head. "It seems nonsensical, if you ask me."

"Only to the untrained mind, Mrs. Knightley," the doctor replied in haughty tones. "Those of us who deal in such matters, however, can see what others cannot."

Sadly, what she could see was that Mrs. Elton's murder investigation had now descended into the realm of farce.

# Chapter 22

When Emma rejoined her husband in the drawing room after dinner, he put aside his book and stood.

"Is your father settled for the night?" he asked. "Or is he still fretting about the murderous inclinations of the poultry thief?"

She scowled. "I would dearly love to give Dr. Hughes a piece of my mind for spreading about his idiotic theory these past two days. The entire village has been abuzz with it. Fortunately, I was able to persuade my poor father to drink a glass of ratafia while he reads his book. That should help him sleep, and Simon will check on him in a bit."

"Then all is well. Now, come sit with me. It's a beautiful evening, and the fresh air is delightful."

He drew her to the sofa. Now that her father was in bed, George had dared to open the French doors so they could enjoy the rose-scented breeze drifting in from the gardens. Emma gratefully let go the stresses of the day and drank in the evening's quiet beauty as dusk descended on the landscape and transformed the oaks into shadows that towered toward the azure-blue sky.

After turning slightly to study her husband, she took in the abstracted frown marking his brow. "What are you thinking about?"

He glanced at her with a quick smile. "I am relishing the chance to spend a quiet evening with my wife. For once, there are no guests in need of reassurance and no crises looming before us."

"Indeed. We managed to go an entire evening without resorting to smelling salts or restorative glasses of brandy."

"In my case, sometimes more than one restorative glass," he dryly replied.

"I confess to being tempted to reach for the smelling salts more than once."

"Then we must hope those trying days are now behind us, and that life will soon return to normal."

She waggled a hand. "We can hope that, but is it likely?"

A grimace was his answer.

After a few moments, she gently poked him in the shoulder. "So, you're not really enjoying the peace and quiet. You're thinking about the investigation."

"Yes."

"Dearest, what part in particular troubles you?"

He lifted his brows. "Why do you think I'm troubled?"

"Any sane person would be. The entire thing has turned into a farce, thanks to our coroner. Besides, I can always tell when you're troubled or frustrated."

Since she'd been a major source of frustration for George in times past, Emma had come to recognize the signs.

He kissed her hand before rising to his feet. Despite his claim to the contrary, he had been restless since returning from Donwell before dinner.

After wandering over to the open doors, he braced a hand on the frame and gazed out into the deepening dusk. Emma took a few moments to appreciate her husband's broad shoulders and tall, masculine physique.

"I suspect you would also feel a certain degree of frustration if you'd spent much of the morning with Dr. Hughes and Constable Sharpe," he said, glancing over his shoulder. "Frankly, I barely managed to keep my temper."

"You're the magistrate, dearest. You're not allowed to lose your temper, no matter how silly or irritating people might be."

His smile was wry as he turned to face her. "A particularly annoying aspect of the position."

"Can I assume that Constable Sharpe agrees with Dr. Hughes regarding the poultry thief turned cold-blooded killer?"

"Yes, although he resisted the theory for quite some time. Dr. Hughes was not pleased about that."

Sharpe's change of view was surprising. "How astonishing. I had not supposed Mr. Sharpe capable of such a sensible view. But he did capitulate, obviously."

"I believe it stemmed mostly from the fact that he is lacking in credible suspects. He's even given up on Miss Bates, although not for want of trying. Fortunately, I managed to finally disabuse him of her purported guilt."

She rolled her eyes. "Then he's not so sensible, after all, if he could go straight from one silly theory to another."

"Dr. Hughes didn't leave him much choice."

"Has either of them provided an explanation as to why a common poultry thief would even be in the church, much less murdering Mrs. Elton?"

"Sharpe did venture the possibility that the thief was already lurking about the vicarage gardens, preparing to raid the chicken coop."

"In the middle of the day?" she asked, incredulous.

"I also expressed my skepticism, but Dr. Hughes reminded me that the thief had already mounted a prior attack during the daylight hours."

Despite her irritation, she couldn't help but laugh. "Mounted an attack? Did he truly say that?"

"Our coroner does have a flair for the dramatic."

"Particularly when it comes to his speckled hens. But according to Mr. Weston, that earlier theft was on a farm set back from the road, with the coops behind the barn. The kitchen gardens at the vicarage are easily seen from the lane, the churchyard, and the house."

"I also raised that point, without success."

Emma huffed. "Such nonsense. So, his theory is that the thief was lurking about the kitchen gardens, and then what?"

"According to Sharpe, he must have spied Mrs. Elton entering the church and seized the opportunity to rob her."

"Thus going from stealing chickens to bashing a woman over the head with a brass candlestick. It is beyond improbable, George."

"I agree, but Sharpe has charge of the investigation, and on this point, he has the full backing of Dr. Hughes."

She rose and went to the sideboard to fetch him a brandy and also thought to pour a sherry for herself. He accepted his glass with a smile and a kiss, and then they both settled back on the sofa.

"I devoutly hope we never see another murder in Highbury again," she commented as she nestled under his embracing arm. "A proper investigation, and the application of any degree of common sense, seems beyond the capabilities of those charged with seeing justice is done."

"Accept my sincere apologies for disappointing you," her husband wryly replied.

"Don't be silly. Of course I wasn't referring to you."

"I'm teasing, my darling. But it may be that Sharpe's original conclusion was the correct one."

"That Mrs. Elton was killed by a random thief?" She wrinkled her nose. "Perhaps, but there are so many unanswered questions, such as the state of Mrs. Elton's finances."

"Those unanswered issues may simply be coincidental."

Painful experience had taught Emma to distrust the appearance of coincidence. For instance, she'd once thought it entirely coincidental that Frank Churchill had spent so much time with Jane Fairfax and the Bates ladies last year.

"While I hate to admit that Constable Sharpe could be right," she said, "I suppose there's nothing to be done about it. Mr. Elton is extremely closemouthed when it comes either to his finances—"

George suddenly shifted to frown down at her. "When were you discussing Mr. Elton's finances with him?"

She mentally winced at her slip. "It came up *entirely* by chance. Mr. Elton stopped by Hartfield a few days ago, hoping to make a social call. As you can imagine, Father was quite upset and asked me to make it clear to Mr. Elton that his presence was not welcome."

"But I thought you'd already explained that to him?"

"I did, but Mr. Elton was very persistent. I was forced to explain *again* that it would be best if he refrained from calling at Hartfield for the present."

"So you went to the vicarage instead of sending a note?"

"I knew he would be distressed, so I thought it best to deliver the message in person."

"And during this visit the state of his finances just happened, quite by chance, to come up," he responded in a sardonic tone.

"Well . . ."

"Emma . . ."

She sighed and put down her glass. "I did pose a few questions—very discreetly—but he was markedly disinclined to discuss anything to do with his finances."

He snorted. "One can hardly imagine why."

"Really, dearest, it's not as if you aren't digging into the man's finances. I simply tried to take a more direct route."

"Obviously, with little success."

"Yes, although he did mention one thing I thought rather odd."

"Just one thing?"

"There's no need to tease, George. You've made your point."

He finally cracked a smile. "All right, what did he say that struck you as odd?"

"He said that when it came to financial matters, he relied entirely on Mr. Suckling for guidance. That statement, however, runs counter to what I heard during the funeral reception." She twirled a hand. "You remember, when they were fighting over money. At the time, Mr. Elton seemed to be blaming Mr. Suckling for mishandling some aspect of Mrs. Elton's finances. So, why would he subsequently tell me that he relied so heavily on his brother-in-law?"

George frowned at his now-empty glass. "I have no answer to that. But I'm not surprised by Elton's reluctance to discuss money matters with you. Most men of my acquaintance are quite private in that regard."

"Unlike Mrs. Elton, who was quite forthcoming in letting everyone know how much money she had."

"Or did not have."

"Or did not have," she admitted. "Has John discovered anything about their financial situation—or Mr. Suckling's, for that matter?"

"He has not, although he wrote to say that he will continue to investigate. I think we must be prepared, however, to accept that there is little fruit to be harvested from this line of inquiry. It could very well be that Mrs. Elton was murdered by a thief, now long gone."

All her instincts rebelled against such a simple explanation. "If only I could get into Mr. Elton's study again, I feel certain I would find something."

George put down his glass with a decided clink. "You are to attempt no such thing, my dear. And, for once, I need you to listen to me."

Emma adopted what she hoped was a suitably wounded expression. "I always listen to you, George."

"But this time I need you to actually *do* what I am asking of you. In fact, I think it best if you no longer call at the vicarage by yourself."

She was slightly startled by his serious tone. "Why ever not?"

"It's not appropriate."

Emma stared at him, perplexed. "But that makes no sense. I'm a married woman, and he is our vicar. George, if I didn't know better, I would think you were jealous of Mr. Elton. Which is—"

"Ridiculous," he replied. "My dear, I am not jealous, but have you forgotten that Elton was once your suitor? The current circumstances have generated a great deal of gossip in Highbury, some of it centered around you."

"It's hardly my fault that I discovered the body. As to the other issue, no one knew Mr. Elton was courting me. *I* didn't know Mr. Elton was courting me."

"Some did. John, for one."

"John is hardly about to exchange lurid tales with anyone in Highbury."

"Regardless, I think it best if you place a bit of distance between yourself and Elton. I fear he leans on you too much for support—and that *will* generate gossip."

"If people are going to gossip about anyone, it's Mr. Elton and Harriet. He seems to be quite taken with her, and she with him. Given their previous history, I find it entirely bizarre."

"I imagine it would be even more bizarre for Robert Martin," he replied. "I would therefore advise that Harriet distance herself from Elton, too."

"I have already made that suggestion."

"Sound advice, my dear. Please apply it to yourself, as well."

Emma thought about it for a few moments and then shrugged. "I suppose you're right. I truly feel for the poor man, but he certainly made a nuisance of himself over Miss Bates and Dick Curtis."

"Precisely. By the way, I spoke to Elton today."

She raised her eyebrows. "You did? And did he say anything about me that gave you this present cause for concern?"

"He did not, but I did ask him why he excluded Dick Curtis from the parish poor roll."

"Goodness, that must have been awkward."

"Thankfully, Elton acknowledged his error in keeping him off the roll in the first place. He takes full responsibility for subsequent events, and he told me that he has already written to Curtis to express his sincere regrets."

"One would hope he would make his apologies in person," she replied, feeling rather severe. "Given that his actions resulted in the poor fellow getting carted off to prison."

"I suspect our vicar is a trifle leery of meeting with Curtis in person," George dryly replied.

She had to agree, since Mr. Elton had never struck her as a man with a great deal of physical courage.

"Did he give a reason for keeping Dick off the roll in the first place?" she asked.

"Only that he objected to Dick's rough manners and rudeness."

That was certainly the old Mr. Elton, and not the new. "It hardly seems fair to expect a farm laborer to have the manners of a gentleman."

"Elton seemed sincerely apologetic and readily agreed to put Curtis on the roll."

"I'm glad to hear it. Now, I'd best check on Father and see that all is well."

As she started to rise, her husband wrapped his hand around her wrist and pulled her gently back down.

"I saw Mr. Suckling today, as well," he said.

She raised an enquiring brow. "So, he's back in Highbury. I take it that Mrs. Suckling did not accompany him?"

"No."

"I wonder why he returned. Oh! Perhaps he came back to help Mr. Elton with some financial matters."

If so, that might give her an opportunity to—

"I doubt it," her husband replied in a dampening tone. "What he did request, and quite vociferously, was an update on the investigation. He and his wife are impatient to see progress."

Emma sighed, disappointed. "I suppose I cannot blame him, although I'm not sure why he couldn't write to Mr. Elton for details."

"He wished to speak to Constable Sharpe in person. And to me," he added with a long-suffering look.

"I take it that he was not best pleased with your report."

"With Constable Sharpe's report, more to the point. He found the notion of the poultry thief as killer to be entirely risible."

"While Mr. Suckling is a very unpleasant man, he is certainly not stupid. I hope he didn't blame you for this silly state of affairs."

"He certainly did. In fact, I got quite the lecture on the incompetence of country magistrates."

Emma bristled on her husband's behalf. "I hope you put him in his place."

"I doubt he would have cared. Elton did try to manage him, but Suckling would have none of it."

She rested a hand against his cheek. "My poor George, what a day you've had."

When he took her hand and kissed her palm, the tender caress evoked a delightful sensation. "True, but dinner was excellent, and I have an evening alone with my enchanting wife."

"Then your enchanting wife will check on her father and return to you forthwith. She also promises to cease talking about murders and investigations, at least for the rest of the evening."

"Then I shall look forward to your return with great anticipation."

She rose and was halfway across the drawing room when the door flew open and Simon rushed in.

"Goodness," she exclaimed, stumbling to a halt. "What's the matter, Simon?"

"Begging your pardon, Mrs. Knightley, but it's your father," the footman blurted out.

Emma's heart skipped a beat. "What's wrong?"

"Mr. Woodhouse fell out of bed, and I can't wake him up."

Emma quietly closed her father's bedroom door before turning to see George coming up the stairs.

"Perry is gone, I take it," he said as he joined her. "Can I assume all is well?"

"Yes, thank goodness," she replied.

She handed an empty breakfast tray to Simon, who'd kept watch by the door all night with steadfast loyalty, ready to assist at a moment's notice.

"Thank you, Simon," she said to their senior footman. "That will be all for now, but have someone bring up a fresh pot of tea in an hour."

"I'll bring it myself, Mrs. Knightley."

Emma wagged a finger at him. "You kept watch all night, and now you should retire for some rest. Thomas or one of the kitchen staff can bring the tray up."

"Don't you be worrying about me, Mrs. Knightley," the young man stoutly replied. "I'll be fine."

Once Simon had retreated downstairs, George gently stroked

Emma's hair. "He obviously takes after the mistress of the house. Did you get any sleep, my darling?"

She rubbed the back of her neck. "More than I expected, although I cannot say that a leather club chair is particularly conducive to a comfortable rest."

George grimaced. "I would have sat with him, you know. There was no need to wear yourself out like this."

She patted his arm. "I'm just a bit creaky, which is nothing a hot bath cannot fix. Besides, I wished to be there in case Father woke up and was confused."

"Did he wake up during the night?"

"No," she ruefully replied. "As Mr. Perry predicted, he had a sound sleep."

*Very* sound, due to a quantity of laudanum large enough that Mr. Perry had initially feared it would send her father's heart into a fatal spasm. Fortunately, she and the apothecary had finally managed to rouse Father from his stupor. A purgative had been administered, and nature had then taken its course. A few hours later Mr. Perry had pronounced him out of danger, and he had subsequently passed a peaceful night in a deep but natural sleep.

Emma would never forget those terrifying moments when she and George had rushed upstairs to find the old darling unconscious, his breathing labored. A footman had run to summon Mr. Perry, who'd arrived with remarkable speed and swiftly diagnosed the condition, concluding that Father had ingested a fairly substantial dose of laudanum.

How he'd managed to do so, however, was a question yet to be answered.

"How is Henry, now that he is awake?" George asked.

"Much better. In fact, he managed to eat both a coddled egg *and* a bowl of gruel. I was quite surprised."

"I'm glad to hear it. I'm sorry I missed Perry, but I knew he would not leave your father if he had any lingering concerns."

She smiled. "Not surprising, since Father is his best patient."

While most of her father's complaints amounted to nothing more than minor ailments, last night's incident had been anything but minor. Mr. Perry had not departed Hartfield until the longcase clock in the hall struck two and his patient was clearly out of danger. He'd then returned before breakfast and stayed until satisfied that Emma's father was well on the mend.

"I think Henry gave even Perry a scare last night," George commented. "I've never seen him so concerned for your father's health."

She had to stifle a yawn. "Thankfully, he believes Father will not suffer any lasting effects."

George studied her with concern. "Emma, you must be exhausted. Why don't you lie down for a rest? I will sit with Henry."

"Thank you, dearest—perhaps I will later. First, I want to hear what you discovered."

He hesitated for a moment. "I think we must talk to your father, and hope that he will be able to shed more light on the situation."

She sighed. "So the servants have no idea how it could have happened?"

While Emma had spent the morning with her father, George had investigated the unnerving incident. There were a number of medicinal tinctures and concoctions in the house, most of which were in the stillroom and carefully supervised by Serle. It was possible, although hard to imagine, that someone might have inadvertently mixed up one medicinal with another. But her imagination could not supply the means by which the laudanum had then found its way into her father's wineglass.

"Unfortunately, no," George replied. "Serle was beside herself at the notion that anything coming from the kitchen or stillroom might have poisoned your father."

*Poisoned.*

The word hit like a hammer blow to the chest.

"*Poisoned* is a very strong word, George."

"It is accurate nonetheless." He put out a quick hand to stem her protest. "Although I believe it was entirely accidental."

Emma struggled with a brief surge of panic. "If Mr. Perry hadn't acted so quickly—"

"Thankfully, he did."

"Did you check the decanter in the drawing room?"

Emma had poured her father's ratafia from that decanter last night, but it was hard to believe that could be the source of the contamination.

"Unfortunately, because it was near empty, Thomas removed it last night and brought it to the kitchen to be washed and refilled."

"And neither he nor the scullery maid noticed anything amiss with the decanter?"

"They did not. Serle also checked the bottle of laudanum in the stillroom, and it seemed untouched from the last time it was used."

Emma nodded. "That makes sense. Father only occasionally takes the drops when his nervous stomach plagues him, but he's been ever so much better in that regard. I don't think he's had even one drop for the past few months."

George looked thoughtful. "Serle said that, as well. But your father has been very anxious about this murder business. Is it possible he put the drops in his glass last night and miscalculated the dose?"

"He does keep a small bottle of laudanum in his room, so it's possible. But it's normally Serle who adds the drops in his tea, which she sweetens with honey."

Since the drops themselves tasted bitter, they required a sweetener or other flavorings to make them palatable.

"Then the most reasonable explanation," George responded, "is that your father must have self-administered the drops last night and miscalculated. It seems all but impossible that one of the household staff could be responsible, even inadvertently."

She held up her hands. "Well, none of the servants have ever wanted to murder Father before, even when he was at his most fretful. So I doubt they would begin now."

When her husband's eyebrows all but shot up to his hairline, Emma winced. Clearly, Mr. Elton wasn't the only person whose mind had become unhinged by this summer's unfortunate events.

"How *dreadfully* inappropriate of me," she said. "My apologies, dearest. You may blame my ridiculous comments on lack of sleep."

He stooped and pressed a kiss to her lips. "There is nothing to forgive, my love. And one might also note that your observation is not entirely without merit."

She swatted his arm. "You're almost as bad as I am. What is the world coming to when Mr. Knightley loses all sense of propriety, just like his wife?"

"Marriage was bound to have some effect on my character."

"Not for the better, apparently," she wryly replied. "But I suppose we'd best go in and speak with Father."

"Is he well enough to discuss the situation?"

"I left him reading in his chair, and he seemed quite content. I do hate the idea of upsetting him, though. He'll be mortified if he did this to himself."

George held out his hand. "I know, but it must be done so the same mistake cannot happen again."

She briefly squeezed his fingers, drawing comfort from the warmth and strength of his grip, and then opened the door.

"You have a visitor, Father," she announced in a bright tone as they entered the room.

Her father, seated by the fireplace in his dressing gown and cozily wrapped in a cashmere shawl, looked up from his book with a gentle smile.

"Ah, George. I was hoping you would come to see me. I must apologize for putting everyone to such trouble. My poor Emma spent the entire night by my bedside." He reached for her hand. "I only hope she does not fall ill from holding such a strenuous vigil."

She stooped to press a quick kiss to his forehead. "You're not to worry about me, dearest. I'm perfectly fine."

"I insist that you rest this afternoon, my dear. George, tell Emma that she must rest."

"Not to worry, sir. I will see that she does so."

"Father, do you feel well enough to talk about what happened last night?"

He sighed. "George, will you please fetch Emma a chair and put it next to mine, right by the fire? I do not wish her to catch a chill."

Emma would have preferred to open a window, since the handsome room was quite warm enough, even without a fire.

As befitting the private domain of Hartfield's master, the bedroom was the largest in the house. After Isabella married John and moved to London, Emma had undertaken a flurry of renovations, including papering her father's bedroom and installing a new carpet and draperies in lovely shades of cream, gold, and cerulean blue. Ever resistant to change, Father had naturally objected. But no major refurbishing had been undertaken since the death of her mother, and Emma had found her father's room to be a trifle gloomy. Now, though, it was a cheerful, comfortable retreat, calculated to lift his sometimes depressed spirits.

Still, as she got a good look at the curtains in the bright morning light, she thought the gold fabric was looking a little faded. Perhaps it was time—

"My dear?" George said in a quizzical tone as he set a padded rosewood chair next to her father. "Would you like to sit?"

"Forgive me, George. I was woolgathering."

Her father sighed again. "About me, I suppose. What a trial I am to you both."

She winced, embarrassed that she'd started to mentally redecorate the room instead of attending to her father. But one couldn't spend *all* one's time fretting about one crisis or another. Doing so would be a very tiresome way to conduct one's life.

"You are never a trial," she said as she took her seat. "And we're very relieved that you're ever so much better this morning."

"Perry counseled that I am not to leave my room until after luncheon, and to avoid any strenuous activity for the rest of the day. So, I'm afraid we will have to forgo our walk around the garden, my dear."

Emma bit back a smile, because only he would regard their leisurely strolls around the rosebushes as strenuous activity.

"Never mind. You can always spend the rest of the day up here, where you won't be disturbed."

"I will certainly come down after luncheon," he replied, "since Miss Bates will be calling this afternoon."

Of course Miss Bates was coming. Emma could hardly remember the last time a day had passed when the spinster had *not* called at Hartfield.

"I'm sure Miss Bates would understand if you wished to stay up here and rest, Father."

He shook his head. "She will fret if she hears I've been ill. I do not wish to worry her."

In days past, it never would have occurred to him that his various ailments were a cause for concern for anyone beyond his immediate household.

"Only if you feel up to it," she dubiously replied.

He graced her with a beatific smile. "I will be perfectly fine, my dear."

She and George exchanged an incredulous glance. Normally, an episode of this magnitude would have prompted her father to take to his bed for a few days, at least. She hardly knew what to make of him anymore.

"Then since you are feeling better, sir," said George, moving to the side of the fireplace, "I hope you won't mind discussing what happened last night."

"Indeed, no," he replied. "Unfortunately, I can hardly remember a thing."

Mr. Perry had warned Emma that such might be the case. Under the circumstances, that was most unfortunate.

"Father, how did you feel when I escorted you upstairs?" she asked. "You seemed fine when Simon came in to help you prepare for bed."

He nodded. "I was a trifle fatigued, I will admit. All this murder business and that dreadful poultry thief cannot help but weigh on one's mind."

"Perfectly understandable," George said. "In fact, one might even expect one's sleep to be disrupted."

"Dear me, yes. How can one properly sleep knowing that such a desperate villain is at large?"

"Which is why I suggested you have a glass of ratafia," Emma said. "I thought it might help you relax."

"It seemed a sensible suggestion, my dear. But I did feel quite woolly-headed after I drank it." He grimaced an apology. "After that, I seemed to have dozed off in my chair. Simon helped me to bed, but I have only the vaguest recollection of him doing so."

Emma put up a finger. "You didn't finish your glass. Do you remember that?"

He'd left the wineglass, almost half-full, on the round table beside his reading chair. That was how Dr. Perry had been able to ascertain that the ratafia had contained a fairly large dose of laudanum, one that—given her father's age—could have caused a fatal heart spasm if he'd imbibed the entire thing. That horrible image made her blood turn icy, and for once, she was grateful for the warmth of the fire in the grate.

Her father frowned, as if struggling with the question. Then his brow suddenly cleared.

"I remember now. I didn't finish the drink, because it tasted rather odd. I thought perhaps that our wine supplier had sold us an inferior bottle." He shook his head. "You must speak to him, Emma. We cannot be serving inferior wine to our guests."

"It was the laudanum that altered the taste," she patiently replied. "Remember?"

"Oh, that's right. My memory is so frightfully bad. I don't know how you manage to put up with me."

She patted his hand. "We do so very well, I assure you. Now, this is important, Father. Do you think it's possible that you might have put the laudanum drops in the ratafia yourself and perhaps miscalculated the dose? You've given yourself laudanum in the past, usually just a few drops, when you had trouble sleeping. Perhaps you were afraid that you would lie awake and worry?"

He frowned again. "I must have, even though I have no recollection doing so. How else would the drops have gotten in my drink?"

George crossed to her father's dressing table. It held a large silver tray containing several small bottles of various tinctures, as well as packets of headache powders, provided by Mr. Perry.

After selecting a small dark brown bottle, he returned to them. "Is this it?"

Emma nodded. "Yes."

"Do you recollect how full it was before last night?"

She took the bottle and studied it, willing her brain to dredge up the memory. Alas, her brain was refusing to cooperate. "No, unfortunately. How frustrating."

"Please do not fret yourself, Emma," her father said. "Since neither you nor Serle nor Simon administered the drops, the only explanation is that I did so myself. I shouldn't be surprised at all, since one cannot possibly think clearly with dangerous villains running about Highbury. I'm sure I was distracted and simply failed to properly count the drops."

George nodded. "That is the most reasonable explanation. In the future, however, it might be best to have only Emma or Simon administer your drops from this bottle. Then you may be sure the dosage will be correct."

Her father looked rueful. "How very foolish of me. I shouldn't be surprised if you're both very angry with me for causing such a commotion."

Emma leaned forward and pressed his arm. "Dearest, of course we're not angry! We simply wish to make sure that nothing like this ever happens again."

He pressed her hand with his own. "With you and Simon taking care of me, not to mention George and Serle, I'm sure it will not. You always do everything so perfectly, my dear."

She mustered a smile, even though she couldn't shake the feeling that she had somehow failed him—and failed to get to the heart of yet another mystery. Even within the domestic sanctuary of Hartfield, the truth was proving elusive.

# CHAPTER 23

Emma stifled a yawn. Although she'd wished for nothing more than a quiet afternoon and no visitors, her father had felt otherwise. After a modest lunch, he'd insisted on coming downstairs to await the arrival of Miss Bates. Resigned, she'd thought it best to join them to keep a weather eye. She was determined Father not wear himself out.

Thankfully, she'd not been expected to join the conversation. After serving the pair tea, she'd retreated to a corner with her needlework to watch discreetly. Father seemed fine, listening attentively to Miss Bates's musings and observations while adding his commiserations and consolations, as required.

And there were many observations and many commiserations. Emma was ready to stuff cotton batting into her ears to avoid hearing yet another discussion of the combined perfidies of Constable Sharpe and Mr. Elton.

Although to be fair, Miss Bates displayed a truly Christian charity toward Mr. Elton by explaining away his actions as the confusion and distress of grief. Father, however, was not so ready to forgive. Despite Emma's best efforts to justify Mr. Elton's behavior to her parent, she suspected it would still be some time before the vicar was again welcome at Hartfield.

In the occasional idle moment, like now, she tried to imagine how she would respond if George were murdered. She doubted she would adopt Mr. Elton's model of patient suffering. In fact, Emma thought it highly likely that she would transform into an avenging harpy, albeit one in widow's weeds and armed with only a sharp-ended parasol. Since she looked dreadful in black and would probably grow queasy when stabbing villains with her pointy parasol, she could only be thankful that the odds of George getting murdered were extremely slim. After all, everyone loved him—unlike the poor departed Mrs. Elton.

"Emma," her father said, breaking into her silly imaginings, "you have let your tea grow cold. You must have a fresh cup and something to eat."

Miss Bates clasped her hands together in an earnest manner. "Indeed, Mrs. Knightley. Your father has been telling me how you never left his bedside last night. Such devotion is beyond anything, I vow. I will be sure to tell Mother all about it. She will be amazed, as will Jane. But you have always been the most devoted of daughters." She smiled at Father. "You have been so fortunate in your daughters, sir, as I have been so fortunate in Jane. She is like a daughter to me, you know, and none could be more devoted than she—except Mrs. Knightley, of course. No one can compare to Mrs. Knightley. But how terrified you must all have been! I should have been in a dreadful fright to see you brought so low, Mr. Woodhouse."

"I can hardly fathom how it could have happened but for my own foolishness," he replied. "Thank goodness for Mr. Perry and my dear Emma. She is patience itself, Miss Bates, even though I must greatly try her at times."

"Father, that is entirely silly," said Emma when she was finally able to put in a word. "No one could have a better parent.

And I know that Jane feels just the same about you, Miss Bates. We are both of us fortunate in our families."

The spinster gave her a sweet smile. "Dear Mrs. Knightley. Indeed, Jane is the kindest girl one could ever hope to meet. Why, I remember one time—"

"And how is Jane?" Emma interrupted, hoping to forestall another anecdote detailing Jane's many virtues. "I've not seen her in two days. I hope she is feeling well, and I trust that Frank is taking good care of her."

"Indeed," Miss Bates replied, properly diverted. "Randalls is the perfect place for a good rest, you know. Such a healthful environment—quite the best one could imagine. Except for Hartfield, of course. No house could be more conducive to one's health than Hartfield."

Emma's father looked much struck. "Very true. Randalls is well enough, and dear Miss Taylor—"

"Dear Mrs. Weston," Emma automatically corrected.

"Keeps a fine house," her father serenely continued. "But Hartfield has Serle, and that makes all the difference."

The two friends then embarked on a lengthy discussion about Jane's health, the merits of Hartfield's cook versus Randalls's cook, and the sorts of food most appropriate for a woman in the family way. Emma was once more able to let her mind wander as she pretended to do her needlework.

She'd almost fallen into a doze when the door opened and George entered the drawing room. Quickly rousing herself, she rose to her feet.

"Good afternoon, dearest," she said. "Are you joining us for tea, or must you be off to Donwell?"

"Neither. Constable Sharpe has come to call, and I'd like you to join us in my study."

She sighed. As if this day hadn't been trying enough.

Miss Bates, who'd also stood when George appeared, sank back onto the settee, pressing a trembling hand to her throat.

"H-how distressing," she stuttered. "Constable Sharpe. Dear

me, whatever can he want? I hope I don't have to speak to him, Mr. Knightley. Perhaps I should go. If only I can do so without seeing him. It is foolish of me to be so nervous, but I cannot seem to help it."

Emma's father now came to his feet, the picture of genteel offense. "George, I will *not* allow that man to continue to persecute Miss Bates. He believes he can come into my home at any time and attempt to frighten us. It must stop, or I will be having words with him."

"I'm sure there's nothing to worry about," Emma hastened to reassure. "No doubt he's simply stopping by to discuss some small detail of the investigation."

At least she hoped so. If he tried to arrest Miss Bates again, she would be tempted to stab the dratted man with a very pointy parasol, even though he was a constable.

George held up a calming hand. "You need have no fears, Miss Bates. In fact, Constable Sharpe has arrested Mrs. Elton's murderer, or so he believes."

His announcement produced a stunned silence.

"Never say it's the poultry thief," Emma finally exclaimed.

Her husband cast her a sardonic glance. "I'm sorry to disappoint, but no."

Father looked affronted. "You mean that villain is *still* at large? I must speak to the constable, George. This state of affairs is deplorable."

Emma had to press a finger to her lips to hold back a laugh. Only her father could so dramatically miss the forest for the trees.

"Perhaps it might be best if we defer that discussion for now," she said. "George will be sure to raise it at the appropriate time."

"The poultry thief is, of course, very frightening," Miss Bates ventured in a tentative voice. "But can it truly be that Mrs. Elton's murderer has finally been caught?"

George nodded. "So it would seem."

The spinster clasped her hands in a prayerful attitude, her cheeks flushing a bright pink. "Heavens, what a blessing! I do not mean to complain, Mr. Knightley, but I have been in such a terrible flutter, no matter how hard I try to be brave. And poor Mother and Jane! It has been such an ordeal for them both. If not for the support of all my dear friends, especially Mr. Woodhouse—" She broke off, overcome with emotion.

Emma's father sat and took her hand. "You have undergone a great trial, Miss Bates. Who could blame you for possessing such feelings?"

"Your trials are now over, ma'am," George said. "There is no further cause for alarm."

The spinster drew in a shuddering breath. "I hardly know what to think. Dear me, should I thank Constable Sharpe? It is such a relief, you know. He has been so very annoyed with me."

"I hardly think that's necessary," Emma said. "He was wrong to suspect you in the first place."

Besides, if Miss Bates were to engage in one of her lengthy apologies, Constable Sharpe might never get around to telling them who the murderer was.

"You will certainly *not* apologize," said Emma's father. "Mr. Sharpe acted in a very low manner and treated you most improperly."

"But if he caught the killer, should we not thank him?" she asked. "It seems the Christian thing to do."

"If you wish to thank anyone, thank Mr. Elton," said George. "He's the one who identified the killer and saw to his arrest."

That led to another stunned silence. Emma practically had to push up her sagging jaw with her thumb. "What? How?"

"Mr. Elton!" cried Miss Bates. "How very courageous of him to capture his wife's killer. I can hardly bear to think of the perils he must have faced in doing so. He has always been such a kind and mild person, but to hear that he faced down a ruthless killer . . . one hardly knows what to think."

"Most irregular," huffed Father. "I'm not sure I approve of such doings."

*God, give me strength.*

"George," Emma said from between gritted teeth. "Who is this blasted killer?"

Her father regarded her with dismay. "My dear, such language."

Emma ignored him to scowl at her husband. She had the clear sense that he found this absurd conversation amusing.

"George," she said in a warning tone.

He gave her a slight smile. "The constable has arrested Mr. Suckling. Apparently, he has been found in possession of Mrs. Elton's necklace."

As Miss Bates let out a squeak, Emma found herself once more gaping at her husband. It took a moment to gather her startled wits.

"How did this revelation come to light?" she asked.

"Apparently, one of Mr. Elton's servants found the necklace in Suckling's luggage."

Emma plopped down in her chair, turning that bit of news over in her head. "But if he killed Mrs. Elton and took her necklace, why would he leave it where someone could find it?"

Much less cart it about with him, waiting for it to be discovered. It seemed entirely deranged. Then again, most killers probably *were* deranged.

Miss Bates flapped her hands like an agitated goose. "Mr. Knightley, how can this be? The Eltons and the Sucklings were so very close. Mrs. Elton was forever speaking of their intimate relationship and of the beauties of Maple Grove. Why, it was a second home to her. And Mr. Suckling is such a genteel man and so very distinguished."

Father harrumphed. "I never liked the man. He was quite rough in speaking to Mrs. Goddard at the inquest, and he insisted the windows be kept wide open. So reckless a man could be guilty of anything."

Emma had now overcome her shock and rose from her chair. "We'd best go speak to Constable Sharpe. I hope he will be able to shed some light on the matter."

"That is my hope, as well," George dryly replied.

"Miss Bates and I will wait for you, Emma," her father said. "I will wish to hear everything. And please ensure that the constable leaves as soon as you are finished speaking with him. Miss Bates should not have to see him."

The spinster gave him a misty smile. "Dear, dear Mr. Woodhouse, always so concerned for my welfare."

"It is my pleasure, dear lady," said Father, taking her hand again.

A rather alarming thought popped into Emma's brain, but she batted it away. It was a silly notion. Besides, there were much more important matters to attend to.

After promising to return as soon as possible, she and George left the room.

"It would seem you were correct in your assessment of Suckling's character," her husband said as they headed toward his study.

"I believe we shared that assessment, but I never thought him a murderer."

"Apparently, he is."

She waggled a hand. "I neither like nor trust the man, but that doesn't mean he's a killer."

"Hopefully, Constable Sharpe can provide more detail."

When they entered the study, Sharpe rose from his seat in front of George's desk. His attitude was somber, and he even forgot himself enough to give Emma a respectful bow. He remained standing while George moved behind his desk and Emma took one of the chairs in front of it.

"Constable, where is Mr. Suckling now?" George asked as he settled into his chair.

"On his way to Guildford, sir. Dr. Hughes is taking him to

be placed in the gaol. The doctor took his own carriage, along with Mr. Elton's footmen to keep the prisoner under control."

George's eyebrows snapped together in an intimidating frown. "He is already being transferred to prison? When was he arrested?"

"First thing this morning, Mr. Knightley. The incident occurred right after breakfast—"

"By the *incident*, you mean the discovery of the missing necklace?" Emma interrupted.

"Aye, Mrs. Knightley. That and the fight between Mr. Suckling and Mr. Elton. That's when the vicar's footman came running to fetch me."

"Why was I not told of this?" George sternly asked.

The constable grimaced an apology. "Begging your pardon, sir, but we knew Mr. Woodhouse was feeling poorly, so I thought it best to send for Dr. Hughes first. And then he said we shouldn't be bothering you." He twirled a hand. "On account of Mr. Woodhouse being taken so ill."

"It is not the coroner's job to arrest suspects," George replied, clearly annoyed by the abrogation of his authority.

The constable shook his head. "No, sir, but it is my job, and I would have done it without any say-so from Dr. Hughes."

"They why is Dr. Hughes escorting the prisoner to the gaol, and not you?"

Sharpe's thin features pulled downward into a sour expression. "I made that point myself, sir, but Dr. Hughes insisted he accompany the prisoner. He said he was best placed to take Suckling's statement. That way, he would know it to be accurate for the indictment."

"Coroners do not issue indictments, either," George replied in a clipped tone.

"Don't I know it," muttered the constable.

George tapped his desktop. "I will want a full report in writing from both you and Dr. Hughes."

Although loath to overstep her husband's authority, Emma couldn't wait a second longer. "And speaking of reports, what happened? Did Mr. Elton and Mr. Suckling actually get into a fight?" She twirled a finger. "As in fisticuffs?"

Her mind was still attempting to conjure up the image of their weedy vicar engaging in a physical contest.

"More like a beating, Mrs. Knightley," the constable grimly replied. "Mr. Suckling tried to throttle poor Mr. Elton."

Her mind was instantly catapulted back to the church and the bruises on Mrs. Elton's throat. Emma felt her stomach revolt.

"Good heavens," she managed.

George looked astonished but quickly recovered. "Constable, why don't you start at the beginning? How did all this come about?"

"It was all a bit garbled, sir, with the vicar being so distraught. Mr. Suckling gave the poor fellow a right good crack to the jaw before he got his hands around his throat." He shook his head. "Mr. Elton was a terrible sight, Mr. Knightley. That was another reason I sent for Dr. Hughes straight off. Mr. Elton was fair knocked about."

Emma pressed a hand to her throat, which suddenly felt too tight. "How dreadful."

George nodded. "Under the circumstances, it certainly made sense to send for Dr. Hughes. But let me try to understand. You said one of the servants found the missing necklace in Mr. Suckling's luggage?"

"The housekeeper did. Mr. Suckling was to return to London first thing this morning, and Mrs. Wright was bringing some fresh laundry up to his room. That's when she found the necklace."

Emma frowned. "Just sitting in his luggage, waiting to be discovered? Why would he not hide it someplace safe instead of carrying it about with him?"

"Mr. Elton says Mr. Suckling probably thought it was safest close by or on himself. He said no one would think Mrs. Elton's own brother-in-law would kill her."

Emma shot a glance at George, whose skeptical expression probably mirrored her own.

"And what was Mr. Suckling's response to the discovery of the necklace?" George asked.

"I told you, sir. He tried to throttle Mr. Elton."

"But surely he didn't immediately launch himself at Mr. Elton," Emma impatiently said. "Did Mr. Suckling not have anything to say for himself first?"

"I was just getting to that, ma'am, if you'll let me finish my report," Sharpe replied in an aggrieved tone.

"It would certainly be helpful if you could relate the events in order," she said. "You seem to be working back to front."

Bristling, the constable opened his mouth as if to rebut her, but George swiftly intervened. "It would be useful to know what happened before the assault, Constable. I assume Mr. Suckling and Mr. Elton exchanged words."

Sharpe threw Emma a disgruntled look before returning his attention to George.

"They did, sir. Mr. Suckling claimed he had no idea how the necklace got into his luggage, and told Mr. Elton he was a fool for thinking he had anything to do with Mrs. Elton's murder. According to Mrs. Wright, things got right heated after that, and Mr. Suckling accused Mr. Elton of being a traitor."

Emma raised her eyebrows at George. "A traitor? What could he possibly mean by that?"

The constable shrugged. "You'll have to ask Mr. Elton—or Mr. Suckling."

"I intend to," George replied. "What happened next?"

"Mr. Elton accused Mr. Suckling of killing his wife. That's when Mr. Suckling attacked him. By the time the footmen got into the room, he had the vicar down on the floor with his hands around his throat. Took two of them to pull the villain off poor Mr. Elton."

Emma could barely fathom what she was hearing. She'd certainly not found Mr. Suckling a trustworthy or likable person, but to learn that he was capable of such violence was appalling. Even so, it simply made no sense. What motive could he have for murdering his sister-in-law?

"Did Mr. Elton have any explanation for why Mr. Suckling would murder his own wife's sister?" she asked.

"The oldest in the world, ma'am," the constable replied. "Money."

She frowned. "Did it have something to do with Mrs. Elton's money troubles? We know that she was experiencing a degree of agitation in that regard, but surely that is hardly a rational motive for her murder."

"Murder is never rational, Mrs. Knightley," Sharpe pedantically replied. "It's the foulest of deeds and springs from a disordered mind."

Mr. Suckling hardly struck her as someone with a disordered mind, despite this morning's violent episode. "I'm sure that is often the case. But if the motive is strong enough, it might be considered an entirely rational act—at least from the killer's point of view."

"When it comes to murder, I believe I have a greater knowledge of the criminal mind than you, Mrs. Knightley," Sharpe huffily replied.

Emma graced him with her sweetest smile—so sweet it made her teeth tingle. "Mr. Sharpe, with this one exception, no one has been murdered in Highbury in our lifetimes, much less during your term as constable."

He drew his lanky frame to its full, offended height. "I'll have you know, ma'am, that I have studied the subject at great length, and—"

George rapped his knuckles on his desktop. "May I suggest

we refrain from embarking on theoretical discussions of the criminal mind and stick to the matter at hand?"

Emma wrinkled her nose at her husband in silent apology.

"Just as you say, sir," the constable stiffly replied.

George nodded. "Then please continue. You stated that money was the motive for Mrs. Elton's murder. In what way, exactly?"

"Mr. Elton believes that Mr. Suckling was in the River Tick and—"

"What does that mean?" Emma interrupted.

"It means he was in debt," George explained.

"Really? What an odd expression."

"As I was saying," Sharpe said in a long-suffering tone, "Mr. Elton is now convinced that Mr. Suckling has substantial money troubles and is trying to hide them. He believes that Mrs. Elton had discovered what was going on, and was going to tell her sister and then expose Mr. Suckling's chicanery to the world."

Emma all but goggled at him. "That makes *no* sense. While I can understand Mrs. Elton wishing to inform her sister—assuming Mrs. Suckling wasn't already aware—publicly exposing Mr. Suckling would ruin not only his reputation and standing but his wife's, as well. That is hardly an act of sisterly charity."

If her own brother-in-law were to find himself in the River Tick, Emma would move heaven and earth to protect Isabella and the children. Mrs. Elton had her faults, but surely she would protect her sister, with whom she had—by all appearances—a close relationship.

"What proof did Mr. Elton provide that would bear his theory out?" George asked.

Mr. Sharpe held up a finger. "The vicar discovered some letters between Mr. Suckling and Mrs. Elton—very suspicious letters."

They both waited for Sharpe to elucidate at greater length.

The constable, however, simply regarded them with a triumphantly smug expression.

"And what did these letters say?" George finally asked.

"I wouldn't know, exactly," Sharpe admitted. "Dr. Hughes took them with him."

Emma's patience fully deserted her. "George, this is utterly ridiculous. Dr. Hughes has absconded with all the evidence, leaving us with nothing but vague theories and accusations."

Her husband looked as irritated as she felt. "It's certainly an irregular way to conduct an investigation."

"Begging your pardon, Mr. Knightley," the constable said, "but it's not my fault if Dr. Hughes took the evidence with him, and poor Mr. Elton was in no shape to give a clear account of events. I'm not best pleased about the state of things, neither."

Emma felt a twinge of sympathy for Sharpe. Clearly, he was no happier with Dr. Hughes than they were.

"How very annoying of him to run off with both the evidence *and* the suspect," she said. "I cannot think what got into him."

"I can," George sardonically replied.

Enlightenment dawned on Emma. "Ah, I suppose he wishes to take the credit for solving the murder. I must say that's not very charitable of him."

Sharpe again fell to muttering under his breath, clearly aggrieved with his crime-fighting colleague.

"Constable, do you have anything else to add?" George asked.

"No, sir. I've told you all I know. For more, you'll have to wait until Dr. Hughes returns this evening."

Emma thought for a moment. "We could call on Mr. Elton now."

The constable looked startled. "He's a right mess, Mrs. Knightley. Took quite a beating, he did."

"Then all the more reason to visit," she briskly replied as she rose to her feet. "The poor man will need our support after suffering such a harrowing experience. George, I'll just nip down to the kitchen and ask Serle to put together a basket of nourishing foodstuffs. And I have a very effective tincture for pain and bruising, so I'll fetch that, too."

Her husband stood. "My dear, I'm sure Mrs. Wright has everything she needs to—"

"Nonsense. One cannot depend entirely on servants in cases such as this. Mr. Elton needs his friends right now. He needs us."

Emma truly believed that. She also believed they wouldn't get any straight answers about Mr. Suckling until they heard it directly from Mr. Elton himself.

She began to mentally tick off a list of necessary supplies. "George, perhaps you can pop in and explain things to Father while I gather up what I need. I'll meet you in the entrance hall in a half hour."

He eyed her with a skeptical expression and then simply shrugged his acquiescence. Emma graced him with an approving smile as she hurried from the room.

# Chapter 24

"It would make life easier if Mr. Suckling were indeed the murderer," Emma said to her husband as they walked toward the vicarage. "But there are so many unanswered questions."

"Such as?"

"For one, Mr. Suckling was ostensibly in London that day. How could he slip in and out of Highbury unnoticed? That would take a great bit of luck."

"Presumably, he came by horse, which would mean only one animal to keep out of sight for a short period of time. It's possible that someone did see him, especially on the road, but would not remark on it. Remember that it was a very hot day, and few people were out and about. You mentioned that yourself, as I recall."

He shifted the large basket of supplies to his other arm.

Emma frowned, momentarily diverted. "George, you should have allowed one of the footmen to carry the basket. I'm sure it's much too heavy."

He cast her an amused glance. "My dear, I know I strike you as a weedy sort of fellow, but I am well able to carry it."

She scoffed, since her husband was one of the tallest and fittest men in the parish and had a fine set of shoulders, which she admired on a regular basis. "I simply don't wish you to get overheated."

"I am hardly likely to get overheated by walking a scant ten minutes to the vicarage. Although it does appear that you emptied half the contents of the medicine chest into this basket, as well as most of Serle's baking."

"Perhaps I did overdo it, but poor Mr. Elton! Under the circumstances, one feels one cannot do enough."

He immediately sobered. "Yes, it's truly hard to believe."

That reminded her of another niggling doubt. "Why do you think Mr. Suckling was so secretive in his meeting with Mrs. Elton? Surely he didn't travel to Highbury with the express intention of killing her."

"He might well have."

She let that horrid thought settle for a moment. "Very well, let's say that is so. Why would Mrs. Elton agree to meet him secretly? And in the church, of all places?"

"Perhaps because she didn't wish her husband to know about their meeting. And barring a secluded country lane or a spot in the woods, I can think of few places more private than the church on a quiet Saturday afternoon."

"She was also to meet Miss Bates, don't forget."

"I imagine that Suckling didn't realize his sister-in-law would be meeting Miss Bates."

"George—" She broke off to acknowledge a greeting from Mrs. Peters, who was out tending the small vegetable garden in front of her cottage.

"Mrs. Peters seems a great deal improved," commented George as they passed by.

"Yes, she was able to return to work at Ford's last week."

"That is excellent news."

Emma eyed her husband. After his brief spasm of irritation

during the interview with Constable Sharpe, he had reverted to his usual state of calm. In fact, one might call him positively phlegmatic—quite a mental feat given the dramatic events of the day.

"George, what aren't you telling me?"

He lifted both eyebrows in exaggerated surprise. "Are you suggesting I would withhold information from my beloved wife?"

"If you're implying that *I* withhold information from *you*, that is simply untrue. I always tell you everything."

"Eventually," he wryly replied.

She couldn't really deny the point. "I would still like to know what you're thinking."

"I'm surprised it hasn't already occurred to you."

"Please humor me."

"Very well. I'm thinking how easy it should be to ascertain Suckling's whereabouts on the day of the murder. If he was in London, he should be able to prove that."

She sighed. "I don't know why I didn't think of that."

Undoubtedly, the shocks of the past twenty-four hours, coupled with lack of sleep, had addled her brain.

"Mrs. Suckling should be able to account for her husband's movements," George added.

"But could be she counted upon to tell the truth if it casts her husband in an unpleasant light?"

"We shall see if Mr. Elton can shed light on some of these questions. If, that is, he is well enough to receive us."

"He'll see us." Even when Mrs. Elton was alive and relations were frosty, Mr. Elton never turned down an invitation to Hartfield or refused to see Mr. Knightley.

They walked in silence for a few moments, with only the twitter of sparrows disturbing the quiet of Vicarage Lane.

"George, do *you* believe Mr. Suckling is the murderer?" she finally asked.

"I reserve judgment, but the presence of the stolen necklace, for one, seems rather definitive."

The necklace did rather trump other considerations.

"He's certainly an unpleasant person," Emma mused, "and it's become clear that he and Mr. Elton had a troubled relationship."

"One that now seems to have extended to Mrs. Elton, as well."

"What a tangled web," she said with a grimace. "If he did murder Mrs. Elton, I cannot help wondering if Mrs. Suckling knew. Perhaps that's why she never came down to Highbury. She couldn't face Mr. Elton."

"An excellent question."

Another thought darted into her head, and she grabbed her husband's sleeve. "George, what if she *does* know and *approves* of Mr. Suckling's actions? Wouldn't that implicate her in the crime?"

He shot her a startled frown. "That's a grim thought. But a wife cannot be made to testify against her husband, which would make it difficult to arrive at the truth in that regard."

Emma blew out a frustrated sigh. "How convenient for them. So, they could give each other an alibi for that day?"

"Correct. Under the law, husband and wife are considered to be one person, and one cannot be forced to testify against himself or herself."

"That's annoying."

"It wouldn't matter, anyway. In criminal cases a wife is not considered competent to give reliable testimony."

She stopped dead in her tracks, irritation turning to disgust. "You're joking."

"I'm the magistrate, my dear. I would never joke about something like that."

With the vicarage now in sight, she took his elbow and began to march forward. "Believing a wife is not competent to testify is a completely antiquated way of thinking, George. I hope you realize that."

"I do. And if I am ever on trial for committing a crime, I will make it clear that any evidence you wish to present against me is completely reliable."

"Are you trying to annoy me?"

"The opposite, my Emma. You've had a trying time of it these past few days, and I do not wish you to fret unduly. I assure you that I will do everything in my power to see that justice is done."

Her flashed of irritation evaporated. "I know you will, dearest. I have complete faith in you."

They walked up the short path to the vicarage door, but when Emma reached for the knocker, George stopped her.

"If Sharpe's account of this morning's events is accurate, Mr. Elton will likely be in a poor state," he said. "You should prepare yourself and try to temper any shock you may feel."

"Oh dear. Of course you're right. It would be upsetting for poor Mr. Elton if I displayed too great a degree of distress."

"I do not wish *you* to be unduly distressed, either. If the situation proves too much for you, please find a way to communicate that to me."

She went up on tiptoe and kissed his cheek. "I will be fine, dearest. I promise."

He looked skeptical but reached for the door knocker.

George had barely rapped before the door was yanked open by a rather disheveled-looking footman.

"Mr. Knightley, Mrs. Knightley," he exclaimed.

When he continued to peer at them, as if mystified by their presence, Emma and George exchanged a glance.

"Is Mr. Elton at home?" George finally asked.

The footman roused himself. "Begging your pardon, sir, but we wasn't expecting visitors today, to tell you the truth."

Emma eyed the nasty bruise on the young man's right cheek. "I'm sure it's been a terribly difficult day."

"Indeed, ma'am. I never thought to see the like." He grimaced. "First, Mr. Suckling murders poor Mrs. Elton, and then he attacks Mr. Elton, then me, then poor Joseph. A body hardly knows what—"

"That will be all, Percy," snapped an imperious voice.

As if summoned by a wizard, Mrs. Wright appeared out of nowhere—a talent she seemed to possess in abundance.

In his haste to scuttle back from the door, Percy almost tripped over his feet. "Yes, Mrs. Wright. I was just telling Mr. and Mrs. Knightley—"

"So I heard," she coldly interrupted. "Please keep your attention on your work instead of gossiping about matters that are none of your business."

When the poor fellow turned a bright pink, Emma leveled a disapproving frown at the housekeeper. But the woman, impervious to that sort of thing, ignored her to run a contemptuous eye over the footman instead.

"Go to your room and make yourself presentable," Mrs. Wright said. "Immediately."

When Percy bobbed his head, clearly mortified, Emma couldn't help but bristle. She'd always considered it the height of rudeness to embarrass a servant in front of guests.

"Thank you, Percy," she called after him as he hurried away.

He flashed a grateful smile over his shoulder before disappearing into the back hall.

Mrs. Wright dipped into a shallow curtsy. "I beg pardon for any offense, Mr. Knightley. We were not expecting visitors."

"There was no offense taken," he replied. "A degree of disruption is not to be wondered at, given the events of the day."

"You are very kind, but there can be no excuse for slipshod behavior."

Emma could barely refrain from rolling her eyes. "It's not every day that one stumbles upon a murderer, who then tries to throttle the master of the house. That would be bound to upset even the most experienced servant."

When the housekeeper transferred her stony gaze to Emma, George stepped into the breach.

"Is Mr. Elton well enough to receive visitors? We do not wish to disturb him if he's indisposed."

The stony gaze flickered back to him, displaying not one iota of emotion. In fact, it struck Emma as rather fishlike—a dead fish.

"I will enquire with Mr. Elton." She reached for the basket. "Allow me to take that, sir."

George handed it over. "Please tell Mr. Elton—"

The woman pivoted on her heel and marched from the hall.

"Good God," Emma exclaimed. "She had the nerve to upbraid that poor footman, then turns her back on you and leaves us standing in the hall."

"She was no doubt offended by your pointed observation," George replied with unimpaired calm. "Still, her response certainly left something to be desired."

"Rather more than something. She's almost as annoying as her former mistress. I suppose Mrs. Elton's behavior must have rubbed off on her."

"That must be a comfort to Mr. Elton, then."

Emma tried to stifle a laugh. "George, that is too bad of you."

He placed his hat on a side table by the door. "I am simply following your lead, my dear."

"Don't expect me to apologize. The dratted woman couldn't even take your hat."

"It's no matter."

While they waited, Emma drew up a mental list of questions she hoped to ask Mr. Elton—all with sensitivity, of course. She wished she could also speak with the servants, since they were often highly useful sources of information. Their days were tightly stitched into the lives of their employers—so much so that their presence was often forgotten. Who knew what they'd overheard these past few weeks inside the walls of the old vicarage?

Finally, they heard a quick footstep, and Mrs. Wright reentered the hall. "If you will please follow me, Mr. Elton will receive you in the family parlor."

"Goodness knows why that took so long to arrange," Emma whispered to her husband.

"Perhaps he was making himself presentable," he murmured back.

She felt a twinge of guilt. As much as she wanted answers, Emma didn't wish the poor man to further injure himself on their account.

Mrs. Wright led them to the parlor and announced their presence. Mr. Elton, seated in the wingback chair by the window, flung off the shawl covering his knees and painfully clambered to his feet.

"Dear sir and madam, come in," he said in a raspy voice. "Do forgive me for not coming out to greet you. As you can see, I am not at my best."

When Emma came to a dead halt inside the doorway, it forced George to take a quick step to the side to avoid bowling her over. She barely noticed because she was utterly horrified by the sight of their vicar.

He was ashen but for the left side of his jaw, which was colored in lurid shades of purple and blue. His lower lip had been split and was swollen. Emma winced in sympathy, as Mr. Suckling had obviously delivered some hard blows before attempting to throttle Mr. Elton. The soft woolen scarf wrapped around his throat in place of a cravat or clerical collar was no doubt due to that assault.

"Good heavens, Mr. Elton," she said with dismay. "Are you

sure you should be receiving visitors? Do you wish us to go away?"

With surprising alacrity, he advanced upon her, both hands outstretched. Instinctively, she mirrored the gesture, and he grasped her hands—rather a bit too firmly. But the poor man was obviously distraught and much in need of comfort.

"I cannot think our call is well timed, sir," George added in a concerned voice. "It's clear you are sorely in need of rest. I can return tomorrow to discuss the situation and lend any assistance you may require."

Mr. Elton glanced at George and attempted a smile, which immediately transformed into a grimace of pain. He waited a few seconds—still gripping Emma's hands—until he collected himself.

"Your visit is most welcome, Mr. Knightley. And, Mrs. Knightley, your kindness always lifts one's spirits, especially after so harrowing a day."

"Mr. Knightley and I are happy to help in any way that we can," she replied as she discreetly tried to reclaim her hands.

Thankfully, as he had in the church after a distraught Mr. Elton had thrown himself on her bosom, George came to her rescue by taking the vicar gently but firmly by the elbow.

"Mr. Elton, you must not be standing about in your condition," he said. "Allow me to escort you back to your seat."

The vicar finally released Emma's hands, now looking rather embarrassed. At least, she thought he looked embarrassed. It was hard to tell, given the sorry state of his features.

"Madam, please forgive my excess of emotion. I hardly know what I am about. It is a cruel blow, a very cruel blow. I cannot imagine how I will ever recover."

"Your feelings are completely natural," she replied. "But my husband is correct. You must take care not to unduly exert yourself."

As George solicitously guided the vicar back to his chair, she turned to address Mrs. Wright, who had remained out in the hall. But words died on her lips, and her mind went blank with shock. The housekeeper was regarding her with a truly venomous expression that could only be described as hatred.

Then, almost instantly, the woman's expression transformed into a bland visage, though something still lingered in her pale gray eyes. That something sent a shiver down Emma's spine.

"Did you wish something, Mrs. Knightley?" the housekeeper asked in a toneless voice.

Emma mentally shook herself. "The tea tray, please. And the tincture in the blue bottle that is in our basket."

"Would that be a goldenrod preparation, madam?"

"Yes."

"Dr. Hughes has already left treatments," Mrs. Wright replied, her tone now haughty.

*Heavens.* What was wrong with the dratted woman?

She narrowed her gaze. "Nonetheless, I would ask you to bring it."

Mrs. Wright seemed to struggle with herself for a moment but then inclined her head. "Very good, madam. Is there anything else?"

"No." Then Emma shut the door in her face.

As she turned back to the men, it occurred to her that *she'd* just embarrassed the housekeeper in front of the woman's master. Sadly, she couldn't find it in herself to feel guilty.

Although George was regarding her with some amusement, Mr. Elton grimaced.

"Please forgive Mrs. Wright's behavior," the vicar said. "My wife's death has left her feeling very low, and I believe this morning's incident was too much for her. In fact, she has given her notice."

Emma blinked in surprise. "She gave her notice this very morning?"

"Oh, no. It was a few days ago." He sighed. "It's for the best, I suppose."

"I'm surprised she would abandon you so precipitously," she replied, irritated on his behalf. "Surely she could have waited until you found another housekeeper."

"You are very kind. However, I doubt I will be hiring another housekeeper. At the moment, I have no need for a large establishment. Events have also shown that I must . . . economize."

It seemed matters were indeed as bad as Constable Sharpe had suggested. She was tempted to ask Mr. Elton exactly how his finances stood, but a glance from George warned her that such a question would be premature.

"Dear me," Mr. Elton said. "My manners have gone completely begging. Mrs. Knightley, Mr. Knightley, please do sit."

Once they were seated, an awkward silence ensued. After all, it wasn't every day that one was almost throttled to death by one's brother-in-law. It certainly wasn't a topic that lent itself to an easy discussion.

Mr. Elton finally bestirred himself. "Mrs. Knightley, I must thank you for the generous provisions that you and Mr. Knightley brought with you. I find myself deeply moved by your consideration. But then you are always so kind."

She gave him an encouraging smile. "I hope you will find them a comfort. Serle had just prepared some lovely, nourishing custards. They are very well tolerated when one has a . . . er, sore throat."

"I am sure I will find them delightful. Everything Serle prepares is excellent, under your careful supervision, of course. Everything at Hartfield is done so well, thanks to you."

While she knew he was simply being polite, she couldn't help wondering if Mrs. Elton had spent much time in the kitchen, since the mistress of a household generally did not. Serle would have Emma's head on a platter if she even tried.

Fortunately, she never felt the impulse.

"Mr. Elton," said George, "while we have no wish to cause you any additional distress, Constable Sharpe gave us only a very basic recounting of events. Would you feel up to answering a few questions about it? I would have gone to Dr. Hughes instead, but he is unavailable today."

"Transporting my brother-in-law to the gaol," he replied, his voice suddenly bitter. "And may he rot there for a good long time."

"He will do more than that if found guilty of your wife's murder. You may be sure of it."

"He is guilty, sir. You may be sure of *that*, too."

Emma thought back to the strange argument between the men after the funeral. "Mr. Elton, Constable Sharpe gave us to understand that there may have been a financial dispute between Mrs. Elton and her brother-in-law. Was that indeed the case?"

"I'm afraid so. Horace was heavily invested in a new bank in Bristol, but unfortunately, the bank failed a few months ago. As a result, he lost a great deal of his fortune."

"And that also affected Maple Grove?" she asked.

"From what I've been able to glean from my wife's letters, Maple Grove was heavily mortgaged, which was a matter of great concern to Horace."

"Ah, the letters," said George. "Can you tell us about them?"

The vicar looked perplexed. "It was my understanding that Dr. Hughes was going to show them to you."

"He has not yet had an opportunity to do so," George dryly replied. "I would therefore be grateful if you could briefly apprise me of their contents."

"Of course. However, you must understand that I discovered the letters only last night. I had not yet had the fortitude to go through Augusta's personal correspondence. But after yesterday's events, I felt I had no choice."

"To what events are you referring?" Emma asked.

Mr. Elton was silent for a few moments, as if collecting his thoughts. "When Horace arrived in the early afternoon, he was in a mood and was very short with me. Naturally, I did my best to ignore such unfortunate behavior, although I was certainly embarrassed by his rudeness toward you, Mr. Knightley. I took him to task after you left, but he was unrepentant."

George put up a commiserating hand. "Give it no thought, sir. What happened next?"

"He demanded that I turn over the entire contents of Augusta's jewelry box to him. At that point, I was obliged to take a stand."

"All of Mrs. Elton's jewelry?" Emma asked, surprised. "Surely he had no right to demand that of you."

"Particularly in the absence of a will," added George. "Did Mr. Suckling say why he wanted all the jewels?"

"He claimed that Augusta would wish her sister to have them. I said I would be happy to select a few special pieces for dear Selina, but Horace was adamant that he must have all the jewels." He tugged at the scarf around his neck, as if it had grown too tight. "He said I was not to be trusted after the theft of the necklace."

Emma couldn't help but gasp with outrage. "What nerve, considering that he is apparently the thief."

"He no doubt wished to sell the jewels to help pay off his debts," George said.

"I believe that is true," said the vicar. "Horace is clearly in desperate need of funds."

The door opened, and the other footman brought in the tea tray, pausing their discussion. Emma was thankful that Mrs. Wright had taken the hint and made herself scarce.

After serving the tea, she took up where they'd left off. "What happened when you refused to turn over the jewels?"

Mr. Eton's expression grew ever more grim. "Horace became very angry with me. I'm afraid harsh words were exchanged. I am not proud of that, nor of the fact that the servants undoubtedly heard us raise our voices."

"Come, Mr. Elton," she gently chided. "You can certainly be forgiven for that, since the provocation was so great."

When he smiled at her again, she rather wished he'd stop doing so. With his bruised and swollen face, it looked excessively painful and made her wince every time.

"Thank you, dear lady," he replied.

George glanced at Emma, his expression enigmatic, before redirecting his attention to the vicar.

"Mr. Elton, I assume you discovered Mrs. Elton's letters after the argument with your brother-in-law?"

"Correct. It was quite late by that point, but I was too disturbed to sleep. I must also admit that certain remarks Horace made—both last night and in previous conversations—had aroused my concern. As difficult as it was, I felt it time to look through my wife's correspondence. I hoped to find some answers there regarding Horace's disturbing behavior."

"And you obviously did," Emma said.

He nodded. "There was correspondence between Augusta and Horace going back several months. As I mentioned, he was heavily invested in a bank in Bristol—one of the principal shareholders, in fact. Unfortunately, he had also pulled my wife into the scheme, and she had granted him permission to invest on her behalf. Not all her funds, mind you. Augusta was too wise for that. But Horace, who managed her accounts, took it upon himself to invest the *entire* amount without her knowledge."

Emma was torn between pity and anger, both for Mr. Elton and for his wife. As a woman of means herself, she'd always cherished her independence. To be so cheated by someone you loved and trusted would be a betrayal beyond compare.

"How utterly appalling," she said. "And poor Mrs. Elton! She must have been devastated."

He sighed. "She was. Their final exchange of letters makes it clear how deeply it affected her."

No wonder she'd been pestering both Miss Bates and Mrs. Goddard. Although her treatment of those two ladies had bordered on cruel, Emma could now have some degree of sympathy. Mrs. Elton had undoubtedly been in a state of panic.

"Mr. Elton," said George. "Did you have any knowledge of your brother-in-law's precarious financial situation before your wife's death?"

"I did not."

"Mrs. Elton never discussed it with you or acted in any way so as to cause you concern regarding her relationship with Mr. Suckling?"

He hesitated. "Toward the end I sensed that something was not right between them. But one must step lightly when it comes to in-laws, Mr. Knightley. My wife was very close to the Sucklings, and I did not wish to interfere. I also suspect Augusta was loath to cause me anxiety and was therefore shielding me from such troubling news."

George looked frankly skeptical at that explanation. "But surely she couldn't have hidden such news forever."

Mr. Elton's shoulders rolled forward and his chin disappeared into the voluminous scarf. An image flashed through Emma's mind—that of a turtle retreating into its shell.

"As I have mentioned before, my wife managed most of our affairs," he replied. "She—" He broke off with a sudden cough.

Emma hastily took the teapot and replenished his tea. The vicar nodded his thanks and took a cautious sip.

"Thank you," he hoarsely said when she'd returned to her seat.

"Mr. Elton, we can defer this discussion if you feel too un-well to continue," said George.

"No, I am better now. As I was saying, my wife managed most of our affairs and never wished to disturb me with finan-cial concerns. I imagine she was attempting to arrive at some kind of compromise with Horace before . . ." He trailed off, as they all knew what *before* meant.

"I imagine that was why your wife and Mr. Suckling were meeting that day," Emma mused.

"Yes, I believe so, Mrs. Knightley."

"But why in the church?"

"I can only surmise that Horace asked to meet somewhere private." His expression grew suddenly dark. "One can now see why, of course."

"You're suggesting that Suckling came to Highbury with the express purpose of murdering your wife?" George asked.

"What else can one think, Mr. Knightley?" he bitterly re-plied.

Emma still found it hard to imagine such a cold-blooded course of action. "Is it possible that they argued and Mr. Suck-ling lost his temper? After all, he attacked you when he lost his temper."

"While that is true, I remain convinced that Horace traveled to Highbury that day with the express intention of murdering my wife. Why else would he go to such lengths to remain un-seen?"

His point was difficult to deny. Even though Emma had al-ways harbored doubts that Mrs. Elton's death was an impul-sive act committed in the course of a robbery, to have it all but confirmed that it was a cold, premeditated killing turned her stomach.

"The poor woman," she whispered.

George glanced at her, clearly troubled by her reaction. When he briefly covered her hand with his, she mustered a reassuring smile.

"I'm fine, really," she said.

"You needn't sit through this, my dear," he replied.

"My only concern is for Mr. Elton."

George directed a look at the vicar. "Sir, are you sure you are well enough to continue? As my wife noted, we have no wish to cause further distress."

Mr. Elton, who'd been silently watching them with a strangely dull expression, seemed to rouse himself.

"If Mrs. Knightley is able to bear it, then I must, as well," he responded.

Emma mentally frowned. It seemed an odd thing to say, but George simply nodded and carried on.

"Constable Sharpe suggested that Mr. Suckling's financial woes triggered the final dispute with your wife."

"Yes."

"What, exactly, do you think caused him to take so drastic and irreversible an action? From what you and the constable have told us, if anyone had the right to be outraged, it was Mrs. Elton, not Mr. Suckling."

Emma mentally blinked. Now that George had voiced the thought, it was blindingly obvious.

"You're right," she exclaimed. "Under the circumstances, Mrs. Elton would certainly be more justified in killing Mr. Suckling than the other way around. At least one could understand the desire to do so."

As soon as the words dropped from her lips, she froze. As true as they might be, they were ones that should have remained unsaid. She had little doubt that George would scold her for such a thoughtless remark, and she wouldn't blame him in the least.

Her husband breathed out a quiet sigh, while Mr. Elton looked . . . stunned.

She grimaced. "Do forgive me. I cannot imagine why I would say something so dreadful."

"Were you able to ascertain the specific motive from the correspondence, Mr. Elton?" George asked, clearly deciding to carry on.

When the vicar didn't reply, continuing to stare at her, Emma felt a painful heat rise into her cheeks.

"Mr. Elton," George sharply said.

The vicar startled. "Oh, I beg your pardon, sir. Motive, you say? Yes, I believe I found one. From what I could glean from Horace's final reply to Augusta, she had apparently expressed great dismay with what she deemed his *criminal* behavior and his refusal to assist her. It also seems clear that Horace was hiding the magnitude of his losses from dear Selina, and Augusta intended to correct that."

George's expression was politely skeptical. "While it would certainly be distressing for Mrs. Suckling to hear such news, it hardly seems a reason to commit murder."

"And would not Mrs. Suckling wish to assist her husband in his difficulties?" Emma couldn't help asking. "She would gain nothing by exposing his troubles to the world."

"True, and Selina *is* very loyal," Mr. Elton replied. "It would seem that Augusta was hoping to enlist her sister's help in gaining restitution from Horace. His response to that declared intention was . . ." He pulled a grim face but then winced and gingerly patted his jaw before continuing. "Strongly worded, to say the least. He also feared Augusta would publicly expose him, which, of course, would have had a dire effect on his reputation and bring creditors to his doorstep."

Emma frowned. "Please believe that I have no desire to offend, sir, but would Mrs. Elton expose her sister to such a scandal? Because her actions would surely do so."

"My wife was a woman of great integrity," he said with quiet dignity. "If she felt a wrong had been done—and it clearly had—

she would seek to correct it. Horace lied to Selina and the Lord only knows whom else. That is not something my wife could tolerate."

That was certainly an inspiring characterization of Mrs. Elton. Unfortunately, it hardly squared with the woman that Emma had come to know.

"If what you say is true—" George started.

"It is," the vicar tersely interrupted.

George nodded. "Then no doubt Mr. Suckling was in fairly desperate straits. Mrs. Elton was threatening to expose him to his wife and potentially to his creditors, as well."

While that was all true, some part of it still didn't make sense to Emma. "But wouldn't his losses all come out, anyway? One can hardly cover up a bank failure."

"Bank failures are not uncommon," her husband replied. "Others have survived such occurrences if they have the opportunity to retrench. Perhaps Suckling was trying to secure additional funding to cover the losses or needed time to manage his creditors. Mrs. Elton's actions would threaten that. If Mrs. Elton was insisting that Mr. Suckling make her whole, that would make it more difficult for him to recover his situation."

"I suppose so," she replied, though doubts remained.

But if nothing else, she would have to defer to her husband's superior knowledge of the issue.

"I believe that is the correct interpretation, Mr. Knightley," the vicar said with a nod. "Do not forget that my wife's fortune was quite large. Her insistence—" He broke off, as if momentarily overcome with emotion. "I truly believe she did it for my sake. If only she had come to me, I would have helped her. I would have gone to Horace on her behalf. And I would have assured her that the greatest treasure resided in our matrimonial bond. That, you know, mattered most."

Emma had to struggle to hide her skepticism, since she imagined the old Mr. Elton would have been *quite* upset to see his wife's fortune evaporate. Still, losing one's spouse to a vicious act of murder would be bound to change one's attitude. Perhaps in looking back, he now realized that their relationship did indeed matter more than their financial standing.

"Mr. Elton," said George, "did you intend to confront your brother-in-law after you found the letters?"

"I thought to do it first thing in the morning. The letters explained many things about Horace's recent behavior—although, of course, at that point, I did not even consider that he could have killed Augusta. But before I could speak to him, Mrs. Wright discovered the necklace in his valise. As you can imagine, that caused the situation to change quite dramatically."

"Mr. Elton, forgive any impertinence," Emma began.

The vicar pressed a hand to his chest. "Mrs. Knightley, you could *never* be impertinent. Please ask whatever questions you wish."

Emma had to avoid her husband's ironic eye. "Thank you. I was simply wondering about the circumstances surrounding the discovery of the necklace."

"Ah. Horace had dropped a handkerchief in the dirt when he was out in the garden. Naturally, Mrs. Wright had it washed, and she brought it up to his bedroom. His valise was badly packed—he did not travel with his valet—so she thought to repack it for him. That was when she discovered the necklace and alerted me. I then confronted him."

"Mr. Elton, would it not have been wise to then immediately send for Constable Sharpe?" George asked.

The vicar sighed. "Yes, but I regret to say that I lost my temper. Reason flew from my head, and I could think only of confronting Horace at once. I went straight down to the dining room and did so. Foolishly, as it turned out."

"Perhaps, but it certainly was an understandable reaction," Emma sympathetically commented.

She had a feeling that she would likely do the same if anyone ever hurt George.

He gave her a wan smile. "Thank you, Mrs. Knightley."

George glanced at her before addressing Mr. Elton. "Thank you, sir. I believe we have imposed on you enough for one day. We will leave you to rest."

The vicar held up both hands. "Mr. Knightley, you and Mrs. Knightley could never be an imposition. I am eternally grateful for your support during these difficult days."

"And you will have our continued support," he replied. "When you are feeling better, I will speak with you about the trial and what might be expected of you there."

Mr. Elton looked vaguely alarmed. "The trial. I had not even thought of that. Poor Selina. I must write to her immediately."

"I would advise against that for now, since the investigation is still ongoing."

When the vicar issued another weary sigh, Emma couldn't help but attempt to console him. "Your instinct to give Mrs. Suckling comfort is a great credit to you, Mr. Elton. One can only imagine her distress when she hears this news."

"Indeed, it is a cruel blow to both of us. I cannot think how she will manage."

George stood and held out his hand to Emma. "Are you ready, my dear?"

There were a few questions that niggled, but it was clear Mr. Elton would be unable to provide the answers. That being the case—

"The tincture." She glanced down at the tea tray. "Mrs. Wright must have forgotten to send it up. You must be sure to take some, Mr. Elton. My father swears by it for bruises and pain. I'm sure it will give you some relief."

When he began to struggle to his feet, she held up a restraining hand. "Please do not get up, sir. You are ill and must rest."

He sank back into his chair. "Mrs. Knightley, you are an angel of mercy. I will partake of your medicinal immediately. And please give my regards to your esteemed father. I hope to see him quite soon, and I pray he will forgive me for my earlier blunders."

"I'm sure he will."

"Are you sure Henry will forgive him?" George quietly asked after he ushered her into the hall. "It would not do to give Elton false hope."

"I certainly hope he will. Under the circumstances, it seems foolish to hold on to a grudge. And Mr. Elton does look ghastly, George. Even Father couldn't help but be moved by his situation."

"Perhaps then he should visit your father before the bruises fade."

She threw him a wry glance. "I should scold you for that remark, but it's a very sensible suggestion. Father would happily commiserate with his woeful state."

George declined to respond, since Mrs. Wright stood waiting for them by the front door.

"I understand you're leaving Mr. Elton's service," Emma said.

"That is correct, ma'am," she replied in a colorless voice.

"I'm sure he will miss you very much."

"Thank you, though, in fact, I was here for Mrs. Elton. Now that she is gone, there is little point for me to remain."

Emma was surprised by such a forthcoming admission.

"Yes, it's been a distressing time," she cautiously replied. "This morning must have been extremely trying."

The woman's gray eyes suddenly glittered with something akin to malice. "With Mr. Suckling, you mean. That man—" She suddenly stopped, but her jaw kept working as if she were chewing on gristle and bone.

"What about Mr. Suckling?" George prompted.

Her lips momentarily rolled inward, as if holding back more words. "Nothing, sir, except to say that I hope he gets everything he deserves and then some."

"I suspect he will," George calmly replied.

"When do you leave, Mrs. Wright?" asked Emma.

That cold, fishlike gaze settled on her, and an uncomfortable shiver ran across the back of Emma's neck.

"First, I must record my statement for the constable," the housekeeper replied as she opened the door. "And then I will leave as soon as I can."

George gave her a courteous nod. "Then we will bid you goodbye, Mrs. Wright. And better luck in your next posting."

"Luck has nothing to do with it."

And with that enigmatic reply, the housekeeper all but slammed the door in their faces.

# CHAPTER 25

"Another cup of tea, my dear?" asked Mrs. Weston.

"You've already stuffed me with tea and cakes," Emma replied with a rueful smile. "Father would be most alarmed to see me consuming queen cakes in the middle of the afternoon."

"You've had a difficult week, Emma. You deserve a little pampering."

"If anyone deserves pampering, it's George. That poor man has been run from pillar to post for three days now, ever since Mr. Suckling's arrest. But I will happily stand in for him."

After a morning spent immersed in the household accounts, Emma had decided to reward herself with a visit to Randalls. Once her father was settled after lunch, she'd set out on the gloriously sunny afternoon. The clear skies and a crisp feel to the air signaled that the end of summer was approaching.

It had been rather marvelous to indulge in a leisurely stroll, secure in the knowledge that no crisis demanded her attention. Although Mr. Suckling's trial loomed on the horizon, and many questions were as yet unanswered, today she could put all that aside and simply enjoy an afternoon with friends.

As luck would have it, the men were out, which left the ladies to the pleasures of a comfortable chat. By tacit agreement, they'd so far avoided the subject most on their minds. Instead, they'd discussed Mrs. Weston's plans to refurbish the dining room, agreed that little Anna was the prettiest baby in the world, and debated how long Jane and Frank should remain in Highbury before returning to Yorkshire.

It was a blessedly normal day, the first she could remember in weeks.

"You must admit that the queen cakes are delicious, though," said Jane as she selected one from the oak tea tray. "It's dreadful of me, but I cannot resist another one."

Mrs. Weston gave her a fond look. "We're so happy you've regained your appetite. You should eat as many cakes as you like."

"I seem to be famished these past few days," the young woman admitted. "If I go on like this, I shall grow as big as a house."

Emma smiled. "But that is the natural order of things, is it not? Truly, Jane, you look splendid now. We were all quite worried when you arrived."

Compared to the wan-faced girl who could barely keep anything on her stomach, Jane now brimmed with life. Her complexion had regained its lovely bloom, and her gray eyes their sparkle. It was a tremendous relief to see her looking so well.

Mrs. Weston nodded. "Mr. Perry sees the return of Jane's appetite as an excellent indication of her general health."

"I am sure he's correct," Emma replied. "I also suspect Jane has improved thanks to her aunt and grandmother's relief from their burdens."

Jane finished her last bit of cake before replying. "To know that Aunt Hetty is no longer under suspicion has been a tremendous relief, I will admit. Although she remains a trifle anxious regarding the promissory note and the monies owed to

Mrs. Elton—or to Mr. Elton, as the case may be. I have tried to convince her not to fret, but you know how she is."

"There is no debt attaching to her name," Emma firmly replied. "Rather, it is she who is rightly owed money by Mr. Suckling—or Mr. Elton. However, I imagine it's unlikely she will ever recoup it from either one."

"Frank has made it clear to Aunt Hetty that she is not to worry about that, either. We will cover any loss incurred." Jane sighed. "Although, of course, she feels terribly guilty about that, too."

Mrs. Weston tsked. "Miss Bates did nothing wrong. Both Mrs. Elton and that dreadful Mr. Suckling took advantage of her. One is, of course, very distressed by Mrs. Elton's death, but it was quite shocking of her to impose on your poor aunt in such a fashion."

"I've always wondered why Mrs. Elton did so," mused Emma. "It seems so odd to ask someone like your aunt to invest in a financial scheme."

"I was mystified, too," Jane replied. "But after discussing it with Aunt Hetty, Frank has come to the conclusion that Mrs. Elton was hoping that we could be persuaded to invest in Mr. Suckling's banking venture, as well."

The light dawned for Emma. "Ah, I see. If the initial investment was successful, Mrs. Elton hoped that Miss Bates would persuade you and Frank to invest."

Jane nodded. "Yes, and also Frank's uncle, Mr. Churchill."

"It all seems rather convoluted to me," said Mrs. Weston.

Emma waggled a hand. "Mrs. Elton no doubt wished to curry favor with her brother-in-law, and it likely never occurred to her that the venture would prove so risky. I suspect she was blinded both by the magnificence of Maple Grove and Mr. Suckling's self-importance. So, to have it end in such a dreadful fashion—murdered by the very man she hoped to please—is truly an irony."

"It makes one reluctant to trust anyone," exclaimed Mrs. Weston. "To be murdered by her own brother-in-law, one can hardly imagine anything worse."

"With the possible exception of being murdered by one's own spouse," Emma dryly replied.

Mrs. Weston grimaced. "My dear, what a dreadful thought. I cannot begin to imagine it."

"That is because you're married to the kindest man in the world. And I'm sure none of us need worry in that regard, either."

"I do feel dreadfully sad for Mrs. Elton," Jane quietly said. "She was kind to me, you know."

*Kindness* was not the word Emma would have used to describe Mrs. Elton's behavior. *Patronizing* and *pushy* were the terms that still sprang to mind. But since she'd made so little effort to befriend Jane when the young woman was most in need of friendship, it was best not to voice such opinions.

"Emma, are you and Mr. Knightley certain that Mr. Elton will not attempt to recover any funds from Miss Bates or Mrs. Goddard?" asked Mrs. Weston. "It would be dreadfully awkward if he did."

"You need have no worries. Mr. Elton places the entire blame on Mr. Suckling and now heartily regrets the distress he caused Miss Bates." Emma smiled. "Besides, my father would have something to say if Mr. Elton dared to broach the topic with Miss Bates."

Mrs. Weston pressed her hands together. "Ah, Mr. Woodhouse. Mr. Elton was to call on him yesterday, was he not? I do hope your father wasn't unduly distressed by his visit."

"It was rather more distressing for Mr. Elton, I imagine. It took some persuading on my part to secure Father's agreement to see him."

"Aunt Hetty certainly holds no grudge against Mr. Elton," said Jane. "She even expressed admiration for his courage in confronting Mr. Suckling."

"What about Mrs. Bates?" Mrs. Weston shrewdly asked. "Is she also as forgiving?"

Jane hesitated. "I think it might take my grandmother longer to reach a similar state of charity with Mr. Elton."

Emma couldn't help but laugh. "I think your grandmother would like nothing better than to crack Mr. Elton over the head with her cane—after dishing out the same punishment to Constable Sharpe."

Jane smothered a giggle.

"I hope Mr. Woodhouse did not resort to such measures," Mrs. Weston said with a wry smile.

"He was inclined to be stuffy at first, but he did unbend—especially in light of Mr. Elton's injuries. There is nothing more certain to gain my father's sympathy than one suffering from a physical ailment. Father delivered a lengthy discourse on the benefits of poultices versus ointments for bruises, and he even wished to send for Mr. Perry. He was persuaded against it only by Mr. Elton's earnest promise to visit Perry at the first opportunity."

"That would certainly endear Mr. Elton to your father."

"Mr. Elton delivered a very sincere apology, I must say," Emma added. "It was lacking in his usual flourishes and seemed to genuinely come from the heart."

In fact, Mr. Elton's visit had gone even better than she'd hoped for. His humble apology, combined with his dreadful appearance, had done its work. The initial visit, expected to last only fifteen minutes, had extended for over an hour. Mr. Elton had patiently listened to her father recount his own ailments and various treatments and had even eaten a bowl of Serle's gruel.

Well, he'd managed to choke down half a bowl, anyway. Emma had made sure to whisk it away as soon as her father was distracted, replacing it with newly baked scones and excellent strawberry jam.

When the visit had finally drawn to a close, it seemed that

past sins were forgiven. Father had sent Mr. Elton off with a packet of his own headache powders and extended an open invitation to visit Hartfield. Mr. Elton, overcome, had lapsed into old habits and expressed his gratitude in flourishing terms. It was rather silly but obviously well meant, so Emma had sent him on his way with another basket of goodies from the kitchen. That had also cheered him greatly.

"Mr. Woodhouse and Mr. Elton are friends once more, then?" asked Mrs. Weston.

"It appears so. In fact, Mr. Elton is sitting with Father this afternoon. He stopped by Hartfield to return the basket just as I was about to set out for Randalls. He offered to escort me, but I suggested instead that he sit with my father. When I left them, Mr. Elton was regaling Father with the details of his visit to Mr. Perry this morning."

"That must have pleased Mr. Woodhouse."

"Indeed. I couldn't escape quickly enough."

The ladies laughed, but then Jane grew serious. "I must confess I'm relieved that Mr. Elton didn't escort you to Randalls. Frank is not best pleased with him, and I'm not entirely certain he would be quite so polite."

Mrs. Weston breathed out an exasperated sigh. "I'm afraid Mr. Weston feels the same way, which is most unlike him."

"Ho, now," said the man himself, walking into the room. "Do I hear my name taken in vain?"

Frank followed closely on his heels. It took a few minutes for husbands to kiss wives, for greetings to be exchanged, and for tea to be served to the gentlemen.

When they were all settled again, Mr. Weston regarded his wife with an enquiring expression. "I believe you were discussing Mr. Elton when Frank and I came in. I hope there's nothing amiss. We don't need any additional troubles on his account, do we, Frank?"

"Certainly not. And if Elton has any intention of trying to

reclaim money from Aunt Hetty based on that blasted promissory note, he shall have me to deal with."

Since he was looking rather severe—and Frank was generally not one to be severe—his wife hastened to reassure him.

"Nothing of the sort," Jane said. "According to Emma, Mr. Elton wishes most heartily to make amends for the unfortunate events of these past weeks."

"I should bloody well hope so," he replied.

"Frank! Such language in front of ladies," Mrs. Weston scolded in her best governess voice.

He flashed her a rueful grin. "My apologies, dear ma'am. But one can't help feeling rather warm on the subject."

"There's no need to worry," Emma said. "All is well. I even left Mr. Elton at Hartfield, keeping company with my father."

"Oh, ho," exclaimed Mr. Weston. "So Mr. Woodhouse has forgiven our vicar. Well, then, I suppose the rest of us must, too."

"Ha," muttered Frank, obviously disgruntled.

Jane touched his hand. "Dearest, if my aunt can forgive him, then we should, as well. Mr. Elton has very sincerely apologized. We must not hold grudges."

"When I see the effect of his actions on you and on your family, I most certainly can hold on to a grudge. The fellow's a pompous ass, and we all know it."

Mrs. Weston looked pained. "Frank, that is most unchristian of you. The Lord does call on us to forgive."

As Frank reached for a scone, he looked not the least bit perturbed by his stepmother's reprimand. "That would require one to believe Elton is truly a changed man. And you'll forgive *me* if I withhold judgment in that regard."

"I say, Emma, what is the latest news on Suckling?" asked Mr. Weston in a rather obvious attempt to divert the conversation. "Mr. Knightley went down to Guildford the other day to question him, did he not?"

Mrs. Weston frowned. "My dear, I'm not sure we should be

quizzing Emma on the legal elements of the case. Mr. Knightley might not approve."

"No, it's fine," said Emma, waving a hand. "Everything will come out at trial, regardless."

"Then do tell all, Mrs. Knightley," Frank said, his good humor apparently restored by the scone. "The locals are agog with curiosity."

"I'm afraid I cannot tell all that much," she confessed. "Mr. Suckling was exceedingly rude. He refused to tell George where he'd been on the day of the murder, claimed that everyone in Highbury was a fool and a scoundrel, and was adamant that he would speak only to his solicitor and his wife. He even swore at George, if you can imagine."

Mr. Weston huffed with disgust. "Outrageous. Man's a thorough cad!"

"It was a great waste of my husband's time, certainly," Emma replied.

When George returned home two evenings ago after a long day, he'd been thoroughly out of sorts. He'd opined that Mr. Suckling was either quite mad for refusing to talk to him or was indeed Mrs. Elton's killer.

"What will you do now?" Emma had asked him.

"I believe I must ride into London tomorrow and attempt to speak with Mrs. Suckling. Surely she will be more forthcoming and would at least wish to provide her husband with an alibi."

That venture, unfortunately, had also proved less than satisfying.

"And what of Mrs. Suckling?" asked Mr. Weston. "I assume she's still staying in London, in that town house they rented. Was Mr. Knightley able to speak with her?"

"George was kept waiting in the hall for twenty minutes, and then a servant informed him that Mrs. Suckling wouldn't speak to him," Emma dryly replied. "If I didn't know better, I might even begin to think the woman doesn't exist. After all, none of us have ever laid eyes on her."

Frank shook his head. "Another sad waste of a day for Mr. Knightley."

"Not entirely, because he stopped in Brunswick Square to speak with his brother, John, who has been looking into Mr. Suckling's finances. Apparently, he *has* suffered substantial losses and will be forced to retrench. John is of the opinion that he might even be forced to sell Maple Grove."

"I doubt there is a bank or an investor in England that would be willing to lend him the necessary funds at this point," commented Mr. Weston.

"Emma, do you truly think Mrs. Suckling was unaware of her husband's financial difficulties?" asked Mrs. Weston. "Given that the situation is apparently so dire, that would seem hard to believe."

"Mr. Elton is convinced she didn't know. He said Mrs. Elton was determined to apprise her sister of the situation and enlist Mrs. Suckling's help in recouping the funds, regardless of the consequences."

Jane put down her teacup. "Are you suggesting that Mrs. Elton would have been willing to expose Mr. Suckling's financial troubles?"

"So Mr. Elton believes. He claims it was the reason behind her murder in the first place."

Jane firmly shook her head. "Mrs. Elton would never have exposed her sister to scandal or treated her so shabbily. They were exceedingly close. I believe she would have done everything she could to protect Mrs. Suckling, not humiliate her."

Mr. Weston smiled kindly on her. "You would think so, my dear, but you have a very tender heart. Whatever good one might say about Mrs. Elton, one would never call her tender or sentimental."

"No, I agree with Jane," Frank put in. "Whatever her faults—

and they were many—Mrs. Elton was genuinely devoted to Selina. She also set great store in her sister's elevated status in society and would do everything she could to protect it."

"Even at the expense of her own status and financial standing?" Emma asked.

"I believe so. After all, she stood more to gain by Mr. Suckling successfully retrenching than from going bankrupt. For one thing, how could she ever recover any of her lost savings if he did not?"

That observation struck Emma with significant force, as it cast an entirely new light on the situation.

"That's very true, Frank," she said. "What would she gain by exposing Mr. Suckling if he would then be unable to repay her?"

"Nothing, as far as I can see."

"But the necklace," said Mrs. Weston. "It was found in his luggage. Surely there could be no doubt about his guilt, given that evidence."

Emma hesitated but then voiced an idea that until this moment had been nothing more than an ephemeral wisp dancing at the edge of her thoughts. "Unless someone planted the necklace in his bag, hoping to divert suspicion."

That stunned the others into silence.

Mrs. Weston recovered first. "But who would do such a thing?"

"Possibly the person who found it," Emma slowly replied.

Mr. Weston goggled at her. "Mrs. Wright? You cannot mean it."

Emma hesitated. "I don't know that I do, but her behavior has been so odd. For instance, why did she take it upon herself to repack Mr. Suckling's luggage? It was rather forward of her."

Frank shrugged. "Yes, but that's not entirely unusual. Servants pack our luggage all the time."

"True," said Jane. "But not just any servant. Only my maid

attends to my things, and when you don't travel with your valet—as you did on this trip—you pack your own bags."

"Very badly, I might add. Any self-respecting housekeeper or maid would take one look inside my bag and immediately give her notice," he jested.

"The point remains that Mrs. Wright took it upon herself to repack Mr. Suckling's valise without his permission," said Emma. "At which time she conveniently found the necklace."

Mrs. Weston held up a hand. "But why would she murder her own mistress?"

Emma tapped her forehead, as if in doing so, she could break free the tangle of questions that bedeviled her. "For the necklace, one might suppose. But then why give it up?"

"Perhaps she sensed she might be falling under suspicion?" mused Jane. "And that it would be discovered among her things?"

Mr. Weston looked dubious. "I don't think anyone has raised any suspicions against her. Certainly, there was no question in that regard during the inquest."

Emma sighed. "You're right, of course. But she *is* very angry about something, or at someone. Mr. Suckling, for one. And why has she so precipitously abandoned her position, especially when she has no other employment? Mr. Elton certainly had no intention of letting her go. Even though he needs to economize, he made it very clear that he depended greatly on her."

"It is rather dodgy for her to scamper off like that," mused Frank. "Never took to the woman myself. She's rather a grim sort, don't you think, Jane?"

His wife nodded. "Yes, and I must confess that she has been rude to me on more than one occasion when Mrs. Elton was not in the room."

"What?" Frank exclaimed. "Why the devil was she rude to you? And why didn't you tell me?"

Ah, now it made sense.

"I'll wager she was rude because she was jealous of Jane's relationship with Mrs. Elton," Emma said.

Jane wrinkled her nose. "I thought that might be the case, although it seemed so silly at the time. Why would a housekeeper be jealous of me?"

"The woman is clearly deranged," Frank said with disgust. "Perhaps she had something to do with the murder, after all."

Emma cast her mind back, searching for the relevant conversation. "Dr. Hughes did tell me it was possible that Mrs. Elton was murdered by a woman."

"Good gracious," exclaimed Mrs. Weston. "For all her faults, I cannot believe that Mrs. Wright is guilty of murder. Mrs. Elton spoke so highly of her. And by all accounts, Mrs. Wright was devoted to her mistress."

"It does seem rather far-fetched," added Mr. Weston. "If robbery was her motive, Mrs. Wright wound up leaving empty-handed."

For all her theorizing—and admitted flights of imagination—Emma could not disagree.

"You're right, of course," she replied. "All the evidence points to Mr. Suckling. Still, there are many unanswered questions. How was he able to escape detection that day? He presumably traveled on horseback, so where did he stable the animal? And we have just heard confirmation of how unlikely it was that Mrs. Elton would expose her sister to scandal and disgrace, which suggests a lack of motive on Mr. Suckling's part."

Frank nodded. "True. Mr. Cole also informed me that Suckling has apparently hired a Bow Street Runner to try to clear his name. Seems a silly thing to do if he's actually the guilty party."

"That might be for show," Mr. Weston pointed out. "Suckling is paying the fellow, after all. He can send the runner off in any direction he likes."

"Is it possible there might be more than one person involved in the murder?" Jane asked in a hesitant tone.

Emma blinked. That possibility had never occurred to her. "Are you suggesting that Mr. Suckling had an accomplice in Mrs. Wright?"

Jane waggled a hand. "Perhaps. As you pointed out, she has been behaving most oddly. And the coincidence of finding the necklace does tax credulity."

"But if such is the case," said Mrs. Weston, "why would Mrs. Wright then implicate him in so direct a fashion?"

Frank snapped his fingers, looking almost gleeful. "Perhaps they were lovers, and Suckling betrayed her. She sought her revenge by planting the necklace in his valise."

"By Jove, I think you could be right," exclaimed Mr. Weston, eagerly catching the scent. "That would wrap it all up rather neatly, wouldn't it?"

Mrs. Weston directed an incredulous stare at her husband. "Why in heaven's name would Mr. Suckling have an affair with Mrs. Wright, of all people?"

Emma didn't know whether to laugh or recoil in horror. "Mr. Weston, I would suggest that this notion is significantly more far-fetched than anything I have proposed."

"I don't know," said Frank. "They're both very unpleasant people, which would make them perfect for each other."

"I simply cannot envision Mrs. Wright engaging in such behavior," said Jane in a frankly skeptical tone. "With anyone."

Emma pulled an exaggerated face. "Indeed. The notion leaves one feeling rather queasy."

"Perhaps Suckling made monetary promises to her and then reneged," Frank replied. "He used Mrs. Wright to help him carry out the deed but then up and betrayed her."

"But then why wouldn't he simply accuse her of murder?" asked Mrs. Weston.

Emma shook her head. "He would still be implicated in the crime. No, as disturbed as I am by Mrs. Wright's behavior— and as much as I agree that she is thoroughly unlikable—I'm afraid we're probably drawing too long a bow."

Frank gave a good-natured shrug and reached for another scone. "I suppose you're right, although I'd like nothing better than to see the blasted woman punished for the way she treated my poor Jane."

"Going to the gallows for murder seems a bit of an excessive punishment," Emma wryly commented.

Still, she couldn't rid herself of the sense that Mrs. Wright was indeed involved in the web of lies and mysteries that surrounded the murder. She just couldn't fathom the ways and the whys of it.

"I suppose we just have to accept the fact that all the evidence points to Suckling," said Mr. Weston as he selected a cake from the tea tray. "After all, he's the one who stands to benefit the most from Mrs. Elton's death."

"That is true," Emma replied. "If Mr. Elton is to be believed in this matter."

*If Mr. Elton is to be believed.*

For a moment she felt an odd swooping sensation, as if she'd just lost her footing and taken a tumble down a hill. She'd said the words almost absently, but now they seemed to lock into her mind, holding her thoughts in a fast grip.

Mrs. Weston frowned at her husband. "My dear, that is your third cake. You'll ruin your appetite before dinner."

"I'm a former military man," he drolly replied. "Nothing ruins our appetites. In fact, I think I'll have one of those scones after I polish this off."

Mrs. Weston tsked at him, while Frank began to tease his father about his sweet tooth. But to Emma, the room and the voices had faded away as one idea after another spun madly in her head.

Jane's voice called her back to the moment. "Emma, is something wrong?"

Emma glanced up to meet her friend's concerned gaze. Dredging up a smile, she tried to force the alarming but surely ridiculous notion out of her brain. "Not a thing. I'm simply thinking . . ."

Frankly, she didn't know exactly what she was thinking.

"It's very frustrating, isn't it?" Jane replied in a commiserating tone. "Not having all the answers."

"Very. But as my husband has reminded me, we must let justice take its course, and hope that all questions will then be answered."

Her remark captured Mr. Weston's attention. "I, for one, am looking forward to putting this business behind us. After all, there's that blasted poultry thief still running about. The sooner Constable Sharpe can turn his attention to that matter, the better."

Emma widened her eyes at him. "I'd forgotten all about the thief. Has he struck again?"

Mrs. Weston grimaced. "I'm afraid so. He got into Mrs. Cole's chicken coop the other evening. The man grows bolder by the day."

Mr. Weston patted her hand. "I'm sure Constable Sharpe will run him to ground soon enough, now that Suckling is behind bars."

Frank snorted. "Doubtful. The man's clearly a fool." Then he flashed a grin at Emma. "Perhaps the magistrate should look into it."

"The magistrate has quite enough on his plate, thank you," she tartly replied.

"And he certainly has better uses for his time," added Mrs. Weston. "I'm sure he's very busy at Donwell, since the harvest is approaching."

"Indeed," Emma replied as she stood to take her leave. "He has missed a great deal of work, thanks to the demands of this investigation. William Larkins is most displeased with him. I expect he'll keep my poor husband working right through dinner."

George had indicated as much when he'd set off this morning for Donwell.

"You are certainly welcome to stay here for dinner, my dear," said Mr. Weston, also rising. "Frank can then walk you home."

Frank hopped to his feet and gave a dramatic bow. "It would be my great honor, Mrs. Knightley."

She had to smile. "Thank you, but I must get back to Father. If news of Mrs. Cole's chickens comes to his ears, he'll be in a terrible fret."

Farewells were exchanged, after which Mr. Weston walked her to the front door.

"Try not to trouble yourself over this murder business, Emma," he said. "All will come right in the end."

"I'm sure that is true."

But as she set off down the drive, Emma knew she didn't believe that. And one question in particular now came to the fore. It was a simple one but went to the heart of the matter. In the murder of Mrs. Elton, who stood to benefit the most?

# CHAPTER 26

The walk home from Randalls was decidedly less enjoyable than the walk over. Emma was once again bedeviled by questions, and she was increasingly disconcerted by thoughts that persisted in raising doubts about Mr. Suckling's guilt. Given the preponderance of evidence against him, questioning his guilt seemed absurd. If Mrs. Elton had intended to expose her brother-in-law's nefarious deeds to the world, it would surely follow that he would have become desperate, and desperate men took desperate measures.

Yet, as Frank had pointed out, if Mrs. Elton had pursued that course, the end result would have been the downfall of the Sucklings and the loss of any opportunity for her to recoup her monies. And would Mrs. Elton truly have brought the righteous hand of vengeance down on her errant brother-in-law? Emma suspected that the woman's intense regard for her own social standing would have made her reluctant to do so.

Heartily sick of her circling thoughts, she entered the house and handed her bonnet and gloves to the waiting footman. "Thank you, Simon. I take it that Mr. Elton has departed?"

"Yes, Mrs. Knightley." He glanced at the longcase clock in the entrance hall. "He left at about quarter past the hour."

That meant the vicar had spent almost two hours at Hartfield, a surprisingly long visit for her father. "Is Mr. Woodhouse in the drawing room, or has he gone upstairs to rest?"

"He's still in the drawing room, madam, writing letters."

"I'll join him, then."

"Can I bring you a fresh pot of tea, Mrs. Knightley?"

"No, thank you."

She hurried down the hall, eager to discover what her father and Mr. Elton had found to discuss at such great length.

Her father was seated at the escritoire in the window alcove, busily writing away.

"Good afternoon, dearest," she said, crossing to give him a kiss. "I'm sorry to have been away for so long. Apparently, you had company for most of the afternoon."

Father put down his quill and allowed her to help him up.

"Indeed, I thought Mr. Elton would never leave," he said with gentle complaint. "While one must exercise the virtues of forgiveness and charity, I do hope we will not suffer him spending half the day at Hartfield from now on. I would find that very tiring."

She could sympathize, because she felt rather the same about Miss Bates.

"I suspect he's very grateful to be able to visit with you again and so is perhaps a trifle enthusiastic." She helped him settle in his armchair by the fireplace and then draped a light cashmere shawl over his knees. "No doubt he is low about everything and much in need of company."

Her father rearranged the shawl to his liking before answering. "To be sure, he was excessively grateful to be here again. But I believe he was also waiting for you. He asked when you would be returning from Randalls and wondered if he should go there and escort you back home. I told him that it was unnecessary, since Frank Churchill or Mr. Weston would certainly escort you to Hartfield."

Emma slid past the need to tell her parent that she had walked herself home from Randalls. Still, she was grateful that his misapprehension had spared her the vicar's company.

"It was rather odd of Mr. Elton to think he needed to do that," she commented, taking the chair opposite him. "Especially since it would have taken him out of his way."

"It seemed a bit strange to me, as well. I suppose he simply was wishing to be polite."

More likely, the vicar was trying to curry favor with her father. Given the events of the past few weeks, it was understandable.

"Mr. Elton has always been excessively polite, and with very nice manners. Until he accused Miss Bates of murder, that is," her father added on a darker note. "I still cannot comprehend why he did so."

"He didn't actually accuse her of murder," Emma patiently explained for perhaps the hundredth time. "He only shared what he thought was information relevant to the investigation. It was actually Constable Sharpe who accused Miss Bates of murder."

Father held up a minatory finger. "But Mr. Elton gave that dreadful Sharpe person the idea. While I have forgiven him, it is very hard to forget that he caused Miss Bates a great deal of distress. We can only hope she will recover without any lasting effects to her nerves."

"I'm sure she'll be fine. And Mr. Elton is truly sorry, so we must do our best to forgive and forget. To dwell on such unhappy events will serve no good purpose, nor will it help Miss Bates to recover a more peaceful frame of mind."

"I suppose you're right, my dear, as you so usually are. But I do not know if I will ever forget the terrible trials of this unhappy time. One wonders if Highbury will ever be the same."

Emma mentally grimaced. As curious as she was about Mr. Elton's visit, it was time to direct her father's thoughts along more cheerful lines. And perhaps she also needed to think less about their vicar, the murder, and the entire nasty business, since it was beginning to grow more than a trifle wearisome.

"To whom were you writing when I came in?" she brightly asked.

"Ah, yes, my letter. I was writing to Isabella, but I will have to finish it this evening. She will no doubt be shocked to hear of Mr. Suckling's arrest. I hope it does not upset your poor sister too greatly. Like me, she has a very delicate constitution. Nevertheless, I feel it better she receive the news from me than from the common gossips of London."

She leaned forward and patted his knee. "You may be sure that John has already told her, so it will not come as a shock."

Besides, Isabella wouldn't give two figs about Mr. Suckling, other than how his arrest might affect the residents of Hartfield. Emma's sister was a lovely, kind woman, whose preoccupying interests were her husband, her children, and her life of quiet domesticity in London—well, as quiet as life could be with five children to manage. When Isabella married John Knightley, she'd readily left Highbury behind. While always entering into the immediate concerns of her family and close friends, she no longer possessed more than a passing interest in the people from her former life in the country.

"Ah, but she will not have heard about that dreadful poultry thief," her father proclaimed in a portentous tone. "Isabella will be shocked to hear that he has struck again. Why, she might even be afraid to bring the children down for Christmas, and then what shall we do?"

So her father had already heard about the stupid poultry pilferer. That fellow was growing even more tiresome than the departed Mrs. Elton.

"I'm sure the thief will be long caught before then, Father. Christmas is many months away."

"But poor Mrs. Cole! Her best laying hen taken right from the kitchen garden coop, which is very close to the back of their house. I cannot think how I will sleep tonight, knowing that such a ruthless predator roams free."

Emma would have been tempted to laugh at her father's high dramatics but for the fact that his fears *would* keep him awake for most of the night. And that was exactly why she'd wished to break the news to him first.

"Father, how did you find out about Mrs. Cole's chickens?"

"From Mr. Elton. On his way to Hartfield, he met Mr. Cole, who was excessively disturbed and told him everything. Both he and Mr. Elton are of the opinion that the thief is getting very bold, and that we must all be sure to check our doors and windows before we retire every night. Mr. Cole also told him that Dr. Hughes remains greatly upset, although one does not generally set any store by the doctor's opinion."

Emma was beginning to feel quite out of charity with Mr. Elton. He was well familiar with her father's frets and fears and should have known better than to stoke them.

"Dearest, you know that George always checks the windows and doors before he retires to bed. Besides, the thief steals only poultry. He has never made any attempt to break into a house."

Her father began fussing with his cashmere shawl, never a good sign. "Mr. Elton is very worried, though, which is not to be wondered at. First, Mrs. Elton's murder, and now the threat of this villainous person to contend with."

Emma stared at him, astonished that he *and* Mr. Elton would make such a leap. "Surely there can be no connection between the robbery and murder of Mrs. Elton and the theft of some chickens. I would be very disappointed to hear Mr. Elton draw such a connection."

Her father hesitated. "He didn't precisely make that connection, but he did say he would be securing the cabinet locks in the vestry. He is nervous the thief may try to steal the church's silver. And if he is so bold as to do so, who knows what he will do next? The villain might even try to break into Hartfield," he replied in a genuinely unhappy tone.

Emma briefly rubbed a spot in the middle of her forehead, where a headache was starting to form. Mr. Elton had always been sensitive to her father's nervous disposition but was clearly in need of a reminder.

"I'm very certain the *poultry* thief will not start breaking into houses or the church," she responded in a soothing tone, "since he has never done so. But I will speak to George. We can always have one of the footmen stay up and keep watch the next few nights, just in case."

Her father graced her with a relieved smile. "I think that would be very wise. And I do hope Constable Sharpe can attend to this business now that Mr. Suckling has been detained."

"No doubt that will be the case. Now, surely you and Mr. Elton had other things to talk about. Something a little more cheerful, perhaps? He is in great need of cheering up and should not be dwelling on morbid or disturbing subjects."

"We did speak of other things, although our conversation took a rather odd turn, I must say."

*What now?*

"How so?"

"Well, first, he said it was a great relief to speak with me, because I better than anyone could understand his present state." He waved a vague hand. "He meant as a fellow widower, of course. But he has such a different view of the matter than I. After losing your dear mother, I never contemplated the wedded state again. After all, how could one replace such a woman? To even consider it at that time was out of the question."

Even though Emma had been very young when her mother died, she could still recall the depth of her father's grief. And she'd been living with the aftermath of that grief and the effect on his temperament for all these many years.

"That was perfectly understandable," she replied. "But how does his view differ from yours?"

"Mr. Elton said that, despite his grief, he had too great a regard for the married state to remain a widower. In fact, as a cleric, he felt it his duty to remarry as an example to his parishioners, preferably sooner than later."

Something instinctively recoiled in Emma, giving her pause.

"I'll grant that it was strange for him to speak of such matters so closely upon the heels of his wife's death," she cautiously said. "But perhaps he was simply rambling. He's been somewhat scattered since Mrs. Elton's passing."

Father shook his head. "No, he spoke quite decisively about it. He expects to remarry within a year's time, and he seems certain to find a lady of equal stature and standing as Mrs. Elton."

Emma felt her eyes go wide. In fact, she rather imagined them popping right out of their sockets. This sounded much like the Mr. Elton of old, the man who had betrothed himself to Augusta Hawkins within weeks of swearing undying devotion to Emma.

"What an extraordinary thing to say," she managed.

"I was surprised, as well, my dear. Indeed, I was so astonished that I quite forgot myself and asked him a rather impertinent question."

Emma waited, but he simply gazed at her pensively.

"Father, what was the question?" she finally prompted.

"I suppose it wasn't so much a question as an observation," he replied.

"Which was?"

"That despite one's obligations to one's vocation, one should never rush into these matters. I advised him that the widowed state could indeed be preferable, especially for a man of the cloth. Having once lost a spouse, one doesn't wish to take the risk of losing another. That would be *most* regrettable."

She had to stifle an inappropriate impulse to laugh, since he made it sound as if Mr. Elton had simply misplaced Mrs. Elton as one would a set of keys. But lurking underneath that impulse was something decidedly lacking in humor. Uneasiness was growing within her, and it was of a piece to the unsettling conversation she'd had with Frank and the others at Randalls.

"I strongly advised Mr. Elton to resist any such decision for two years, if not longer," her father added.

"And how did he respond to that advice?"

"He said he could not afford to wait."

Again, she felt that strange sense of disorientation come over her, as it had at Randalls.

"I assume he was referring to his financial situation?" she asked. "Did he discuss that with you?"

Her father grimaced. "Indeed he did. I fear Mr. Elton is in very straitened circumstances, Emma. I believe *impoverished* is the word he used."

"But how is that possible?" she exclaimed. "Of course the loss of his wife's fortune was a terrible blow, but he has his own independence—and his living as Highbury's vicar. He will be forced to economize, but he is hardly penniless."

"Not according to Mr. Elton. Apparently, Mr. Suckling invested and lost his money, too."

Emma now felt like she was wading through a field of mud. "Do you mean Mr. Elton's personal independence? Because I understood that was separate from Mrs. Elton's fortune."

"I must admit he was rather vague on that point," he replied. "And it was such a muddle that I grew quite confused. He said so many things, Emma. I confess they didn't all make sense to me."

Or to her, either, which was immensely frustrating.

"It certainly sounds confusing," she replied as she struggled to maintain a calm demeanor. "But I do wonder how this came about, and how Mr. Elton was apprised of the loss of his personal funds."

"Ah, I do know that," her father replied with a triumphant air. "He happened upon a letter from Mr. Suckling to Mrs. Elton that was tucked away in the corner of her—"

"Another letter?" she exclaimed. "Good God, they seem to appear in a remarkably convenient fashion."

"You mustn't interrupt, my dear," Father replied in a gently chiding tone. "It's impolite."

*So much for remaining calm.*

"I beg your pardon, dearest. Please continue."

He opened his mouth but then shut it, looking suddenly perturbed.

"What's wrong?" she asked.

"Mr. Elton told me about the letter in strictest confidence. He has not even shared it with Dr. Hughes, and I believe he does not wish to do so."

"Why not?"

"Out of embarrassment, I suppose. I imagine that he is reluctant for others to realize the extent of his financial woes."

If that were the case, why then would he confide in her father? As the Woodhouses were the first family of Highbury, Mr. Elton had always valued his relationship with them and had clearly regretted losing the favor of Hartfield's master, even if only temporarily. But his attitude toward Father had always possessed an awkward element, one both patronizing and obsequious. After his marriage to Augusta Hawkins, Mr. Elton had become more patronizing and less obsequious.

Somehow, she'd forgotten that, like she'd forgotten how greatly his manner had annoyed her. With all the changes that had come with her marriage to George, the behavior of Mr. and Mrs. Elton had become much less important. And the death of Mrs. Elton had produced a revolution of sorts in all their lives. The past hadn't seemed to matter so greatly, and Mr. Elton himself had been metamorphosing into a new sort of man.

But now . . .

In an attempt to mask her increasingly disturbed state of mind, Emma mustered a reassuring smile. "I feel sure Mr. Elton wouldn't mind you telling me about the letter. He's been very forthcoming with me—and with George, as well. Indeed, he relies greatly upon George's advice, and I have no doubt he'll soon share the particulars of his financial situation with him."

Her father looked dubious. "Are you sure, Emma?"

"Absolutely," she replied, mentally crossing her fingers. "Did Mr. Elton relay any of the specifics contained in the letter?"

He frowned, as if trying to recall the details. "He noted that Mrs. Elton had generally managed their various financial accounts—just as you have done with ours these past several years. That included his independence and the funds from his living. As a man of the cloth, he had no head for such things, you see." He smiled. "In that we are much the same, although, of course, I am not a cleric."

Mr. Elton had made similar claims in the days following his wife's death. Emma had found them just as strange then as she did now. The vicar had always been a man greatly concerned with money. She'd learned that lesson the hard way when he'd so callously rejected Harriet, horrified at the very notion of an alliance with a girl of uncertain parentage and no real fortune. As George had once said, although Mr. Elton might speak sentimentally, he would always act rationally. He had always possessed a good opinion of himself and would be highly unlikely ever to make what he would consider an imprudent match, or indeed act in any way that diminished his standing in the community.

But perhaps after his marriage to Augusta Hawkins, a woman of considerable fortune, he was less concerned with financial matters. After all, he'd become a wealthy man. And although his wife may have generally controlled the purse strings, she was no pinch purse. They'd always lived in an elegant and sometimes even extravagant fashion. Since that was the case, perhaps Mr. Elton had been content to leave the disposition of their fortune in the hands of his wife. As a vicar, he would not wish to appear overly concerned with money, despite his obvious enjoyment of the luxuries obtained on his marriage to a wealthy woman.

"I assume Mr. Elton discovered the loss of his personal funds via this recently unearthed letter from Mr. Suckling?" she asked.

"That's it exactly, my dear. Mr. Suckling invested the entirety of Mr. and Mrs. Elton's monies. And it was all lost in the collapse of that dreadful bank." He suddenly grimaced with apprehension. "I do hope that will never happen to us, Emma. I could not bear it."

She hastened to reassure him. "George and John would never allow that to happen. You know how careful they are in their investments and management. They would never risk anything happening to Isabella and the children, or to you and to me."

He visibly relaxed. "We are indeed fortunate in our in-laws, are we not? Mr. Elton lamented that such was not the case for him, and one can hardly blame him. Not that he blamed Mrs. Elton—quite the opposite. He said that Mr. Suckling had greatly imposed on her, taking advantage of her trusting nature. He was not angry with her in the least."

"That is very charitable of him," she dryly commented. "Especially since the poor woman has been murdered."

"Very true, my dear," her father said, oblivious to her gentle sarcasm. "Mr. Elton greatly regretted that his wife hadn't alerted him to their troubles. If she had done so, he felt he might have been able to protect her from Mr. Suckling. He said he would not make such a mistake again."

She frowned. "What mistake? Not manage his own finances?"

He shook his head. "I believe he was referring to their reliance on Mr. Suckling. He stated that when next he married, he would be a great deal more careful in his relationship with his in-laws."

Again, Emma experienced an instinctive recoiling. "For such a recent widower, he seems already obsessed with the notion of marriage. I find that very strange indeed."

It was also highly reminiscent of the old Mr. Elton and his speedy engagement to Augusta Hawkins after Emma rejected his impertinent proposal. In this case, however, his behavior was even more startling.

"What can one say, Emma? As I mentioned, I cautioned Mr. Elton against making any rash decisions." Father sighed. "I truly wish people would stop getting married. There have been too many weddings in Highbury this past year. I find it all very fatiguing."

A quick perusal of her father's face convinced her that he was genuinely worn out by his bizarre discussion with Mr. Elton.

She stood. "I'm not surprised that you're tired after such a long visit. Come, Father, let me help you upstairs. I think you should take a bit of a rest before dressing for dinner."

As Emma escorted him to his bedroom, she forced herself to speak cheerfully on other matters, particularly the decision by Jane and Frank to remain for some time in Highbury. Father agreed that they should host a dinner party for the Churchills very soon—as long as no cake was served. Under the influence of her soothing patter, he was soon stifling yawns. By the time she covered him with a blanket, he was already dozing off, with all thoughts of Mr. Elton or the poultry thief apparently forgotten.

Unfortunately, she could not forget so easily. The more she thought about her father's conversation with Mr. Elton, the more disturbed she became. Fetching a light shawl from her bedroom, she decided to take a turn around the garden, now cooler and long with shadows in the late afternoon.

As she wandered aimlessly between the neat rows of rosebushes and shrubbery, her head buzzed with questions. When answers slowly began to rise up, in hardly more than whispers, at first, she pushed back, hating what her mind insisted on telling her. But as she sorted through everything she'd heard this day, both at Randalls and from her father, she could no longer keep her thoughts at bay. Pieces began to fall into the empty spaces of the puzzle. They were small pieces, to be sure, the little niggles that others had brushed aside.

But Emma could no longer brush them aside, because they *fit*. And she *hated* that they fit.

Perhaps she was wrong. Perhaps she was letting her imagination run away with her again, because the logical conclusion of her thoughts seemed too horrible to be true. George would certainly advise caution, as he'd done so many times in the past. She could envision the skeptical slant to his eyebrows and his growing incredulity as she made her case that Mr. Suckling had *not* murdered his sister-in-law, after all. Her husband would likely shake his head and gently scold her for letting her imagination run wild. More than anything, Emma would love to agree with him.

But her theory made too much sense to ignore, because it came down to that critical question again, which was, who stood to benefit the most from Mrs. Elton's death? And perhaps even more important, who had been most harmed by her actions? Who had lost the most? At first blush, one could certainly say it was Mr. Suckling. He had indeed lost a great deal. But someone else had lost more. Someone else had lost everything he prized—money, social standing, even his ability to advance within his profession. Now that was all gone because the person closest to him had betrayed them both and risked everything, lost everything.

She sank down onto the bench under the oak tree and held her head in her hands. So much of what they knew about the murder, or what they *thought* they knew, came from one source. They'd thought that source to be unimpeachable, beyond question. But he more than any other had controlled the information, doling it out in bits and pieces, pointing first in one direction and then another. And although she and others had certainly had their doubts or, like her father, had vociferously objected, no one had questioned the man's motives. It had never even occurred to any of them to do so.

And yet, it *all* came down to motive. Who among them had the strongest motive? It wasn't Mr. Suckling—Emma was almost certain of that now. No, it was the one they'd never suspected, the one she had truly come to believe was a changed man.

She thumped a clenched fist against her forehead. How had she allowed it to happen again? How had she allowed him to misdirect her *again*?

Unable to bear her own company a moment longer, she swiftly rose and set off through the gardens, heading for the gravel drive that would take her into Highbury and thence to Donwell. She needed to speak to George at once. He would listen to her, certainly with skepticism, but he would listen. She *needed* him to listen.

If her theory proved to be correct, it would upend everything in ways that were hard to imagine—not only for them but also for Highbury. And only George, her unshakable, levelheaded magistrate of a husband, could be trusted to put it right again.

# CHAPTER 27

By the time Emma reached Donwell, she was dust covered and breathless. She'd all but raced past Randalls, where, for a fleeting moment, she'd considered stopping to enlist Frank's support. But a disconcerting instinct had told her that she couldn't afford the time, so anxiety had driven her on, like the gusting winds that foretold the approach of a storm.

She paused for a few moments, bracing her hands on her knees as she sought to catch her breath. It wouldn't do to rush into her husband's study like a madwoman. She probably looked like one, though, so she took a moment to smooth her hair and shake the dust from her skirts.

As usual on a summer's day such as this, Donwell's oaken front doors stood open to let in the fresh air. She hurried through the great hall to the corridor that led to the east wing. Unless he was out in the orchards with William Larkins, George was most likely down there in his study, working on the abbey's accounts.

Thankfully, all seemed quiet. There were very few servants at Donwell these days, and most of the rooms were shut up, the furniture under Holland covers and the drapes tightly drawn. Abovestairs, only the great hall, the library, and the study were cleaned on a daily basis.

As she entered the corridor, she nearly ran into Mrs. Hodges coming from the opposite direction.

"Mrs. Knightley." The housekeeper's gaze tracked over Emma. "Goodness, madam! Is everything all right?"

Clearly, she'd not done as good a job restoring her appearance as she'd thought.

"I'm fine. The walk from Hartfield was simply a bit dusty and warm."

Mrs. Hodges peered toward the hall and frowned. "Now, where has that dratted footman gone off to? I told Harry to keep watch by the front door. I apologize, madam. Can I bring you something to drink?"

"Is Mr. Knightley in his study? If so, you can bring a pot of tea up there, if you wouldn't mind."

She nodded. "He is. And I'll bring up a pot of—"

A startling boom echoed along the corridor, freezing them both. Emma's heart skipped a few beats, then started pounding with urgent intensity.

That boom came from a gun.

"Heavens!" cried the housekeeper.

Emma grabbed her arms. "Where is Larkins?"

Mrs. Hodges gaped at her. "I . . . I believe he's out by the stables."

"Go there right now and tell him to come to the study. And tell him to bring a pistol or shotgun."

"Mrs. Knightley, what is happening?"

Emma gave her a little push. "I don't know, but hurry! Mr. Knightley might be in danger."

The woman picked up her skirts and ran. Emma did the same, plunging down the long corridor. After the startling report of the weapon, an ominous silence now filled the air, broken only by the soft slap of her footsteps.

That silence terrified Emma.

She skidded to a halt at the door of the study and grabbed the doorframe to steady herself. Relief flooded her body. George was standing behind his desk. While he was clutching one arm, he was alive and whole otherwise. But he might not be alive and whole for much longer. Standing several feet in front of the desk was Mr. Elton, holding two pistols.

As she watched, he dropped one to the floor—obviously the one he'd just fired—and transferred the other weapon to his right hand.

George grimaced as he let go of his arm and held up a hand. "Philip, you don't want to do this."

A patch of the green woolen fabric of George's coat sleeve was dark, obviously with blood. Emma's head swam, and black dots swarmed across her vision.

*Don't faint.*

She forced herself to suck in a deep breath. Then anger rushed in and cleared her gaze.

"Not true, Mr. Knightley," Mr. Elton replied, sounding almost gleeful, as he pointed the weapon at George. "I definitely do want to do this."

Emma stepped through the doorway. "Mr. Elton, you will stop right now!"

He jerked and then spun to face her before pointing the weapon straight at *her*. Then he stumbled back a few steps.

"Mrs. Knightley!" he exclaimed in a horrified tone. "What are you doing here?"

George sucked in a startled breath. "Emma, my God!"

When her husband started for her, Mr. Elton snarled at him. "Not another step, Knightley, or I *will* shoot you."

"You will do no such thing," Emma snapped as she stalked

over to her husband. "Mrs. Hodges has already now run to fetch help, so you'd best put that pistol down while you can."

Mr. Elton looked momentarily disconcerted before lifting a defiant chin. "I very much doubt that, Mrs. Knightley. When I approached the house, I checked to make sure that none of the servants were in the vicinity of the study."

She ignored that bit of nonsense as she gingerly touched George's injured arm.

"He only winged me," he said in a low, urgent voice. "You must leave right now, my Emma."

When he tried to push her toward the door, she resisted. "I'm not going anywhere, and certainly not while Mr. Elton is pointing a gun at you."

"You'd best do as he says, Mrs. Knightley," Elton replied. Clearly, he'd recovered from the shock of her surprise entrance. "My business is with your husband."

She rounded on him, fixing him with a ferocious glare. "Your only business here should be to surrender to him. I know that you killed your wife and tried to cover it up by blaming others. Well, you will not get away with it. If you have a shred of integrity left in your character, you will put down that gun and submit yourself to justice."

Far from being intimidated, he gazed at her with rapt attention and a feverish intensity, which raised the hairs on the back of her neck. It occurred to her that his senses had indeed become utterly disordered.

"Dear, dear Mrs. Knightley," he said in a disconcertingly fond tone. "You should do as your husband advises and leave immediately. I should hate for you to see anything that would cause you distress."

She stared at him. "Mr. Elton, have you gone entirely mad?"

"Not helpful, Emma," George said through gritted teeth.

The vicar heaved a sigh. "Certainly not. That is most unkind, Mrs. Knightley. I expected better of you."

"Good God! You murdered your wife and seek to murder my husband, and yet you expected better from *me*?" Then her mind suddenly switched tack. "Wait, why do you want to murder George?"

When he cast her an indulgent smile, Emma began to wonder if she was the one losing her mind.

"Madam, I should think it obvious," he gently chided. "I told you once how ardently I adored you, and that has never changed. You will *always* be the sole object of my affection, no matter what obstacles might stand between us. I seek only to eliminate those obstacles so we might have a future together."

She gaped at him for an astounded moment before replying. "That obstacle obviously being my husband."

"A husband who does not love you as you deserve. Knightley reprimands you, even in public, and lords it over you. Surely you can see that I'd never do that, Miss Woodhouse. I would treat you with the reverence and respect you so richly deserve." He sneered at George. "Something your husband has failed to do."

Emma exchanged on incredulous glance with George. Clearly, their vicar *had* gone insane.

"It is *Mrs.* Knightley," she said. "And it escapes me how you could have failed to see that I am very happily married. Until a short time ago, we thought you were happily married, as well."

He casually waved his free hand. "After your cruel refusal, I had no choice but to look elsewhere. For a time, I found a degree of contentment with Augusta. But it was a false contentment, as I soon discovered. Having loved you, no other woman could ever measure up. You must believe me when I say that my affections for you are eternally fixed."

Emma could only stare at him, horrified by his unnervingly placid smile. All these weeks she'd disciplined her imagination, avoiding flights of fancy. Apparently, she'd not been fanciful enough.

"And here I thought you were falling in love with Harriet," was all she could think of to reply.

"Ah, Miss Woodhouse," Mr. Elton soulfully said. "Who can think of Mrs. Martin when you are near?"

Was it only a few days ago that George had cautioned her against spending too much time in the vicar's company? She'd thought her husband's concern an overreach, but he'd had the right of it. Still, no one could have anticipated *this* deranged an outcome.

"She is Mrs. Knightley," George said in a cold tone as he tried to pull Emma behind him. "And it is clear that you married Augusta Hawkins for her money. When she lost her money, you murdered her, and now you seek to murder me in the absurd hopes of persuading my wife to marry you. You will never succeed, Philip."

Emma resisted George's attempts to shield her with his body. She was quite sure Mr. Elton would not shoot her. Logically, he'd also lost his chance to shoot George and get away with it, but logic was clearly not top of mind with the vicar at the moment.

"George is correct," she stated. "It's . . . it's . . ."

She stuttered to a halt as a truly sickening notion leapt unbidden into her head. Her chest grew so tight she could hardly squeeze out the words.

"You tried to poison my father, didn't you?" she said with a gasp.

George let out a startled hiss before wrapping a protective arm around her waist and pulling her against him.

Mr. Elton simply shrugged. His manner suggested she'd accused him of some minor infraction, such as stealing apples from the orchard.

"What else could I do? Mr. Woodhouse was keeping us apart. If it's any consolation, I'm pleased he survived the . . .

episode. Your father clearly regrets his treatment of me and has recognized the error of his ways."

When Emma thought of how closely death had stalked her father, her blood seemed to crystalize into icy little shards. "You are *utterly* insane."

Something dangerous and ugly sparked in the vicar's gaze. George's arm tightened around her waist in silent warning.

"I have to say that you certainly fooled all of us, Philip," her husband said in a conversational tone. "How did you manage it?"

Mr. Elton blinked, and the nasty gleam in his eyes faded, replaced by something like a smirk. "It was quite simple, really. I knew only Mr. Woodhouse drank the ratafia, and always from the decanter in the drawing room. He also told me once that he occasionally resorted to the drops. While you were all at dinner, I slipped in from the gardens into the drawing room. It took only moments to dose the decanter, and then I departed the same way."

He all but preened with appreciation for his own cleverness. Emma was tempted to pick up the heavy brass inkwell on the desk and throw it at the vile man's head.

*Actually . . .*

Perhaps that was not such a terrible idea. Holding a pistol for so long was bound to be tiring, and Mr. Elton's arm must surely soon droop or waver. When it did, she would take her chance. They simply needed to keep him talking until the opportunity presented itself.

"I do not entirely comprehend your plan, sir," she said with forced calm. "You intended to kill both my father *and* my husband, after which you expected me to marry you?"

He held up his other hand. "Yes, but after the appropriate mourning period, of course. I feel certain we would have grown very close during that time, as two bereaved spouses. Soulmates in tragedy, as it were."

Disbelief got the better of her. "But with Mr. Suckling in prison, how could you possibly explain my husband's murder?"

"The poultry thief, of course. He's grown very bold, as you know. Mr. Knightley's study contains several fine pieces, like that silver clock on the mantelpiece. It should not be difficult to make the case."

"The poultry thief?" she exclaimed. "The man steals only *poultry*. Even my father wouldn't believe it."

*Well, perhaps he would just a little.*

"That is as ridiculous," said George, "as your assertion that you love my wife. What you love is money and position. That is why you murdered Mrs. Elton."

"I *am* in love with your wife," Mr. Elton coldly replied. "But I will not deny that Augusta's foolish behavior—not to mention Horace's bungling—was the precipitating event."

Emma had to ask. "How did you find out that Mrs. Elton had lost everything?"

A shadow seemed to flit across his face. "It doesn't matter." He gave the gun a little jerk, gesturing toward the door. "I will again ask you to leave, madam, and allow me to conclude my business with your husband."

"Emma, please go," George urgently murmured.

Of course the darling man wished to protect her, but she had no intention of leaving.

Still, she pretended to consider the vicar's demand. "Mr. Elton, I will certainly not leave until you have answered my questions. You owe me that, if nothing else."

The more he told them, the more time they would have.

He studied her, as if to measure the sincerity of her words. Emma kept her own gaze steady, while praying that William Larkins would soon come to their rescue. By now, Mrs. Hodges should have been able to run into Highbury and fetch half the town to help them.

Mr. Elton shrugged. "Very well, I will answer your questions. But then you must leave."

She dodged making a promise. "Then I will ask again how you found out about the loss of your funds."

"Some weeks ago, I began to harbor suspicions that all was not well. Augusta had grown strange by then, and she became particularly secretive around questions of money."

"So," George said, "Mrs. Elton did manage your finances. That was not a tale made up to divert suspicion."

He sneered. "It was a mistake I shall not make again."

*Dead men can't make mistakes.*

At this point, Emma would happily escort him to the gallows herself. "Why didn't you manage your finances yourself?"

"Augusta insisted that she and Horace be allowed to continue to manage her fortune. It was a condition of our union, you see, and included in the marriage settlements. In return, she agreed that I would inherit everything if she predeceased me, with nothing directed to Selina or even any children she might bear. The fact that she was in no great hurry to write a will was a show of her trust in me." He snorted. "She thought herself so magnanimous, so much the great lady. But she was just a great fool to place herself in the hands of a scoundrel like Suckling."

"And that letter you mentioned to my father. Is that how you found out that Mr. Suckling's investments had failed?"

"Yes, although I found that letter before our . . . altercation in the church, obviously. It made it clear that Horace had no intention of helping us, since the state of his financial situation had made it impossible." A ferocious scowl distorted his features, rendering him almost unrecognizable. "That was a lie, of course. It was to be expected from a man without an ounce of integrity running through his veins."

"At least he never killed anyone," Emma retorted.

George gave her another warning squeeze.

"Not that it matters," she hastily added. "So, you found the letters, and then what? You confronted Mrs. Elton?"

Elton eyed her with suspicion but eventually nodded. "I demanded a full explanation. Initially, she was quite evasive, but I soon managed to get the truth out of her."

An image of Mrs. Elton sprawled in a bloody heap on the floor filled Emma's mind. Her heart ached with sympathy. The moment when the poor woman realized she was married to a madman must have been horrible indeed.

"How did you get her to go to the church?" George asked.

"And why was she wearing her pearl necklace?" Emma added.

Mr. Elton shifted, rotating his right shoulder, as if his arm was finally getting tired. But although his gun hand drooped a trifle, it was steady enough. Still, Emma casually dropped a hand down to the desk and rested her fingertips only inches from the heavy inkwell.

"I discovered the letters in the morning, while Augusta was out," Mr. Elton replied. "By the time she returned home, I was quite . . . perturbed."

"Of course you were," she sarcastically replied.

Elton smiled approvingly, obviously taking her comment to be one of understanding. "Indeed. We had a tremendous row about it. Since I did not wish the servants to overhear us—at least more than they already had—I insisted we go to the church for privacy's sake."

Another piece of the puzzle slid into place for Emma. "And Mrs. Wright overheard you."

He scoffed. "Some of it, yes. Fortunately, Augusta reassured that interfering old biddy that it was nothing. My dear wife didn't wish to be embarrassed in front of the servants, you see," he said in a sarcastic tone.

"Mrs. Wright was obviously very loyal to your wife," George commented.

"She should have been loyal to *me*," the vicar snapped. "Instead, she caused a great deal of trouble, filling Augusta's head with her nonsense."

Emma tapped the top of the desk, a bit closer to the inkwell. "Did Mrs. Wright suspect that you had, er, feelings for me?"

That would certainly explain the woman's ill will.

"Probably. Toward the end, Augusta accused me of caring more for your good opinion than hers, which she likely heard from Mrs. Wright." He preened a bit. "Of course, that was true."

It took a moment for Emma to wrestle her rising temper under control. "So you went to the church for privacy. But, again, I must ask why Mrs. Elton was wearing her pearls."

"Ah, yes," he replied with a genial nod. "Thank you for reminding me, dear madam."

*Mad as Mrs. Radcliffe's monk.*

"I insisted that Augusta hand over her jewels, as I would need to sell them," he explained. "She must have feared I'd make such a demand at some point, because she'd taken to always wearing her best pieces or carrying them about in her reticule. But I had no intention of letting her escape with any of her jewels. They were all we had of any value besides her gowns and our silver service and china."

Emma frowned. "Escape? What do you mean by that?"

"She threatened to retire to Maple Grove to live with her sister. Astonishing, really, that she would live with the man who'd ruined us all. You may be sure I forbade her to do so. I also informed her that I would do my best to ruin Horace and her blasted sister, just as they had ruined us."

"I imagine she didn't like that," George quietly noted.

Elton's gaze once more grew flat and hard. "She did not."

"How did she respond?"

"She cursed at me and then slapped me." He shook his head. "She was always a vulgar woman, but even I was surprised by such behavior. Apparently, my influence was not enough to temper the flaws in her character."

*Unbelievable.*

Emma had to steel herself to ask the next question. "And how did *you* respond?"

He frowned, as if the question made no sense. "How do you think? I struck her back."

"Good God," George muttered, his voice heavy with disgust.

Just then, Emma caught a slight movement out on the terrace. Through the open terrace doors, she saw a shadow cast onto the stones just beyond the doorframe.

*William Larkins.*

Some relief flowed through her, making her painfully aware of how tightly she'd been holding her body. Finally, help was nearby.

A gentle squeeze at her waist communicated that George had also noted the movement. Larkins, an intelligent and sensible man, was no doubt waiting for the opportune time to strike. Now they had to continue to keep the vicar distracted.

"I assume that was when Mrs. Elton fell and bumped her head?" Emma asked.

"No, that happened when I took the necklace. We had a bit of a struggle, and I was forced to be quite rough. She fell, but it was really her fault. She should have done as I asked. After all, it's a wife's duty to obey her husband." He again flashed her that bone-chilling smile. "It's in one's wedding vows, as you know."

The deranged reply unleashed emotions Emma could no longer contain.

"But why?" she exclaimed. "Why not just let her go? Instead, you *murdered* her. And please don't say that you did it for love of me, because I will *not* believe you."

He bristled, clearly annoyed by her response. "She threatened to lodge a complaint against me to the bishop. She said she would ruin me as much as I had ruined her." He chopped down his free hand. "Nonsense, of course. I have been the victim in all of this. I ask you, Mrs. Knightley, how did *I* ruin *her*?"

"You married her," she tersely replied.

"And it was *your* refusal that sent me off to her. You should have accepted me when you had the chance."

Emma goggled at him. "So this is my fault?"

His calculating expression sent a chill deep into her bones. "In one sense, I suppose it is."

If not for the gun, she would have picked up the inkwell and thrown it straight at his evil, swelled head. Again, a small squeeze from George urged caution.

"I imagine that made you quite angry," he said in a steady tone of remarkable self-control. "Such a report from your wife—combined with the general scandal surrounding the Sucklings—would have been most distressing for the bishop."

Mr. Elton shifted his shoulder, wincing slightly. "Yes, of course," he replied. "Such a complaint would have destroyed any opportunities for advancement. I might have even lost the living here in Highbury. I could not allow that to happen."

"So you had to kill your wife," said George.

"What choice did I have? Surely you can see that, Mr. Knightley."

He was a monster—a murdering, deranged monster hiding behind the mask of a grieving widower and mild-mannered cleric. Unbelievably, he'd convinced himself that he was the victim, and that all his subsequent actions had been justified by the wrong he thought done to him.

"There is always a choice," George sternly replied.

"Says the wealthiest man in the parish. Mr. Knightley, you have no idea what it's like to be raised as a gentleman and yet always forced to scrape by. Always forced to toady to the likes of you. Or to a man like Cole—or Horace Suckling," he said, his tone thick with contempt. "I had finally escaped that life of constant little humiliations, and I have no intention of going back to it."

George scoffed. "The only place you'll be going is to the gaol."

Mr. Elton narrowed his gaze. "Do not forget I am holding the pistol, sir."

"I would suggest that *you* not forget you have only one try with that pistol," Emma snapped. "You cannot shoot both of us."

For a moment, he appeared genuinely shocked. "Dear madam, I certainly have no intention of shooting you."

"Well, I'm certainly not going to let you shoot my husband, either."

Unfortunately, Mr. Elton took that as a challenge, since he began to move around to the side, as if trying for a better angle to take a shot. Emma attempted to wriggle out of George's grasp, hoping to use her body to shield him.

Unfortunately, her overprotective husband was doing the exact opposite and trying to wrestle her behind him.

"Stop it, George," she ordered.

"Yes, George, stop it." Mr. Elton sarcastically echoed her. "Only a few more inches will do it."

"For God's sake, how do you think you're going to get away with this?" she exclaimed.

She surreptitiously glanced toward the terrace doors, but the late afternoon sun reflected off the windows. Where was Larkins, and why was he waiting?

"Larkins can't get a clear shot," he whispered in her ear, reading her thoughts.

"What are you saying to her, Knightley?" snarled the vicar.

"He's simply trying to reassure me, sir," Emma hastily replied.

Mr. Elton waved the gun. "Mrs. Knightley, you will—"

"I'm curious," she said, interrupting him in a desperate gambit. "Why did you blame Miss Bates for your wife's murder when you clearly intended to level that accusation against Mr. Suckling?"

He blinked a few times, as if taken aback. "At the time it hadn't occurred to me to frame Horace for the crime. And if you'll recall, I never truly accused Miss Bates."

"Come, Mr. Elton. You did everything you could to cast her in a suspicious light."

He scowled. "That stupid woman with her constant chattering. And that mother of hers, always silently comparing me to her husband—and finding me lacking, I have no doubt. Sadly, Augusta insisted on befriending them." He waggled the gun again. "They caused me a great deal of trouble, along with that stupid Jane Churchill. So, when that promissory note came to light, you may be sure I was happy to take advantage of it."

"But when that didn't hold," said George, "you decided to plant the necklace on Suckling. A very neat trick, since it would be returned to you, anyway, along with all your wife's personal belongings."

The vicar flashed an odd little smile. "Yes. It was worth a beating to see Horace hauled off like a common thief—which, I might add, he is. But even so, the jewels and the rest of it weren't enough. I was certainly not exaggerating when I said I was near to impoverishment."

"So you decided to kill Mr. Woodhouse and then me."

"I already stated that I am thankful Mr. Woodhouse survived. You, however, do need to be removed. How else can Mrs. Knightley and I be together?"

"Good God," Emma exclaimed. "You truly are deluded."

Mr. Elton glared at her. "Deluded? Hardly. Every action I've taken has been carefully thought out, and with one goal in mind."

"Not getting caught," she retorted.

He narrowed his gaze on her. "If I got caught, then how could I marry you?"

Emma's temper finally boiled over. "You are a small, contemptible toad of a man, and the very sight of you makes me ill. And you dare to compare yourself to my husband? It's utterly ridiculous."

His face darkening with fury, the vicar took a menacing step toward her. George pulled her back and around the other side of the desk.

"Are you going to shoot me?" she challenged, glaring at Mr. Elton.

"Get out of the way," he barked. "Now."

William Larkins stepped into the room, armed with a shotgun. "Ho, Elton," he called.

Startled, the vicar spun around, almost tripping over his own feet. He jerked up the pistol and fired, but Larkins had already ducked behind a settee. One of the terrace doors exploded, glass raining down as the pistol's echo reverberated around the walls.

As George pulled her to the floor, Larkins was already moving. In a blur of motion, he swung up the butt of his gun and smashed Mr. Elton in the face. Without a sound, the vicar crumpled to the floor.

For a few moments, they all remained frozen, as if in a tableau.

"Good God," Emma whispered.

George enveloped her in a fierce embrace. "It's over, my darling. You're safe."

She twisted around to face him. His features were set in pale, strained lines.

"You've been shot," she said as anxiety broke through her shock. She touched his shoulder. "I think you're still bleeding."

"He truly did only wing me. I promise I'm fine."

Holding on to each other, they clambered to their feet and

Murder in Highbury 373

made their way to Larkins. The sturdy Irishman stood over Mr. Elton, gazing at him with undisguised loathing.

"I don't think he'll be waking up anytime soon," said George.

"Better if the sneaky little bastard didn't wake up at all." Then Larkins glanced at Emma and grimaced. "Begging your pardon for the language, Mrs. Knightley."

Emma huffed out a shaky laugh. "No apology necessary, Mr. Larkins. You have expressed my feelings precisely."

# CHAPTER 28

Emma and her father entered the drawing room, with a solicitous Mrs. Weston in their wake. Since the evening had grown cool, one of the footmen had built up a blazing fire in the grate and strategically placed screens around the chairs and settee.

"How cozy," Emma cheerily said. "We can be perfectly comfortable while we have tea."

Just now rising from table after a light supper, they were awaiting George's return from Donwell Abbey. He'd warned Emma that he might be very late. It would be necessary to interrogate Mr. Elton—once he recovered from his well-deserved blow—and then appropriate legal processes must be followed in dealing with their criminal vicar.

Her father sighed as she tucked his lap blanket around him.

"I don't know if I shall ever feel cozy again," he dolefully said. "Mr. Elton trying to shoot George . . . He must be mad, Emma! No sane person would ever wish to hurt George."

"It is indeed shocking," Mrs. Weston noted as she adjusted one of the screens. "But from what Emma tells us, Mr. Knightley is perfectly well."

"But why must he stay away so long?" Father replied. "Donwell is a very fine house, but it is drafty and quite damp in the evenings. It would be a terrible thing if George were to catch a chill. He might fall into a fever, and then what should we do?"

Emma patted his shoulder. "I promise you that George is perfectly well. It was a very slight graze, and Mr. Perry himself said there was no danger of infection or fever."

"Then I suppose we must thank the good Lord that Mr. Elton was as bad a shot as he was a vicar," he said. "That was indeed a blessing."

Mrs. Weston made a slight choking noise. Emma studiously avoided looking at her friend, since doing so might trigger a bout of semi-hysterical laughter.

"Yes, we were very fortunate in that regard," she replied instead.

Her father mustered up an indignant look. "Still, to think of all our kindnesses to Mr. Elton and how often we had him to dinner. I will never be able to forgive him, Emma. Please do not expect it of me. Trying to shoot George is even worse than what he did to poor Miss Bates."

"No one will expect us to forgive him, dearest. After all, he *is* a murderer."

Mrs. Weston sat in the opposite chair. "Forgive? No, but I suppose we must make allowances for the fact that he is obviously mad. Mr. Elton certainly had his flaws, but one never expected him to be a lunatic."

Emma shrugged. "I imagine that development came later."

His thwarted ambitions, fueled by rage, had propelled the vicar down a dark path that led to madness and death—first, for his wife, and then no doubt eventually for him at the end of a hangman's noose.

"You may be sure I will be writing to the bishop," Father

sternly added. "I cannot imagine what he was thinking to send us a lunatic for a vicar."

"I'm sure the bishop had no idea at the time," Emma said.

"He should have known. It was most irresponsible of him, which I will certainly make clear."

Emma and Mrs. Weston exchanged a glance. Clearly, a diversion was necessary.

"Mr. Woodhouse," said Mrs. Weston, "you hardly touched your food at dinner. Perhaps you would allow Emma to bring you a lovely scone and jam, and a nice cup of tea. I'm sure it will do you good."

He blinked, appearing vaguely alarmed by the suggestion. "I think not, although I thank you for your concern. I could barely swallow a morsel at dinner, not even the coddled eggs. No one makes coddled eggs like Serle, as you know. I'm sure your cook does her best, Mrs. Weston, but no one coddles an egg like Serle."

"Very true," she replied with a smile. "Then might I suggest a small glass of ratafia? I'm sure it would be just the thing for your nerves."

"Just so, Father," Emma chimed in. "I'm sure you would find it restorative."

He breathed out another lugubrious sigh. "If you say so, my dear. And please bring one for Mrs. Weston, too. She no doubt needs a restorative, as well, after this shocking day."

"Nothing for me, thank you," Mrs. Weston hastily replied. "I'm perfectly fine."

Emma flashed her a wry smile. Her former governess had always viewed ratafia with horror, a sentiment Emma certainly shared. But a large glass of sherry might be in order. Today's events had left her feeling like a shuttlecock batted about one too many times. Even now, she hardly knew what to think—not that she'd had any opportunity to stop and think, much less sort through the emotions that had spun her from one moment to the next.

Once Larkins had vanquished Mr. Elton, things had moved very quickly. George had ordered Larkins and Harry, who had finally reappeared after an unfortunately ill-timed nap, to lock the vicar in the pantry. George had then dispatched a groom to fetch Dr. Hughes and Constable Sharpe, while Emma had sent the stable boy running for Mr. Perry. Her stubborn husband had insisted that his wound was only a scratch, but she'd refused to be deterred. Ignoring his protests, she had helped him take off his coat and had ruthlessly sliced open his sleeve with his desk scissors. Thankfully, the wound was indeed superficial, and she and Mrs. Hodges had made short work of cleaning and dressing it.

After George went upstairs to change his shirt, the magnitude of what had happened—what *could* have happened if she'd not arrived at Donwell when she did—finally hit her. She was forced to sit down and put her head on her knees while a concerned Mrs. Hodges patted her back. Thankfully, a cup of tea soon set her to rights. By the time George returned, Donwell's lone housemaid was sweeping up the broken glass, and Emma and Mrs. Hodges were returning the rest of the room to order.

At that point, George insisted she return home.

"Talk of this unfortunate scene will begin spreading very soon," he warned, "much of it no doubt exaggerated."

Emma almost gaped at him. "Mr. Elton attempted to murder you, George. I hardly think one can exaggerate *that* particular detail. It's quite dreadful enough without embellishment."

"That being the case, I urge you to return to Hartfield immediately. You can hardly wish for your father to learn of this from one of the servants or Miss Bates."

Emma was forced to admit the soundness of his logic. After giving him a fierce and prolonged hug—mindful of his injured arm—she hurried out. She made a quick stop at Randalls to enlist Mrs. Weston's aid in breaking the news to her father, since she felt quite unable to walk through that emotional quagmire on her own. Jane expressed her great shock, Frank roundly stated that he'd known Elton was a villain all along, and Mr. Weston hurried off to Donwell to lend George his support. Frank and Jane then decided to walk into the village to inform and manage the Bates ladies, while Mrs. Weston accompanied Emma back to Hartfield.

And never had Emma been more grateful to her former governess. Even though they'd left out as many grim details as they could, the tale was still one of violence and evil. Her father had been so upset that Emma had been tempted to send for Mr. Perry. Fortunately, Mrs. Weston had performed her gentle magic, and her kind but firm reassurances had restored Father to a semblance of equanimity.

"Emma," he said as she went to the sideboard to fetch their drinks, "Simon brought up a fresh decanter of ratafia this afternoon, so you need have no concerns that there are any contaminating substances. He opened the bottle himself, and it was perfectly good."

She mentally grimaced. In her recounting of the scene at Donwell, she'd left out the detail that Mr. Elton had tried to poison her father. The poor dear would have to be told soon enough, but he'd had enough shocks for one day. Of all the villainous actions their murderous vicar had committed, the attempted poisoning of her father—a kindly elderly gentleman who'd never hurt a soul—struck her as truly heinous. In fact, just looking at the ratafia decanter made her feel rather queasy.

After a steadying breath, she poured the beverage into a small crystal wineglass. After she poured a rather larger glass of sherry for Mrs. Weston, she decided she would quite like a brandy. While Emma did not generally drink strong spirits, this one would surely be medicinal in nature. Even Mr. Perry would approve.

After setting the glasses on a small silver tray, she carried them back to the fireside. Mrs. Weston did raise an eyebrow at the size of Emma's drink but declined to comment. Father, thankfully, didn't notice.

The French bracket clock on the mantelpiece chimed out the hour.

"Eight o'clock already?" her father fretfully said. "And George still not home? Perhaps we should send James with the carriage to fetch him, so he doesn't catch a chill on the walk from Donwell."

"Mr. Weston will take care of Mr. Knightley," Mrs. Weston said with a comforting smile. "You needn't worry in the slightest."

"George will be home soon enough," Emma added as she took a seat. "As magistrate, it is his responsibility to oversee this situation, so there are many details to attend to with Dr. Hughes and the constable."

Her father tsked. "I do not approve of either Dr. Hughes or Constable Sharpe. If they had performed their jobs in a proper fashion, you would not have been placed in such a dangerous situation and poor George would not have been shot."

Emma didn't entirely disagree with her father's assessment. But since she'd also failed to put all the pieces together until it was almost too late, she supposed she shouldn't find too much fault with their local representatives of the law.

To her credit, though, at least she'd never believed that the poultry thief was the killer.

When she heard voices in the hall, she jumped to her feet. "Thank goodness. I think the men are finally home."

The drawing room door opened, and George and Mr. Weston walked into the room.

As she hurried over to greet them, Emma took in the grim cast to her husband's countenance.

"Dearest, what an ordeal for you," she exclaimed as she took his hands. "You must be positively exhausted."

He raised her hand to his lips and kissed it, his somber gaze lightened by a small smile. "I will admit it has been a difficult afternoon, but now I am all the better for returning home to you."

"Difficult?" exclaimed Mr. Weston. "It's been nothing short of a dashed nightmare. I don't know when I've ever been so appalled by anything. Mr. Elton is a thorough villain, and the sooner he's swinging from the hangman's noose, the better."

"Now, my dear," Mrs. Weston admonished as she joined them, "I think we can spare Mr. Woodhouse such distressing observations."

Her husband winced. "Forgive me, sir. Sometimes I let my feelings run away with me."

Father waved a dismissive hand. "No apology is necessary, Mr. Weston. Mr. Elton has caused a great deal of trouble, and the sooner he is dispatched, the better off Highbury will be."

Emma exchanged a startled glance with Mrs. Weston. Apparently, all the mayhem in their little village had produced a bit of a ruthless streak in her mild-mannered parent.

"Where is Mr. Elton now?" Mrs. Weston asked.

"Constable Sharpe and William Larkins took him to the vicarage and placed him under guard," George replied. "Sharpe will be transferring him to the gaol in Guildford first thing in the morning."

"He should have been tossed into the cellar at the Crown for the night," Mr. Weston put in. "That's certainly what he deserved."

"I understand the sentiment," George replied. "But holding Mr. Elton at the Crown would have created a considerable commotion. The villagers will no doubt become greatly upset when the facts are fully known, and I would prefer to have Mr. Elton safely away to Guildford before that happens."

"A very sensible course of action, to be sure," Mrs. Weston said.

"Dash it, I suppose Mr. Knightley is right," Mr. Weston replied with a gleam of humor. "Which is why he's the magistrate and not me."

Emma patted her husband's arm. "George is always right. And if you have any doubts on that score, he will be sure to tell you so himself."

That produced a genuine smile from him, just as she'd hoped.

"We should be off, Mr. Weston," his wife said. "It's been a dreadfully fatiguing day for Emma and Mr. Knightley, and they must get their rest."

Emma hugged her friend, murmuring her heartfelt thanks. The gentlemen shook hands, farewells were made, and the Westons departed for Randalls.

"Father," Emma said as the door closed behind their friends, "I think you should retire early. This has been a very trying day for you, as well."

"I do not deny it, my dear," he replied as she helped him up from his chair. "But I fear I will not sleep a wink, thinking about how you and George were in such mortal danger."

"There were a few tricky moments," she admitted as she escorted him to the door. "But the danger passed very quickly. Mr. Elton could never get the best of Mr. Knightley, you know. The notion is entirely inconceivable."

Thankfully, her father smiled at her bit of foolishness. After promising to check on him shortly, Emma handed the old dear off to the ever-faithful Simon, who was waiting in the hall.

When she returned to her husband, he raised his eyebrows, his expression frankly skeptical.

"What?" she asked.

"Only a few tricky moments?"

"Father was so distressed that I thought I should avoid the most gruesome bits. I hate to think how he'll react when he hears the full story, since he no doubt will from Miss Bates," she ruefully said.

"That is a worry for another day. Right now, I have a few things I wish to say to you."

She crinkled her nose, recognizing the signs of an impending lecture. "May I at least fetch you a brandy first? I'm sure you stand in need of one."

He expelled a sigh and ruffled a hand through his hair, making it stand straight up. It was so endearing and so unlike him that she couldn't resist going up on tiptoe and kissing him. His arm slipped about her waist as he responded with a tenderness that brought a mist to her eyes.

When he finally released her, she had to rub her nose.

"Goodness," she said, "I'm turning into a watering pot. Whatever will you think of me?"

"What I think is that you were decidedly reckless this afternoon," he replied, adopting a severe expression. "I cannot be happy that you placed yourself in such danger, Emma. To say I was alarmed by your sudden appearance—and your refusal to leave the study—is to greatly understate the case."

She took his arm and towed him to the settee, then gave him a little shove onto the cushions.

"How could I possibly leave? He would have killed you, George," she said as she went to pour him a brandy. "And that very likely would have killed *me*."

Emma knew she would not have recovered from such an unthinkable loss. That moment she saw Mr. Elton pointing his pistol at her beloved husband had been the worst of her life.

"Besides," she added, as she returned to him, "you know very well that Mr. Elton would never have killed me. He said so himself."

George took the glass Emma proffered and put it down, then grasped her wrist and gently pulled her onto the settee beside him.

"Yes, because he loved you," he said. "I suppose we must be grateful for that."

"As much as a madman can love anyone, I suppose. I've been pondering that very point, though. I think his emotions had a great deal more to do with his own amour propre than with any true feelings for me. Mr. Elton simply couldn't understand how I could reject him. You heard him—he was absolutely convinced I would return his affections once you were disposed of."

George shook his head. "The man was clearly living in a fantasy world to believe such a thing."

"Lucky for us that he was." She rested a palm flat on his chest. "Still, it wouldn't have mattered. I would never have left the room, no matter what Mr. Elton threatened to do."

He studied her for a long moment, the warmth in his gaze igniting an answering glow in her heart.

"Then despite my dismay that you were forced to witness so horrific a scene," he said, "I cannot be anything but grateful for your courage. You were truly heroic in the face of danger, my Emma. I stand in awe of you."

His praise made her blush. "You are too kind, sir. But let us not forget that Mr. Elton, murderer though he is, still has his standards. He would *never* murder a lady."

George snorted. "The man truly is deranged, so I cannot begin to fathom his thought processes."

"Poor Mrs. Elton. She must have known before the end that her husband viewed her with contempt."

And that fact, she couldn't help thinking, was very sad indeed.

"Yes, it's quite awful." George gently brushed a stray lock of hair back from her cheek. "Emma, I hope that, in time, you will be able to forget this day. It wouldn't do to let it weigh on your thoughts."

"I'm afraid there's no forgetting this day, George. Although we must take consolation in the knowledge that Mr. Elton can never hurt anyone again."

"Highbury's nightmare is finally behind us."

Not the scandal, though. That was just beginning, and it would no doubt provide fodder for gossip for months to come.

She imagined there were very few villages in England that could lay claim to having a murderous vicar.

For a few minutes, they sat in blessed silence, George's uninjured arm resting gently around her shoulders as they stared into the dying fire.

Her husband finally stirred. "I have been wondering about one thing."

"Just one?" she ironically replied.

"For now."

"And that is?"

He tilted his head to gaze at her. "Despite the shock of encountering your husband facing the business end of a pistol, you didn't seem shocked that it was our vicar holding the other end."

"Of course I was shocked, George," she exclaimed. "Mr. Elton had just shot you."

"But you weren't shocked that it was *him*, were you?"

"Not really," she admitted.

"How did you know?"

"You must understand that I wasn't entirely sure until I saw him pointing that pistol at you. I was simply planning to speak with you about, well, a feeling I had about him."

"It must have been quite a strong feeling," he replied. "According to Mrs. Hodges, you were in quite a fluster when you arrived at Donwell."

"Something I heard at Randalls this afternoon raised my suspicions. Mr. Elton had stopped by Hartfield to visit with Father, so I took the opportunity to pop over to Randalls for a visit." She grimaced. "I feel terrible now, knowing that I left Father alone with the man who tried to kill him. It's *too* hideous, George."

He gave her a gentle squeeze. "Try not to think about it. Just tell me what you heard at Randalls that gave you pause."

"We were discussing Mrs. Elton's apparent threat to expose

Mr. Suckling, regardless of the consequences. Both Jane and Frank were adamant that she would never treat her sister in so shabby a fashion. According to Jane, Mrs. Elton was truly devoted to Mrs. Suckling and would never hurt her. Frank also made the very cogent point that it made little sense for Mrs. Elton to ruin Mr. Suckling in so spectacular a fashion. Because if she did, she would lose any chance of recouping her lost funds."

"How clever of Frank to note that," George sardonically replied.

Emma poked him in the thigh. "Even you must admit that Frank had the right of it."

"I will concede the point, and I will also concede that I am annoyed he thought of it first."

"It's very lowering, isn't it? It had never really occurred to me, either. But once the point was made, I was forced to reorder my thinking about motives. If Mrs. Elton was not threatening to expose Mr. Suckling, why bother killing her?"

"So then the question became, who truly stood to lose the most from the destruction of Mrs. Elton's fortune?"

"Mr. Elton."

He nodded. "I also concede that point, but the case against Suckling *was* strong. The necklace and the fact that he refused to even speak to anyone but his solicitor or his wife. The evidence clearly seemed to indicate his guilt."

Emma clapped her hands together. "That reminds me! When you questioned Mr. Elton, did he reveal why Mr. Suckling behaved so strangely? Why *did* he refuse to tell you his whereabouts on the day of the murder?"

"I do know the answer to that, although my source is Dr. Hughes. Suckling's solicitor sent him an express post this morning, explaining his client's whereabouts at the time of Mrs. Elton's murder. The solicitor claimed to have proof that Suckling was indeed in London that day, meeting with a potential investor, something his client did not wish to become widely known. Apparently, Suckling still hoped to keep the extent of his losses secret, so as not to frighten off other potential investors. He was confident he could get clear of the murder charge, but he needed to avoid revealing the dire state of his finances."

She frowned. "I suppose if one squints hard enough, his logic might make sense. But, George, why did Dr. Hughes fail to share this information with you immediately? In light of today's events, it strikes me as a most egregious oversight!"

"Dr. Hughes claims he was busy with patients all morning and intended to call on me later in the day to discuss the matter. You may be sure I had a few words to say to our good coroner about that. I also asked him why Suckling's solicitor was writing to him instead of me."

Emma frowned. "That does seem very odd. What was his answer?"

"Since Dr. Hughes had taken it upon himself to both interrogate and transport Suckling to the gaol, the solicitor made the reasonable assumption that the doctor was in charge of the case," he dryly replied.

Indignation flushed her cheeks with warmth. "Dr. Hughes has puffed himself up throughout this entire investigation, and to no good effect, as far as I can see. Truly, George, I think you must find a new coroner. He's both narrow-minded and pompous and seems to be good only for tending to his speckled hens."

"And do you also hold the same opinion of Constable Sharpe?" he asked with some amusement.

"Of course I do. I hope they were both properly mortified when they finally learned who the killer was."

"I believe they were. Dr. Hughes was stunned into silence for a good two minutes."

"That must have been refreshing."

Her husband laughed. "I will admit to a degree of satisfaction in that moment. And now that we've disposed of Mr. Suckling, tell me more about your suspicions regarding Mr. Elton. Surely one conversation at Randalls was not enough to convince you of his guilt."

"No, but it led me to think about our primary source of information during this entire affair—the person who, more than any other, controlled what we knew and what we didn't know."

"Ah, of course. Elton."

"Yes, including the appearance of the incriminating letters. Oh!" She tapped his thigh again. "And Mr. Elton told Father that he'd found yet another letter, one that presented even more damning evidence against Mr. Suckling. I found that extraordinarily convenient timing."

"And had anyone else seen this new letter?"

She rolled her eyes. "Of course not. But that's not all, George. Mr. Elton had the oddest conversation with my father."

As she related the details of that encounter, a thunderous expression descended on George's brow. Emma certainly couldn't blame him. It was beyond outrageous that Mr. Elton could so calmly relate his plans to her father, knowing he would soon be off to Donwell to try to kill George in the delusional hopes of claiming his wife.

"That conversation truly alarmed me," she finished. "At that point, I couldn't wait for you to come home. I had to see you immediately."

His arm tightened around her shoulders.

"I owe you a great debt, my Emma," he gruffly said. "Although I still cannot be happy that you placed yourself in such danger."

"George, I would happily face down a band of Cossack marauders if it meant saving your life."

"Thankfully, Cossacks are rarely seen in Surrey, so you may stand down."

"Yes, although I admit I was ready to run Mr. Elton through

with a saber myself, if one had been at hand. As it was, I was preparing to throw your brass inkwell at his head at the first opportunity."

When her husband was silent for a moment, she gave him a questioning nudge.

"And I was ready to kill the blighter with my bare hands for putting you in such danger," he said in a somber tone. "I am shocked to discover that I felt no qualms at the prospect, nor do I now. And that is a less than comfortable feeling."

Emma's throat suddenly grew tight, and it took a moment to answer. "George, you were trying to protect me from a deranged killer, one who actually *did* try to throttle his wife. And do not forget that he also tried to murder my father. I will be most displeased if you dare to feel one iota of guilt over what you wanted to do to that dreadful man. He isn't worth it."

"You are too kind, my dear. Still, a magistrate should be above such primitive emotions."

She scoffed. "Not when the murderer is also trying to kill the magistrate. George, you have been an absolute paragon throughout this gruesome affair, despite all the challenges you faced—including two inept officers of the law. I cannot decide who was worse, Constable Sharpe or Dr. Hughes."

"Regardless of their failings, I do think they tried their best."

"Their best almost got you killed," she pointed out.

"True, but Elton managed to fool all of us."

She let out an exasperated sigh. "I cannot believe I allowed him to pull the wool over my eyes *again*."

"My darling, unlike the rest of us, you managed to put the pieces of this mad puzzle together. I, for one, stand in awe of your detecting skills."

"Jane and Frank deserve praise, too, though. Without them, the idea that Mr. Elton was the killer would never have entered my head."

"But you saw what the rest of us failed to see."

She waggled a hand. "I failed to see that he was in love with me."

"Yes, but I believe he was also greatly driven by love of money—your money, specifically." He gently kissed the tip of her nose. "Not that I blame the villain for being in love with you. Any man would be, given the slightest chance."

She graced him with a smile. "Thank you, dearest. But I still maintain that it was really love of self. Mr. Elton simply refused to accept that I could ever reject him. His mind could not contemplate such a thing."

"Nor could he accept the loss of his social and financial standing."

She tapped a finger to her chin. "A few weeks ago, Mr. Elton quoted scripture to me. He said that the love of money was the root of all evil. How ironic that he was speaking of himself, although I suppose he was too deluded to recognize that at the time."

George nodded, holding her close. Outside, night fell softly over the gardens, a gentle benediction after the horrors of the day. Emma let the peace of the late summer evening rest upon her. In the days to come, she would no doubt think much on these events and how they had affected and would continue to affect her family, friends, and indeed all of Highbury. For now, though, she was content in the knowledge that her loved ones were safe and whole.

After a few moments, George stirred. "I will likely be gone for most of the day tomorrow."

Emma sighed. "Drat. I suppose you will be going to Guildford again. How tiresome for you."

"It is, but I still have questions for Elton, ones necessary for preparing the indictment. Constable Sharpe quite rightly wishes to transfer him to the gaol as soon as possible, and I think it best if I accompany him."

"I do not envy you such a grim task." She suddenly pulled

out of his loose embrace. "I forgot to ask you. What of Mrs. Wright? Did Mr. Elton have anything to say about *her* odd behavior?"

"I did ask him, particularly in regards to her feelings toward Suckling. Apparently, Mrs. Wright was resentful on Mrs. Elton's behalf, both because Suckling lost her fortune in the first place and because he was then unable to provide any assistance."

"So her hatred toward all of us was the result of her loyalty to her mistress. I'm surprised, though, that she never mentioned anything about the Eltons' argument on the day of the murder. That seems odd."

"Mrs. Wright will be required to testify at Elton's trial, where I'm sure that question will be raised. One can only assume, however, that if she had any suspicions about her employer, there was no proof to support them."

Emma nodded. "And Mr. Suckling was a very handy suspect, which no doubt colored her thinking. That makes sense."

"Yes." George glanced at her with a slight grimace. "I'm afraid you might be called on to testify, as well. You must prepare yourself for that."

She'd already anticipated that such would be the case. "That is certainly annoying, but at least I have the satisfaction of knowing that I solved the murder."

And that, she had to admit, was *quite* satisfying.

George smiled. "That you did. I am hopeful, however, that your detecting days are over. Unless, that is, you wish to take on my duties as magistrate. I should be grateful for the break."

She couldn't resist flashing him a cheeky grin. "That is much too high-minded for me. I think my skills might best be employed assisting Constable Sharpe. He isn't having much luck with the poultry thief, is he? Think of the speckled hens, George. Think of poor Dr. Hughes. We cannot allow this crime spree to continue unchecked."

Her husband looked pained. "My dear, I beg you to refrain."

Emma laughed. "Poor George. You have nothing to fear, I'm sure. Soon enough, Highbury will return to its sleepy old self, and nothing remotely as dreadful as these past weeks will ever happen again."

He raised a hand, as if taking a vow. "From your lips to God's ear."

"You may be sure of it. After all, I am always right, am I not?"

George chuckled, but in this case, Emma felt certain she was correct. Lightning never struck twice, and in Highbury neither would murder.